Acknowledgments

My many thanks are offered to my partner Joan and our very good friend Peggy for their welcome help in the writing of Pinkeens to Diddies and to artist and designer Patricia Faraday for front cover.

PINKEENS TO DIDDIES

A Boyhood in Ireland

David R. McCabe

Eloquent Books

Eloquent Books
An imprint of Strategic Book Group
P.O. Box 333
Durham, CT 06422
www.EloquentBooks.com

ISBN: 978-1-60976-254-4

Printed in the United States of America

Contents

Introduction

Brendan woke with a start. What was that noise?

The large room was filled with flickering shadows from the sunlight forcing its way through the dirty window. Brendan pulled up his father's overcoat that had been used as a blanket, sat up in the bed, and peered around.

Golly! he thought to himself. *What's the noise? It's scary! Where am I? Where's Ma? Gotta go to the lav. Where is it? Gotta go quick.*

"Jono, Jono," he called out, shaking his brother's shoulder. "Jono, are you awake? Where's the lav? What's that noise?"

"Out there somewhere, now leave me alone," was the grumpy answer from the sleepy eight-year-old.

Brendan, six years old, tall and thin for his age, with a pudding-basin haircut and fringe over an enquiring fresh face, scrambled out of the warm bed. With the heavy overcoat trailing after him, his stockinged feet caught in the torn lino as he groped his way toward the side of the room. His outstretched free hand touched a wooden door.

"Where's the handle?" he muttered under his breath as his groping fingers touched a smooth enamel strip on the tall door. He sighed with relief as they found the round porcelain doorknob. The heavy door creaked on its hinges as he turned the large knob and peered apprehensively out into the dark hallway. His eyes were drawn to the right by the gathering daylight gleaming through the oval shape of the fanlight above the distant front door. The high-pitched sound which had awakened him continued. What was it?

That must be the front door. I remember the lav was down there, he thought as his eye caught a slight glimmer of light in the surrounding gloom to the left. He stepped tentatively out onto a worn strip of Axminster in the hallway, his free arm out in front of him, and moved forward into the shadows. His foot touched cold concrete as his body moved into the darkness; his hand felt a rough wall to his left. The subdued light ahead drew him forward. *The lav must be there*, he thought, and made his way slowly into the shadows, the coat trailing behind him. By now he was feeling quite apprehensive.

What is there in front? Golly! It's cold and I need the lav!

His outstretched hand glided into the beam of soft light permeating through the gap in the darkness; there was nothing under it, no wall. He stepped back, startled. Where had the wall gone? Was there a big hole? He looked over his shoulder; the light from over the front door was creeping slowly along the walls. The large cupboards to each side seemed to be closing in on him. The noise continued—a painful, screeching sound. He shuddered and pulled the coat tightly around himself. He was in no man's land. He felt very alone and began to shiver violently. The centre of his world was the ray of light that seemed to be beckoning him. Dare he seek where it came from?

Taking a deep breath, Brendan pulled himself to his full height, a good four-feet plus, and tentatively looked into the pale beam of light, his hand in front of his body to ward off any danger. This outstretched hand found a yielding door, which opened into a small, dimly lit room. With great relief and in the difficult light, he saw the lav.

The high bowl had a large, heavy wooden seat, polished by constant use, resting on the stained ceramic sides. He gratefully stepped forward, letting the coat fall from his shoulders, and used both hands to lift and push the heavy wood against the rusty downpipe. With the ever-increasing need to relieve himself, the boy stood on tiptoe, aimed his stream into the bowl and, with a large sigh, found the shivering lessening and the gloom less menacing. The screeching sound from outside was as loud as ever, but now it was a lot less frightening.

Brendan, his needs satisfied, recovered his father's coat from the floor, wrapped it around his cold body and peered out into the shadowy passageway. Wide awake now, he went out into the long hallway with its high ceiling and silent cupboards. *Where's Ma?* he wondered anxiously as he tiptoed along the worn carpet runner, past the tall thin cupboard doors. Thin shafts of dusty light peered spookily through the dirty fanlight over the large entrance door leading to the hall.

Would they be in there? he wondered. Grasping the round white doorknob, he turned it with both hands and pushed the door open into a dark room. There was the sound of steady breathing and he could see the shape of the bed with his parents asleep in it. He quickly ran around the bed, pushed past the large cot that contained his baby brother Billy, and climbed in under the eiderdown to snuggle up against his mother's warm body.

"Ma, what's that noise?"

"It's only the birds," came the sleepy reply. "In the country the birds get up early. Now go to sleep."

But the noise, it's awful loud, thought Brendan. Birds only go "tweet tweet." He pulled the blanket over his head to lessen the sound of the bird song and warmed his shirt-clad body against the comfort and protection of his mother.

His mind fell back to the excitement of the day before. The car his father had borrowed was huge and smelled lovely. He had wanted to know what all the levers and lights did. This excitement had been increased by the journey from the house in Dublin.

He remembered travelling through the narrow streets in the city, out to the docks, through the posh areas like Blackrock, and into the country. The car was going very fast, and he and Jono were on the edge of their seats as they stared out at all the new sights.

"Look! Look! What's that, Pop?" Brendan had shouted. "Look at the ships! Gosh! Look at the houses! Are we goin' to live in one of those, Ma? Pop, look at the cows!"

Nearly asleep, Brendan was disturbed by movement in the bed and glanced up to see his Pop getting dressed. He heard him whispering to Ma, "It's getting late, I'll go and start the brekkie and leave the young fella to get his rest."

As his father made his way out of the room, instinctively bending his head as he passed through the door, Brendan leaped out of the bed and followed the broad-shouldered figure down the hallway. With a wide grin on his weather-beaten face, gained from the many hours in all weathers on the Gas Company bicycle, his father turned and playfully lifted Brendan from the floor, carried him into the bedroom, and dropped him on the bed beside Jono.

1

Oh! For a Better Life

Henry Harris was a good-looking man with a head of close curly hair. In his late twenties, he weighed in the region of fourteen stones, was over six feet in height, and strode rather than walked, putting his size thirteen feet positively in front of his large body. Rather than make decisions, he smiled his way through adversity. Always dependable, he was the rock to his wife's sometimes wilful ambitions.

"Get yerself dressed, Brendan, an' I'll put a boiled egg on fer you. Do you want one, Jono?" He called out as a long thin arm uncoiled from under the cover and pulled the overcoat over his head.

"No! I wanna sleep. It's Saturday, isn't it, Pop?"

"It's a lovely day out there, Jono. I've got the day off this Saturday an' there's lots of work to do. So up you get then."

"Come on Jono," encouraged Brendan, hastily donning his shorts and pulling up the woollen, lumpy, darned grey socks. "Come on an' git up, there's lots to do. Look, the sun's shinin', come on."

Looking at the two boys, Henry Harris took a deep breath and strode out of the room considering his responsibilities: three youngsters—these two and the baby—and a house with a large mortgage on it. Had he made a mistake letting Alice push him into buying this large, dilapidated cottage in the middle of nowhere?

Henry's parents had died when he was a youngster and he had been sent to live with relatives in the country. With a very basic education and no professional qualifications, he had returned to the city at the age of fifteen to find work. He managed to gain an apprenticeship with the Dublin Gas Company and scraped a living until he met Alice Ryan. They fell in love and married.

Alice Ryan was a woman with ideas of her own, a woman who was ahead of her time with her independent views. Henry was loath to admit it to himself, but he knew he needed someone to push him, as he would prefer the easy life, but it did annoy him at times when she made the running.

Alice, a couple of years younger than Henry, had been brought up in a Protestant enclave in the midlands of Ireland. Her father was a tenant of a large farm owned by wealthy farmers and there were always workers from the Catholic community in the background. Alice, however, had rebelled against the thought of marrying a farmer and living the rest of her life in the middle of nowhere and moved to Dublin where she had met and married Henry in 1936. They bought a small terraced house on the outskirts of Dublin with a loan from Alice's father shortly after they married.

Their life settled, uncomfortably for Alice, into a drab existence. Henry would leave early in the morning and take the bus into work in the city, where he would collect his bike from the depot in Dolier Street and cycle around his "patch," emptying the gas meters of their farthings and pennies. Alice found the days long and the house small; after the large farm she had lived in, the clutter of houses around her was claustrophobic. However, life went on and, in 1937, she became pregnant and produced Jono; three years later, Brendan arrived. Life continued its drab existence.

Alice was a tall, slim woman with a well-formed figure, long ash blond hair and attractive, striking features. She and Henry were an impressive pair when seen together. With Henry's rugged good looks and tall, well-built figure, they caught the eye. Alice did, however, make Henry's life quite difficult at times, embarrassing him with her modern ways. She was one of the first women in Dublin to wear slacks, to smoke a cigarette in public, and possibly one of the first wives to tell her husband's employer he should be paid more for the dedicated hours he worked. She was forever annoying friends through her outspoken views. Not being very well educated, her views were sometimes confused and often resulted in Henry later apologising to the indignant recipient.

There was one particularly embarrassing occasion, amongst many, incurred on him by Alice. In the very male-orientated workplace of the day, wives were meant to support their husbands, smile when expected, and, especially in the Gas Company, to stand by their husband's side, but to stay in the background. Alice, ever the exhibitionist, could never be sidelined. Hearing from Henry that he had been invited to an office party to celebrate the marriage of a working associate, she turned up at the stag party in her new slacks and wowed them all with her rendering of "The Woman with the Wooden Leg" whilst, of course, smoking a cigarette.

One day, during the early part of 1945, while Jono was in school and Henry was at work, Alice, ever impetuous, decided she would like to go into the city with Brendan to do a bit of window-shopping. Whilst there, she would go into Clearys Department Store and maybe see Kathleen, one of the sales girls. Alice, before marrying Henry, had worked as an assistant in the store and had made a few friends. Little chance of finding anything I could afford there, she thought, but it would be nice to see a few of her old friends.

"Come on, Brendan, let's go to town. Here, put on your best clothes and clean up your shoes. Oh! There's a hole in that one! Here, I'll put some cardboard in. Don't walk in any puddles!" She laughed as she pulled up his long stockings, adjusting the garters and folding the top of the stocking over the strip of elastic.

"Not too tight are they, Bren? Don't want your legs to fall off." She laughed. "Oh! That we could afford some decent clothes for us all. Look at myself, painting my legs brown to look like I have stockings on. Are my seams straight? The dress I got last year seems to be getting a bit tight. I missed last month and late again. Oh God! Must be pregnant again," Alice mused, as she eased the waist on the dress of the grey suit bought some years ago. "The jacket is also a bit tight around the shoulders. Shoes are okay, thank God. A bit of spit will get rid of that mark. Right, now the coat, that brown colour looks a bit old-fashioned. Covers over everything, anyway." She looked disdainfully at the faded brown cloth of her coat.

"Look at me, Brendan. Aren't I the belle of the ball!" she called as she put her hands on her slim hips and swung her tall figure in a circle, allowing the loose coat to pull out from her.

"Let's away then Brendan, me boyo!"

"Okay! Ma, are we goin' on the train?"

"Yep! And maybe see the ducks in the green."

Brendan was very excited. He had only been on a train once before and a trip into Dublin was always special. The short walk down to the station was followed by a long flight of wooden stairs that seemed to reach to the moon. Arriving at the platform amidst the sharp smell of soot and loud noises, he pulled Alice to the edge to see a large black shape covered in swirling white clouds of steam rounding the entrance to the station. They stepped back as the engine braked alongside the platform. With gushes of white steam enveloping them, the carriage doors opened and passengers clambered down calling for a porter, or hurried past with important-looking briefcases under their arms.

Amidst shouts, clanking trolleys, and hissing steam, they climbed the high steps into the carriage. Brendan pulled the door behind him with a very satisfying "clunk!" and wondered how to open the window. Alice showed him how to release the long, well-worn leather belt supporting the heavy window. She sat down on the narrow passenger seat alongside the door and Brendan leaned out to watch the surrounding activity.

"Put your head in, young fella. Or you might be after losin' it," admonished the uniformed guard as he went past, slamming any doors left open. Reaching the rear of the train, he waved his flag, blowing a shrill whistle at the same time and leaped aboard.

With more hissing steam and loud clanks and clunks, they started to move. A short journey through side streets and back gardens brought them into the city station and, with a loud whoop and whistle, the train shuddered to a halt. Jumping down from the carriage, Brendan grabbed Alice's hand as they pushed their way to the exit.

"I can hear chukki hens. Where are they?" exclaimed Brendan. Rounding a stack of timber, they saw, against the station wall, rows of hessian sacks with anxious calves' heads sticking out from them, all parcelled up and labelled with their destinations. Crates of chickens with their nodding heads were stacked up alongside, all with labels. Apparently, there being no goods train to the south of the country, the passenger train was used to transport livestock. However, as the authorities forbade the carriage of such livestock, the senders wrapped their live goods as parcels and claimed they were presents for their relatives.

Surrounded by hurrying people, loud noises, and the smell of soot, Brendan held tightly to Alice's hand and they made their way along the side of the River Liffey to O'Connell Bridge to cross down to Clearys.

"Ma! Look, the bikes, there's hundreds of 'em an' the buses, an' all the people," exclaimed Brendan as they walked over the bridge towards the wide O'Connell Street, with the imposing tall Nelson's Pillar catching the eye.

"Gosh! Wow! Ma!" exclaimed Brendan. "Isn't it great?"

"Sure, Bren. Now hang on to my hand," Alice instructed as they made their way towards their target, pushing and dodging the hurrying people.

Ah, memories, she thought as she pushed her way into the quieter, muffled sound of the store. The traffic sound was taken over by voices. The smell of oil and exhaust fumes were replaced by that of clothing, polish, and people.

"Still the same," she said out loud. "There's Paddy the floor walker. Hi Paddy!"

"Well, would ye ever, it's young Alice Ryan. My, you're lookin' well, an' is this young fella' yours?" said Paddy, his eyes never still. "Sorry lass, can't stay." He moved away, acknowledging the beckoning hand signal from another walker.

"Now, where's Kathleen? Oh! Hello, Mrs. Rooney. Still here then? Do ye know where Kathleen Donovan is now?"

"Kathleen Donovan, now where would she be?" replied the small, well-dressed woman. "She's not on my department. Maybe ye will find her in underwear. Remember yer face now, was yer name Ryan?"

Smiling to herself and pleased that she had been remembered, Alice made her way through the crowded floor towards the busy ladies wear counter to see her friend Kathleen waving to her.

"Come on, Bren," she encouraged. "I'll say hello to Kathleen an' then we'll go and have a cake in the café."

"Ma! Me shoes are hurtin' an' I want to go to the lav."

"How are you? Kath!" Alice smiled across the counter to the smartly dressed woman some three years older than her.

"Look Alice, God it's luvely to see you again. Can't speak with you now. I'll have a word with Mrs. Gorsuch for an early break."

"Janey Mac, is she still here?" exclaimed Alice. "Thought she would be dead by now."

"No! She's still goin' strong the ould . . . Remember Maeve Devlin? She's still waitin' for her promotion. Look, hang on a mo."

"Won't be long now," consoled Alice, patting an impatient Brendan on his head.

"That's okay, Alice," said Kathleen, returning. "I can take an early mornin' break. Now, who is this fine lookin' fella?" she enquired, placing her hand on Brendan's shoulders.

After introductions, they made their way to the café and joined the long queue, eventually sitting down with their coffees and plate of biscuits and a large cream bun for Brendan.

"I just love these Mikado biscuits with the jam and coconut," announced a grinning Alice. "Now, how are you Kath? An' how's Clearys treating you?"

With the two women talking animatedly between themselves, Brendan, having eaten his cream bun, thought he would like another and left the small table.

"How's married life treatin' you, Alice? An' how's that good-lookin' fella ye married?" enquired an enthusiastic Kathleen.

"Oh! Married life? Kath, it's tough at the moment. Henry is hard to get movin', but we're getting by," replied an unenthusiastic Alice. "How are things with you?"

Their conversation continued for some time until Alice sensed a returned Brendan sitting down alongside her.

"Look, Alice," laughed Kath, "he's got another cream bun."

A triumphant Brendan with a mouthful of creamy bun and a big smile pointed to the cream bun display. "Got it there, Ma."

"Anyway, Alice, I've got to go. Lovely to see you again," said Kath, standing up. "Bye Brendan, enjoy your bun."

"Come on Bren, let's get out o' here before the police come," grinned Alice. "Let's go see the ducks in the green."

Meandering back across the river, past Trinity College on their way to Stephen's Green, they entered Grafton Street. Grafton Street, the expensive part of Dublin where window-shopping was the only exercise Alice could consider. Looking enviously at the display in Brown and Nolans, she heard a cultured male voice behind her enquire how Alice Ryan was keeping. Startled, she looked around to see a smartly dressed, tall, smiling young man standing behind her.

"Good God! It's Sid Matthews. Well, well! Sid, how lovely to see you," enthused a delighted Alice. Sid Matthews was an old beau Alice had known before meeting Henry, and she sometimes wondered how life would have been if things had developed with him.

Looking back at her reflection in the store window, she quickly adjusted her hat, smoothed down her dress, and turned back to face this memory from the past.

"So you married him then. Always thought Henry Harris was a lucky man."

"Yes!" replied a slightly flustered Alice. "We have two boys now. How are you?"

"Look Alice, I've got half an hour. Let's have a coffee in Bewleys at the top of the street. The young fellow can have lemonade. How are you then, young man?" The tall, rather portly newcomer enquired as he leaned over to shake Brendan's hand.

"That's Brendan. Say hello to Mr. Matthews, Brendan. Oh, yes! We've got time for a coffee."

Talking together, the two adults made their way to the café whilst a disconsolate Brendan followed, thinking there wouldn't be much chance of seeing the ducks now.

Sid, realising Alice and the young fellow had not had any lunch, offered them a sandwich each along with their drinks and had a small snack himself.

Whilst the pair talked animatedly together, Brendan sniffed the coffee-scented air, kicked his chair and, after a short while, pulled at Alice's dress.

"Ma! I wanna go home. I'm fed up. Ma, I wanna see the ducks."

"Oh! Sorry, young man. I'm ruining your day out. Would you like a drive in my car, though? Bet you would, better than looking at some old ducks. What do you think?"

"Yes! That would be great, Mister Matthews. Let's go now!" an excited Brendan replied. "Come on, Ma!"

A surprised Alice looked enquiringly at Sid.

"That's all right, Alice, I'm my own boss. My car is parked close by and I could drop you at your house in Ranelagh—it is Ranelagh, isn't it?"

The professional businessman looked directly at the flattered housewife, a woman somewhat bored with her life and looking for something to happen.

"Yes! That's right, Ranelagh," she replied, but thinking she daren't let him see the little house she lived in. "Yes! That would be lovely, Sid. You could drop us off at the shops."

God! What does the man want? she thought. *Is he making a pass at me?* Quite flattered with the attention, Alice rose from the table and, feeling she was the centre of attention, made her way out of the upmarket café alongside Sid, with Brendan hurrying along beside them.

The car was parked in a small street off Grafton Street. Alice settled in the passenger seat of the four-door Wolseley car with an excited Brendan in the back.

"Sorry about the car, Alice," apologised Sid needlessly. "This is just a substitute until I have my Rover delivered."

Alice, beginning to realise Sid was perhaps a bit of a fake, commiserated with him whilst moving his left hand from her right knee, looking him in the eye with a glance to the rear seat. Sid, getting the message, rolled his eyes and grinned in recognition of the implied promise.

That evening, Henry arrived home late from work. Poor old Mrs. McGuire had lost her son through the diphtheria, and he couldn't very well leave her in her lonely misery while she wept on his shoulder. This meant he was too late to bank his takings and leave his bike in the company shed, so he had cycled home in the teeming rain.

After a hurried meal, Henry started stacking the dirty copper coins in neat order on the kitchen table. Alice, quite frustrated after her day of hidden promises, pulled up a chair to the kitchen table opposite him. She leaned over and took the copper-stained hands into her own.

"Henry!" she said, looking him in the eye. "Henry! My dear, we've got to do something. We've got to get out of this miserable life we're leadin'."

Henry sat back in the creaking wooden chair with a weary smile; he patted Alice's slim hand with his large stained fingers and, with a tone of defeat and some small frustration, replied in his soft, deep voice.

"Whatever you think, Alice. Whatever you think. Now!" he continued, pointing to the untidy pile of copper coins. "I've got to get all this money bagged up and left in the office by nine in the morning."

"Henry!" shouted a frustrated Alice, annoyed by Henry's dismissive attitude. "Forget your stupid money. I'm bored; I'm fed up. The house is too small, I hate the neighbours and . . . Henry, I'm pregnant." She lowered her voice and, with great deliberation, repeated the words. "Henry, I'm expectin' again. We've got to do somethin'."

"All right, all right Alice—that's life!" he replied, raising his hands in resigned defeat. "Now, let me git tis copper out of de way an' we can talk about it." He started counting the coins again into stacks of twelve, placing them alongside the orderly rows of half pennies and farthings.

"Oh! I giv' up," Alice called, throwing her hands in the air and knocking over the neat row of coins. "I giv' up, giv' me strength. Giv' me strength."

"Alice, look wha' you've done," remonstrated Henry, looking aghast at the untidy heap of coins. "I've gotta start all over again."

Muttering under her breath, Alice ran her hands down the sides of her print dress as she stood up in frustration.

"Henry Harris," she announced in a deliberate and threatening voice, "if you're not bothered, I am. An' I'm goin' to do somethin' about it. So there!" she stormed as she strode across the kitchen, slamming the door behind her.

Henry continued counting the pennies, muttering under his breath. "Haven't I enough to do? We're all right where we are. But another child. She's right; the house will be too small. Must get this money counted though, now. That's seven pounds fifteen shillins and tuppence."

2

Laurel Cottage

The following morning, after an unsettled night, Henry left the house on his bicycle with his large Gladstone bag full of parcelled coins and headed into the office. He was hoping to get in before management noticed he hadn't dropped his collections off the previous evening.

Alice was in a determined mood. Having waved Henry off, she walked Jono to school and left Brendan with a neighbour, then took the bus out to Dunlaoghaire to discuss her problems with her good friend, Sheila Elder.

"A new start Alice, my dear, is what you need," advised Sheila later that morning. "Move house, get your man to change, don't have any more childer. Perhaps you won't have the great fortune I've had marrying the Managing Director of a successful business, but you can still do it. Scare the life out of him. He's a lovely man but he needs a kick up the bum, Alice. You're the leader, hav' a go."

Alice had known Sheila from childhood. She had been to her wedding, an extravagant affair, a number of years earlier, and admired her attitude to life.

"Yes, Shelia. He is a lovely guy, but I could kill him sometimes. Yep! After I have this one," said Alice, patting her stomach, "no more, finito. It's going to be difficult, but I'll work out sometin'. Thanks Shelia. Anyway, when are you goin' to hav your first?"

"No idea, Alice. George an' I are practising a lot," Shelia replied with a rueful smile. "But nothing's happening."

Sheila was a year older than Alice and had lived on a neighbouring farm in the Midlands where the two of them, when children, had become great friends. They had met their husbands at a party in Dublin and their weddings were held within six months of each other. However, due to their partners' circumstances, their paths diverged and Sheila now lived in a large Edwardian house with sweeping views of Dublin Bay and Dun-laoghaire Harbour, quite different to Alice's small terraced house.

Sheila gave her a letter of introduction to a firm of solicitors in Dun-laoghaire and Alice steeled herself to call on them. Solicitors, accountants, and bank managers were a breed apart from normal people.

With some apprehension, Alice had called into the solicitor's office on the main street and profferred her letter of introduction. To her surprise and delight, Sheila had already phoned and Mr. Tierney saw her immediately.

"Yes! Mrs. Harris, we can act for you on the sale and purchase," agreed the grey-haired pillar of society. "We will, of course, have to meet with Mr. Harris to confirm what you have told us. But yes, we see no dif-ficulty in acting for you."

Right, Alice thought to herself as she boarded the bus on her way home. *I'll have this youngster, six months t' go, and get Henry in the mind to move.*

Buoyed by her decision, Alice settled down over the next few months to save whatever money possible. Henry gave her his pay packet each week. She was able to hide the letter from the solicitors confirming their meeting. "Keep it until the right moment," she said to herself.

Later that year, delivery time arrived and William, a seven-pound male, was born. With the birth of William, very quickly shortened to Billy, Brendan and Jono had to make way for the newcomer and things became very cramped in the two-bedroom house. Alice, after a short period of recuperation, decided to re-approach Henry about moving house.

Over the months of Alice's pregnancy, Henry had put the thought of an addition to the family to the back of his mind and had resigned himself to his lot. He knew Alice would probably bring up the need to move house one day, but he would worry about that problem when it occurred.

On a particularly wet and cloudy Saturday in November, Alice's pa-tience snapped. She had had a miserable morning contending with rain in the bedroom from a broken roof slate, from Brendan wetting the bed, from next door complaining about the noise, from feeding the new youngster, in fact, from the sheer boredom of her life.

Henry had barely got in the door and was feeling somewhat sorry for himself. The morning's work had not gone too well: the bike had got a puncture and Mrs. Connelly, one of his regulars, had just lost her hus-band through the consumption, which meant he spent more time than he could afford listening to her misery. And Maeve Fitzgerald, a good-looking, well-built country girl living on her own, had taken off more than her cardigan before he had been able to escape.

"Henry! Is that you?" was the call from the back yard. "I'll be in, in a minit, got sometin' I wanna talk to you about."

Oh no! Henry thought as he draped his wet raincoat over the back of a wooden chair in the kitchen. *Is this wha' I have been afraid of? The move?*

Noticing Billy, gurgling happily to himself in the corner, a smile softened his face. "Hello little fella. How are you?" He smiled again as he patted the baby in the tall pram.

"Hello Brendan, Jono. What have you there?" he asked as the two boys burst through the kitchen door from the hallway, each with a sheet of white paper with crayon drawings on them.

"Look at mine, Pop! I drew it at school," demanded Brendan.

"No, mine first, Pop! I'm the eldest," argued Jono.

With a big grin, Henry took both sheets of paper and, whilst he was complimenting his sons on their efforts, the door to the yard opened and Alice, wearing an old rain-soaked overcoat with a headscarf around her long hair, stumbled into the crowded and steamy kitchen carrying a bucket of coal in both hands.

"There you are, Henry. Here, take it from me," Alice ordered, placing the heavy galvanised bucket on the lino-covered floor. "Oh! The rain, will it ever stop? Jono, Bren, out of the kitchen now. Hen' will you take the coal into the front room? How'd your day go? Oh! What a mornin' I've had!" Alice exclaimed as she wiped her forehead with her sleeve. "Henry, where are you goin'? We've got to talk."

"Jus' takin' the coal in," stuttered Henry.

"Oh! Forget about the coal. Sit down an' lissen to me."

"All right, Alice, what is it you want to say?"

"Oh! Giv' me strength," Alice cried out in exasperation. "Henry," she pleaded, "look at me. Look at us. We're goin' nowhere. The house is too small, it smells, I'm always tired, we never go out, it's always raining, you're always workin', and I want us to do somethin'. I want to move or I'll go mad." After her tirade, Alice slumped in the kitchen chair alongside the Formica-topped kitchen table and rested her head in her arms, willing Henry to agree to a move.

"But, but Alice, I want to," Henry stuttered again, "I want to do whatever is best. But could we afford to move?"

"We can do it, Henry," replied Alice, as she stood up from the table and put her arms around the large man standing abjectly in the centre of the small kitchen.

"Yes! We can do it, Hen'. I've been able to save up a bit, an' we could get a mortgage, an' Pa Ryan has said he could loan us a few hundred pounds. The farm has been good over the past year. What do you say? Com on, say yes, say yes. Hen'."

"Okay, Alice, let's see what we can do," agreed Henry resignedly and somewhat relieved as he gave Alice a hug and kissed her upturned face.

With Henry resigned to the possibility of a move and the three boys all growing up, Alice, to save money, had cut back on new clothes and budgeted severely on food. There was not much variety in foodstuffs in any event with the rationing in England, which also reduced the choice in Ireland. Alice, to keep her dream of moving house alive, made a telephone call to the solicitors from the pub close to the house and made arrangements for her and Henry to visit Mr. Tierney.

"Henry, you have to take some time off from work. I've arranged to see the solicitors in Dunlaoghaire. You did agree to do sometin' about moving," she reminded Henry, as he looked at her slightly taken aback.

"Time off! How can I do that? A trip to Dunlaoghaire would take the best part of the day. Solicitors!" he exclaimed. "Alice! Couldn't we write to them? Do I have to go?"

"It's all right, Henry. All they want is to meet you, I'll do de talkin', don' worry," mollified Alice. "I've arranged we see Mr. Tierney at eleven next Wednesday. So take the day off. This is important."

"Okay, Alice, I'll see what I can do," Henry offered in defeat.

Early in the morning under a cold, snow-filled sky in January 1946, Alice and Henry took the bus on its circuitous route to Dunlaoghaire and met Mr. Tierney. Tierney, in his late fifties, was initially very off-hand with the two of them. But with Henry's charming, if innocent, attitude and Alice's flirtatious approach, albeit restrained, she helped Henry to prove their ability to afford a mortgage and Tierney's attitude mellowed to some degree. They left the office with the promise that Mr. Tierney would do his best for them.

Rather exhausted after their long meeting and not too satisfied with the outcome, they made their way to the bus station, taking turns in carrying the baby, to start the long process of returning to Dublin.

Henry, relieved that he would not have to do anything more, returned to work whilst Alice, quite dismayed by the lack of decision from the "bloody" solicitor, resigned herself to await a letter from him. She thought it would do no harm, in any event, to get the house smartened up and bought some white paint. The two boys helped where they could. Brendan, who seemed to have a flair for painting, splashed some paint around and Jono was given the task of tidying up the garden.

Alice started looking out for something to buy. *You never know,* she thought. *The solicitors might come up trumps.* She took the bus into the city and went around some auction rooms and agents, but could find nothing they could even consider. Towards the end of January, the long-awaited letter arrived from the Solicitor, suggesting a bank loan of up to £1000 could be considered and that the bank awaited their call.

An overjoyed Alice, and perhaps a less than pleased Henry, visited the bank and were offered a mortgage amount not exceeding £1000—a small fortune.

"Now to sell Ranelagh Road, Henry. Daddy said that Michael Dowdall was interested. Remember him, Henry?" she asked, looking at him "he's son of the man that owns the next farm in Mullingar," Alice said on their way back from the bank in Donnybrook. "Daddy said he was interested in buying somewhere in Dublin. Anyway if he buys we can buy a house for over a thousand quid, Henry. A thousand pounds!" she exclaimed, gleefully rubbing her hands together, not only in satisfaction, but to warm them in the freezing January air.

"A thousand pounds, Alice. It's an awful lot. Can we afford it? I'm only getting eight pounds, ten shillin's a week," replied a somewhat startled Henry.

"Don't worry Hen', I'll work it out. I'll get in touch with Daddy. Now we can really start looking for a house. Come on Hen', give me a smile," Alice pleaded. "This is our chance, you big lump. Come on, cheer up, let's see a big smile," she said, catching Henry's big hands in hers while looking into his eyes.

Henry, reacting to Alice's enthusiasm and confidence and mentally crossing his fingers, gave a resigned, yet rueful, grin in return.

"Okay, Alice! Okay! Let's do it. I could do with a bit of excitement. God help me."

That night, Alice settled down to write to her father in Mullingar to tell him the good news and to find out if Dowdall and his family were still interested in moving to Dublin.

A few days later, becoming frustrated at the lack of progress in the house hunting, Alice decided to contact Shelia again. She knew Shelia's husband, George, was a big noise in a business based in Dublin. Maybe he could help, so she rang Shelia from the phone in the nearby grocer shop.

"Yes, Alice, I'll have a word with George," Sheila had replied. "You never know. How are you and the family keeping? Give me a ring the day after tomorrow an' I'll tell you any news."

Some two days later, Alice called back to the shop and rang Sheila.

"Alice, thanks for ringing. No, I'm sorry, George can't help. He has no contacts in the housing market. However, there is a large cottage, just outside Dunlaoghaire, he says, that has been derelict for a few years, just beside a pottery works—sounds awful. His firm had to close down the pottery a few years ago and the owner used to live in the cottage."

"I could do with a day out, Sheila. Let's go and have a look."

"Could be wastin' our time."

"I know Shelia, but there's nothing else an' I'd like to meet you again anyway."

"Okay! I'll get the address from George and see you next week."

The following week, Alice made her way out to Dunlaoghaire with the three boys and arrived at Shelia's large house on the harbour front.

"We'll leave the boys with Mary, Alice, so that we can have a few hours out on our own," suggested Sheila, nodding to her full-time maid.

"A great idea," agreed Alice. Oh! That I could have such a luxury! A maid. "Now, where are we going? You said this cottage was just outside town."

"Yes, a village called Killoughlin, on a Red Clay Lane, about a mile an a half away on the Dublin bus. We can be there an' back before dark."

The two women, in their mid twenties and well dressed for the winter weather, waved good-bye to the boys as they set off to board the Dublin bus.

After a short journey through the suburbs of the town, moving cautiously past the mounds of snow at the roadside and stopping every so often to take on or drop off passengers, they heard the conductor announce in his broad Dublin accent that they had arrived at Moran's.

"This is us," advised Shelia. "The conductor said when we boarded that Moran's, whatever that is, was our stop. Morans must be in Killoughlin. Come on, let's get out."

As they dismounted from the relatively warm bus onto the cold pavement, the conductor called out to them.

"Yeh! Der ye are den ladies, Moran's Pub, de centre of Killoughlin," as he pointed towards a sullen building standing some twenty yards away at a crossroads. "Der's snow forecast fer tonight ladies, so git back inter civilisation as soon as ye can."

Slightly apprehensive, the two young women linked arms as they watched their warm, well-lit contact with the world slide its noisy way to Dublin.

"I hope there will be one going to Dunlaoghaire when we want it," Alice muttered "Now, where's the cottage? Let's see if there is anyone in the pub. Come on."

Wondering why they were doing this, but enjoying the novelty, the two of them held on tightly to each other as they giggled nervously and nodded in agreement to enter the pub. The pub was the province of the male species: women could only enter where the male deigned to allow them.

The narrow, uninviting and well-used door swung back and the two explorers stepped into a dimly lit large room filled with the smell of porter and cigarette smoke. There were two elderly, scruffily dressed male customers at the bar. They turned in unison at the sound of the door and grinned at each other upon seeing the two women. Alice strode over to the bar, a well-scrubbed wooden top, nodded to the two bar fixtures and called out.

"Barman, are you there?"

"He's out in de bac' den, missus," informed the nearest fixture, as it went into a bout of cigarette-induced coughing.

"Do ye know where Red Clay Lane is then, mister?" asked Alice in her best accent. "Laurel Cottage?"

"Oh! Ye mean de cottage, down past the 'V' house, beside the shop, missus. What would ye be wantin' with a place like dat? There's nobody there. Ould Fagan died years ago. Didn't he, Sean?" the fixture asked, bringing his compatriot into the conversation.

"Excuse me den, missus," fixture one asked as he hawked and spat a lump of smoky phlegm into a tin can on the bar beside him. "Sorry bout dat, miss, but it's better out dan in, innit?" he laughed, going into another bout of coughing.

"Yeh! He did now, died of the consumption, ye kno," nodded Sean through the woodbine dangling from his lips. "Yeh! God res' his soul de ould bugger. Oh! Excuse me language der, miss, and you too young lady," he offered, looking toward Sheila.

"That's all right, sir," agreed Sheila, trying to hold back the laughter. "Come on, Alice, it'll be dark soon an' we've got a lot to do."

Laughing under their breath, the two women left the warm smoky atmosphere and started to make their way along the slippery, roughly laid pavement.

"Do ye get that smell, Shelia?" asked Alice as she stopped, sniffing the air. "Smells like something burning, and what's that clanging sound?"

"Yes! I get it, could it be from that building over on the left? Look, it's a forge. Well, would ye believe it? Look at the furnace and that must be the farrier." Peering in through the large doorway, they saw the shape of a male outlined against the red furnace, hammering a horseshoe on a large anvil.

"There's a horse in there, look Alice. Look, the fella is waving," giggled Sheila. "Look! He doesn't have a shirt on."

Laughing together, the two women returned the farrier's welcome wave and continued cautiously along the broken pavement, past a shop on the left to see a single-story house situated on the "V" where the road split to the left and right of it.

"That must be the 'V' house," said Sheila, pointing to the whitewashed building. The two women walked as briskly as the slippery laneway allowed, Sheila in fur-lined leather boots and Alice in her rubber Wellingtons, and made their way down the unpaved roadway to the right of the "V" house.

"There's the shop de old fellow mentioned, an' look, there's a door in the wall under that long hedge," Alice exclaimed excitedly. "This is getting interesting. Wonder what it's like behind the wall."

"Come on quick, Alice," encouraged Sheila. "It's going to be dark soon."

The shop looked deserted with rubbish in the window. They walked alongside the tall, whitewashed, ten-foot wall, to a small green door recessed in the brickwork. There was a stained brass plate attached to the door with the name "Laurel Cottage" etched into it.

"Go on, Alice. Open it," smiled Sheila standing back. "You never know, this could be your future."

Alice, shivering a little in the cold air, pushed at the door. It needed an extra effort, as some branches on the laurel hedge behind the wall obstructed the door. As she stepped through, she was taken aback to see a wide, overgrown lawn stretching some thirty yards in front of her bordering a narrow gravel path. The path led to a wide, single-story building with large multi-paned windows on each side of a huge door. The walls were covered in Virginia creeper and there were large chimney stacks on each side of the roof.

"Good God, Sheila! The size of it," exclaimed Alice, as she stood in the pathway leading to the front door. "It's huge. Look at the hedges. Oh! There's an orchard."

To the side of the front garden, over a small hedge, was a large expanse of land stretching back into the gloom dotted with many fruit trees all bare of foliage, their branches rimmed in frost.

"Look at the front door, Sheila, it's massive. And the knocker! It's a brass lion's head!" Alice exclaimed, pointing toward the door. "Let's see in the window. Giv's a hand." Supported by a smiling Sheila, Alice stepped up onto the rocks on a flowerbed to peer through the paned window.

"It's big, but there's nothin' in it. No! There's an old bed against the wall. Come on, Shelia, let's look at the back. Gosh! It's getting cold."

With the light dimming, they walked past a broken gate into a large expanse of overgrown land with fruit trees and various fruit bushes that dotted haphazardly in the hard ground.

"An' now we enter the well-kept and bountiful orchard of Laurel Cottage," announced Sheila in a BBC voice. Laughing, Alice walked briskly along the side of the tall, one-story building, peering into darkened windows. Out of the orchard and through another gateway, they noticed some ramshackle sheds and some scurrying shapes.

"Look, they're cats. Gosh, there are lots of them," exclaimed Shelia. "Have you seen enough yet, Alice?" she asked, wishing she could start for home. "No! Let's go around the back. Come on, don't be a spoilsport, this is great."

The sheds and open areas reminded Alice of her childhood in the country. They rounded the rear of the cottage, stepping over crumbled walls and high weeds.

"Watch the nettles, Sheila," Alice cautioned and stopped suddenly. "Look! Look at the trees." Stretching to the right of the two women was a row of immense tall pine trees reaching up into the darkening cloudless sky.

"There's another line of trees on the other side of the field. Is this still part of the cottage? Gosh, it's huge," Alice said in wonder. It was getting quite dark and cold, and both women were shivering as they made their way back to the road.

As they stepped into the dimly lit lane they were halted by a herd of cows returning from a day out in the fields.

"God, look at them, Alice. There's hundreds of 'em," exclaimed Sheila. Snorting and farting with their tails swishing, the shuffling and rolling sea of cows filled the road with a cloud of steam rising from their hot bodies.

"Oh! Isn't that lovely! Cows! Gosh! They remind me of home," exclaimed Alice.

"Watch yerself den, ladies," called the youngster herding the cattle, hitting the road with a large stick. "Away wi' ye now," he shouted at the slow-moving herd.

"Oh! Alice, do we have to walk after them? They are doing their things on the road an' I'm wearing my good boots."

"Come on, we'll walk at the side, should miss most of the dung," suggested Alice, catching Sheila's hand and pulling her purposefully along the grass banking at the roadside.

After waiting some twenty minutes, the bus from Dublin to Dunlaoghaire arrived. As it was full, they had to stand most of the way in the jolting, steamy, overloaded interior and arrived back to the house cold and weary. Alice was quite exhilarated with the day and, after another long bus journey, she and the boys arrived home wet, weary, and cold.

"Henry, you've just got to see it. The house is lovely, it's bigger than 'tis and there's lots and lots of land. You always wanted to grow your own veg. Let's borrow Sid Matthews' car; he said we could have it whenever. I'll telephone him, and we could get a key for the cottage. I've worked out how we could pay for it."

With some further cajoling, Henry raised his hands in defeat and agreed to have a look at the cottage whenever it could be arranged. He hated having anything to do with Sid Matthews. Sid was a racy bachelor who used people and always had eyes for Alice. However, Alice could match Sid, played along with him in his approaches, and felt it did no harm to Henry, as it would keep him on his toes.

Late the following Saturday morning, Henry, having travelled to Sid's home in the north of the city to collect the car, arrived at the front door in Ranelagh in a smart Connaught Green Wolseley 12 with imposing headlights and gleaming body.

In great excitement, after a quick lunch, the family climbed onto the green leather seats Jono and Brendan in the back, and Alice in the front with the baby. Henry fitted his large body behind the steering wheel and the five of them headed out of the city suburbs and into the country.

For the two boys, the journey seemed to go on for hours; they passed smoking factories and waste ground. They drove along narrow streets with rows of houses on each side; they passed churches, lots of shops, overtook a few horses and carts, drove alongside a railway line, along the sea shore and onto wider roads with big houses on each side. They drove past fields, white-rimmed with frost, hedges, trees, and lots of birds waving at them from the cloudy sky.

"We're nearly there," announced Henry over his shoulder, as he took the Bray Road avoiding Dunlaoghaire.

"There's a sign to Killoughlin, Henry. Should be near it now."

They turned down a wide road with smart houses on each side.

"There's Moran's, the pub. Now down to the right past the shop. Stop at the green door in the wall."

"Okay! Okay! I've got it," Henry retorted and pulled in alongside the grass verge.

Henry, with a resigned smile, began to accept the inevitable and became interested nevertheless. He unhinged his large frame from the small car and stood beside the two excited boys, both jumping alongside Alice and the baby. He smiled at Alice and looked down at the two boys.

"Boys! This is Laurel Cottage. This could be our new home. Let's go and have a look."

Brendan made it to the gate before Jono. He turned the handle and pushed. The door wouldn't open.

With a resigned sigh, Jono pushed Brendan aside with a loud grunt and attempted, but also failed to open the door.

"Let a man do it," laughed Henry. With both hands, he pushed the door against the low-lying branches of the laurel hedge and was the first to step into the garden.

Not usually a demonstrative man, Henry stopped and exclaimed, "Alice, I see what you mean. Isn't it smashin'? Look at the house, the size of everything."

As the two adults stood in the gateway savouring the scene, the two boys ran forward.

"Careful you don' slip," called Alice as Jono fell forward onto the icy grass and hastily got to his feet again to catch Brendan. Both boys disappeared, whooping and shouting around the back of the huge cottage. They raced through the orchard, dodging around the fruit trees. They ran past derelict sheds, a row of tall pine trees, and down a long path to a big gate, which they clambered over and they were on the road again.

"Gosh! Isn't it great, Bren?" gasped Jono, catching Brendan's hand as they ran back up the road to join their parents standing in the front garden, looking up at the cottage.

"Isn't it lovely, Henry?" enthused Alice. "Look at the creeper on the walls, look at those windows, look at the trees, look at all the grass, all the bushes. Hear the birds. We'll make this a wonderful home, Henry, won't we?"

Nodding in affirmation, Henry, with a big grin on his face, produced a large brass key and entered it into the keyhole in the tall, heavy door. The original wood peered through the peeling green paint. The grinning lion's head holding the heavy doorknocker seemed to welcome them as the door opened with a push. The two boys raced into the dark interior, followed by their smiling parents.

The hallway they entered was narrow with large, wooden doors on each side painted a hideous green. There was white paper hanging from the ceiling with a water stain in the middle of the well-worn Axminster. The doors opened into huge rooms with stained carpets and dispiriting wallpaper. They moved further down the hallway, Henry looking somewhat aghast at the condition.

"God, Alice, it's in poor condition, isn't it?"

"Henry, we can afford it. It's going cheap and with a bit of paint here and there, it will look fine. Look, the boys love it. Could you take Billy for a while? My arms are aching," she asked, passing the sleeping baby over to Henry.

"Now boys, follow me. This will be mine and Daddy's bedroom, and this will be the sitting room. Do you want this room, Jono?" And so Alice walked through the four large rooms of the main building, getting more and more enthusiastic with the size of the place. There was a bathroom, two flush toilets, and a large kitchen—all cold and weary-looking. The rain had come in through the roof in many places, and there were a further three rooms off the kitchen, all needing decorating and cleaning.

"It's great Ma," called Jono. "When are we goin' to live here?"

"Let's go down the back. You okay with Billy, Henry? I'm goin' t' see what's in the kitchen."

"Sure, Alice, I'll look around the rooms. There are some lovely fireplaces. Did you see the one in the front room? It was all black marble."

For the next hour they walked from room to room, marvelling at the size and at the huge kitchen with its range and ovens. They found the water pipes were all frozen and Henry made sure all the taps were turned off.

"You never know. After the thaw, this place could be flooded."

They walked around the large building, peered into sheds, and chased the feral cats. Brendan disappeared for a while in one of the sheds. Jono started to climb one of the pine trees. They looked, gasped, and talked excitedly about how lovely the place was and how much better it could be with its apple trees and gooseberry bushes.

"Let's buy it, Henry," pleaded Alice. "I know it's damp and big and needs a lot of work done, but we can do it."

"Now calm down, Alice. Calm down," Henry mollified. "We've got a lot of thinkin' to do. What about the children an' school? An' it's another ten miles to work from here as well."

"But you'll maybe say yes, will ye Henry? Oh please, the solicitor said we could afford it," pleaded Alice.

"I might say no," pronounced Henry, as he looked at his wonderful wife, the two eager boys, and the baby in his arms, knowing in his heart what the answer had to be. "An I might say yes. Let's away home now, it could start snowin' soon an' we've got a long trip ahead of us."

"Right boys," called Alice, knowing she had nearly won the battle. "Let's hit the trail. We'll come back again. What do ye think? Jono? Brendan?" Alice asked, smiling in response to their resounding "Yes!"

3

The Move

"Are ye all ready? Hav' you all got everything? We're goin'. We're on our way, Henry."

"Okay, Alice, we are on our way," replied Henry, as the borrowed green Wolseley 12 pulled out into the road.

"Full speed ahead, Pop," Jono and Brendan called out in unison. "Laurel Cottage, here we come!"

Alice looked back to see the last of the Dublin house. The rows of houses were all the same, the untidy streets crowded with tired people.

"Wave to Mrs. Temple, boys," she instructed, "an' Mrs. Jones. There's Michael outside the shop. Give him a wave, Brendan. Good-bye everyone, thank God. Good-bye."

"Bye, Mick," shouted Brendan as the car turned the corner.

"Bye, Bye," called Jono to all.

"Sit down, boys. I can't see out the back window," remonstrated Henry as he changed into top gear, directing the car and his family to their new life. "Fred is followin' us in the truck with the furniture, an' I don't wanna lose him."

Have I done the right thing? he wondered. It was now well into June 1946 and after some surprisingly quick negotiations, the sale of the house had been completed and the purchase of the cottage had gone through, all mainly due to Alice's initial planning. He now had a mortgage of £1200 pounds and had to find £25 every three months. At least the loan from Pa Ryan, Alice's father, was interest-free. I know I'll pay that £200 back fifty times over, he thought to himself. At least I have some of the roof leaks done on the new house and the weather is improving. Where am I goin' to find the money for the mortgage? Ah well, what of it, Alice? We'll work out somethin'.

Henry cheered up and began to enjoy the feeling of change. He had a week's holiday ahead of him and Sid, who had left for a holiday in England, had said they could have the use of the car for the week. *I wonder what his motives are?* Henry thought to himself. *I'd love to own a car like this. Ah! That's only a dream.*

In a more cheerful frame of mind, Henry gave Alice a sideways grin. She patted his knee in agreement and smiled in satisfaction as she settled the youngster on her lap.

With Fred and his son in the Ford truck labouring behind them, Henry and the family followed the now familiar route to the cottage. Fred, a fellow meter collector in the gas company, had offered to help in the move. He and Henry had been friends for many years. The journey took over an hour, with Fred having to stop a couple of times to secure flapping wardrobe doors and save iron bedsteads from falling on the road.

As they pulled up outside the cottage, Fred, in his cloth cap and normally an undemonstrative chap, glanced over to his son.

"Johnnie me lad, I wonder what's behind that green door."

"Yeh! Wonder," the teenager grunted in reply.

"Come on, Fred," encouraged Alice, inviting Fred to step through the door. "Come on an' tell us what you think."

Eagerly, Alice and Henry stood back as Fred stepped up to the door and pushed it open, taking his cap off at the same time.

"Well, what do you think then, Fred?"

"Come on," called Alice with an anxious smile on her face. "Come on, Fred. What do you see?"

"Well," replied Fred, turning around in the doorway while scratching his head. "I see in front of me a pair of right eejits. Look at the size of the place. It's a monster. But I know ye, Alice Harris, ye'll make it into a palace so gud luck to the pair of ye. Now," getting a bit embarrassed, Fred stepped back onto the road and bellowed. "Johnnie, git yerself down on the road. We've got a lot of moving te do."

"Yeh! Fred, you might be right there," agreed Henry as he stepped in the doorway to look across the overgrown lawn and at the impressive frontage of the house and the pine trees in the skyline to the right. "There's a lot of everything an' a lot of it needs mending."

The next few hours were spent moving the few pieces of furniture from the truck and showing Fred and his not-so-interested son around the cottage.

As he climbed back into the truck to return to the city, Fred leaned out from the cab and patted the grateful Henry on his curly head.

"As I said Henry, I repeat, after seeing the mansion, you're a greater pair of eejits tan' I thought at first, but anyway good luck."

"Thanks, Fred," replied Henry with a rueful smile. "See you in a week."

Having waved Fred away, Henry returned to help Alice sort out the bedding and get the iron beds erected. The older boys' bed was placed in the rear room with a blanket over the large window to keep out the light. The cot for the youngster was put at the end of their own double bed in the front room.

After their exhausting day, the new owners of the cottage, with its acres of ground, trees, sheds, weeds, broken roofs, water-stained ceilings, and hanging wallpaper, went to bed.

Before lying down to sleep, the two adults looked at each other and, in one voice, exclaimed, while breaking out into laughter, "What in the name of God have we done?"

"Shh! We'll wake the baby," admonished Alice with a grin. With that, they snuggled down together and slept until Alice awoke the next morning to find Brendan climbing in beside her.

After their breakfast of boiled eggs, fried bread, and mugs of tea with sugar, Henry fetched his ladders and tools to climb on the roof to replace some loose slates, whilst the two boys started to explore. With the radio tuned into the light programme with the melodious voice of Donald Peers singing "In a Shady Nook," they brought life back into their new home.

While the boys went exploring the grounds of the cottage, Henry took Alice's hand and, leaving the baby in the pram shielded from the sun, walked her to the orchard.

"Look at that, Alice. Look at the apple trees. Is that a pear? There must be a dozen gooseberry bushes. Look, even loganberries and blackberries. We should have a fair crop of apples in a couple of months."

"Yes!" agreed Alice enthusiastically. "There's a plum tree, no there's three of them. Gosh! Henry, isn't it great? How big is it?"

"The orchard, ye mean? Must be sixty yards long and twenty wide. God! There's plenty of work, look at the weeds. Anyway, Alice, must get up an' finish the work on the roof before it rains."

"Before you move, you big hulkin' beast," commanded Alice, standing on her tiptoes and putting her arms around Henry. "Giv' us a big kiss. Isn't it all exciting?"

"Yeh! But can we afford it?" Henry replied.

Whist their parents were wondering whether they had made the right move, the two boys were exploring the grounds. Jono, a tall gangly boy with tight curly black hair and features similar to his father's, was answering a shout from Brendan.

"Jono, come here quick!" shouted Brendan. "Come an' look at this."

Dropping the odd-shaped piece of wood that had caught his eye, Jono followed the sound of Brendan's voice coming from behind a tall hedge.

"Look at this, Jono," Brendan exclaimed again as Jono reluctantly rounded the hedge, wondering what the youngster wanted. Standing in the centre of a tiled square Brendan was pointing excitedly towards a dilapidated shed.

The square had been formed with black and white tiles, like a draughts board. Some of them were cracked with weeds forcing their way through. Two wooden doors in a broken red brick wall attracted the eye to the left, looking as if they had not been opened for years. The sagging roof of grey slates looked ready to collapse. The large shed was filled to its gaping roof with old sheets of corrugated iron, lengths of wood, old cart wheels, piles of bricks, and weeds sprouting from every open crack in the walls. What had caught Brendan's eye was a small jaunty cart with broken shafts and wheels, its spokes missing.

"Maybe we could get it to work. And race it"'

"Don't be daft," scorned Jono. "We don't have a horse. Wonder what's behind that door?" he queried, pointing to the red brick wall.

Using a stick to push aside the large stinging nettles guarding the first of the closed doors, they tried to open it. It was jammed shut.

"Give it a push, Jono," Brendan suggested, rubbing the painful red lumps on his arm caused by brushing against the nettles. The door wouldn't budge.

"Look, there's a rat," called Jono. A large sleek rat had raced out from under the door, disturbed by the movement, but before they could react it had disappeared under the other closed door.

Moving to the rat's sanctuary, Brendan gingerly turned the door-knob and pushed; the door creaked open and he peered into the musty interior. There were old newspapers on the floor, and a rusty linked chain with a wooden handle hung from a stained ceramic tank above a lavatory bowl with a broken wooden seat. Cobwebs were everywhere. When Jono pulled the chain, the handle broke off, the tank jolted sideways, and the startled rat raced out between their legs. They both jumped back, laughing, and ran out into the sunshine.

"What are you two divils up to?" shouted Alice from the kitchen, coming out into the yard to see what her boys were laughing at. Noticing Brendan rubbing the nettle stings, she went into the kitchen to get some lotion to ease the irritation. A voice warned from the roof.

"Look out below," and with that some large tufts of grass and weeds came flying through the air, landing on the broken flags in the yard.

"Let's go on the roof and see what Pop's doing," shouted Jono, running towards the wooden ladder that was leaning against the kitchen wall. Brendan was just about on the third rung when Alice caught his leg.

"Hold on, what's the rush?" she asked, laughing. She pulled him back to earth and applied lotion to the many nettle stings. "Jono, come down and I'll do your stings as well."

By then Jono had reached the roof valley and was asking Henry if he could help. Impatient to see the action, Brendan shrugged the medication off and started up the ladder again.

The kitchen and sheds were the older part of the building, with ridged roofs of heavy tiles separated by lead-lined valleys. Some of the tiles were cracked and most were covered in moss. Each ridge had a line of shingles with a red ornamental edge atop. Some of the shingles were broken, but were really in surprisingly good condition.

Henry was busy clearing the valley of weeds and grass so the two boys decided to do some more exploring up there in the sky. Clambering up the slope of the roof on his hands and bare knees, Brendan reached the top to see yet another valley of weeds and a higher ridge ahead with large chimney stacks towering over the roofs.

"Let's go over the next one," suggested Jono and, with that, he ran down the slope and raced half way up the other side. There was a roar from behind.

"Come back here, the pair of you, before you break your necks!" Brendan scurried back to Henry who was looking anxiously over the roof ridge.

"Where's Jono?" questioned Henry.

Brendan pointed to the waving figure as it disappeared over the next ridge.

"You go back down the ladder, Brendan, and I'll go and get him back."

"What's all the racket?" came Alice's voice from ground level.

Brendan slid down the ladder, glad to reach ground level and told her. A call came from the front of the cottage. Henry wanted the ladder to be brought around so that he could avoid clambering back over the roof and possibly breaking a few more slates.

The day followed with further discoveries and more dangerous moments. Climbing one of the pine trees bordering the paddock, for example, was a bit scary.

"Bet I can get higher than you!" taunted Jono as he swung up into the lower branches of what looked like a thousand-foot high tree with a trunk more than fifty feet wide. Not to be beaten, Brendan found a foot-hold on a narrow branch and pulled up to about twelve feet above the ground, whilst Jono disappeared amongst the foliage above. Brendan's hands and clothes were streaked with sticky pine sap from the branches. He was feeling a bit scared.

"I can see the top of the house," Jono called down. "There's pop on the roof."

With that, there was a sudden flurry in the greenery above and Jono's body came sliding down the sloping tree trunk to stop abruptly, a leg each side of a friendly branch. He was in a greater mess than Brendan. Somehow, they both got to ground level, a bit shaken, but feeling proud of themselves.

The pine tree they had climbed was one of a row of twelve, all about thirty feet high, bordering a plot of scrubland they later called the paddock. On the other side of the paddock, about seventy feet away and parallel to the row of pine trees, was another row of dense tall pines.

"Let's go see what's behind those other trees," shouted Jono.

The two boys in their corduroy shorts, thin string vests, and "runners"—canvas shoes with rubber soles—scrambled their way across the straggly mounds of grass and weeds, avoiding the clumps of nettles, potholes, and pieces of broken pottery.

Jono pushed his way through the low branches of the green wall of trees followed by Brendan, and immediately became covered by thick red dust that covered the branches.

"Hey! Brendan, the trees are covered in dust, look! There's a factory over der. Look at all the piles of pots."

As the two boys pushed under the branches of the line of pine trees and peered through the wire fence, they could see a derelict building with rusty machinery all precariously balanced on the side of a shallow pit. There were columns of flower pots stacked against the walls of the dilapidated building. Everything was covered in a red dust.

"Let's go tell pop," shouted Jono, wiping the dust from his face and nose.

"Look at your face, Jono, it's all red. Gosh! Look at your vest. What'll Ma say?"

"Golly! You're right Bren. Look at yourself, you're covered as well," exclaimed Jono, starting to brush his vest with his stained hands.

"You're makin' it worse, Jono. You're all red streaks. Maybe Ma won't notice."

Turning suddenly, Brendan shouted "Yippee!" and started galloping back across the lumpy ground, striking his left buttock with his left hand, his right hand in front holding the imaginary reins. "I'm a Redskin on a mustang, bet ye can't catch me!" he shouted back to Jono.

Leaping upon his imaginary horse, Jono drew his six-gun and started galloping after Brendan, making gunfire noises.

Covered in sweat and dust, the Cowboy and Indian reined in their horses at the kitchen door, hitched the reins over an imaginary rail, and swaggered into the kitchen laughing with the sheer exhilaration of being young—the sheer delight of space to run was intoxicating. Compared to the confined garden in their previous house, this was wonderland.

"Look at the state of the pair of you," admonished Alice as the two boys dashed into the kitchen.

"Look at you! You're both filthy. What's all the red dust, Hen?"

"Must be the old pottery behind the trees, Alice. The trees were planted years ago to protect the house from the dust. They've stopped making pots now, thank goodness."

"Of course, Hen', we're on Red Clay Lane. You know clay for pots," admitted Alice with a grin. "Anyway, you pair keep away from those trees an' go an' wash yer hands."

"Okay, Ma, anytin' you say," laughed the boys in unison and then attempted to wash their hands in the high kitchen sink, but found it difficult due to the sticky pine residue on their fingers.

They sat down at the large wooden table in the kitchen, settled into their meal of sausages and mash, and talked about the adventures they had had and the plans for the afternoon.

The kitchen, the largest room in the cottage, extended the whole width of the building and stretched some twenty-five feet long by twelve feet wide and ten feet high. The high walls were covered in stained, peeling distempered paper. The ceiling of narrow wooden planks, again in mottled white distemper, was festooned with dirty smoke-laden cobwebs. There was a large, ancient black oven recessed into the wall with rust patches and two chipped and rust-marked gas cookers balanced against the walls, their bare copper pipes lining the dirty walls.

"Right, you pair of divils," said Alice with a smile, after they had finished their meal. "You've had your fun. Now for some work. There's a couple of brushes out in the yard. Git sweepin'!"

Muttering together, the two boys picked up the long-handled, well-used brushes and, before long, were having a great time moving the dust and rubbish around the yard. Jono found an old rickety wheelbarrow that helped to move the rubbish out to the back. There was a bit of an argument over who wheeled the barrow. Jono won as he was the biggest, but Brendan decided what was to be put in it as he had found a shovel. Before long, the heads fell off the brushes, which gave them the excuse to down tools and do some more exploring.

After a long and busy day, Henry got a fire lit in one of the large rooms where the five of them sat talking about the day and the plans for the future. The lack of ready money was a great drawback to all the aspirations of Henry and Alice. The cottage needed a lot of money spent on it. The three boys would all require schooling and, whilst the state provided a basic education, they wished for a better opportunity in life for their children. Henry was not on a great salary. Alice, ever the opportunist, had started entering crossword competitions in the Sunday and weekly papers which offered the life-saving amount of £500 to the winner. There was the well-known Irish Sweepstake based on the Grand National, and a pound a year would be tried on that. Borrowed money was another option, but hard to come by.

The best thing was to knuckle down, make the cottage liveable, and maybe develop the plots of land in the orchard and sell some vegetables. The family wouldn't starve and, with a lovely summer expected, there was a lot to look forward to.

To the boys, life was wonderful. Whilst some new clothes and the odd new pair of shoes would have made life easier, they knew no difference and every day was an adventure.

4

Exploring

"Ma!" called Jono from the orchard. "Ma! Bren an' I are goin' to explore the fields opposite."

"Okay!" agreed Alice dismissively as she passed the wet bed sheet through the mangle in the back yard. "Now, don't go into the woods, an' be back by dinner time."

Sweating profusely in the summer heat, Alice, after bidding good-bye to Henry as he left for work earlier, had stripped the beds and decided to wash the sheets. This, of course, meant boiling pots of water on the gas stove; the Ascot boiler wasn't working, so she had to carry the heavy pot over to the Belfast sink. Soap flakes were shaven off the large Life-buoy soap bar, mixed with the water in the sink and the bed sheets then washed, wrung out by hand and then put through the mangle.

"I'll get these on the line in the back yard an' get a bit of shopping done," she muttered.

She thought about Henry and how he had mended the puncture on the bike. *Hope it's okay. Wonder what the two boys are up to. Must find a school for them. Oh God! There's the baby crying. We'll have some eggs for dinner. God knows what I'll do for tea tonight. Isn't it a lovely day though!*

So, talking to herself, Alice dried off her hands and went to comfort the baby.

The two lads, after bidding good-bye to their mother, had made their way out onto the traffic-free lane and climbed over the high stone wall, into a field up the lane from the cottage. The gate would have been much easier, but there was a large challenging vertical pipe alongside the gate with bulges and ridges on its circumference.

Reaching the top of the wall, the drop on the other side was quite daunting. Using breaks in the stones, Brendan started to clamber down and fell the last few feet. Jono came tumbling after him and, laughing in

the sheer enjoyment of the day and life, they raced across the field to the
nearest haycock, a tall half-globe of mown grass. They threw themselves
against the yielding soft cushion, reaching the top of the stack then sliding
down with a whoop. They knew they shouldn't do this, but there were
dozens of haycocks in the field.

The stack was getting a bit dishevelled and, feeling somewhat guilty,
the two of them started to replace the wads of loose hay. Suddenly there
was a roar from the bottom of the field. It was the devil himself, a stick-
wielding monster. It was authority; they were in the wrong.

"Run for it Bren!" shouted Jono. "Get away, don't be caught!"

Racing back to the wall, Brendan surprised himself with his sudden
ability to scramble over it, followed by a panting Jono. Fleeing down the
lane at a hundred miles an hour, they turned into the cottage, flew up "the
avenue" at the side of the cottage, and shot up a pine tree. Alice insisted
in calling this lane "the avenue," as it was at the side of the house and
had been used by a car. There were tracks in the soil leading up to a shed
alongside the cottage.

They were safe. Hearts thumping, they looked over the roof of the
cottage to see the threatening figure walking away up the road, muttering
to himself. Giggling in relief, they slid down the tree—their new haven,
their harbour from the grown-ups. Later they found the "stick wielding
monster" was the farm manager, Jerry Duffy, renowned for his bad temper and dislike of youngsters.

The day the hens arrived was quite an event. For some weeks Henry
had spent time preparing for the delivery of six chickens and a rooster. At
the rear of the cottage, the land rose gradually to a stone-built wall edging
the main road some two hundred feet from the cottage. There was a row
of sheds in poor repair to the side of this land with a large green hedge
facing them. This overgrown piece of land, about fifty yards by ten, had
apparently been used in the past as a small garden. Now it was covered
in weeds and a profusion of nettles with wild blackberry and gooseberry
bushes fighting to survive.

With a hammer, a few nails, a rusty saw, and some woven wire, the
sheds were beaten into shape, nests arranged, and a "hen run" made to
fence the chickens in until they got used to their new home.

The big day arrived. A small lorry pulled up at the front gate and a
large man in a brown coat and cap strode up the garden path, nodded to
Brendan, and asked if his daddy was in.

"Follow me, mister," Brendan instructed and ran in through the
porch door, down the hall, and into the kitchen shouting. "The hen man is
here! The hen man is here!" He raced out the back door, along the orchard
and back into the front garden again, as running everywhere was better
than walking.

"Mammy is comin'," he said to the smiling, bemused "hen man."

Whilst the grown-ups were talking, Brendan went down onto the lane and climbed up the side of the lorry to see bundles of large, red chickens with their legs tied together lying on the floor, all clucking away miserably.

"Are they Rhode Island Reds?" Brendan asked the returning driver. "My dad says they should be."

"Dat dey are, young fella, de finest pedigree hens ye can git. Now, hop up into de cab an' I'll take dem up the avenue." Raising his voice on the word avenue he continued. "Tis a grand place ye have here now, with yer avenue."

At the top of the avenue, Brendan leaped out and helped to carry the frightened and squawking hens around to the run where the hen man then untied their legs and let them loose. Brendan tried to stroke them, but they ran away, clucking frantically.

Having seen the hen man away, Alice came and stood by Brendan. With her arm around his shoulder, she pointed out the cockerel and started to tell him the difference between the cocks and hens and where chickens came from. Brendan paid little attention to this, his one and only lesson on reproduction.

The two of them waited anxiously all day for their first egg, but nothing happened; the hens wouldn't sit on their nests and the cockerel spent all his time strutting around, crowing his head off. However, the next morning when the two boys raced up to the run, they found a few of the hens clucking away contentedly. There were two, lovely, speckled-brown eggs in the straw. Lightly boiled egg with toast was their breakfast that morning.

During the same wonderful summer, the two boys "helped" Jerry Duffy and his workmen winch the semi-dried haycocks in the haycock field onto the horse-drawn hay bogies. There was always a race to be the one to ride on the back of the bogie up to the farmyard, and then stand proudly beside the driver, on the empty flat wagon, as he drove the horse and wagon back to the field. The rumbling noise made by the tireless wheels became a regular and familiar summer sound.

Alongside the haycock field there was a large wood. To the boys it was a forest, or perhaps it was a jungle. It was full of large trees and tangled bushes. There were lots of birds, rooks, and jackdaws, all calling out and swooping down into the field, daring the boys to explore. Rabbits raced away at their approach, stopping to look back from behind the tufts of grass and cowslips with their noses twitching in surprise.

There was an overgrown ditch separating them from this wall of darkness. What was in there? Dare they go in? Their ma had said not to go into the woods. What should they do?

"Come on, Bren," encouraged Jono. "Let's jus' go in an' hav' a quick look, there's no one around." Brendan, not wishing to be a spoilsport, agreed and after checking there was no one watching, they slid down into the deep ditch amongst the nettles and brambles. They jumped the small puddle of water at its base and scrambled out on the dangerous side. What was in there behind the bushes and trees? Were there any lions or tigers? Dare they step into the unknown?

They crept in under the bushes and around the tree trunks and came to a small opening never before seen by Man. The treetops seemed to touch the sky and they felt they had stepped into a fairy tale. Shafts of dusty sun-lit air stretched down from the gaps in the foliage; there were shadowy areas behind the bushes and ferns, small birds darted across their vision and there was the noise of a small animal pushing through the undergrowth.

All this lent to a feeling of wonderment. They pushed forward, swiping the heads off the dandelions with the pieces of branches they had broken off. They picked a few blackberries, but spat them out, as they were quite bitter. They came to a lighter area amongst the trees and, before stepping out into the open, Jono whispered, "Shush! Quiet Brendan, there might be natives around, or a tiger or two."

Peering through the undergrowth into the area lightened by dusty beams of sunlight streaming through the trees above them, they noticed a large ornamental bowl in the centre amongst the tangled weeds and flowers.

"Janey Mac, Jono. What is it?" whispered Brendan.

"It's a fountain," answered the knowledgeable Jono. "Saw a picture of one in a book."

The "fountain" in the centre of the bowl was some ten feet high with statues of little naked, fat boys around the centre pillar, all with open mouths, leaning over a green slimy pool of water. The pool was some twelve feet in diameter, surrounded by a delicate carved stone wall with four statues of lightly robed angels dancing on the edge.

"Look, you can see that one's diddies," Brendan exclaimed, pointing to one of the angels with her arms open wide and only a cloth covering her bottom half.

"Look! They're all the same," called Jono in delight.

Giggling, the two of them ran around the pool pointing to each statue, shouting the forbidden word. "Diddies, diddies! Look at the diddies!"

"I wonder if there are any fish in the water. Let's have a look," Jono suggested, as he pushed aside the rotted leaves and green goo with a stick. The dark, smelly surface parted slightly, but nothing could be seen in the dark water.

"Pinkeens couldn't live here anyway, Brendan, but wouldn't it be great to sail a boat?" Jono said.

They continued with their exploring and discussed what boats would be suitable. An overgrown path, bordered on each side by large,

wild, rhododendron bushes, covered in pink and white blossom, suggested further adventures.

"Let's go down there," they whispered in unison, suddenly becoming more cautious. They swiped the heads off the many blossoming dandelions with their sticks.

"Don' pick one up or you'll wet the bed tonight," cautioned Jono as
they came to a sudden halt. There in front of them, with stone banisters
and statues of cupid smiling down at them, was a set of imposing granite
steps. The steps led to a large overgrown lawn split by a wide path, which
brought the eye to the entrance door of a huge, forbidding-looking house.

The boys hid in a large laurel bush at the bottom of the steps, just
in case anyone was around. Could Jerry Duffy possibly live here? Should
they run for it? Maybe it was a gangster's hideout!

As everything was so unkempt and wild, they considered the place
must be empty. So, full of bravado, but with their nerves tingling, they
climbed the steps up to the gravel path. With the sudden loud noise of the
stones scrunching under their feet they both jumped onto the grass and
ran, crouched, over through the weedy grass up to the large and impressive studded black door.

Brendan looked at Jono.

"Should I knock and see if there's anyone in?" he whispered. "What
if someone comes to de door? What do we do then?"

"Run for it," answered Jono, as he reached up to lift the elaborate
lion's head knocker in the centre of the high door. He leaned against
the door to support his body when it suddenly creaked open under his
weight.

Startled, their hearts thudding, both boys jumped back. They looked
at each other and ran back into the bushes. Nothing happened, and after
a couple of minutes they crept out from their hiding place and ran over to
peer through the crack between the door and the wall. With a gentle push,
the door groaned opened a further twelve inches. Jono peered inside.

"Can't see anything. Come on, let's go in."

Both were feeling a bit scared but, like all youngsters with the thrill
of the unknown and the lack of grown-ups to tell them what to do, they
were encouraged to step into the dark hallway.

"Golly! Look at that!" exclaimed Brendan, pointing to a staircase
with elaborate banisters and a large picture window at the summit. There
were doors everywhere with dusty carpets and mouldering sheets over
objects in the hallway. The smell of stale air and decay filled their nostrils.
There were cobwebs hanging from everything. The whole place had a sin-
ister attraction to the two boys. Dare they go further?

Their nerve-ends tingling, they made their way to the first door,
startled by the sudden creak of a loose floorboard. Jono started to turn the
handle when Brendan gave a sudden dust-filled sneeze. Jono jumped in

fright. Brendan tried to say sorry, but leapt back, scared out of his wits as a couple of small black shapes came flying out of the newly-opened door.

The boys raced like startled rabbits out of the front door, only to see a tall black-garbed figure striding up the granite steps. They turned and raced down a side path, dodging around mounds of weeds and rubbish and ducked under low-lying branches.

Their heads down and running for the lives, they saw their escape route at the end of the path: double iron gates leading onto the road. However, when they reached the gates they found, to their great dismay, they were locked with a large bolt and padlock.

"Golly, what are we going to do?" panted Brendan. "He's going to get us, Jono. What are we going to do?"

"Look there," replied the panting Jono, pointing to a tall side gate. He tried to pull it open. It wouldn't move.

"Look! There's a catch, pull on it," shouted Brendan. "Jono, quick!" Picking up a large stone, Jono hit the bolt, knocking rusty paint off it. It didn't budge. In desperation, he hit it again. It was immovable.

"Belt it, Jono. Hit it hard. He's comin'!" Brendan cried in desperation, looking over his shoulder.

"There! Got it," Jono cried out in triumph, as the force of the heavy stone freed the bolt.

"Giv' us a hand Brendan, the gate's stuck in the weeds."

With their combined strength they pulled the gate open far enough for their thin bodies to squeeze through and looked back to see the black-clad figure, none other than Jerry Duffy, standing at the edge of the undergrowth, its hands on its hips, laughing.

"Look, Jono, he's snarlin'. He's a monster. Run fer it."

Turning their backs on the apparition, the two boys raced down the road past the familiar Moran's Pub, the forge that had a couple of horses outside, down past the Vee Cottage, past the shuttered shop and on to the green door leading into the sanctuary of their front garden. Relief and exhaustion took over, and the pair of them threw themselves down on the grass, their chests heaving, their hearts thumping, their nerves tingling.

"Wow! That was scary," panted Jono. "Wonder if it was Jerry Duffy?"

"Don't know," answered Brendan. "But I'm not going there again. Look!"

He pointed to the green door under the laurel hedge.

"Look!" he called in horror. "Jono, the gate! It's opening. Is it Jerry Duffy?"

Both boys leaped to their feet, ready to run again, but were greatly relieved to see the front wheel of their mother's bicycle as she pushed it through the garden door.

5

Summer Days

The summer days were never-ending. Brendan spent many hours wandering through the neighbouring fields, fishing for pinkeens in the ditches, chasing rabbits and looking out for different birds. He had been given a book on birds of the British Isles for his sixth birthday and had started to record, in a small notebook, what birds he had seen and to try and collect as many eggs as possible. The sky was filled with flocks of starlings, swallows and swifts darting through the air, and seagulls from the nearby coast called out with their raucous shouts.

The garden was full of sparrows hopping around, with the odd thrush hitting a poor snail against a stone. There were blackbirds with their yellow bills disputing their territory, agile blue tits hanging from branches, and magpies strutting around looking for something to thieve. There were always the odd visits from colourful finches, the attractive wagtails, and independent red-breasted robins searching newly turned earth. He was sure he had seen a hoopoe in the orchard he recognised it from its fan-like crest.

His collection of eggs started and remained with the one egg he found under the bush in the front garden. He recognised it as that of a song thrush—light blue, spotted with black dots. When he discovered a blue tit's nest in a hole in the garden wall—there were six little white eggs with red spots—he felt he could not disturb them, particularly as the mother was frantically fluttering in the vicinity and, in his mind, he knew it would not be fair on the little birdie.

There was always the sound of birdsong in the air. The trilling of finches, the chirping of sparrows, the "pink pink" sound from tits, and the rich, flute-like sounds from blackbirds. Starlings would interrupt the song with their shrill alarm calls when disturbed. Butterflies, in their many varieties and colours, fluttered around the garden, while bees and wasps carried out their duties buzzing from flower to flower.

Brendan revelled in the warm, scent-filled air. He touched, heard, and smelled nature. He was stung by the odd wasp and bitten by insects. He fell out of trees, and scraped his knees on gravel; he cut himself with broken glass, picked up fleas from the neighbouring dog, and survived the many cuts and bruises incurred. It was an idyllic time for a youngster. However, amongst this world of burgeoning growth and exhilaration of life, Brendan's young mind was suddenly brought back to reality.

He was passing the Vee Cottage while returning from the sweet shop one afternoon after realising his pocket money of three pence didn't buy very much. He was quite surprised when one of the two old ladies who lived there appeared from behind the cottage door and, in a pleading voice, called from behind the low wall bordering the road.

"Hello der young mister, would you like to be after earning a penny?"

Brendan's foot stopped in mid air. *What is it she wants?* he wondered. A penny would buy four Sharps toffees, a large lollipop, or even a sherbet bag with a liquorice stick.

Yes! Brendan thought to himself. He looked over at the old lady who was pointing to the small gate in the wall and motioning for him to follow her into the cottage. *Into the Vee Cottage!* thought Brendan. *Nobody goes into the Vee Cottage.* In fact, nobody but the two old ones had ever been in there. What does she want? There were stories about the Vee Cottage. It was haunted. It was full of dead people.

Noticing Brendan's hesitation, the old lady, dressed in a long blue gown that reached the ground, with a dirty white shawl around her shoulders and a pink bonnet on her head, held up her hand with two pennies. Two pence! He could get a sherbet and toffees for two pence.

His mind made up, but feeling a bit scared as he had heard about witches, ghosts and evil spirits, he followed the old lady through the entrance door, leaving the bright sunlight behind him with the warm smells of summer.

As he stepped into the dark entrance porch, he was immediately met by a sour smell of unwashed bodies and the acrid smell of wee. The old lady pulled aside a heavy curtain and he reluctantly stepped into the dark room. The smell was stronger; the room was gloomy, with drawn curtains and a large, wooden-framed bed against the opposite wall. By now the smell was becoming quite suffocating. Brendan looked to retreat, but the old lady pushed him forward.

He had begun to notice there was a body on the bed, a stained brown blanket covered the thin form, and an emaciated face with high cheekbones and narrow, bloodless lips was propped up on a mound of lumpy white pillows, with feather ends sticking out from them. Skeletal hands rested on the thin blanket with rosary beads held in the fingers. A small statue of "The Holy Mother" attached to the wall to the side of the bed threw a low blue light onto the whole scene. The dreadful smell of death filled the room.

In a plaintive wheedling voice, the old crone pleaded with Brendan.

"Will ye now be after gettin' down on your knees and prayin' for Mary, me poor sister. She died so young. God help her, Jesus, Mary, and Joseph. Pray that her soul goes to heaven." These were the weeping words from behind him as the old lady rattled her rosary beads, crossing herself frantically.

Brendan's immediate reaction was to run for it. The smells, the darkness, death, the strange religious overtones—it all frightened him. He held his breath, afraid he was going to vomit; he turned away from the apparition in the bed and pushed his way past the old woman, not looking at her. Escape and fresh air were what he needed.

He dropped his loose coins in his haste and, rather than look for them in the dark room and thinking two pence wasn't worth it, raced out onto the road, taking a deep breath.

"Janey Mac, wait until I tell Jono. God! She was dead; the old woman was dead—dead! Gosh! The smell! Golly! She was dead. Better tell Pop, he'll know what to do."

Later that day, an ambulance took the body away. He never saw the old lady again, nor did he see his pocket money or, of course, the two pence.

Henry and Alice would occasionally meet up with some of the neighbours. Next door, on the other side of the avenue, there were the Fagans, a family of five girls with their mother and father. The father was a large, dour man, a member of the Garda Siochana, or police. Next to them were the Morrisons; Michael, the father, ran his own decorating business and had two sons. The Dolans were next to the Morrisons; Mr. Dolan and Mollie lived with their four teenage offspring. Mr. Dolan was an odd job man. He helped Henry with the repairs to the cottage. These neighbours all lived in small detached houses with long, wide, back gardens that backed onto the paddock at the side of the cottage.

The summer months drifted by. The two boys wandered the fields, climbed trees, picked blackberries, scratched their knees, tore their clothes clambering through brambles, and became friendly with a few of the neighbours' children. The Fagan girls, all five of them, aged from five to twelve, took a shine to Jono and Brendan and loved looking after Billy, the baby. Shelia, the eldest of the girls, tall, slim, and an organiser, would decide the games they played. The "house" game was where Jono and she were the parents and would order the children around. They were owners of the pretend shop, selling stones as sweets and sand flour. Brendan wanted to organise his own business and, along with Ada, a very attractive ten-year-old tomboy, opened a drapery shop selling buttons and old clothes.

The Fagan family were very staunch Catholics and Betty, their mother, would troop off each Sunday morning to Mass with her brood of chickens and tut-tut at the Harris family for being Protestants. To the girls, Brendan and Jono were different from the other local boys because they were Protestants. To the two boys, the closest reference to religion was the odd time their Ma dragged them to church on a Sunday morning. However, the five girls were steeped in the religious beliefs of the Catholic faith and were aghast at the lack of "faith" of the two boys. Ada told Brendan he would go to hell if he didn't have communion and all proddies were heathens anyway. However, like all children, they overcame their supposed differences and continued in their innocent games.

Over the summer months, Henry and Alice worked hard in the cottage, preparing it for the coming winter months. A lot of work was required. Apart from the many loose slates and tiles, the gutters needed attention, the brickwork required new plaster or pointing, all the windows needed realigning and puttying, and so on. Henry did what he could but, apart from the time required, money was also needed, so he patched up what he could.

Otherwise, life was quite relaxing. The family got to meet the neighbours and found their way around the locality. Unfortunately, when it rained, buckets and saucepans were necessary to keep the lino dry. The mind numbing "drip, drip, drip" of the water falling from the whitewashed ceilings was a constant reminder of the work to be done.

Alice, ever the opportunist, kept doing the prize crosswords to realise her dream. Jono and Brendan were the envy of the local boys, as they didn't go to school. When asked about schooling, Alice would say, "Soon, next year." The subject was a great problem in Alice's eyes. There were some small, state-run Protestant schools in the vicinity, but she wanted the best for her boys and was holding back until she had time to look at all the alternatives and find the finance.

6

The Win, the Hoolie, and Winter

Whilst the children continued in their innocent enjoyment of life, Henry and Alice were constantly seeking ways to save on spending and to finance the cottage repairs. Henry was quite exhausted, rising at six every morning to take the bus into Dublin, an eight-mile journey of some forty-five minutes. He then collected his bike and bag and cycled out to empty the gas meters on his round. There was always the risk of being relieved of the day's collections by thieves, or certain offers by desperate housebound women when the meter was short of money.

He had a monthly call to Fintan Villas, a block of tenement flats on the north side of the city. The buildings were of drab grey concrete, four stories high, and separated by unattractive dirty grey, weed-strewn slabs. Each building was the same with rows of small windows and small balconies balanced under them. Washing lines crisscrossed between the flats, holding them together. Radios could be heard, competing with each other to be the loudest. There was always a group of youngsters kicking a soft leather football on nearby waste ground, or some shawl-covered women either shuffling by with their shopping or talking in loud voices.

Henry invariably placed his bike against some rusty railings and nodded to Colum, who had sauntered over from the waste ground. Colum was a youngster of indeterminate age, certainly in his teens, with cropped hair, a dirt-engrained face, a mouthful of irregular soiled teeth, and an air of invincibility that accepted no compromise. Colum had already laid the rules on a previous visit.

"I'm de bicycle polis, mister. I'll guard yer bike fer ye for sixpence," was conveyed in a tone of voice which offered no alternative.

Henry resigned to the rules, yet knowing his bike would be safe, handed over the agreed deposit of three pence and made his way to empty what meters he could.

The door of number 301 was immediately opened when he rang the bell. Maggie Dolan, a small woman with stringy grey hair, a sagging body and an equally saggy smile, welcomed him.

"Hello der big fella, do cum in. I saw ye leave yer bike," she would offer in her flat Dublin accent, standing back from the door to allow Henry into the untidy apartment. Apart from the sheer mess the room was in, with a smell of rotting food, dirt and unwashed clothes, there was an overpowering smell of cats.

Breathing through his mouth to avoid the stench, Henry, ever polite to his customers, acknowledged her welcome and hurriedly made his way to the gas meter, pushing aside the cats rubbing against his legs.

Invariably, after counting the contents of the gas meter onto the kitchen table, there would be a shortage.

"Maeve, you're two bob short this time."

"Ah! Shure isn't it only money den, big fella, an' shure aren't I worth a bob or two?" the untidy woman would retort and commence to take off her cardigan, looking at Henry with a toothless seductive smile.

"No! No! Maeve! Stop it. We can't be havin' any of that nonsense now. I'm a busy man an' I'll leave the money until next time. Now put yer jersey bac' on. No! I won't have a cup of tea. Now I warn you, you'll be cut off if you don't pay."

Overwhelmed by the smell and clawing cats, Henry would scramble out of the flat as quickly as he could and collect his bike from the "bicycle polis."

Other instances occurred where the housewife concerned was more likely to approach him for a bit of company.

There was Mary McLaughlin, a twenty-five year-old, whose husband went to sea and who was constantly making suggestions.

"Cum on, Henry, den," she would offer, smiling her lovely smile. "Dere's no one around."

Henry, embarrassed and somewhat tempted, would smile his way through the confrontation, and whilst flattered by the offer, was more concerned with the complications which could result, and got out of the flat as quickly as possible.

Cycling all day was followed by a tiring long bus ride home, arriving back at seven in the evening. A car would be the answer, but was quite impossible.

Life in the cottage was basic. Whilst there was a bath in the bathroom—a ceramic boat some six feet in length with two large brass taps and a complicated plug—it was only used once a week. The family of five would take their turn. First Alice and the baby would splash around in the first four inches from the Ascot boiler. Jono and Brendan would follow with another inch or two of hot water added, with Henry after them in the remaining well-used pool.

Henry was often struck with large red boils on the back of his neck. Alice suffered from backache and the boys were forever coming down with infected sores and colds. Alice arranged an account with the local grocery shop and made the most of the few pounds Henry earned each week. Basic foods were plentiful and there was a great supply of fruit from the many apple and pear trees and fruit bushes from the orchard.

In the later months of 1946, however, fate came to their aid. The weather at the end of that year was particularly miserable with snow and ice. The roofs of the cottage were leaking worse than ever. Everyone was down with dreadful colds. Money was in short supply. Henry was taking the bus into work each morning in the dark and coming home exhausted.

Early one evening, in a particularly cold and sharp November, Brendan was out in the orchard chasing Podge, the pup, when it suddenly veered off course and raced over to the front garden gate with its tail wagging, barking a greeting. Brendan opened the gate to see an important looking grown-up in a grey suit with a briefcase under his arm, shutting the door of a small saloon car.

Turning around, Mr. Grey Suit, in a marked Dublin accent, asked if Mrs. Harris lived here. Sensing this was serious, Brendan turned and ran back to the cottage, with Podge racing ahead to warn Alice there was a suit coming to see her. By the time he had reached the back of the cottage, there was a ring on the porch doorbell and, as Alice was in the front of the house, she answered the door before Brendan had a chance to warn her.

The important man in the suit had a serious but welcome message that would help map out the future for the boys of Laurel Cottage.

"Would you be Mrs. Harris, den?" enquired the grey suit as Alice opened the front door. Grey suits and briefcases signalled officialdom, and officialdom signified trouble.

"Yes," said Alice, backing away from the door.

"Don' be after worrying yerself, Mrs. Harris," said the grey suit, noticing her wariness. "Me name is Patrick Walsh and I'm from the Radio Review. I could have some good news for you."

The Radio Review, Alice thought to herself. *Could it be . . . ?*

"Come in, Mr. Walsh. Come in, would you like a cup of tea?" Catching the now grinning grey suit by the arm, Alice ushered it into the front room. Pushing it into the best armchair, she ordered Brendan to make a cup of tea for the suit and sat down opposite this now wonderful fella bearing good news. Brendan stood at the door to overhear . . .

"Yes, Mrs. Harris, I have some good news for you and, rather than write to you, my paper has asked me to come and tell you personally . . ."

Come on, come on! How much? Alice thought.

". . . that your entry for the weekly crossword competition was successful and as you were the outright winner . . ."

Outright winner of the Radio Review. That could be £500, thought Alice, getting quite excited.

". . . and I have a cheque made out in your name for . . ." Pausing for effect, the grey suit produced from his briefcase a large colourful piece of paper and, with a dramatic flourish, handed it over to Alice.

". . . five hundred pounds."

"Pay Mrs. Harris the sum of £500," read Alice. ". . . the sum of £500." Leaping to her feet, she hugged the smiling suit and raced over to Brendan, jumping up and down.

"Five hundred smackers, five hundred pounds, wait till Henry knows. Where's Jono?" Catching Brendan's hand, Alice raced down the hall.

"A cup of tea for the nice man. No! No! Maybe he would like a drink?" Turning in one movement and leaving Brendan in a heap on the floor, she raced back to the front room.

"So sorry, Mr. Walsh. Let's have a drink to celebrate. Would you like some Irish?"

"If it's a drop of whiskey you're offerin', I'm your man," agreed the newfound friend. The many crosswords she had done had finally borne fruit.

Later that month, Alice and Henry held a "hoolie" in Laurel Cottage to celebrate the win. There were friends from the Gas Company, new friends from Killoughlin, the Garda (police) from the local Garda station, and relations from both sides of the family.

Quite a party, it started at eight o'clock on a Saturday evening. Prior to eight, there had been a delivery from Moran's Pub, the local public house, of crates of Guinness, other beers, whiskey, gin, and brandy. Spare glasses were brought in by the neighbours.

Alice had spent the day making sandwiches and sausage rolls. The boys helped where they could to butter slices cut from the pans of bread. The butter was always hard and a lot was wasted. Henry always made a lovely mix of hard-boiled egg, sliced tomato, and slices of ham, all cut as small as possible and mixed with salad cream and a bit of salt.

Just before the party, Alice took both boys aside to tell them there would be a lot of people coming to the house. There would be lots of noise, and that they were to be on their best behaviour and not to cause any trouble. Brendan was instructed to look after the baby, who was a year old now, and whose cot had been put in his bedroom.

The doorbell started ringing shortly after eight o'clock and hundreds of noisy grown-ups were introduced as Uncle this and Auntie that. They patted Brendan on the head and said how big he was. They shouted hello to each other, passed over bottles wrapped in brown paper, they called for a drink, and they laughed loudly. Doors slammed, toilets flushed and, of course, the baby awoke and started yelling. Alice told Brendan to go down and see to him.

Feeling a bit lonely, he looked at the squalling baby and got a stool to stand on, leaned over, and poked him to see if he would stop crying. It just made it worse. He patted him on the head, which increased the noise. What should he do? Take the baby out of the cot and pat his back to make him burp? Or maybe rock the cot? Rocking the cot was out of the question as it was big and heavy.

He leaned over further to see if he could pick the baby up, but his feet slipped off the stool and he buried his head in the blanket covering the baby. It was all wet and smelled awful. A smelly nappy, yes! Its nappy needed changing. That would shut him up. The crying was getting louder, the doorbell kept ringing, and there were raised voices in the hall with doors slamming. Brendan wanted to see what was going on. He was missing all the fun.

"Stop crying, you little divil. Shut up!" he shouted and rattled the cage, annoyed at this smelly monster demanding his attention and spoiling his fun. "Shut up!"

"It's okay! Brendan, I'll take over." It was Henry, who put his arm around him and hugged him as he started to cry. He was only six and a half and it wasn't fair.

"Go up and get your Ma," instructed Henry, as he wiped Brendan's eyes with his hankie.

Opening the door, Brendan looked up the hallway. There was nobody there. He crept tentatively towards the door of the sitting room, where all the talking and laughing came from. Jono, carrying a tray, suddenly burst forth from the doorway.

"Come on Brendan, I need your help to get some more Guinness from the kitchen," he instructed in his grown-up voice.

"Where's Ma?" Brendan asked.

"In there," answered Jono, pointing into the smoke-filled room as he skipped down the hallway.

Peering into the laughter and conversation, all Brendan could see were crowds of grown-ups blowing smoke into the air and drinking from glasses. Alice was standing in the middle of the room talking animatedly to a group of admiring men. He felt like running back to his pop, but slid his way between the bodies and pulled at her dress.

"Well, if it isn't wee Brendan," called a loud voice behind him, catching him under the armpits and lifting him head high to the adults.

"Put me down," Brendan cried, becoming quite frightened.

"It's al'right Brendan, it's only Uncle Sid. Put him down, Sid, ye might drop him," laughed Alice whilst passing her whiskey glass to another partygoer.

"Ma, Billy's dun a dirty. He smells. Pop wants you, Ma," Brendan cried and pulled her towards the door. Apologising all around, Alice followed him to see Henry on his way up the hall.

"Go in an' make sure everyone has a drink, Henry. I'll go sort out the youngsters."

"Wait a moment there, Alice," suggested Henry in a disapproving voice, catching Alice's arm. "I see the charmer Sid has arrived. He's always botherin' you. Do ye want me to have a word with him?"

Alice was taken aback by Henry's sudden possessiveness; she had been quite enjoying the attention from Sid and the others. To gather her thoughts, she patted Jono on the head as he passed, carrying a tray with bottles of Guinness on it.

"Good boy, Jono. Are you busy?"

"Very busy, Ma, ye go look after the baby. I'll keep 'em filled up." Stopping suddenly, Jono called back. "Ma, I heard a man say something rude. He was in the kitchen lookin' for the lav and said he was hopin' to get really—" Looking around, he whispered, "pissed. What did he mean, Ma?"

"Go on Jono, ask yer Pop."

Laughing, she took Brendan's hand and put her other hand to Henry's face.

"Hen', leave Sid to me, I know what I'm doin'. Now, go an' tell Jono what pissed means." She laughed again, smiling at Henry. "Come along with me, Brendan, me boyo. Let's stop the baby cryin', an' get you to bed."

The party had been going full swing for some hours and Brendan was fast asleep when he sensed the door opening.

"There's no one here, Paddy," whispered a female voice, as its dark shape became outlined against the window. A larger shape pushed in and the two bodies wrapped around each other, whispering and kissing.

"There's a bed," stated an excited male voice as they moved towards it.

"Go away! Go away!" Brendan cried to himself as he pulled the blanket over his head. "Go away."

"Wait Paddy! There's someone in the bed," whispered the woman.

"God! It must be wee Brendan. Sorry, young fella, we just got lost," apologised a gruff male voice as the two shapes disappeared back through the door.

In the half world of sleep and awareness, Brendan heard the hum of voices and laughter raised as the party door opened, hushed as it closed. There were loud whispers of people passing the bedroom door, making shushing noises, the sound of the lavatory flushing every few minutes. Sleep was behind his eyes when the door suddenly opened and Jono came stumbling in, muttering that he didn't want to go to bed.

The following morning he awoke with Jono fast asleep beside him and silence throughout the cottage. Bird song filled the air outside, while bright sunlight beamed through the large dusty windowpane. He slid out from under the overcoat and peeked out into the hallway. Nobody around. Somebody had been sick and had half missed the bowl in the lav. Oh! The smell! He washed some of the yellow vomit off the side with his stream, making patterns in the congealed mess. He couldn't flush the lav, as the chain had broken off at the cistern arm.

As he crept up the hallway, he could hear loud snores from his parent's bedroom, but was more interested in finding out who was snoring in the front room. Tiptoeing up the hall in his bare feet, wearing only his shirt with the long tails, he sidestepped the broken glass tumbler on the floor and turned up his nose at the smell from the overfull ashtray on the hall table. There was half a cigarette with lipstick stains on its tip on the side table. Picking it up, he sniffed the tobacco and pretended to smoke like the grown-ups did. A lady's cigarette. What did lipstick taste like? Pushing the sitting room door open, he peered inside with the cigarette dangling from his lips.

The smell of cigarette smoke and stale beer filled the air. There was a grown up, a bald man wearing only a shirt, underpants and socks, spread-eagled on the settee. Disturbed by Brendan's presence he grunted, sighed, and rolled off the seat onto the floor on his face. His short hairy legs stuck out from under his shirt, each leg dressed with elastic suspenders supporting his black socks, just like Pop wore. Brendan wondered where the man's trousers were.

Hearing a muffled snort and spluttering sound behind the settee, and now feeling quite superior at seeing a grown-up in such an undignified position, he saw what apparently were the man's trousers being used as a pillow for one of the aunties he had been introduced to, who he remembered was Auntie Molly. He was fascinated to see she was only wearing her knickers, a blouse and long nylon stockings, one torn and pulled off at the garter around the top of her leg. Her hair was over her eyes and her face had lipstick painted everywhere but her mouth. Her blouse was off one shoulder, showing the top of a diddie cover.

With an effort, he tore his eyes away from the forbidden sight, the knickers and diddies, garters and a lady's legs. *Gosh! Wait until I tell Jono,* he thought, looking around the room. There were half empty Guinness glasses and a partly eaten sandwich, one of Pop's specials, on the piano keyboard. Stubbing the cigarette out on the nearest ashtray, Brendan sat on the piano stool with his bare legs swinging and took a bite from the sandwich, followed by a mouthful of stale Guinness. Whilst the sandwich tasted fine, the Guinness caught at the back of his throat and, mixed with the rich mayonnaise and tomato, came gushing out of his mouth and through his nose, making him snort out loud.

The baldhead grunted and stretched its legs. The woman's sleepy eyes peered over the back of the settee.

"Hello, Auntie Molly!" greeted Brendan.

"Oh God! Ye didn't see?" she exclaimed in a smoke-induced croak, looking down at her legs and knickers. "Ye didn't see? Oh! Christ. Look. It's Jack, Jesus look at the man. Where's me skirt? Me blouse is torn."

Looking on in astonishment that grown-ups could be so undignified, Brendan offered Aunt Molly a drink from the glass of Guinness. She would surely like it, as didn't grown-ups drink Guinness all day?

"No tank you, Brendan," slurred Auntie Molly as she groped around the carpeted floor on her knees, searching for her skirt. The baldhead woke up, put its hands up to cover its eyes from the daylight, and stood as erect as its large belly allowed it.

"I'm burstin," he exclaimed and felt his way out to the hall. He stumbled into the hall table, knocking over the framed photo of the family and all the ashtrays muttering, "Where's the bloody bog? I'm burstin'.'"

"Where's me skirt?" queried a now desperate Molly, panicking, while trying to cover her modesty with her hands at the same time.

"Bren, I'll give ye a shillin' if ye can find me skirt for me. It's green with flowers on it. I tink. Me purse is in me bag. Where's me bag? Oh God! All me money's init," she cried in desperation.

Enthralled by the sight of a grown-up, and a woman at that, displaying her secrets with such abandon, he dismounted from the piano stool and started looking for anything green and worth at least a year's supply of Sharp's toffees. There was a small cushioned bench in the window recess, which looked promising; behind it on the floor was the lost skirt with a large leather handbag. He sat down on the bench.

"Auntie Molly is your bag a big brown one wi' a big yella buckle? An' your skirt green with roses on it?" questioned the smiling Brendan.

"Hav' ye found it? Brendan boyo, hav' ye?" came the desperate cry from the other side of the settee as Molly, in relieved desperation, came stumbling towards him.

"There's your bag, Auntie Molly. Is your purse innit?"

"Yeh! Tank God," answered the half-dressed grown-up. "Where's me skirt, Brendan boy?" Molly asked whilst reaching out a plump arm for the large handbag.

"Hav' you got two bob den, Auntie? I've got your skirt as well."

"Oh! Alright ye little bas . . . Oh! Alright Brendan," agreed Molly handing over a florin, not realising she was also offering young Brendan a close-up of the hidden secrets of female underwear and women's naughty bits as a she stood before him reaching out for the skirt.

"God bless ye, Brendan," said a grateful Molly. "Now don' ye be after lookin' while I get dressed."

7

Starting School

"That was one hell of a party last night, Henry, wasn't it? How many came? Didn't Molly Coyle look cute in her short skirt? An' Bob O'Neill— what was he up to with Mavis Baker?"

So laughed Alice, over a cup of tea, the morning after the "hoolie." Henry was quieter than usual and smiled in agreement. They had both had a few drinks the previous night and Henry was, apart from slightly hung-over, loath to confront Alice with his thoughts. What had she been up to with Sid? She seemed to have been flirting with him. Sid, the rich philanderer, was nothing to look at with his baldhead and paunch, a big talker. What was the attraction to her?

Alice, well aware of what was going through Henry's mind, decided to put his mind at rest.

"Hope he didn't crash the car," she suddenly announced.

"Who? Sid? Why does that bother you, Alice? You sure gave him a lot of attention las' night," accused Henry, glad to bring the subject out into the open.

"Yes! It does bother me, you big lump. He's just bought himself a new car. Going to get it in a few days and will let us have the Wolseley. Isn't that great, Henry? He's lookin' forward to hearin' from you in the next day or two."

Henry was quite taken aback by this disclosure. Once again, this woman he had married had done something without consulting him; once again, she had out-thought him. The Wolseley was a great car, though—so comfortable. *I could use it to get to work. Maybe go down to see Tom in the Deerpark*, he thought.

"Yes, Alice, what a great idea," he replied. "What price did you come to? I'll ring him on Monday. It's a lovely car. Well done, lassie. You. You . . . don't really like him, do you?"

"Hen'," answered Alice, leaning over to kiss him, "you're the only man for me. You're a pain in the arse at times, but you'll do. Now, here's his phone number. Come on, we'll go up to Moran's, phone him from there, an' have a drink or two to celebrate."

With the deal agreed, Henry took the bus into Dublin the following Monday. He met Sid's employee, who passed him the keys and logbook and took Henry's cheque for payment.

Henry walked around the car. He noticed a few scratches in the paintwork, but the tires looked okay. Pretty good for the price. A little bit of paint would spruce her up. He climbed into the driver's seat behind the large shiny steering wheel. He took a deep breath to savour the smell of leather and steel, that unique aroma so indicative of a modern car.

Just as he was revelling in the ownership of this wonderful toy, Sid's employee opened the door and pointed to the cheque.

"Look, surr, this is dated for next month."

"That's fine, young man," replied Henry. "Everything's fine. Nothing to worry about. Now I must get away and complete the insurance."

"If ye say so, surr," acknowledged the employee. It was nothing to do with him anyway, and went to catch the bus.

That post-dated cheque will give me a few days to look over the car and, if necessary, put a stop on it, Henry thought to himself. *Sid! Me boyo! You're dealing with Henry Harris here. Now, let's get it insured.*

That evening when Henry arrived back at the cottage in the car, he took the family for a drive down to Dunlaoghaire and along the coast road. *Better not go any faster than forty miles an hour. Might strain the engine,* he thought.

"Let's go as fast as we can, Pop," encouraged Jono. "Put your foot down."

"Will it do, fifty Pop, or even sixty? Go on, Pop," questioned an excited Brendan. "Look, the speedo is showing forty-five."

"Slow down, Henry, we don't want an accident," cautioned Alice in the front passenger seat. "I've got Billy here on my lap an' we don't want to end up goin' through the window."

"All right then, everyone, I'll do no more than forty until I get used to her," agreed Henry as his wonderful new acquisition sped up and down the hill. They swept past the striking scenery along the Vico Road, and bounced over the cobbles on the main street of Dalkey, out onto the sweeping view of Dublin Bay, back into Dunlaoghaire and then the last mile to Killoughlin.

"The engine seems fine. She may need a couple of new tires an' the bodywork has just a little rust," mused Henry as he stood admiring his new possession.

"Come in the lot of you, before we freeze to death," called out Alice to her three men standing in the frozen weeds, all looking at the shiny green car that was now beginning to show a light film of white frost. "Come on you lot, race you back to the house!" challenged Alice picking up Billy who was now getting quite big.

"No! I'll take the youngster," called Henry. "It's freezin' now. I'll come back out an' cover the engine with an old carpet. Maybe should drain the radiator. Doesn't the car look well?" A pleased Henry stood again admiring his new toy whilst the others hurried back down the frost-covered grass and weeds that constituted the "avenue."

The cold weather continued over the next months, bringing severe frosts and large snowfalls into the New Year in 1947. Henry had to clear out the shed at the top of the avenue to shelter the car from the severe weather and took the bus into work again. The water pipes in the cottage all froze up, and most of the chickens died in the cold.

The snow drifted to some eight feet against the cottage and had to be shovelled aside. The cold was intense, but they were fortunate to have plenty of wood from the trees around the cottage to warm some of the rooms, as coal deliveries were few and far between. Alice made her way to the nearest shops, sliding on the icy pavements to buy whatever food-stuffs were available.

As the weather improved with the thaw in March, Henry started to use the car and, as things settled back into normality, the question of the children's education arose. Could they afford the school fees to send the boys to the grammar school in Dunlaoghaire?

Alice had made her way to Dunlaoghaire, met the Headmaster of the school, and obtained an agreement in principle that the two boys could be considered, but he would have to meet them first. They could probably start after the Easter holidays.

"Now boys," said Henry in a commanding grown-up voice. It was unusual for him to make statements or issue orders or opinions of any sort.

Brendan knew it must be something special, and looked at his father with renewed interest. A meeting had been called, or rather, Alice had told everyone to be in the sitting room on Saturday morning, as Henry had something to tell them.

"Your Mammy and I have decided the two of you will be going to school after Easter."

Now both seven and nine years old, and with the neighbours' children all asking why the boys didn't go to school, this was a momentous moment.

"Will we be going to the same school as Fintan?" asked Jono. He dreaded the thought, as Fintan was the pompous eldest son of a neighbour.

"No, Jono," replied Alice with a chuckle. "No need to worry. Fintan goes to a Catholic School and, as you know, you will go to a Protestant school."

"We're not going to the National School in Dunlaoghaire, then, are we? Is that Catholic?" asked Jono. Schooling in Ireland in the 1940s was primarily run by the Religious Orders and, in the state school where the Catholic priests ruled, there were stories from the youngsters in the area that the priests were very strict and wielded their authority by the cane. The building housing the National School was down a side street in Dunlaoghaire, a very forbidding red brick edifice with small windows that gave the appearance of a jail.

Laughing, to dispel their fears, Alice put their minds at rest, and answered in a pleased and satisfied voice.

"You're both going to the grammar school in Dunlaoghaire. So we'll be goin' into Dublin to buy some new clothes for you both before you meet the Headmaster next week."

The dream of both parents was to give their three boys the education that they never had as children. The crossword win was giving them that opportunity.

The week following their visit to the city, Henry took time off from work and the five of them made their way down to the school in Dunlaoghaire to meet the Headmaster. The two boys were very self-conscious in their new, dark grey worsted short trousers and jackets, white shirts, and ties. They were also finding it difficult to walk in their shiny new ill-fitting black leather shoes.

"Don't worry, boys," Alice consoled them. "Your feet will get used to them. I'll put a bit of stickin' plaster on your heels when we get home."

Henry parked the car outside the Headmaster's house, next door to the school, and they made their way up the impressive steps to the large Georgian house. Alice was talking rather loudly to Henry, who was not looking forward to the interview.

"I'll leave it up to you Alice," he advised as he rang the shiny doorbell.

"Oh! Do come in sir, madam, I shall tell the reverend you have arrived. Do take a seat in the drawing room."

The very smart lady who answered the door directed them into a large, quiet room decorated with dark wallpaper and furnished with an immense sideboard covered in books, and a huge round table in the centre with magazines on it. The smell of furniture polish was very prominent and the shiny wooden floor was quite daunting. Walking with exaggerated careful steps, Brendan made his way over the slippery floor and threw himself onto a large leather armchair that squeaked when he bounced on it.

"Hush child, sit still," Alice admonished in a nervous voice. "Jono, sit."

"Ma, listen to this," interrupted Jono as he slowly walked across the shiny floor. "Listen to the shoes. They squeak. Listen."

"Enough of that, Jono. Sit down and keep quiet," ordered Alice, sitting herself nervously at the centre table with Billy in his one-piece blue suit standing unsteadily beside her.

Noticing one of the magazines on the table had a yellow cover like the one at the doctor's, Brendan slid off the squeaky leather seat, pulled the magazine off the table and, with great excitement, opened the *National Geographic* magazine to see the wonderful coloured pictures of foreign countries and black people. Forgetting the reason for their visit, he became engrossed in a map of South America. The feel and smell of the smooth shiny pages entranced him.

"Brendan, get off the floor and sit back in the chair."

Alice, in exasperation, caught him under the arms and pushed him back onto the leather armchair. Still engrossed in the magazine, Brendan was now in the jungle, riding on the back of an elephant, the leaves from the tall trees shaded the sunlight. He was leading an expedition into the jungle. He was Tarzan. He was . . .

"Come this way, sir, madam. The reverend will see you now," announced the smart lady. Patting their hair into place and needlessly straightening their ties, Alice prodded the two boys into the hallway, following the rapidly disappearing guide. Henry had taken Billy up in his arms.

When shown into a further large, high-ceilinged room, a small, black-garbed man with a bald head and white dog collar rushed out from behind a mountainous desk and welcomed them all into his domain. He greeted Henry, who towered above him, with hands outstretched, and greeted Alice, also shaking her hand. Then, stepping back, he looked Jono and Brendan up and down and offered his hand to each, who shook it tentatively. He then invited them to sit and disappeared behind the desk. Within seconds, the small head and dog collar arose again above the vast expanse of paper-covered green baize.

As the grown-ups talked amongst themselves, Brendan noticed that one of the Reverend's eyes was half closed, with the skin all wrinkled and puckered in varying shades of blue and purple. Brendan wondered if someone had hit him, or maybe he had walked into a door or perhaps he had caught malaria in the jungle. Concentrating on this and trying to catch Jono's eye to see if he had noticed, he missed the Reverend asking him a question.

"Answer Mr. Sweeny, Brendan. Mr. Sweeny would like to know what you expect from school?" ordered Alice in her posh voice.

"To learn, sir," Brendan replied apprehensively.

"Very good. May I ask what your favourite subject is, young man?" enquired the dog collar.

"Jungles, sir," was the prompt reply.

"Humph! Very interesting. What about you, young man?" the bald head enquired of Jono.

"Body building, sir," replied Jono. He had recently seen an advertisement about Charles Atlas, the famous American body builder.

"Humph, Humph," were the critical sounds from the Reverend. After a further short conversation between the grown-ups, the door opened to admit a smiling gentleman wearing a green corduroy suit. This turned out to be the deputy head, Mr. J. Blazer.

Jono and Brendan, with Billy between them, were then passed into the hands of the smart lady whilst the grown-ups continued their discussion. Shortly afterwards, a satisfied Alice and Henry collected the three of them and, on the way back home, advised Jono and Brendan they would be starting school in two weeks' time.

So, in early April 1947, dressed in their second-hand school blazers, navy blue with silver coloured edging, white shirts, black and white striped ties, and re-cycled school caps, all bought from the local outfitters, the boys entered the grounds of the grammar school. Alice had left Billy with one of the neighbours and Henry had gone to work so, in the early sunlit morning, she self-consciously walked her two boys through the imposing gates into the school grounds.

She threaded her way through streams of boys and girls, all dressed in their smart school uniforms and most pushing bicycles, through the manicured garden and towards a large, forbidding-looking building with paned windows.

Brendan was introduced to Miss Short and Miss Walls in kindergarten, whilst Jono went into the big school. It was a bit daunting for Brendan, being introduced to the class as the new boy, and then being placed under the care of a pretty blonde girl named Georgina.

"Now Brendan," smiled Miss Walls, "Georgina will look after you and tell you what you need to do."

Georgina, who was smaller than Brendan, turned and gave him a dazzling smile, making Brendan blush furiously. He could feel his face getting hotter and hotter and felt he had to sit down. The only seat was a low desk where he had to straighten out his legs to get them under the desktop. Whilst blushing and stretching, he over-balanced and brought the small desk crashing onto the wooden floor. The lid on the desk sprung open and colouring pencils, rubbers, broken rulers, pencil sharpeners, tin boxes and a small, petrified frog all leaped out onto the floor.

There was a gasp from the class and Miss Walls, a redoubtable lady, thank goodness, rushed over and lifted him up, commanding the enquiring faces to continue with their work. If she had not caught him, Brendan would have been out the door like a scared rabbit, never to be seen again.

Settling him into the desk and smiling at Georgina, who also wanted to run for it, she opened a small book with pictures of a chubby boy called Bob kicking a ball and requested the now blushing Georgina to read the words to Brendan. Returning to the front of the class, Miss Walls continued with the lesson and smiled at Brendan over the rows of heads. As he was adept at reading, he skipped through the pages whispering aloud the two and three letter words and felt a lot better, as Georgina seemed to be impressed.

The day passed very quickly and after school the two boys met up, said good-bye to their new friends, and started to walk home, feeling very pleased with themselves. They knew the route home, as the school was in Dunlaoghaire and they had walked it many times when they were unable to afford the bus fare.

Their journey brought them through a variety of buildings and small housing estates, expensive houses, a large church, children's home, the outskirts of a council estate, and past a reformatory school. Whilst strolling along in their innocence and talking about their exploits during the day, they approached a row of scruffy shops with a few bored-looking, cloth-capped men leaning against the local turf accountants wall and a group of scruffy youngsters kicking ball on some waste ground.

"Gawd, will ye be after lookin' at the pair of dem, Sean," laughed the biggest of the youngsters, pointing towards Brendan and Jono. The contrast between the two sets of youngsters could not have been greater. Jono and Brendan looked a right pair of beauties strolling along in their flashy finery, pretty satchels and jaunty caps. They were prime bait for a bit of leg pulling.

Coming towards them, three of the grinning monsters blocked their escape and backed them up against the wall. What were they to do? Brendan was getting a bit scared. Jono stood in front of him. The leader, and biggest, reached over and pulled Brendan's cap off, giving it to one of his supporters who put it on his head and started to swagger about.

"There you are, you little bugger. What are ye going to do about dat?" laughed the leader.

With that, Jono swung his bulging school bag with his pencil case, empty milk bottle, and books and caught the aggressor on the side of the head. Both boys started shouting and kicking out. The largest guy went red in the face and started shouting curse words at them. The two smaller lads encouraged him.

"Go on Mick; beat the s—t out of them."

Mick came back at Jono with his arms flailing widely. Brendan started to run for it, pulling Jono after him. One of the little monsters squared up in the Joe Louis style, but Brendan ran through him, pulling his cap from his head and raced away followed by Jono. Getting around the corner, they stopped to catch their breath. Brendan's heart was beating furiously; he was sweating gallons and felt quite sick.

Making their way home up the long hill, past the Reformatory School, Brendan, in his innocence, could not understand why those boys wanted to hit them. Why did they not like him? He wanted to be their friend. How could he ever go to school again? They would be waiting for him.

By the time he reached home, apart from the emotional upset, his right ankle was red and raw from the hard top edge of his shoe, whilst his neck was sore from the stiff shirt collar. This was an abrupt change from the easy days they were used to and quite distressing for a seven-year-old.

That evening, there was a big meeting after Henry arrived home. Alice was all for going down to the Farm, the local name for the council estate, and having it out with the boys' parents. Henry, being more realistic, suggested they avoid the area and anyway it would be a bit difficult tracing the culprits. It was resolved that the following morning the two boys would take the bus from Moran's Corner to the school. This would be expensive at one penny a trip, but it would avoid the trouble spot.

And so it was the next day after their usual fried breakfast and getting ready for school. Henry had already left for work; now an Area Manager for the Gas Company, he covered the North side of Dublin which was some twelve miles away. Billy was becoming a bit of a handful for Alice forever under her feet and there were eight rooms of the cottage to keep tidy. The slate and tile roofs were forever leaking, the kitchen was the size of a football pitch, there were chickens to feed, a crazy dog to control, three pet rabbits to look after and, of course, what with the resident rats and mice, her day was a busy one.

"Where's my school bag, Ma?" cried Brendan. "I left it in the dining room after I'd done my homework las' night. Where is it Ma? Quick! I'll be late for the bus."

"It's in the hall Bren', ready for you. Jono, are you ready? It's getting late."

"Okay, Ma," replied Jono.

"Right, get out, the pair of you. Here's your sanis and a bottle of milk and your school bags. Now, get goin' or you'll miss the bus."

"Ma! It's Tuesday, I haven't got enough money for the comics," interrupted Jono. He was now over nine years old and becoming responsible.

"Here's a shillin', should be enough for your fare and the comics. Don't forget, I want the change back. Now, get goin' the pair of you."

Both boys, dressed in their school blazers, short trousers, neat long stockings, their school caps stuffed in their pockets because neither wanted the neighbours to see the caps, set off reluctantly. It was a bright sunny morning and there were many more exciting things to do, on such a day, rather than go to school. They crept like snails up Red Clay Lane and past Mahoney's shop.

"Come on, Brendan, or we're goin' to miss the bus," encouraged Jono.

"Come on quick, we better run for it." The bus could be heard climbing the hill on the left and they reached Moran's Pub as the large green double-decker bus rounded the corner. Reaching the stop as the bus pulled in, the two boys leaped on the bus platform and, calling "good morning" to the conductor, climbed the steep stairs to the top deck.

"Hope the front seats are empty," called Brendan as they reached the top of the steps, hanging onto the bars as the bus gathered speed. Making their way between the rows of occupied seats, being jolted from side to side, they settled down on the shiny front seat, right up against the wide window. From this vantage point they could see the road ahead and could pretend they were driving the bus.

"Wow! He must be doin' mor' 'dan sixty miles an hour," exclaimed Jono, as the bus picked up speed.

"Look, there's Sean," called Brendan pointing into the reflection in the glass.

"How are you, Sean?" he called waving into the window.

The reflection was full of people, mainly school children all chattering away, all seen through a haze of cigarette smoke. The few grown-ups dotted amongst the reflection were all smoking. "Smoking upstairs only" was the message when you boarded the bus.

As they rounded the corner at the local dairy with rows of horse-drawn milk floats lined up in the yard, the bus lurched to a stop.

"All 'dose want a bottle of milk dis is yer stop," came the call from the conductor. Ding went the bell and, as the bus sped away, the conductor came up the stairs.

"Fares please. Let's be havin' yer money now."

Whirr-Ding went the ticket machine as the conductor made his way up the bus, commenting, "You're lookin' well today Mrs. Murphy, dat'll be two pence."

Whirr-Ding. "Four pence change. Dunleary, Sir! Four pence to you."

Whirr-Ding. Another ticket.

"Keep quiet, or I'll throw you off the bus," was the admonishment to the noisy schoolgirls.

"Take your feet off the seat, young fella."

"Well, if it isn't two lads from the grammar school," he exclaimed as he approached Brendan and Jono. He pushed his peaked cap back up his forehead, wiped his rather long nose with the back of his hand, and looked at the shilling Jono handed him.

"A whole shillin'. You're in the money today, lads. What are you goin' to do wi' all the change?"

"I'm going to get the Beano and Jono the Knockout from the sweet shop. Do you read the Beano, Mr. Conductor?" answered Brendan.

"Whenever I can, Sonny." Whirr–Ding.

"Your change, surr! There's a tanner, a thru'pence and a penny. Now put it safely in your pocket." Jono took the change and put it carefully in his bag with his sandwiches.

"Any more fares please?"

The bus had now entered the Council Estate where the lads outside the bookies' office had teased the two boys. Keeping their heads down as the bus pulled up opposite the bookies, they peered over the windowsill.

"There's no one there," was the relieved call from Brendan. After the loud ding the bus sped away and the two boys began to enjoy the rest of the drive towards the school.

"Next stop, the grammar school. All gentlemen and ladies fer the higher educatin' please leave the bus," was the loud call from the conductor as Jono and Brendan, self-consciously, made their way back along between the rows of seats.

"Careful, surr," was the smiling caution from one of the smokers as the bus rocked suddenly, putting Jono on his lap. Brendan hung on grimly as they made their way down the narrow steep stairway to the open platform.

"Here you are, young surrs. Got you bags? Now hold on tight."

The swaying bus pulled up alongside the stop outside the school entrance, and the two boys jumped down onto the road.

8

Visit to the Deer Park

"Pop, I'm hungry. How much more to go?"

"Keep goin' Brendan, it won't be long now. We should be across the bog quite soon."

Mollified a little, Brendan took a deep breath, hunched his thin shoulders under his cotton shirt and heavy coat, and continued his careful progress across the lumpy wet ground in his unwieldy Wellingtons.

It was now late spring in 1947 and the severe winter months were at last coming to an end. The mountains of snow around the cottage were turning to slush. Henry's repairs to the roofs during the glorious summer had not been a great success, as most rooms now had a variety of saucepans and pots positioned under the many drips coming through the ceiling. Due to the dangerous conditions of the roads over the winter, Henry had put the car away in the shed and made his way into work in the bus and Jono and Brendan walked to school.

Renewed contact was now being made with the rural communities that had been isolated over the snow-filled months, and Henry was relieved to hear that his near relatives, Tom Pinkerton and wife Jane, were alive and well. Jane was Henry's father's sister and she and Tom were caretakers of the Gate Lodge of a large estate in the Wicklow Hills.

On his parents' untimely death at an early age Henry, being made homeless, went to live with Uncle Tom in the Gate Lodge to the Deer Park, an extension to the large Powerscourt Estate. Life in the lodge was very basic—no electricity, gas, in fact, no power whatsoever. Schooling was in the local church, a two-mile trip across bog land. The nearest shops were some five miles away across narrow laneways through the turf footings. Winters were severe and summers mostly wet.

When he left school at the age of fourteen, Henry was sent to live with an elderly aunt in Dublin, prospects for work being so much better, and started an apprenticeship with the National Gas Company. Now in his mid thirties, and married, Henry had kept in touch with Tom by post and infrequent thirty-mile bus journeys to the lodge.

It was not until late April, that it was deemed safe enough to attempt a car journey due to the late winter snows. There would still be some snow but the Garda, in a small township closest to the Deer Park, confirmed on the telephone that the roads were fairly clear.

With five shillings' worth of petrol in the tank and after a couple of test runs down Red Clay Lane to check all was well, the family, with plenty of warm clothing, some tinned foodstuffs and fresh vegetables for Tom, set out on a bright crisp morning.

They sped along at a steady thirty miles an hour, with the car giving the odd splutter with Henry concentrating on the driving. Alice sitting in the front, with Billy on her knee, reminded them all to be on their best behaviour when they arrived at the Deer Park.

"Pop," asked Brendan, "will there be lots of deers to see in the Deer Park?"

"Don't bother your daddy when he's driving, Bren," advised Alice, turning to face the rear of the car. "But no, Bren, there won't be any deer at all; they were all shot dead by the English when they came over for their holidays years ago."

Brendan was quiet for a moment, thinking how mean it was of the English to shoot the deer.

"Ma! Why did they do that?"

Before Alice could gather her thoughts for a suitable reply, Jono, in his grown-up voice answered Brendan.

"Bren, they killed them for the venison. The meat of the deer, so there."

Brendan looked at Jono and, rather than admit he didn't know what venison was, changed the subject.

"Are we goin' to stay on holiday, Ma?"

"No, Bren, we're comin' home tonight. Just goin' to leave a few things for Uncle Tom, have a cup of tea, and come straight home."

"Now, if we turn right here," muttered Henry to himself, "should be okay. God! Look at the river, boys," Henry exclaimed. "Look, it's in flood. Much more and it will cover the road."

Eagerly the boys looked to the left to see the foaming river racing past with small bushes and trees being tossed on the surface. Leaving the river behind as they crossed another small road bridge, they entered a valley with snow-covered trees stretching to the sky and into the small village called Kilmacanough.

"Now, boys, we're into the real country," Henry announced as he carefully manoeuvred the Wolseley into the Rocky Valley. The narrow road started to climb through the rock-strewn slopes, reaching to the moorland above. After a mile of rising road, some of it quite slippery, it started to drizzle light rain and, close to the top, the Wolsley started to labour badly. Henry already had the engine down to second gear and was becoming anxious. Would she do it? Still a bit of power . . .

"No! She's not goin' to do it," he cried in dismay. "Right, the lot of you, out you get and hopefully the old girl will get to the top!" Pop ordered as the car stopped in the middle of the narrow road.

"All out now," instructed Alice. "Don't mind the rain, just put your coats on. I'll leave Billy in the back seat with pop."

Beneath the lowering overcast sky, the three travellers stepped out into the drizzling rain and waited whilst Henry coaxed the car into life again and called out that he would wait for them all at the top of the hill.

"Come on now, heads down, keep going," called Alice. "Don't go runnin' on ahead too fast, you might slip an' it's a long way down."

"Yes, Ma!" agreed Brendan. "Look at all the snow on the top of the mountains. Are we goin' there?"

"No, Bren," answered Alice. "Hope not anyway. Pop knows. See that mountain? That one's called Djouce Mountain. An aeroplane crashed there years ago."

"Gosh! Ma! Were they all killed? Was that durin' the war? Were they spies?" asked Jono, moving his right hand through the air and making airplane crashing noises.

"Isn't that mountain over the other side called the Sugar Loaf?" he asked knowledgably.

"I can see the Little Sugar Loaf," chimed in Brendan, not wanting to be beaten by Jono in mountain lore. "Pop told me. That one there behind us."

"Yes, boys, that's right. Pop lived down here when he was a youngster like you. Now, keep going, we're near the top of the hill. Yes! There's Pop, you can see him there at the top. Come on, let's run."

The two elder boys ran ahead, as best they could, in their long overcoats and Wellington boots. Both wore black sou'wester hats that covered their ears. Alice trotted behind in her boots and mackintosh.

"Just a minit all of you," Henry cautioned, raising his head from under the open bonnet as they all gathered around the car.

"I'll get her working. Now all stand back now." With the rain running down his face from his soaked hair, Henry pulled the black dripping raincoat tighter around his body, climbed into the silent car, switched on the ignition, pulled out the choke and pushed the starter button.

"There's some life there," he said hopefully as the engine whimpered. After a few futile efforts, the recalcitrant engine turned over and, with a very satisfying roar, fired. Puffs of black smoke belched from the exhaust.

"It's workin'. Climb in everyone," called out a triumphant Henry.
"Next stop, the Deer Park."

For the next ten minutes, the car progressed in the morning rain-filled sky. Past expanses of flat bog land on either side with the Wicklow mountains to the right. The narrow road stretched for miles ahead of them, winding through the gorse and heather. Henry pointed out a small clump of windswept trees to their left.

"Just behind the trees—there, you can see it now—the church spire. I went there nearly every Sunday. Calgary Church. Went to the church school as well. There's Calgary Bog to the right. The Deer Park is about half a mile over the bog. Oh no! What's this?"

As Henry came to the end of the longest speech the children had ever heard him utter, the engine seemed to choke, stutter and then suddenly stop. The silence was deafening.

The car glided to a silent halt.

"Can't get it to start, Alice."

Heehee-Heehee went the engine. Cough-Cough.

Henry resignedly clambered out of the car, lifted the bonnet and poked a few things. "Try the ignition again, Alice."

Cough–Cough. Heehee-He-e-he he-e-he.

"Sounds like something wrong with the engine and the battery is dying. Maybe try the starting handle—that should wake her up."

A resigned Henry discovered a much-used starting handle in the boot and commenced to turn it with some effort. The car engine refused to fire.

"Let's try a push start, Alice. Will you go behind the wheel, please. All out boys and get pushing."

The boys were delighted with the novelty of it all and pushed with all their might.

After a few exhausting and futile attempts, Henry called to Alice.

"It's no use, Alice. Look, the lodge is only a half mile or so across the bog. I'll go and see if Uncle Tom can get some help," suggested Henry.

"No way, Hen!" answered Alice. "Hen', were not staying here, we'll go on with you. We've all got our wellies and the rain has eased a bit. What do you say boys? Forward across the bog."

Henry, aware of the risks of crossing soggy bog land, but very confident in his knowledge of the safe path he had used many times as a child, relented under Alice's determination. Anyway, there were plenty of daylight hours ahead.

"Okay! All get in line. Jono, you take up the rear with Ma, then Brendan, and I'll take Billy. Nobody wander off, now."

Making sure the car handbrake was on and taking out the ignition key, Henry patted the car on the bonnet and, looking across the bog with

Djouce Mountain to his right, like an Indian brave led his band of warriors along the narrow track. They pushed through clumps of bracken, were scratched by the low-lying thorny bushes and stepped into squelching puddles. They passed footings of cut turf left out to dry and edged along holes left in the ground. Brendan got stuck in a boggy hole and the water seeped in over the top of his boots. He pulled himself out of the hole aided by Ma and Jono. After a further ten minutes crossing the bog, squelching along in their heavy Wellingtons, Pop encouraged them all.

"It won't be long now. Let's stop for a wee breather," he said as they rounded a small hump of land. All were grateful for the rest. Brendan's boots had filled with water where he had fallen into the bog hole. Alice was exhausted and sat down on a small stack of turf. Jono was all for running ahead, whilst Billy had fallen asleep on Henry's shoulder.

"Look! Look over there," exclaimed Henry pointing ahead of them. "Smoke from the Lodge. Com'on, keep going. We're nearly there."

"Right! Up you get the lot of you," a much-relieved Alice called to the boys. After a further ten minutes of sticky and uncomfortable walking, they came to a narrow dirt track, which led down to a well-used road.

"The cottage is just over there to the right. Thank God we're here," exclaimed a very relieved Henry, feeling quite exhausted not only with the unaccustomed walking, but also the dead weight of the sleeping Billy over his shoulder.

Jono and Brendan raced ahead and stopped at the large double gate, arching high in the sky above them. They could see the lodge a hundred yards down a cart track with a battered old tractor parked alongside. A noisy stream rushed under the road and down past the lodge. Bracken-covered hills formed a backdrop to the old, one-storey building. There was a welcome light shining from one of the windows of the lodge and a curl of smoke drifted lazily from the slate roof of the lodge.

"Look Brendan, look at the chickens. There's a pony. Look, there's some ducks," exclaimed Jono.

"I see a goat, Jono. Gosh! This looks a smashin' place. Look Pop," said Brendan, pointing out the animals to his father. There was a sudden commotion at the lodge and a large dog came bounding down the cart track, barking loudly. Henry tried the gate and, finding it unlocked, stepped inside and held his hand out in greeting to the large Labrador dog, whose tail started wagging furiously as it recognised him. A shaft of light threw its beam down the track as the door of the lodge opened and a small figure stepped out.

"Chan, Chan, cum here boy. Who is it der, den?" called out the man.

"Come in, come in all of you," Henry called out to the family.

"Is it Uncle Tom there I see? It's Henry here," he shouted out towards the man.

Tom, grey-haired and wearing a heavy, hand-knitted white jersey which stretched down nearly to his knees, welcomed Henry with a big hug.

"God bless us if it isn't wee Henry and his family! God! Look at the size of ye all. Cum in, cum in. Down Chan. Cum on in. Jane will be pleased. Down Chan."

Tom, nearly hopping with pleasure upon seeing Henry, as there were many happy memories of the past they had to share, shook hands with Alice and each of the boys as they made their way towards the lodge.

As they neared the building, Auntie Jane came striding out.

"Who is it den, Tom? It's not visitors is it?" she demanded in a loud voice. Somewhat taller than Tom, with her grey hair held in a severe bun, dressed in a heavy skirt and jersey and smelling of wood smoke, she appeared a very forbidding figure.

"Well, if it isn't Henry an' his family!" she cried out upon seeing the bedraggled group. "Hello, Alice. What are ye all doin' here? You should have tol' us ye were comin'. Cum in cum in out of the wet."

"Hello, Auntie Jane," called Henry as they neared the lodge.

"Here, Alice, will you take Billy? Hello Auntie, how are you?" He put his arms around the tall, thin woman and gave her a kiss on the cheek.

"We've come to see you're all right and brought some supplies. But the car broke down over the way."

Alice received a brush of cheek on cheek and the three boys got a royal wave of the hand. Over a cup of tea from the pot stewing on the stove, Henry told the story of the problem with the car.

"Now look," decided Tom. "Yer'll all here now so why don' ye stay the night? It's beginning to get dark. We'll go and see about the car. Young Murphy in the farm across the hill is a wonder with the engin'. He's kept my old tractor goin' for the past five years. I'll go over and see him."

"Yes, Alice, stay the night, as Tom says," interjected Jane. "I'm sure the boys would like to. What do you say Jono, Brendan, William?"

"Oh yes, lets!" was the eager reply in chorus.

"There ye are den," decided Jane, looking in triumph at Alice.

Alice was not too pleased to have the decision made above her head. It was obvious she and Jane were not going to be close friends but to keep the peace she kept quiet and started to help prepare a meal.

The three boys raced outside to wave Henry and Tom off on their mission to find young Murphy. The tractor roared into life, with Henry standing on the rear step hanging onto the back, and lurched out onto the road, with black smoke belching from the exhaust. Jono shut the big gates and the three boys, as the rain had stopped, took off their heavy raincoats and started to explore.

Where to first? The stream looked great, and where did that path lead to?

"Let's go for a ride on the pony," suggested Brendan.

"That's no pony, ye eejit, Bren, that's a donkey," scorned Jono. Just as they were preparing to do some exploring in the growing gloom, Ma called out.

"Come in boys, your tea's ready."

"Great! I'm starving," exclaimed Brendan. "Race you."

Alice and Jane had prepared a heaped plate of lovely smelling sausages with a bungalow-sized mound of soft slices of white, homemade bread with crunchy crusts and a big pat of butter.

"Help yourselves, boys," ordered Jane. "Who takes sugar in their tea? Careful of the candles."

Some hours later, as the boys were getting ready to retire to their makeshift beds, the tractor was heard returning from its mission of mercy. Running out into the darkness, the boys saw the beam of light of the tractor's headlight approaching the large gates. Jono and Brendan ran to open them and the tractor roared in, towing the car, with Pop behind the driving wheel.

"We couldn't get the engin' to start and young Murphy was nowhere to be found," explained Henry as he climbed out of the Wolseley stretching his arms and rubbing his eyes. "Let's get inside and wait until mornin."

Tom, clambering down from the high seat on the tractor, laughed as Henry walked stiff-legged towards the lodge.

"You're getting soft der, young Henry. City life don' suit ye."

"Yeh! You're righ' there Tom," agreed Pop, laughing as he continued towards the welcoming candlelight flickering in the doorway.

"Right boys, away to your beds," ordered Alice on their return. "Now be careful with the candle." Brendan and Jono made their cautious way down the cold hallway, shielding their spluttering candles.

"I don' like this," complained Jono, rubbing his hands together. "It's cold."

"Nor do I, Jono," agreed Brendan.

Moving slowly down the scary hallway with its flickering shadows, they came to the doorway of their bedroom. The room was filled with odd-shaped shadows rushing to hide from the sudden light.

It's scary. Where's my bed? wondered Jono. On the floor were two mounds of blankets that they adjusted to make into beds and, before settling down, went in search of the lav.

Returning to the kitchen, they were directed out the backdoor to a small shed at the back of the house.

"Can't wait," advised Jono and, joined by Brendan, he watered the small flowerbed, giggling to each other.

Returning to their "bedroom," they settled down for the night. Before long everyone had retired and the lodge was silent, apart from the dog moving around, the owls hooting, the sounds of small animals scratching outside and the kitchen clock ticking every second and striking with a loud DONG! every half hour.

"Cock a doodle doo! Cock a doodle doo!"

Wakening to the sound of the cock crowing, Brendan, through sleepy eyes, looked around the small room and at the dim shapes covered in dust: a battered wardrobe, an old mangle and shelves on the walls covered with dusty newspapers and books. Jono was moving restlessly beside him. Brendan stretched his stiffened limbs under the thin blanket and, donning the short trousers with the tear in the crotch, an elastic belt with the snake-shaped buckle, his well mended socks, crumpled grey shirt and Wellington boots, made his way to the outside.

Hearing noise in the hen coop, a ramshackle little shed away at the back of the lodge, he ran over to see Uncle Tom throwing a couple of dead hens out of the coop. There were feathers everywhere.

"Mornin' Brendan. You're up early den," he said in a resigned voice.

"The foxes have been at it again." Hitching up the loose pair of brown corduroy trousers he was wearing, with the legs tucked into rubber boots, Tom picked up the mutilated chickens by their legs and, swinging them over his shoulder, his grizzled lined face broke into a grin.

"I'll be havin' cooked chickin' for tea tonight. Me favrite."

"Yes, Uncle Tom, I love chickin' too. Can I have some?" asked Brendan.

"Shure son. Have a word with yer Auntie Jane."

Taking a deep breath of the clear air, Brendan looked around him with a feeling of wonder. There was so much of everything, hills and mountains stretching out before him, some with patches of snow, others without. There were very few trees on the windswept gorse and heather-covered hills. The clear blue sky, with a watery sun beginning to show through the early morning mist, seemed to promise a dry day ahead.

A valley behind some straggly pine trees showed promise. Uncle Tom said there was a lake down there and the Powerscourt Waterfall was over there behind the hills. The air was so pure and clear that Brendan took another long pull of it and jumped up and down with delight in anticipation of the adventures ahead.

"Yoo-hoo! Brendan, breakfast!" Auntie Jane called from the lodge.

Wow! Breakfast, thought Brendan. "Comin', Auntie, I'm comin'," he shouted.

Jono was already sitting down at the large table in the kitchen that smelled of fresh bread and fried bacon. Jane was frying some eggs and Henry was talking with Tom. Alice had Billy on a chair beside her and was feeding him.

As he sat down, Brendan nudged Jono and whispered, "Uncle Tom has promised me some cooked chicken tonight."

"You'll be lucky, Bren. Pop says soon's the car's ready we're goin' home."

"Ma! Are we staying for a while? I want to see the waterfall," Brendan called over.

"Shure! Why not Alice?" Auntie Jane interrupted. "Let the wee lad have a look."

"I wanna go too," called Jono.

"It should be all right now with most of the snow gone," suggested Auntie Jane in her positive manner, moving spluttering fried eggs to plates, already half covered in fried slices of bacon.

"Get that down you now, an' there's plenty of bread te eat with it."

Silence reigned for a short while as the lovely smelling, tasty food was eaten. Henry speared his last forkful of creamy egg white and yellow yolk on the thick piece of homemade white bread and, after chewing it thoroughly, as he did with every mouthful, addressed the table.

"Okay! You lot, we'll walk down to the waterfall if there's not too much snow. We've all got our wellies. I'd love to se it. That okay with you all? Okay, Alice?"

With a chorus of "Yippee," everyone agreed.

"Yeh! You go on with them, Henry lad. Young Murphy said he would be here about eleven. The key's in the car."

"Right, Tom," replied Henry, nodding to Aunt Jane as he rose from the table with the tea cup to his lips.

"Thanks Auntie for the breakfast, an' a lovely cup of tea. Are ye comin' Tom?" Henry called out to him as he was heading toward the hen coop.

"For God's sake, don't ask Jane," implored Alice under her breath.

"No, Henry! Tanks, but I'd better sort out the hens."

"Is our bridge still standin' Tom?" called Henry. When as a youngster living in the lodge, Henry had helped Tom had built a bridge over the stream running alongside.

"Yeh, it is, Henry, still there," answered Tom as he waved the five of them off.

"Come on now," called Alice as she and the three boys headed out towards the lake. Wearing grey slacks, which Jane had tut-tutted about, her rubber boots, a cream-coloured roll-necked sweater, which Tom secretly admired, and her long blond hair tied back in a ponytail, Alice looked quite a picture. The boys thought she looked smashin' and Henry, whilst he slightly frowned upon the ponytail, was very proud of her.

Henry, with his commanding height of over six feet, and his dark, curly hair with slight grey tints, wearing grey flannels tucked into his Wellingtons and a suit jacket going slightly threadbare at the elbows, looked very smart albeit a bit overdressed for the countryside.

"Lead on, Mac Duff. Ye know where we're going," ordered Alice, with a beaming smile, as they made their way along an unused path in the wet weeds and grass. They walked onwards towards the rushing stream on its way to join the river, lower down in the valley.

"There's a narrow part where we can cross the stream over the bridge Tom and I built years ago. Here Billy, I'll giv' you a piggy back."

They followed the path between the bracken-covered slopes, ever aware of the increasing roar of falling water. As the ground levelled out, the stream they followed joined a small rushing river racing away to their right. The thunderous sound of falling water ahead of them became stronger as the five of them rounded a large clump of rhododendron bushes.

Henry stopped in mid step.

"Look at that," he called in awe. They all stopped. Brendan and Jono called out in unison, "Janey Mac!" while Alice put her arm around Henry and exclaimed, "Isn't that wonderful."

Some 400 feet above an open glade, a brown-stained stream of water, having gathered momentum on its journey through the heather-covered land above, rushed out from the skyline and fell in a steady stream down the cragged rock face, crashing in a constant rush of water into a pool at the base of the moss-covered boulders. This brown sheet of water was framed on each side by the browns of heather and bracken and the grey boulders clinging to the sides. Unsteady-looking trees clung to the surface in defiance of gravity. The never-ending sound of the water dominated the surroundings. This scene had been constant for hundreds, if not thousands, of years. Brendan stopped in his tracks.

The cascading water seemed to catch its breath in the deep pool at the base of the fall and then continue on its quest for the sea. Sweeping around the boulders and rocks, brushing aside any obstruction on its journey, the swollen stream of bracken-stained water swept along, indifferent to the admiring gazes from the transient onlookers on its bank.

Running forward and joining in the exuberance of the rushing water and the noise of the fall, the three brothers shouted their joy at being alive. They balanced on the slippery rocks, as near as they could to the vertical wall of tumbling water, looking up into the sky through the spray. Henry and Alice stood at the side of the river holding hands and both smiling at the picture. *What of it? If the car doesn't work, what if we're short of money, or the roof leaks?* thought Henry. We're lucky to be alive and to be a part of this wonderful display of nature.

"Come on, boys, before ye all get wet," called Ma, holding out her hands as each of the boys jumped back off the rocks.

"Let's explore," suggested Jono.

"No lads, it's getting late and we have a long way to go. We can come back again."

With the three boys running ahead, they made their way back to the lodge, all tired but quite exhilarated by what they had seen.

Rounding the small hill sheltering the lodge, they saw Tom and young Murphy standing proudly beside a throbbing car, noxious fumes pumping into the air. Henry, with a beaming smile, went over to thank the youngster.

"Jane!" called Alice. "As the engine is workin' we'll go on. Thanks for the meals. Say good-bye to Auntie Jane, boys. All aboard now, let's go home."

"Bye, bye, Auntie Jane, Uncle Tom, see you in the summer," called out Jono and Brendan as Henry got the car moving, and they headed out the open gates.

9

A Visit from Our American Cousins

It was now early 1949; financial circumstances had not changed much in Laurel Cottage. Alice and Henry were both working hard to keep the house going. Henry was now an inspector in the Gas Company, with responsibility for a team of collectors and supplied with a Gas Company van that had to be left at the depot each weekend. The Wolseley was still serviceable; the engine needed constant care, but could still get by with encouragement.

Due to the shortage of money, Alice decided to take in holiday-makers for the summer. A friend who had been on holiday to Liverpool said she knew people in Lancashire who would love to come to Dublin during Wakes week for a few days' holiday. There was a family of four now due the end of July and another group early August. Alice had also decided to offer "teas," as surely there would be some people passing along Red Clay Lane, perhaps on holiday. Maybe they'd like to try her special "Cream Tea"?

Henry had put together a board and painted it green with the words "CREAM TEAS WITHIN" in white. With a rueful grin, he had put the board on the orchard wall facing towards the main road.

The weeks went by without any customers. The sign was beginning to look a bit weather-beaten and Alice had more or less forgotten it was there.

It was a Sunday afternoon in May 1949, a beautiful sparkling day; every tree was bursting with newly grown buds. New grass, and assorted weeds were sprouting up everywhere. Early flowers were showing a carpet of yellow and blue and there was the constant sound of sparrows chattering as they considered where to fly next. Tomtits, thrushes, and blackbirds all added to the background song of peace and tranquillity until, suddenly, there was a call from the orchard.

"Ma! Jono's nose is bleeding real bad. It's gushin' blood. Quick, Ma," shouted Brendan, running in from the orchard where he and his two brothers had been playing cowboys. Jono, as Tom Mix, had fallen out of the apple tree. The cooking apple tree with the low sweeping branches had one branch that was ideal to adapt as a horse. Jono had lost his balance whilst urging the horse to speed up and fallen off onto his head.

"Come on, Jono," encouraged Brendan as he led the blood-streaked victim, his head thrown back to stem the blood flow, into the kitchen.

"Lean over the sink, Jono. Let it run a bit," ordered Alice as she got a cloth to wipe his face. Just then, the doorbell rang.

Billy, who had wandered in wearing soil-stained shorts and an old shirt, with his bare feet dirty from playing in the soil, raced up the hall.

"I'll get it. I'll get it."

"Go up with him, Brendan. See who it is. Hawk it up, Jono, and spit the clot out."

"Arragh! Arragh!" gurgled Jono, spitting out a wad of blood.

"Hold your head back and keep breathing in fast through your nose," instructed Alice, wiping the blood from his face again.

"Who is it, Billy?" Alice asked over her shoulder, as Billy and Brendan returned to the kitchen.

"It's some people come for their cream tea, Ma. Will I let them in? They talk funny," Brendan answered.

"Why have they come for their tea? I never asked anyone. Who are they? No, stop!" she paused as the realisation dawned on her, of course— 'Cream Teas Within.'

"Oh God! Here, Jono, take the cloth, keep breathing in. Brendan, put them in the front room and say your Mammy will be up in a minute."

"I wanna see them, Ma," spluttered Jono, turning away from the sink and running up the hall with his face hidden behind a blood-soaked tea cloth.

Two adults, male and female, and a young girl, all with slightly bemused expressions, were following the two rather dirty youngsters towards the front room. Jono, with his face covered in a bloody towel, opened the door for them and directed them into the ill-prepared room.

There was a table at the window but, as there had never been any customers, the chairs had been taken elsewhere. The boys had been playing in the room and the floor was liberally covered with lead soldiers and dinky cars. The bright sunlight emphasised the dusty window and a sunbeam directed the eye to a rolled back carpet spotlighting the stained wooden floorboards and the watermarks, the result of the frequent rainfall coming through some loose tiles on the roof.

The three customers looked at each other and hesitated at the doorway. Brendan, realising the chair shortage, raced out into the hall and met

Alice running up, looking very smart in a white blouse, her best skirt and her hair brushed.

"I'll get some chairs, Ma," he advised running towards the dining room. Alice, stopping at the door, ushered the three amused travellers into the room, wishing them a "Good afternoon," in her posh voice.

"So sorry about the chairs. We took them out of the room because of the rain, you know." Giving a short laugh, she directed Brendan to put the two heavy chairs he had dragged up the hall alongside the table.

"Jono, go back to the kitchen. William, the people don't want to see your dinkies."

Jono, realising his nose was leaking again, caught Billy with his free hand and reluctantly dragged him out of the room.

"Oh, that's okay, Marm! We think your kids are cute. Isn't that right, Abigail? Thanks youngster," the male member of the trio said, as he took the third chair from the puffing Brendan.

"We saw your notice on the wall, Marm, and thought it would be grand to have some real Irish country tea. Isn't that right, Abigail?" The large male in his flowered shirt, large belly and tight trousers, directed his eyes to the tall, thin, serious-looking woman dressed in a two-piece woollen suit and high heels.

"Yes, Abner. Yes, you did." Directing her eyes to Alice and, in a soft American accent that contrasted with the harsh tone from the male, she continued. "We would like a buttered scone each with our cream tea, please. If you do not mind."

"Tea and scones for three," agreed Alice straightening out the cloth on the table. "Are you here on holiday? You're from America, aren't you?"

"Yep! Marm. Myself an' Abigail and our daughter Nuala here," replied the man, pointing to a scowling Nuala, "are here checking out our Irish relatives."

Alice, eager to know whom they were seeking, thought she had better get the tea and scones together and left the room, pulling Brendan behind her.

"Lucky we've got some scones. Hope they're fresh enough. Is there any cream on the milk, I wonder?" she said to herself as she made her way quickly down the hallway. Filling the large black kettle, she lit the gas jet on the cooker and, placing the kettle on the flame, started to butter the scones from the bread bin.

"Excuse me, Marm," came the American voice behind her. "Excuse me, but where's your john, please?"

"The john? The john?" Taken aback for a moment, Ma scratched her head. Suddenly realising that he meant the lav, she turned and pointed toward the pantry, which housed the lav.

"Oh! You mean the lav-a-tory. You mean the lav-a-tory."

"Yeah, Marm. The lav-a-tory, the john."

"In there, in the pantry," directed Ma, pointing to the wooden door in the side corridor off the kitchen. "Be careful with the chain, it's a bit loose."

"The chain! The lav-a-tory! The pantry! What next?" muttered the puzzled American to himself as he stooped his head to enter the pantry. There in front of him what he could see in the dim light from the small dusty window was the large blue veined porcelain lav. The smell of dust and the sweet aroma from some withered over wintered fruit filled his nostrils. Resting the wooden seat from the lav against the pipe behind the bowl, it fell into two pieces. Henry had stuck the two sides together with glue and one had to be careful lifting them.

"Now, where's that chain?" Abner muttered when he had finished. "The lady said it was loose."

A linked chain hung from the cistern over the lavatory. It had a carved wooden handle tied with string. Abner pulled it gently, but nothing happened. He pulled it twice more. "Better not pull it again, it might break."

"Youngster, will you pull the chain for me? I don' wanna break it," he called to Brendan in the kitchen. Brendan stepped into the pantry, peered around the large American, saw the broken seat and resignedly shook his head.

"I see you broke the seat on the lav. Pop won't like that." He placed the two pieces together and rested them on the basin.

"This is how ye pull the chain, sir," he advised as he pulled it down in two short tugs followed by a longer tug, releasing a large waterfall, which nearly overflowed the bowl. Abner stood looking on in admiration.

"Must try that again before I leave. Thank you, sonny. Wha' a wonnerful country this is," he muttered to himself returning to his wife and daughter.

"Abigail, I've just bin to the john in the pantry. They call it the lav-a-tory. Shucks, I had better write this all down. The folks back home will never believe it."

"Yes, here we are now, your tea and scones, sir, madam," was the announcement by Alice, in her put on voice, the voice used for visitors.

"I have put some extra jam on for the young lady. Made it myself, you know, from our own gooseberries," she smiled, looking at the scowling Nuala.

"Now, Nuala, say thank you to the nice lady," ordered Abigail.

Nuala, a tall twelve-year-old, dressed in a plain cotton dress with white socks and sandals, her mousey hair tied back in a severe bun emphasising a plain, freckled face with big eyes and a tight-lipped mouth, stared straight at Ma.

"Thank you, Marm, fer these lovely . . . scans."

Alice passed the treasured cups and saucers from the tea set received for her wedding, and used for special occasions, placed the plate of halved scones, liberally spread with butter, alongside the silver dish of gooseberry jam.

"You say you are looking for some Irish relatives?" she enquired, looking at Abner.

"Yep, Marm. My great grandpoppy, by the name of Traynor, lived in a place called Mountain View somewhere around here. Would ye know of such a place?"

"Mountain View!" cried out Brendan before Alice could reply. "Mountain View is jus' down the road."

"Yes," interrupted Alice, forgetting her posh accent. "Mountain View is a mile or so down past the fields and the convent. Though, there's a John Traynor lives down the road, he owns the nursery."

"Well, Abigail that could be our man. These scans—have I got that right, lady?—these scans are de-licious, de-licious."

The Americans, especially Nuala and her accent, fascinated Brendan and Billy. They suggested Nuala might like to come and look at the hens and rabbits.

"Wha' a great idea," agreed Abner. "Yep! Finish your scan, Nuala."

"An' keep your clothes clean," ordered Abigail.

"Don' forget, Nuala, keep the . . ." Pointing to his lips, Abner instructed Nuala to be careful what she said to the boys.

"Have you seen any Indians? Does your Pop carry a gun?" enquired Brendan as the children made their way down the hall. Billy, who had run on ahead, came out from the bedroom swaggering, with bowed legs and low-slung holsters with two six-shooters on his hips.

"Put your hands up, missus," he instructed, standing in a crouch in front of Nuala, drawing the two large revolvers from their holsters and pointing them at her.

"What ye want, Billy? We're only poor homesteaders," replied Brendan, cowering against the wall with his hands in the air.

Nuala, looking on in astonishment, decided to play the game. Standing with her hands on her hips, pouting her lips, she replied in a casual drawl.

"Wha' ye want, Billy. De ye wanna kiss? I've got no money."

Billy, taken aback by the reply and certainly not wanting a kiss, holstered his guns with a flourish.

"Let ye off this time. If I catch yuh again' I'll shoot ye."

"Are you really an American? Do you know Hopalong Cassidy? Have you seen any Indians?" queried Brendan, relaxing a bit due to the unexpected new attitude of this strange girl.

"Is your Pop a gangster?" asked Billy.

"Yeh! Does he know Al Capone?" Brendan leaped in, overriding his young brother.

"Hold on, hold on the pair of ye," drawled Nuala. "Lemme see the chickens first. Me Paw is no gangster, though he's a lookin' for one in this here town."

Looking in an uncertain manner at the cobwebs hanging from the kitchen ceiling and the rusty gas stoves, she followed the eager boys out into the back yard. Jono, whose nose had at last stopped bleeding, came out from the breakfast room adjoining the kitchen, not wanting to miss out.

"What's yer name?" drawled Nuala at Jono. "In fac', what are all yer names?" She asked all round as the four of them walked up towards the hen run.

With the three boys listening to her strange drawling voice as she answered their many questions, Brendan asked what gangsters her "Paw" wanted to find.

"We live in Nu York and my Paw's gran'poppy had some money stolen from him by a fella called Sean Traynor. Paw is over here to see if he can get any of it back."

"If he finds Sean will your Paw shoot him?" asked Billy in a hushed voice.

"Yep!" answered Nuala. "He'll ask him for the thousand bucks an' if he doesn't get it Mr. Sean will end up full of slugs."

Brendan, listening intently, immediately pictured Sean Traynor being forced to eat slimy slugs.

"Slugs," he interrupted. "What d'ye mean?"

Before Nuala could tell him Jono replied with a scornful look.

"Slugs are bullets. Ain't dat right, Nuala?"

"Yep! Pump him full of slugs until he rattles."

"Golly," said Brendan thinking he had better warn Sean. Sean was John Traynor's son, who was the same age as Brendan.

"Jono, I'll go and tell Sean," Brendan whispered.

"Okay! Bren, I'll tell Ma," Jono whispered back. "Nuala, have you seen enough of the hens yet?"

"Wanna see your rabbits."

"Okay! Billy will do that. Have to go."

With Brendan disappearing down the side of the cottage and Jono racing down the other side, Nuala realised she had said too much and, leaving a disappointed Billy who was looking forward to showing off his rabbits, raced after Jono to stop him.

With the sudden exertion, Jono's nose started to bleed again and, with his face covered in the bloody towel, called Alice from the kitchen to get her away from the visitors.

By now, Brendan had made his way to the nursery and, shouting for Sean, was stopped in his stride by John, Sean's father. John was not a very pleasant man. He certainly had no time for children, especially that Protestant woman's brats.

"What you want, child?" he asked the breathless Brendan.

"They've come to kill Sean, Mr. Traynor. The American and his gang. They say Sean's granda stole money from him. Where's Sean, you gotta' tell him."

"Now calm down, boy. Who's this bloody 'merican?" Remembering his own grandfather Michael, who had emigrated way in the past, he didn't doubt the man had broken the law. Maybe there was some trouble in the offing.

"Where's dis 'merican now, youngster?"

"He's in the cottage. He's gotta gun. He's goin' to shoot Sean."

"I hope you're not havin' me on, young fella. Now, where's that bloody Sean? Sean! Where are ye boy?" shouted John.

Clang, clang went a bell on the road. Brendan remembered there was an old cowbell at the gate. *Must be Mr. Abner,* he thought. *Don't wan' him to see me.* Looking through a hedge near the gate, he could see the three Americans standing on the lane.

"Golly! There's Mr. Traynor goin' down. Is he goin' to punch him? No!"

Traynor, with a beaming false smile, welcomed the Americans, leading them up the path towards the house.

"Brendan, what's goin' on? Da said to go an' hide." It was Sean looking very worried.

"Yeh! Sean, the 'mericans there are come to kill you. They tol' me."

"Yer jokin' aren't ye? What would they wanna' kill me for? I'm only nine years old."

"Can we get in the back way to hear what they say, Sean? Come on," suggested Brendan.

Following Sean, Brendan sneaked in through the kitchen door to hear raised voices coming from the front room.

"Sean Traynor, me great granddaddy, was a decent god-fearing Catholic when he left our shores all those years ago. It was only you bloody Americans taught him to steal."

"What do you mean to steal, Mr. Traynor?" enquired Abner, slightly bemused.

"I kno' nuttin' about me granddaddy stealin'. T'was the young fella from the cottage saying ye were cummin' to sort me out an' that ye had a gun. Have you got a gun den?" Traynor backed away from the American with his hands raised in mock distress.

Turning to Nuala, Abner asked in a resigned voice, "What have you been sayin', Nuala? Have you been making up stories again?"

"Yeh! Paw thought . . ."

"Quit thinkin' young 'un, look at the trouble you caused."

Turning back to the confused Traynor, he apologised.

"Sir, I'm sorry, this young 'un is always causing trouble with her fancy stories. Abigail, hav' a word with her while I talk to Mr. Traynor here."

Abigail, turning around to face Nuala, resignedly remonstrated with her. Abner pacified Traynor, telling him their reason for calling was to find a relative of the famous Sean Traynor who had saved his, Abner's, great granddaddy from the red Indians in the battle of the Little Big Horn. John Traynor, ever the man to take advantage of an opportunity, agreed with Abner that his granddaddy was probably the same brave man.

"Yeh, the stories me Pa used to tell me by the fireside about his famous relative in 'merica."

There was some truth in the story and Traynor was only too ready to add his embellishments. Brendan and Sean were listening behind the door and, whilst relieved with the outcome, were naturally disappointed there was to be no gunfight. As they both stepped into the room Traynor turned to them.

"You, young fella," he said, pointing to Brendan, "had better stop causin' trouble with yer fancy stories."

Brendan stepped back in astonishment at the injustice of it all.

"Shure, Mr. Traynor, she told me an' I came to warn you."

"Okay, young fella den, okay!" replied Traynor, waving dismissively at Brendan. Turning to Abner, he pointed to a cabinet on the wall.

"Would you be after likin' a wee drop of Jameson whiskey now, Mister 'merican? No hard feelings den."

Relieved at the outcome, Abner chuckled.

"Shure! John, I'd love a shot and no hard feelins here either."

Pouring a liberal amount of whiskey into two glasses, Traynor turned to Abner and, noticing Abigail, offered her the glass, pouring another for himself. Whilst the three grown-ups were toasting each other, Sean and Brendan approached Nuala. The American girl and her accent fascinated both boys. Brendan's curiosity overcame the indignation he had felt at being lied to.

"Let's ha' some lemonade," offered Sean and, whilst the two boys listened to a further list of tall stories from Nuala, the grown-ups were deep in conversation talking about and toasting distant and long gone relatives.

In the midst of a lengthy story about another possible close relative in the States, Abner, with Abigail sitting beside him on the seedy sofa, dozing slightly after the whiskey, suddenly stood up and struck his forehead with his pudgy fist.

"Gee whiz! I forgot, John, my friend. Abigail, we'd better get up an' go. We have to be in Dublin tonight. How are we to get into Dublin? Where are we, John boy?"

Having had a fair few whiskeys, Abner was feeling a big groggy.

"Dat's all right den, Abner. I'll get the young 'un to take ye up to the bus te Dublin," replied Traynor.

"Are ye all right there, Missus?" He leaned over the sofa to the half asleep Abigail.

"Ye gotta go now, missus."

Pulling the slightly tousled Abigail to her feet, Traynor patted her on the bottom and hiccupped, saying to Abner, "Now, be looking after your woman, Abner, an' the next time I'm in Miss-isso-urie I'll gi' ye a call. *Sean!*"

Calling to Sean, he helped his new friends with their coats and, scowling at Brendan, he and Sean ushered the lot of them out the gate and onto the lane.

With the night approaching and the air cooling, the two adults felt groggy and slightly disturbed by the sudden expulsion from their new friend's house. Abner turned to look down at Brendan.

"What's the way to the bus, young fella? God I feel unsteady. Are you all right, dear?"

"I don' feel too well a-tall, Abner. What are we doin' in this god for-saken country? I wanna go home."

"How about you, Nuala?"

"This is terrific. Let's stay."

"You can get the bus up at Moran's' Corner. I'll get Ma," advised Brendan, running ahead in the gathering darkness up to the cottage. He met Alice, who was on her way out to look for him.

"Ma! The 'mericans are on the lane wonderin' what to do. They didn't shoot Sean. Come on, quick."

Wondering what was going on, Alice ran down to the dark lane with Brendan, followed by Jono and Billy.

"Yoo-hoo! Yoo-hoo! Where are you?" called Ma in her posh voice, It was now so dark she could not see anything.

"Here, Marm, over here at the wall."

Following the sound of the strained voices, Ma made out the figures in the dark and, reaching out to touch the dark shapes, she asked if they were all right.

"Fine, Marm," replied Abner in a voice filled with annoyance. "Jus' wanna get my wife an' child back to civilization."

"Come on into the house and have a cup of tea first," offered Ma.

"Very kind of you, Marm," replied the voice in the darkness, "but we have an important meeting in Dublin. Gotta get there soon. Tell us how we can get this bus to Dublin. Is it always this dark? God dam!"

"No need to utter profanities, Abner," came the tired voice of Abigail from out of the gloom.

"We would be grateful, lady, if you could show us the way to this bus to Dublin."

"Certainly. Sir, madam, follow me." Turning on her heel, Ma, followed by the Americans with Billy, Jono and Brendan riding shotgun, marched up the lane toward the street light at Moran's pub.

"Now, the bus comes up the road there, from Dunlaoghaire," advised Ma, pointing to a road disappearing in the gloom to the right of them.

"We'll stay with you until it comes. Every half hour. Are you all right, Nuala? Did you enjoy your visit?" asked Alice, directing her voice to the tired girl standing close to her mother.

"Wanna stay here. Don' wanna go to Dublin."

Ignoring the response, Alice enquired if the Americans had the right bus fare. Delving in his pockets, Abner produced a handful of coins and a crumpled ten-shilling note.

"There you are sir. That florin should be enough to get you all into Dublin. Look, here's the bus."

Directing their attention to the approaching lights, she hustled the three visitors towards the bus stop. The single deck bus drew up with a squeal of brakes. The bus conductor stood back as the three Americans boarded. Alice got on with them, staying the conductor's hand as he went to ring the bell.

"Our friends here are from the United States of America. Will you direct them when you get into Dublin, please?"

"Shure, missus, 'merica it is. Move along the bus den, please. Are ye comin' wid us den, missus?"

"Oh! God no, let me off."

Waving good-bye to the tired Americans, she jumped off as the bell was rung and the bus pulled away from the pavement. Apart from Jono, they all waved good-bye to the visitors from the new world. Jono's nose had started to bleed again.

10

Just William "The Play"

It was now the early months of 1951 and Brendan was approaching his eleventh birthday. Tall for his age and physically fit, he played hockey for the school team and took part in the regular gym classes. He was above average on the sports field, fast in the sprints and excelled in the medium distance races. Cricket, in the summer months, was out of the question due to cost.

He was very conscious of how little he had in material possessions compared to the other children at his school. He was aware other boys were coming to school in full school uniforms, whilst his second-hand uniform clothes were now becoming too small. His school clothes were hand-me-downs from Jono. Very self-conscious, Brendan was prone to blush very easily, especially when near to any of the supremely confident schoolgirls.

Academically, he was holding his own in class, finding it hard in some subjects, while maths was difficult. He coped with geometry, geography was interesting, and he was good at art and French. History was a lot of confusing dates. He ignored Irish language, whilst he revelled in English composition and literature.

It was a Saturday morning. The temperature was below freezing, and the only heating in the cottage was a couple of smelly portable oil stoves and the coal fire in the front room.

Brendan and Jono had finished their homework and had been playing a game of "skeet" on the lino floor in their bedroom. It was becoming a bit boring and their fingers were getting sore. The game consisted of a set of bakelite round counters from a draughts board, with a line of toy soldiers placed on the lino six feet away. The idea was to "skeet" the counter across the lino by pressing down on it using one's forefinger. The harder the "skeet" and the more backspin on the counter, the more dead soldiers.

Brendan's army of ceremonial palace guards, with big bushy helmets, and a tribe of assorted Red Indians, all led by Hopalong Cassidy on his white horse Topper, were becoming a bit decimated. The unerring fire from Jono and his army of farm animals led by Roy Rogers, on his palomino horse, Trigger, was knocking them down easily.

"Hey, Jono," Brendan interrupted the slaughter of his army. "You know Ma and Pop went to a play in Dunlaoghaire yesterday? You know the one, where there are actors on a stage?"

"Yeh! Ma said it was borin' and a waste of money. Whee! Jus' got Hopalong," Jono added, as a skeeting counter-tumbled horse and rider.

"You've only got a couple of Indians left."

"Okay, Jono, I give up," replied Brendan, raising his hands in surrender.

"Why don' we do a play ourselves. We could charge people, say, a tanner each. If ten came that would be—what's ten sixes? That's sixty pennies. Gosh! Five bob. That's two bob each and give Billy a shillin'."

The thought of two shillings made them both think hard.

"If twenty people came that would be ten shillins," said Jono, doing a quick bit of mental arithmetic. "Five shillins each!"

"No Jono, four and six each—don' forget Billy."

"If we got a hundred, golly! That would be an awful lot," enthused Jono.

"Who could we ask? The Byrnes, the Carrolls, the Duffys. There's six of them there, den there's the Flynns, one, two, three."

Brendan scratched his head. "An' Mrs. Flynn and Paddy, that makes another five. How many are we now?"

Counting on their fingers, they were excited to find there were fifteen prospective sixpences.

"We could advertise," suggested Brendan. "Put a card in Mahoney's shop window. Get at least ten from that. What about Mr. and Mrs. Mahony? How many are we now?"

"That's another fourteen. Fourteen and fifteen, that's nine and two tens, that's twenty-nine tanners. Golly, we're goin' to be rich."

Deciding that twenty-nine sixpences made the wonderful total of fourteen shillings and sixpence, they realised they had to find a play to act.

"What about Black Beauty? We could make a play from that story," Jono suggested.

"Couldn't get a horse in the room. Could pretend one tho'. No! No good, the Chap would hav' to be a girl."

"What abt' the Famous Five? There's some great stories there," suggested Jono again.

"They always go out in boats don' they?" replied Brendan.

"No! Not them. I know! The one, the best!" he called out excitedly. "What about 'Just William'? I'm reading the stories and we could make a play out of one of them. I could be William. What about William an' the Tramp? You could be the tramp, Jono. Maybe Declan could be Mr. Brown?"

The thick hardback library book was produced and turned to the episode of William's escapades with the tramp.

"There you are Jono. William and the Tramp. We could work out how many people would be in the story and we could pretend to be different ones. Look!"

There was a sketch of the untidy William defending the right to harbour the ragged and dirty tramp, a dishevelled-looking shyster, to a simpering Violet Bott. With his hands on his hips Brendan, in a voice he presumed would sound like William's, read from the book.

"I tink he's jus' a poor person what wants a holiday an we shud giv' him the spare bedroom to sleep in."

Taking the book from Brendan, Jono, in a plaintive female voice with a lisp, continued.

"I don't think Mummy 'ith going to like him much William. I think thee'th going to think he'th common."

Laughing, the two of them read passages out of the book. Jono enjoyed taking off the voice of the snobbish Violet Elizabeth.

"I don't think Mummy would let him have a bedroomth. Thomeone athked her oneth and thee said thee liked to keep herthelf to herthelf and daddy thaid that an Englithmanth houthe wath hith cathled."

"That's rot," read Brendan in his role as William.

"A house isn't a castle. A castle's got a thing like a frill on the top an' holes to pour boiling oil from. What do ye think, Jono? You be the tramp and dress up as Violet as well. I'll be William and Mr. Brown. Declan could be Mrs. Brown and Violet's Ma. What could Billy be? He's only five,"

"We'll make him William's brother, Robert. I know Robert in the book is older, but who's to know?"

Whilst Jono went off to see if Declan was at home, Brendan started to put some form into the idea. Reaching for his school satchel, Brendan went through his exercise books to find one he could use. *English literature, better keep that one. Arithmetic, that one as well. What about History? No, Mr. Jones would kill me. Euclid, better learn some of that. Irish language, there's nothin' in that. That'll do,* he thought to himself.

Scribbling out the word "Irish" on the front cover of the book and replacing it with the word "PLAY" in bold capitals, he started to put in the characters' names and who was expected to play them. Then, with the Stephens fountain pen he had received as his main present at Christmas, Brendan began the important job of writing the play.

The bones of the story were that a Mr. Bumblebee, an early day, self-styled social worker, was going to stay overnight with the Botts, Violet's parents. Mr. Bumblebee was then going to lecture the Botts and their friends on how they could help the poor and the homeless.

Learning all this from Violet, William happened to meet a Mr. Marmeduke, a tramp, at the roadside and thought the tramp looked as though he needed some help and would probably like a holiday.

Violet, who had been boasting how big her house was, agreed he could stay there. "We've got ten bedroomth and a garath and a coal thed. Maybe Mr. Marmeduke cud stay in one of them. Oh! An', William, Mr. Bumblebee telephoned to say he will be a day late cumin. I haven't told Mummy yet."

William, in his generous way, told Mr. Marmeduke he could have one of the Botts' rooms for that night's holiday and pretend he was Mr. Bumblebee.

"Anything to oblige, young 'un. One halias is the same ter me as another," the tramp agreed in a false posh accent.

So with the bones of the story decided, Brendan started writing the first act. This would start with breakfast in the Brown's home:

ACT 1

Mrs. Brown: William! Stop messin' about with your food.

William: I'm not messin'. I'm pretending that that mushroom on the top of the fried egg is me on the top of a mountain, an I've gotta' get down, an' there's this precipice here an' this swamp there and—

Mrs. Brown (to Mr. Brown):   Don't be late, dear, from golf. Remember we are going to the Botts' to meet Mr. Bumblebee.

Mr. Brown: Who's this Mr. Bumblebee?

Mrs. Brown: He gives his time for good causes and we are invited with . . .

"Brendan, are you doin' anytin'?" Alice called from the kitchen "Will you go an' get the milk from the front, before the birds get them. I'm up to me eyes in washin'."

"Okay, Ma," shouted Brendan, glad of the interruption, as all the writing was a bit tiring. Brendan put the exercise book and pen and the bottle of Quink ink away and raced down the hall, skidded to a halt in the porch and pulled the reluctant door open to see a pair of tomtits flying away with a rush of wings.

"Little divils," smiled Brendan. As he lifted the cold wire bottle-holder containing the two bottles, he noticed that the birds had pecked through the waxed cardboard tops.

"The birdies got the cream, Ma. Look, it's beginning to snow again. Yippee! I'll go see if Jono has asked Dec," advised a hurrying Brendan as he placed the container on the kitchen table.

With a warm jacket on over his jersey, Brendan pulled up his socks. He still wore short trousers. His school shoes were not in too good a state of repair, one of the leather soles had come loose, so he put on the pair of black Wellington boots that had become too small for Jono. Ma, dressed in a heavy skirt and wearing two jumpers to keep out the cold, was busy scrubbing clothes on the washboard over the sink.

"Don't be too long, Brendan. An' mind you don't get stuck in a snow drift," she called out, her breath making puffs of white in the cold air.

"I'll be back in a few minutes, Ma. Going to find Jono. Look, there's lots more snow falling."

With the kitchen door open, Brendan stepped back to show Alice the clean white snowflakes that fell quietly onto the yard. He stepped onto the film of white covering the dirty grey stone flags and looked back at the footprints he was making, marvelling at the transformation of his surroundings. The orchard was covered in a blanket of snow; all the branches on the apple trees were etched in white. There wasn't a sound.

Suddenly, a disturbed blackbird went flashing past in a screeching bundle of black feathers. With a wild whoop of joy, Brendan ran over the white surface, delighting in the exhilaration of being alive. He rounded the gate from the orchard into the front garden. Scuffing his feet in the snow, he reached the front gate, shaking the laurel hedge to dislodge the snow on its branches and dodging the falling wedges of white.

Stepping directly from the gate onto the road, Brendan walked along one of the tracks left by a farm tractor, kicking the packed snow created by the tractor's large wheels. He noticed a hawk hovering in the clear air above the adjoining field. Concentrating on the motionless bird and waiting for it to swoop, he didn't notice Jono and Declan creeping up behind him. Just as the hawk dropped out of the sky, two large snowballs caught him around the head. Turning in fury, he saw the two grinning culprits making a run for it.

Racing down the road as fast as he could, he noticed Sean making a snowman in his front garden. Sean's sister, sensing the start of a snowball fight, came racing out calling to the Duffys, who lived next door.

"Come on, girls, I need your help."

With the added members to his army, Brendan started to advance. The Tallons and the Devlins, seeing the start of some fun, joined in with

Jono. Beginning to retreat, Brendan got some reinforcements from the Flynns and Carrolls and a pitched battle ensued. Backwards and forwards, the laughing red-faced armies flung snow at each other until exhaustion set in.

With the air full of panting breath and children leaning on each other, they suddenly heard the sound of an approaching car. Stepping aside to let it pass, a number of the boys started to throw snow at the enclosed saloon. As the car was going very slowly everybody started to fling snow at it until it stopped and the driver stepped out, receiving a large piece of slushy snow in the face.

"God! It's Sergeant Duffy. Run for it!" was the warning call and everyone ran for their respective homes. With flushed faces and steaming breath, Jono and Brendan returned to the cottage recounting the different snowball successes.

"Did ye see the one that hit Jerry? Right in the face I got him!" beamed Jono.

"Not as good as what I got on Dec," corrected Brendan. "Got him twice in the face. Wow! That was good fun."

Later that day, Brendan's mind returned to his writing. Must do some more of the play, thought Brendan, after Jono had confirmed that Declan would take part. Returning to the blank pages and the story of William, he continued copying lines from the story of William and the Tramp, realising how difficult it was going to be changing scenes and writing all the words. He eventually resolved the scene-changing problem by deciding that he would write on large separate boards the words "Kitchen," "Mrs. Botts' House," and "Garden," and then let the audience use their imagination.

Over the next few weeks, Brendan got Alice to help him, worked out a play of sorts, and eventually got a cast together. Jono and Declan had helped to write out copy scripts and everybody was now ready for rehearsals.

The cast arrived at the cottage for the first rehearsal, all very important, with their copies of the play: Brendan, Jono, Billy, Declan, Sean, Anthony, Pat, Jean, and Scamp the pup.

Brendan, feeling very nervous with the responsibility of getting things going, asked if everyone had read the play. When Billy said he wanted to be William, Brendan told him to shut up and Billy stormed away in a huff. Declan said he didn't want to be Mrs. Brown. Pat, the nice girl from next door, offered to take his part, saying it was not fair on Declan as he was a boy. Sean said he was goin' to be the tramp and was goin' home if he couldn't be. Jean, Pat's older sister by one year, agreed with Sean and asked could she be Ethel, William's sister.

"Okay!" agreed Brendan in exasperation. "Be whatever you want, but I'm goin' to be William and Jono is Violet."

Some instinct within Brendan had realised the saviour of the whole plan was going to be Jono and his part as Violet.

With everybody more or less agreed to which part they were to take, the rehearsals started.

They were all in the dining room where the play was going to be held. The dining room had a door from the hallway and a door directly opposite—all very convenient for entrance and exit. The first scene was to be in the kitchen with William and Robert eating their breakfast and Ethel helping her mother clean up the dishes.

"Pretend you're washing the dishes, Pat. Pretend you have a sink to do it in," pleaded Brendan. "Where's Billy? He's in this scene. Jono, you're not on yet."

Trying to keep control as well as playing the part of William became quite a challenge for Brendan. Jean offered to help, saying she would look after the stage props.

And so the rehearsals continued, with some of the budding actors shining with their ability to act and some floundering. The highlight of the whole morning was Jono in his part of Violet Elizabeth with the immortal sentence. "I'll thcweam and thcweam until I'm tick!"

Alice brought in tumblers of lemonade and a plate of Marietta biscuits. Pat decided she didn't want to be an actor and went home; she lived next door and sent her elder sister, Ada, to take her part as Ethel. Ada immediately tried to take over as she was twelve and had acted in a play at her school so thought she knew everything.

"I took the part of the Holy Mother in the Chapel at Christmas time an' everyone said I was wonderful."

Brendan was quite exhausted after everyone had gone home, but pleased with the result. He had decided to put the play on for Easter. The best day would be the Saturday, as most of the cast said they would be in chapel praying a lot on the Good Friday and the Easter Sunday. This would give them about a month to get everything ready.

Rehearsals for the play were more spontaneous than regulated. Brendan tried to arrange a time that agreed with everyone, but eventually accepted that whatever will be will be. He learned his lines as William as best he could. Ada and Thomas and, of course, Jono took their parts seriously and, working together, they put something together which resembled Brendan's initial intentions of a Broadway hit.

Easter Saturday arrived, the invitations had been delivered, the stage was set and the actors were all anxiously awaiting opening night. Alice had prepared for up to twenty in the audience and had bottles of lemonade ready for the youngsters and something stronger for the adults. The stage was set up in the dining room. Two large bed sheets were to be used as stage curtains. Stage furniture was, apart from easy things like tables and chairs, made up of cardboard boxes with labels stating in black crayon what they represented, such as "Cooker," "Sink," "Oven," and "Wardrobe" to name but a few.

The show was to start at seven o'clock; Brendan had asked Henry to set up a table in the porch to collect the entrance fee of sixpence for adults and three pence for children. At six o'clock the cast, apart from Sean and Anthony, had arrived and were all anxiously milling around in the kitchen asking each other how they looked in their costumes.

Jono looked very funny as Violet Elizabeth, wearing a short dress with black stockings and a pair of Alice's high heels, talking in a lisp all the time. Declan, dressed as the tramp, was very serious and was sitting in the corner repeating his lines to himself. His tramp outfit was immaculate—his mother always made sure he did not let her down. Ada as Mrs. Brown, in the frumpy dress supplied by her mother, looked very much the part—she was a natural. Brendan just wore his usual clothes, comprising short trousers, a striped jumper, and dirty shoes and didn't bother combing his hair.

By half past six, Brendan was concerned as to the whereabouts of Sean and Anthony. Both, however, arrived with their fathers, saying they didn't want to take part but Brendan pleaded successfully with them to stay, promising them an extra sixpence each.

The doorbell started ringing and Pop's voice could be heard directing the customers down the hallway. Ma was settling them down in their seats, very proud that her family was putting on this entertainment for the locals. By ten to seven, some ten people had arrived and the hum of expectancy was affecting the actors. Jean started to cry, saying she was scared and didn't want to do it. Billy, who was not too happy with his one line as the younger brother, immediately volunteered to take her part as Ethel, and went off in a huff when he was turned down.

Peering around the kitchen door looking down the hall, Brendan could see Alice showing people into the dining room and could hear the doorbell ringing.

"Look, there's Mr. and Mrs. Mahony and Mary. Didn't think they would come," Brendan whispered to Jono. "There's old Draper the Vicar. There's Tommy's Ma and Da. There's lots and lots of them. Gosh! It's five to seven."

Alice, after showing Mr. Draper to his seat, came down to the kitchen, where the cast had gathered. She had volunteered to be stage manager and prompt, and had the entire cast sneak along the back way to the stage.

"Jono," instructed Alice, "will you go and tell the audience the show will start in ten minutes?"

"Shure, Ma!" answered Jono, pleased to be doing something so important.

The loud chattering ceased as everyone noticed the strangely-clad Jono step from behind the white sheets into the room, holding onto the broom handle to prevent the curtain falling.

"Ladies and Gentlemen," he announced nervously, "tonight the Laurel Cottage Players present 'William and The Tramp', a play written by Brendan, helped a lot by me, with a cast brought in from far and wide."

As everyone was laughing at his dress, he started to play the fool, strutting up and down in the high heels with a big grin on his face.

"I'm Violet Elizabeth, you know," he announced as Alice's arm suddenly came out through the curtains and pulled him in.

"Stop acting the fool, Jono, an' tell them about the lemonade and biscuits," she hissed at him, pushing him back out before the chuckling crowd of ten.

"Pop will be selling lemonade and orange juice and biscuits in the in-in-tervil," announced Jono without looking up. "I was goin' to say that," he complained, stepping back behind the curtain.

"Never mind, Jono. Get off the stage now," Alice said pushing him away to the side.

"Are you all ready now?" she whispered to the nervous actors all sitting at the table with Mrs. Brown standing at the oven. Receiving nervous nods of agreement, she called out in a loud whisper.

"Pull the curtains, Henry. Are you there, Henry?"

"Henry's in the kitchen," was the laughing reply from the audience.

"Oh God! I'd better do it myself," Alice complained aloud.

"That's all right, I'll do it," came the eager call from the Vicar.

"No, no, not him. Oh God, please not him," she pleaded, rushing out from behind the sheets, just in time to thank him for his offer and stop him pulling the whole lot down.

Alice pulled the sheets back and sneaked away. Henry arrived somewhat breathless and turned off the light, and the room silenced. The audience looked at the nervous actors sitting at the kitchen table and the large cardboard boxes with the words "cooker" and "sink" printed on them.

"William, will you stop messin' with your food," admonished Mrs. Brown nervously, starting the scene.

"I'm not messin'," replied William with dignity. "I'm—I'm—I'm—"

"Pretending," came Alice's voice from behind the red sheet hanging up at the side. This sheet was supposed to be the sidewall to the kitchen.

"Oh, yes!" exclaimed Brendan in a relieved voice. "I'm pretending that the mushroom there is on the top of a mountain an' this is a lake . . . em . . . em."

Mrs. Brown, realising William was in trouble, interrupted with her first line.

"Oh dear," she said, looking at Mr. Brown as he was getting up from the table.

"Oh dear! Don't be late back from golf. Mr. Bumblebee is calling."

"Who's this Bumblebee fella?" Mr. Brown retorted.

"He's, he's, the—the—" stumbled Mrs. Brown.

"He's the President of the Literary Society," came the loud whispered prompt.

"Oh! He's the Present of the Library Society," answered Mrs. Brown, all the time trying to balance the heavy frying pan on the cardboard oven.

'Leave the frying pan' leave it there. You'll knock the sink over," was the frantic call from the prompt. It was too late. The frying pan—not one of your light frying pans, but a large metal dish with twenty years' worth of accumulated residue from fried eggs, bacon, and pork sausages—fell from Mrs. Brown's grasp. Billy, ever the boy for the emergency, threw himself forward, caught the pan in mid air, demolishing the cardboard sink as he fell to the floor. The audience cheered and clapped, as Billy took a bow and returned to his place at the table.

By now the stage props were in some disorder, but with nothing daunted, the actors continued, with the prompt working overtime. The audience were beginning to enjoy themselves now, taking part in the mistakes and prompting the actors. Jono, as Violet Elizabeth, tall for his age, dressed in a short skirt and all the accessories with golden ringlets made of cardboard stuck to his head, entered, stage left, and the audience gave a cheer. The acting continued with Brendan and Jono's big scene.

"Go away," ordered William to Violet. "I'm busy."

Violet retorted, "I'll be buthy, too. I like bein' buthy."

"Then go away and be 'buthy' somewhere else," replied William in a final manner. Violet then came out with the immortal lines.

"If I can't be buthy, I'll scweam and scweam and scweam until I'm tick!"

The audience cheered and clapped as Henry lifted the broom handles with the sheets attached to signify the end of the first act.

There was a surge of conversation amongst the audience as they stretched their legs and took the glasses of lemonade and whiskey being handed around. Mr. Draper, the Vicar, had opened his raincoat for the first time ever, and was in animated conversation with Mrs. Mahony. The air was beginning to get a bit thick with smoke. Charlie was puffing away at his pipe. Francis, his wife, was as usual endeavouring to help in the passing of lemonade, looking askance as Alice passed a large whiskey to the puffing Charlie. Bob, the smiling odd job man who was married to Kathleen lifted his false leg onto a neighbouring chair.

"Sorry, ye kno' the joint aches. T'anks for the whiskey, Henry. It's goin' well isn't it?"

Alice was talking to Paddy, the owner of the local shop; he had his left hand on her shoulder with a whiskey in his right and his eyes dropping to the inviting gap under the carelessly buttoned cardigan.

Sergeant Padraic Duffy, six foot five, taking up the space usually reserved for two average males, was holding forth about the careless parking outside Gerry Mahoney's shop.

"Ye kno' Gerry, ye should be after makin' shure when Murphy and Larkin park their carts dey leave room at the corner. When the cattle are passin' there's a real bottleneck."

"Yer right der Paddy. Keep tellin' dem, de bloody eejits," replied Gerry, scratching a flea bite under his arm. "Dese bloody fleas wil' be de deth of me. We're lookin' after young Michael's greyhound, ye kno'."

Whilst the audience were relaxing, the actors were all frantically working to repair the stage props and change the scenery. Henry tied the ends of the broom handles together and hung them from the electric light flex hanging from the ceiling, and then draped the sheets over the long handles to give the actors some privacy. The next and final act was the audience's introduction to the Tramp and Mr. Bumblebee.

The second act opened with the scenery changed to a relatively clear stage. The props were stacked up at the side apart from two large pieces of cardboard with the words "Field" and "Ditch" printed on them in green crayon. Jono, now dressed as the tramp, was wearing trousers instead of a skirt and had left the cardboard ringlets on his head, as they were difficult to remove. He was eating a piece of bread.

William entered from left. "Good afternoon, sir."

"Good afternoon, young 'un, an' wot can I do fer you?"

"Well," said William. "I was wondering—er—I mean—I was thinking—er—I mean would you be after likin' a holiday?"

"Yes, young 'un, I cud di wi' one. Lead me to it."

The two of them left the stage and Billy came on with another piece of cardboard with the words "Botts' Garden" written on it in red crayon.

William re-entered from the left and a flustered Jono, having run around in front of the stage pulling on Violet's dress, came in from the right.

William told Violet he had arranged for Mr. Marmeduke to stay the night at her house. Violet, quite aghast, replied, "I don't think Mummy'th goin' to like him much. I think thee'th goin' to think he'th common."

Declan, dressed as Mrs Bott, stumbled onto the stage. He tripped over the remains of the oven (which, in the next scene, was going to be a cupboard), and prepared to say his bit.

The audience were now becoming a bit bored as there was so little action compared to the first act, and were beginning to talk amongst themselves. With the scene coming to a hesitant close Jono, whilst the rest of the cast prepared the stage to represent Mrs. Bott's bedroom, stepped out from behind the sheet.

"Gud evenin' ladies an' gentlemen. I am goin' to entertain you for the nex' few minits with a magic trick." Jono had bought a magic card trick from Ellisons, the mail order firm. Holding the pack of cards out, face down, he invited someone from the audience to take a card from the pack. Mr. Draper, now rather red in the face, having drunk an unaccustomed glass of whiskey, stood up unsteadily from the settee.

"Allow me, Jono," he slurred his red face a picture of concentration.

"Excuse me there, Mrs. Mahony," as he pushed past her, stretching his arm out to pick a card from the proffered pack.

"No, don't show it to me, Mr. Draper," Jono instructed.

"Show it to everyone else."

Turning with an embarrassed smile, Mr. Draper held the card up for his fellow spectators to see.

"I don't know what the card is, do I?" Jono called out.

"No you don't, but you're goin' to tell us," was the spontaneous and well-lubricated response.

"Please place the card back in the pack, Mr. Draper."

Jono held the pack of cards out again face downwards and the chosen card was replaced. Feeling quite triumphant, Jono held the pack up for everyone to see.

"I will now shuffle the pack and by magic will be able to find Mr. Draper's card. See."

Hitching up his dress and patting his cardboard ringlets, Jono started to shuffle the pack of cards.

"Is that enough?" he asked the audience.

"Yes, get on with it," was the impatient reply from Bob as he scratched his wooden leg.

With a flourish Jono held up the pack with the back facing the audience and, with his thumb, slowly pushed the chosen card, the King of Spades, which was already turned to face the audience, up out of the pack. As the king's head appeared, Charlie started to clap in appreciation, followed by Mr. Mahoney who called out, "Well done."

"How did he do it?" asked Mrs. Byrne, genuinely amazed.

Bowing to their applause, Jono rushed around behind the white sheet to prepare for the next scene. The lights dimmed and the sheet was pulled back to show Jono, now dressed as the tramp, in Mrs. Bott's bedroom. Brendan addressed the audience to remind them that the tramp, Mr. Marmeduke, was going to pretend he was Mr. Bumblebee, as he was a day late. The audience nodded wisely, not too concerned as they were all, apart from Mrs. Byrne, who had taken the "pledge" not to drink, feeling quite mellow and ready to applaud anything.

Alice was going quite berserk trying to keep them to the script, as Jono lost his curls and Declan arrived upstage as an unexpected Mr. Bumlebee. Brendan was pleading with the cast to stay in character. Pat and Jean, the Duffy sisters, as Mrs. Brown and sister Ethel, came on before their expected entrance.

The audience, by now confused with the story line, but enjoying the mêlée on the stage, were laughing and clapping their hands. Mr. Draper had fallen asleep. Bob had to get up and walk around a bit to relieve the ache in the leg he didn't have. Paddy Duffy and the shopkeeper were beginning to get annoyed with each other about the parking outside Gerry's shop, and the drink was causing them to raise their voices.

Alice decided, having first confirmed with Brendan, to bring forward the last scene and, with great applause and even greater relief, the final curtain was drawn.

She then called all the cast onto the stage and had the audience give them a big cheer. Taking their bows to the applause, the actors called Brendan to the front and told everybody it was all down to him and wasn't he great?

"Gud ould, Brendan," was the call from Bob. Brendan blushed mightily but took the applause. Glasses were refilled. Kathleen, Bob's good-looking wife, started playing some old songs on the piano and Alice embarrassed her family by singing her only song, the one about "de woman with the wooden leg."

"Sorry, Bob," she apologised.

Henry, while disentangling the broom handles from the centre light, pulled the flex out from the ceiling and, of course, fused the lights. Candles were sought and the evening continued into the early hours until everyone wandered off to their homes and respective sleeping places. The takings for the night amounted to five shillings and sixpence.

11

The Cross Country Race

Brendan, now eleven years old, was beginning to realise the disparity between the living standards of those in the other cottages and his own in Laurel Cottage. Whilst life in Laurel Cottage was pretty basic, there was plenty of room with electricity and gas laid on and the luxury of indoor toilets, whereas the other cottages only had earthenware floors, no power, and a communal outside "wash room."

He felt some guilt in his good fortune of going to private school, albeit to some degree poorer than his peers, as he did not have the smart uniform and new schoolbooks the other pupils had. However, there was always a meal on the table and clothes to wear compared to the supposed poverty in the other cottages.

"You're better than them, Brendan. Don't forget that," his mother continuously told him.

Not wishing to contradict, but inwardly not agreeing with her, Brendan wanted to be liked by everyone and did not think he was better than anyone else. When Mickey Farrell, one of the boys who lived in the cottages stopped him on the road, he was quite taken aback. Standing in front of him with his hands on his hips, he stared at Brendan in a pugnacious manner.

"Will ye be after lookin' at his new runners?" the boy spat out. "Who do ye think you are den? A cross-country racer?"

Mickey jeered as he gazed with mock astonishment, but Brendan felt a bit of envy from the boy as he looked at Brendan's new runners. Snowy white with long white laces, they made his large feet look even larger. Made of a canvas with rubber soles, they were the new shoes for everyday wear.

"Aw, you're just jealous, Mickey," Brendan retorted. "Aren't they just lovely? See the way they have been vulcanised?" Having just read the label stating how wonderful this new vulcanising business of sticking two things together was, Brendan thought he would impress Mickey with his newfound knowledge.

"They were vulcanised in America and exported to Ireland. Came in by boat to Dublin only last week. They're waterproof and only cost one and six, so there you are, Mickey. You should get your Ma to buy you a pair. They say you can run like the wind in them."

Looking at Mickey's feet, Brendan saw that the leather shoes he wore were a couple of sizes too big for him, broken down around the heels, and badly scratched.

"Iffin you want Mickey, I'll give you my old runners. They're still pretty good."

"Huh! Runners me ant fanny, I don' need no hand downs. Ye can run like the bloody wind if ye like, but I bet ye I'd beat you in a run any day. I don't need no new fancy runners, me bare feet are good enough for me."

A bit taken aback by Mickey's answer, Brendan quickly thought to himself before speaking again.

"Bet you I'd beat yuh. Bet you I'd beat you over ten miles, uphill even."

Mickey scratched his head and looked up at him.

"Ye may be bigger than me, how old are ye? Bet you still wet the bed. I'm 'leven and a half."

"Well, I'm eleven an' two months, but I'm bigger 'n you and I know how to run. Won a race at school against the senior boys an' I don't wet the bed."

"Ye live in the posh cottage, don' ye?" questioned Mickey as he hitched up his torn, short trousers, held up by a thick piece of baling string.

"Yes!" Brendan replied. "Do you wanna come in and have a look?" They were standing at the edge of the road outside the cottage with the green entrance door behind them.

In comparison to Laurel Cottage, the row of two-roomed terraced buildings that comprised the other cottages built to house the workers for the now closed pottery works were very basic. Each had two rooms, a slate roof with a constant smoking chimney balanced at the edge, an earthen floor, two small windows, and a heavy front door. The toilet facilities were a communal pit behind a brick wall and fresh water came from a tall cast iron pump with a large handle. Apart from the worn paths in front of the cottages, the surrounding uncultivated dusty earth was dotted with weeds and rubbish. Compared to this, Laurel Cottage must have appeared as a mansion to Mickey.

"Yeh! If you like," replied Mickey hesitantly.

"Have you ever been in before?" Brendan asked.

"Saw the house through the gate, t'was nutin."

Not appreciating his reluctance, Brendan proudly ushered Mickey in through the green front gate. The contrast between the dusty lane edged by scruffy weeds and the relaxed green lush lawn with small hedges and imposing ivy-fronted house was very striking. To Brendan it was natural; this was his home, this was where he lived. To Mickey, however, it must have been another world, an unattainable world.

Entering the gate he turned around saying, "It's nuttin, gotta go," and went back onto the lane. Brendan followed, not understanding and asked what was wrong.

"It's nuttin', gotta go," was all Mickey muttered and started down the road, dejectedly scuffing his shoes in the dust.

Brendan went to call him back, feeling there was something terribly wrong. He wanted to be Mickey's friend. He did not realise the gulf between them. Looking at the bowed head over the scruffy clothes and comparing them to his own relatively well-clothed body and his brilliant white runners, he began to realise how fortunate he was.

Slightly disturbed, Brendan went to the orchard where Henry was digging the soil, telling him what had happened and asking him what he had done wrong. Henry smiled.

"Best thing," he said, "is to have a word with your mother. But before you do get a holt of that spade and do some digging."

"I'll dirty me runners and Ma will shout at me, Pop."

"Oh! All right then."

Resigning himself to his lone task, Henry lifted another large cube of black soil and threw it down in front of him, slicing a big juicy pink worm in half with the edge of the spade.

"I'll be back, Pop," Brendan shouted back to him as he ran into the cottage to change.

"Come on, Scamp, race you to the house." Scamp, their new black and white mongrel pup who had been helping in the digging, lifted his head at the sound of his name, leaped over the newly turned soil, and raced ahead of Brendan. Poor Podge, the previous puppy had died after being kicked by a horse.

Taking off his new runners amongst the redundant newspapers and cut logs in the spare room, Brendan replaced them with his old brown shoes. Scamp immediately grabbed the lovely white toy in his mouth and started to shake it like a rat.

"Let it go, Scamp," Brendan pleaded.

Scamp, too young to understand English, raced back into the kitchen with his prize. Oh! The sheer enjoyment! I've got this lovely white tasty piece of whatever it is, let's run, run, run.

Racing after the rapidly disappearing streak of black and white, and hampered by his unlaced shoes, Brendan shouted to Henry.

"He's got my runner, Pop. Stop him!"

Henry, willing to have a break from digging, let out a challenging "whoop!" and started after the very happy little pup.

Scamp raced through the last of the brussels sprouts. He dodged between the stalks into the long grass around the pear tree and tunnelled under the hedge into the front garden.

"Brendan, go around to the left, I'll get him before he goes under the laurel hedge," Henry shouted. Too late. Before they could reach him, his black tail disappeared into the dense foliage. The laurel hedge ran all the way on the inside of the front wall and left very little space for a human.

"Go in after him, Brendan. I'll watch out at the end here," instructed Henry.

Brendan squeezed himself between the wall and the heavy branches of the old hedge and could see Scamp worrying his lovely new runner.

"Let it go, Scamp. Please," he implored. "What will Ma say? They cost a lot of money."

Hearing Brendan's pleading voice, Scamp raised his head, scuffled out under the branches, leaving the badly-stained and torn runner wedged under the laurel trunk, and lay down on the grass panting with his long, pink tongue hanging out of his mouth.

After squeezing over and under branches, Brendan pulled the now very green, half-eaten runner free from the hedge's grip and forced his way back onto the lawn. Both of his knees were scuffed, his clothes were stained, and the runner was ruined.

"Don't worry, Brendan. We'll get you another pair," consoled Henry as he took the battered runner from him and made a pretend kick at the happy little bundle of black and white mischief that rolled over onto his back inviting a tickle.

Upon showing the mutilated runner to Alice, Brendan was mildly ticked off and Henry was told to "Stop grinning and to go back out an' finish de diggin' or there would be no tea."

When asked what he had done wrong with Mickey, Alice, in her certainty that she was right and that there could be no other opinion whatsoever, made Brendan aware of the differences between Mickey and himself—the way he lived and what his parents were like. Mickey's father had no job and spent his time drinking. They were poor and didn't know how to live properly. They needed help and she, lady bountiful, would help whenever possible. Brendan was advised not make close friends or confide with them and "hadn't the young divil himself been caught stealing some sweets in Woolworths?"

"So, there you are now, Brendan. Be careful what friends you make. Now go and help your father with the digging. Tea will be ready in ten minutes."

So that's that, thought Brendan to himself.

"But he still said he would beat me in a runnin' race, Ma."

"Well, did he now? The little divil. Did he now?" Alice muttered as she continued preparing the evening meal.

The early months of the year passed. Henry finished the digging in the orchard and completed planting the potatoes. The blossoms on the apple trees were almost all gone, leaving a colourful mat under the trees, and the evenings were growing longer.

One such evening, after he had done his homework and just before the weekly radio episode of "Riders on the Range," Alice confided with Brendan.

"Remember what Mickey Farrell said about racing you?"

"Yeh! I do. I bet I could beat him."

"Well, what about a cross-country run over the fields? We could have a sports day and have other races on the lane," suggested Alice.

"Yeh! We could have egg and spoon races and maybe a sack race like they do at school. But what about prizes?"

"Leave that to me," replied Alice, thinking she could have a word with Paddy, the owner of the local grocery shop.

"Ma! Hush, it's time for 'Riders of the Range'."

For the next half hour, silence reigned in the house whilst the men listened to and pictured Cal McCord, Jeff Arnold with Luke and Bob, the singing cowboy, going down the Chisholm Trail in search of Billy the Kid. Every youngster at eight o'clock that evening then swaggered out to the hitchin' rail and mounted their horses to go and either round up the cattle for the 6T6 Outfit or have a gunfight with Billy the Kid.

As the summer months approached and the school holidays came closer, Alice arranged the Sports Day for a Saturday in June. Brendan had been practising his running. Mickey avoided him but Mickey's pals, Jerry and Pat, taunted him, saying that Mickey had paid for a trainer and was down in the country running miles.

The chosen Saturday arrived. Brendan donned his shorts, shirt, and a pair of comfortable runners and began to make his way to the fields for the start of the race. On their way down Red Clay Lane, with Henry and Jono as stewards, the youngsters from different houses and cottages began to join in. The Tallons, the Flynns, the Murphys, the Duffys, and Sean Traynor came running out from their homes to join in the excitement, until eventually there were some twenty youngsters with ages ranging from five to twelve gathered behind them.

It was a very hot day with no clouds in the sky. The tar in the lane was beginning to shimmer in the sunlight and those youngsters without shoes were tiptoeing from grass verge to grass verge. Those with shoes would burst into a run ahead of Henry to impress him with their speed.

Henry, in discussion with Jono, decided they would have to work out a handicap system due to the spread of ages. Working on this, they all proceeded past the cottages to the five-barred gate leading into the first large field. The little ones squeezed through the bars whilst the other, more grown-up and athletic racers climbed over the bars and jumped down into the grassy field. Mickey, along with his pals, most of who were in their bare feet, were discussing their plans for the race and kept in a small group.

Thomas, who was the same age as Brendan, was wearing his Christian Brothers School Sports shorts and shirt with special running shoes, as did Fintan and Michael. Sean had his team of seven-year-olds, Anthony and Fergus with Paddy and his twin sisters Finnoula and Mary.

Henry had delegated Billy, who was now six and a half years old, to herd the youngsters of his own age into order and they all made their way down to the start of the race. At the bottom of the first field they had another gate to climb, and then another field with a large drainage ditch which the more able leaped over, while the little ones had to be helped over the green water at its base.

Finnoula slipped into the water and had to be hauled out by Henry. She started to cry as her sister Mary wrung her knickers out with the boys all hooting and laughing. Crossing the final field to the start, some of the girls started to pick the yellow primrose flowers. One of them gave Henry a cowslip flower she had plucked from the side of the field.

When they reached the edge of the last field some half a mile from the finish, Henry had them all gather around to tell them what he and Jono had planned.

"First," he said, "all the young ones will start. You go last of them, Billy. No! Not yet, Peter. Billy, find out what Jacinta is crying about."

Pop and Jono then had little groups of children running up and down the field to see who was the fastest. Having decided a sort of handicap system, they got all the runners to line up. Jacinta was the first to go; she kept looking back and, as no one was following, she came back, crying that nobody liked her. Mary was sent to join her followed by a couple of the younger boys. Billy was kept back until the seven-year-olds were let loose. They all raced away in a group whooping like Red Indians and soon disappeared into the next field.

Next in line were the other girls who raced away, talking together. The field ahead was now filled with bodies running at different speeds. Jono had to run forward to help some of the smaller racers over the ditch.

Then Henry let Tommy, Christy, and Christy's two buddies off before Brendan.

"Yes, Brendan, it's only fair," said Pop in response to Brendan's remonstrations.

He let them get quite a distance before letting Brendan go. By then, Brendan was getting a bit anxious, but he put his head down and started racing after them. He began to overtake some of the little ones. His target was Mickey, who was running like fury ahead of him with his two friends racing behind, looking over their shoulders.

Mickey was getting further away and before long he was over the first gate. Brendan started to run faster and the two "friends" slowed down to let him catch them. In his innocence, Brendan thought they were getting tired and was ready to commiserate with them; however, Vinnie, the larger of the two, suddenly pushed in front of Brendan and tripped him up. Brendan instinctively threw his hands forward, rolled over, and landed on his feet still running.

Gosh! he thought. *This is a bit nasty.* The other "bodyguard" thought twice about tripping him up and went back to Vinnie. By now, Mickey was well over the gate with his bare feet racing through the grass. He looked like a rabbit fleeing a fox. *I'm the fox*, thought Brendan, *so get your tail up Brendan and get after that little rabbit.*

Halfway through the last field he overtook Tommy, who was labouring considerably, and most of the smaller ones who had given up and were picking daisies. Mickey was hampered by others climbing the gate, so Brendan recovered a bit of ground. By now, he was beginning to run out of breath and sweating heavily; in fact, he was feeling a bit sick.

He scrambled over the gate and started up the road to find all the parents had come out to cheer them on. Mickey was having difficulty on the hot road, having to run on the tips of his toes to avoid the hot tar. Brendan started to gain on him. Mickey was slowing down; the heat was too much for him and he had to run on to the grass verge. With his head down, feeling quite sick, Brendan passed Mickey and ran through the tape held by his mother and Mary, the shop owner's wife. Running to the side of the road, he bent over and vomited his breakfast into the dust. He had won, but all he wanted to do was die.

Alice hurried over whilst Mary ran into the shop and returned with a glass of water. They sat Brendan in the shade of the wall and went to look after Mickey, who was nursing his scorched feet.

The remaining contestants all meandered in. Billy came in first of his group of seven-year-olds and sat down beside Brendan. The older girls' race was won by Maeve Duffy and by then, Alice had realised they all needed water, so she and Mary and a few of the other mothers ran a shuttle service to the gasping runners.

Feeling somewhat better after the water, Brendan went over to Mickey who was joined by his pals. They all looked a bit sheepish and would not look at him. Shrugging his shoulders, he went over to Alice who was in earnest discussion with the other parents. Mickey's lot were complaining that Brendan had had an advantage by wearing runners and that it wasn't fair on poor Mickey. Nobody mentioned what he had tried to do to Brendan. It was decided to cancel the rest of the programme as it was too hot and the tar surface on the lane was nearly boiling.

Mary, Paddy's missus, as a consolation for the lack of the egg and spoon race and others, gave everybody the choice of either a lollipop or a bag of Dolly mixtures. A prize of a half a crown had been offered for the cross-country winner with a shilling for the runner-up. Brendan received his half crown amidst some unwelcome boos whilst Mickey, who had tiptoed across the line, collected his twelve pennies, lifting his hand to acknowledge the cheers from his friends.

Brendan told Alice what Mickey's pals had tried to do.

"You won fair and square," she replied. "Don't bother with them. They're not worth it."

So ended Alice's first community experiment. It didn't help to bring the community together; rather, it showed just how different their attitudes were. Whilst she continued her lady of the manor role, Brendan found it more difficult than ever communicating with the Mickies of the neighbourhood.

12

Birthday Party with School "Friends"

Alice decided that Brendan should have a party for his thirteenth birthday and invited a group of girls and boys from the school and a few of the local children. The school children were mostly English or of English descent and Protestant, whilst the locals were a mix of relatively affluent and poor families and 100 percent Roman Catholic.

Ever the aspiring social worker Alice thought she would be helping them all by introducing the Dianes, the Patricias, the Prunnellas, Colins and Winstons to the Seans, Thomases, Paddys, Marcellas, and Marys.

Not only would Brendan have to entertain these opposing camps, but he would also have to speak to the schoolgirls. He had been quite relaxed with the local girls, having grown up with them, played chasing and marbles and girly games like hop skip and jump and house, but he was now noticing differences in their attitudes to him and some confusing feelings within his own body. The girls from the school were a different breed altogether—all beautiful and completely unapproachable. The party was to help Brendan to get to know them in his own surroundings, or so Alice said.

Whilst Brendan wouldn't say a word to Alice, he was also quite conscious of the relative squalor of Laurel Cottage compared to the large, clean, well-tended detached houses of most of his guests.

The school "friends" all duly arrived, beautifully dressed along with their beautifully wrapped presents, whilst the locals turned up in a more relaxed dress style, in white runners, canvas trousers, all very much on the defensive with some very low key offerings.

Alice was at her worst, in her lady bountiful role, putting on her posh accent. Little brother Billy had been delegated to help in the kitchen, whilst big brother Jono was too grown up to have anything to do with twelve and thirteen-year-olds.

The birthday room split into three sections: the girls from the school in one corner, talking in whispers, with the boys from the school talking loudly and showing off to one another and throwing inane comments at the whispering girls. The locals, meanwhile, were grouped together in a defensive wall, saying nothing and wishing they were somewhere else.

Brendan was very self-conscious, being the host, and had no idea how to get the party going. He was afraid of making a fool of himself with the mature girls and was conscious of the resentment beginning to be shown by the locals. The split lino on the floor, the dust in the corners, the unwashed windowpanes and the well-worn pieces of furniture did not help either. In his new pullover and long trousers, he blushingly accepted his presents from the guests—fountain pens, books, a pair of socks, a bar of chocolate, the Beano Annual and a few records. Prunella gave him a seventy-eight-rpm record of "Secret Love" by Doris Day. There were a few hoots from the boys, which made Brendan blush even more.

Maybe if I play a record it will help, Brendan thought to himself. The record player, or "pick-up," made of Bakelite with metal arm and rubber turntable, had been purchased for two shillings and sixpence at a second-hand shop and played very erratically. One could stack up to ten seventy-eight records onto the centre arm, push the drop leaver at the edge of the turntable and, with a loud crash, the first record would fall onto the base and the stylus arm would sweep onto the edge of the spinning record. When each record finished, the next one would come crashing down. Sometimes two or more fell together and the playing arm would go out of sync.

It was with some trepidation that Brendan approached the ready-loaded player and pushed the drop lever. Down crashed the record and, in great relief, he saw the arm do its duty. The swinging sound of Guy Mitchell singing the hit of the day, "Red Feathers and a Hooley Hooley Skirt," came blasting out from the player and there were cries from the knowledgeable.

"Oh! Not him again!"

"Oh! Goody, Guy Mitchell."

A couple of the boys came over to examine the merits of the player, whilst the girls started discussing the singers of the day.

"What about Frankie Laine?"

"Isn't Dicki Valentine dishy?"

"Doesn't Nat King Cole sound lovely?" Conversation began to flow with the records crashing down every three minutes. However, the locals were not having anything to do with this newfound camaraderie and maintained their sullen silence. Brendan, very conscious of their presence, wondered how to bring them into the conversation. Fortunately, there was a loud call from the kitchen.

"Yoo hoo! Food's up! Come and get it."

Oh, God! Brendan thought to himself. *Not the scruffy kitchen.*

From the relatively well-lit birthday room, Brendan led his guests into the hallway and along the threadbare carpet, down the dark red-tiled passageway, and into the large kitchen of many shadows.

Alice, dressed in a long heavy skirt and white blouse, looked very smart and encouraged all the children to take a plate and then help themselves to the food. Whilst the boys picked up any plate, the girls were more particular.

The food, enough to feed the whole of Dublin, was laid out on a large wooden table in the centre of the kitchen. There were plates stacked high with sandwiches filled with chicken, tomatoes, or ham, plates of delicious large pork sausages pierced with cocktail sticks, large buns oozing fresh cream, and cakes with coloured icing all laid out on the bare surface of the table.

In the centre of this bountiful display stood an upturned saucepan with a home-made fruit cake balanced on it, its sides covered in attractive Christmas wrapping, and thirteen large candles stuck in the thick white icing all blazing away.

"Now, who would like some lemonade? Fill your glasses before we all sing Happy Birthday to Brendan," Alice said, smiling

There was a stifled giggle from a few of the girls who only knew Brendan by his surname Harris, and Winston gave him a dig in the ribs, nodding at the girls, and started to sing "Happy Birthday," raising his arms in time to the tune and encouraging the girls to join him. Alice and Billy by this time had passed around the assortment of glasses with lemonade and orange juice and joined in the chorus.

"Happy birthday, dear Brendan, Happy birthday to you!"

"Three cheers for good old BRENDAN," bellowed Winston, raising his glass of lemonade. "Hip hip," and with surprising gusto the rest of the children, all still in their respective groups, followed with a loud "Hurrah!"

Brendan, blushing mightily, leaned over and after some effort, blew out the candles. When Winston demanded a speech, Brendan muttered a thank you and wished he were somewhere else.

Alice tried to break up the separate groups and endeavoured to introduce the girls to the locals, but the Dianas and Elizabeths did not want to know. Pamela, trying to be friendly, said hello to Paddy Cunningham from the cottages, who blushed and stammered something. Marcella gave him a dig with her elbow.

"Com' on Paddy. Now speak to the lady," she said in her posh voice, looking at Pamela with venom in her eyes.

When all had re-gathered in the party room, a couple of the school boys had broken the ranks of the school girls and Sean, a good-looking curly-headed local lad, had opened a conversation with Prue.

To get things moving, Brendan suggested they play some party games and the prepared parcel, for "Pass the Parcel" was duly passed around the critical group. The schoolgirls, apart from Prue, took part grudgingly. The boys from both sides of the divide had now relaxed their defences and started throwing the parcel around. After a rowdy few minutes with newspaper and brown paper tossed around the room, the prize of a pack of crayons was received with a few hoots of derision.

Some writing games were tried without any great success. With the party still lagging, Colin from the school suggested they play Postman's Knock. He had it all worked out—every boy and girl was to be given a piece of paper with a different number written on it. Copies of the numbers were folded separately and placed in a spare saucepan for the girls and a cardboard box for the boys. A boy or girl was then chosen and he or she would go outside the room, pick a hidden number from the saucepan or cardboard box, and close the door behind them. The boy or girl outside the door would knock on the door the number of times stated on the paper; the boy or girl with the chosen number would leave the room, taking a folded number from the receptacle and close the door behind them. Both parties would exchange kisses. The first person would return and the game would continue.

To the shyer person, the game was sheer torture. Winston "the brave" volunteered to start and swaggered toward the door. As he took a number from the saucepan, he looked toward the girls with a threatening grin, opened the door with a flourish and closed it with a bang.

The girls looked at each other. Who was going to be the first? There was a solid knock on the door followed by five more. As each knock passed, there was a sigh of relief from those whose number had gone. Who was number six?

Prue looked aghast at her number and, very hesitantly, made her way to the door. Prue was one of the smaller girls with colourless hair, a cheerful pixie-like face, and a curve-less body. A grey woollen dress that reached six inches below her knees with a pink blouse buttoned to her neck did not help, but her pleasant personality made up for the lack of looks.

Brendan, who had the number ten on his card, had thought to himself that if there was any girl he had to kiss, he would prefer it be Prue, as they got on well together. He had never kissed a girl before and was quite fearful the superior Diana would accidentally pick him. *What do you do? Do you bend your head to the right or left? What do you do with your hands? Do you hug her? Oh God, I want to run,* thought Brendan. *How do I get out of here? Maybe it will be all right. A lot of people do it. They do it in the pictures.*

The door opened within seconds and Winston strode back into the room with a forced grin on his face, obviously disappointed in his chosen kissing partner.

There was a hesitant knock followed by the second; the boys avoided each other's eyes. Who would be the chosen one?

Knock . . . five . . . six . . . seven.

Sean rose from his seat. Known for his ability to throw a stone furthest, Sean went to Chapel three times a week. With a deep breath, the chosen one squared his shoulders and walked purposefully towards the closed door, wrenched it open, and closed it behind him with a bang.

The girls looked at each other—poor Prue! What will he do to her? He's a bit scruffy. Poor Prue. They are taking their time. The girls looked at each other in mock anxiety until almost two minutes had gone by. What's he up to?

The door opened with a "swoosh" as Sean stood aside to allow a smiling Prue to re-enter the room, giving her school friends the thumbs up sign.

Good on you, Sean, Brendan thought to himself. *Now you have something worthwhile to tell your priest at next confession: you kissed a protestant!*

There were expectant, if fearful, glances amongst the girls whilst they awaited the next summons.

One . . . two knocks . . . silence.

Diana rose, tossed her long blond ponytail over her shoulder, smoothed her expensive flowered skirt down her flanks and, without looking to either side, strode purposefully towards the door. The door opened before she reached it; Sean stood aside whilst she passed through, caught Brendan's eye and gave him a wink. There was silence in the room as each imagined what was happening behind the door. Was Diana giving him the cold shoulder? Was Sean forcing her to kiss him? A minute went by followed by another, ultimately followed by a triumphant Sean coming through the door with a big smirk on his face.

"Brendan," he whispered out the side of his mouth, "I've told Diana if she knocks ten times her dreams would be realised."

"Oh God! Sean, that's my number," answered a horrified Brendan.

One knock . . . two . . . eight . . . nine . . . ten . . . silence.

Wow! Here I go, thought Brendan. *Into battle, Diana the female Amazon, the one with the cutting tongue, the best looking girl in the school. Hair like Diana Dors, a body like Marilyn Monroe. Oh God! What do I do?*

Taking a deep breath, the condemned walked towards the door with a forced smile. Sean and the boys were willing him on.

"Go for it, Brendan! It's your birthday."

He opened the door to see the vision of beauty standing in the hallway.

"Oh, it's you. Let's get this over with," were the cold-blooded instructions from the maiden as she stepped forward with her left cheek raised for a sterile peck. Brendan, taken aback, stooped down with his lips pursed. *This is no better than kissing my mother,* he thought to himself.

His lips met the cool cheek and he smelt the trace of perfume. Diana stepped back with a superior smile, asking in a sudden confusing and sultry tantalising voice, "Did you like that, Brendan?"

Brendan, aroused in a way he had never experienced before, looked appealingly at the vision in front of him.

"Perhaps you would prefer this," she then said, standing on tiptoe and kissing him full on the mouth and rushed back through the door.

An astonished Brendan touched his face. *Did she really kiss me? Did that really happen?*

"Golly! Wow! Gosh! I had better knock."

Whatever happened now would be an anti-climax.

He knocked three times and then Marcella came through the door. Marcella from next door, Marcella with whom he had played chasing, conkers, and hide and seek. As the door closed behind her, there was a smothered giggle from one of the wall cupboards behind Brendan.

"Oh no! Not Billy, he's been looking on all the time. The little sod."

Before Brendan could do anything, the cupboard door flew open and Billy dashed out, racing down the hallway and into the kitchen.

Marcella, all of five feet tall and looking quite startled, suggested in an embarrassed voice, "Look, Brendan, we don't have to do anything. Let's pretend."

Brendan, still thinking of Diana's kiss, put both his arms around the thin body and kissed a startled Marcella full on the lips, patted her on the bottom, and re-entered the party room. Brendan had opened a box of variety chocolates and had tasted the one labeled "More."

13

School Sports Day

Run, run as fast as you can, run like the wind, keep going. Your heart is pounding, your legs are weakening—keep going—you're nearly there. One more bend in the track, you can hear them behind you, nobody in front—faster—faster—just keep going, nothing left—no, there is a bit more. Another few steps and you'll have won. You can hear them behind. Energy—energy, a final burst of speed. The tape, arms flung wide, head thrust forward through the tape. You've won! Slow down, catch your breath. Long pulls of air. You've *won*! Gosh! The legs are wobbly, must sit down. Can't stop grinning, you've won.

Yes! It did happen. School sports day, early summer 1953. The Junior 440 yards. One lap of the sports field. Brendan had beaten the best. He didn't even have spikes, just a pair of rubber-soled runners.

Getting to his feet, he trotted nonchalantly over to his parents and brothers who were all smiling at his success. Jono licked his forefinger and chalked up another addition to the total. He had just won the 880-yard run and he and Brendan had teamed up to race in the boys' three-legged race, in which they had come third. Brendan had come a credible second in the egg and spoon race (mixed) behind that athletic, long-legged, blonde Patricia Taylor. Billy had won the obstacle race for the five- to seven-year-olds.

It was a bright, sunny Saturday afternoon. The summer term had ended and this was the annual sports day prior to the long summer holidays. The sky was a lovely, clear blue with just the odd friendly white cloud. Being close to the seaside, foraging sea gulls swooped endlessly in the sky. The smell of newly mowed grass filled the air.

Parents had come from many parts of the country. Leslie Smith's father had even come all the way from South Africa, according to Leslie, and was smartly dressed in a bow tie of all things. Andrew Wood's mother and the Rev Wood, with the glorious simpering Cynthia, his sister, had motored up from Wexford. Cummings father, who played cricket for Yorkshire, palled up with Brendan's parents.

Harold Fitzpatrick, who was no athlete—all legs, thin body, and a chin festooned with severe acne—arrived with his mother, Caroline. Harold (nobody could ever invent a nickname to suit him) was a great brainy bore. He had entered the three-legged race—a stupid thing to do, as he had no coordination at all. His partner, Theodore Render, was shorter and plumper than Harold. They came last in the race, having fallen over at the start, as they could not get their legs to move together.

Mrs. Fitzpatrick, Carrie to her friends, raised her large blue eyes to the skies in mock frustration at Harold's attempts to emulate a human being, tossed her dramatic sun-burnt curls and sat down on the nearest wooden bench, crossing her long and shapely stockinged legs.

Brendan fantasized about Carrie. He had saved her many times from drowning, escorted her to the pictures, kissed her outstretched hand as she presented him with a large cup for some outstanding achievement, and even protected her from the Red Indians.

Yes, he had to pretend he liked Harold.

"Will all competitors for the long jump please now proceed to the long jump area." In its cultivated, if slightly disjointed, voice, the loud-speaker invited competitors over to the side of the sports field where a narrow twenty-foot track of worn grass led to a wooden board on the front edge of a long pit of sand.

Brendan had been practising his jump-off—the toe must not protrude over the front of the jumping-off board. He did not feel very confident. The twelve contestants, including Teddy Render and three other no hopers, were all resigned to failure as Cartwright and Taylor (D), both the same age as Brendan, both athletic and full of confidence, were in the line-up. Cartwright had been short-listed for the county championships and Taylor (D), who stood at six-foot-four in his socks, had leaped sixteen feet without any effort.

The best jump of three attempts would be counted and the leading six would jump off to determine the winners. Moving like veritable panthers, the two favourites left the remaining mediocre humans behind. Brendan finished a creditable fourth. There were handshakes all round and numerous "Well done, chaps."

On to the next event. Feeling fairly pleased with himself, Brendan joined the others to watch Billy win the sack race, and Jono come first in the 100-yard sprint. He failed to be placed in the high jump, but did well in the 4 by 100 relay race. His team finished first.

All was going well. Henry had a go in the fathers' sack race. He came well down the field, as he couldn't find a sack big enough for his long legs.

Alice was leading the mothers' egg and spoon race until a close competitor knocked her elbow and the ceramic egg flew into the air. She made a show of losing balance, staggering around, and eventually falling amongst the spectators, showing a lot of leg and getting a round of applause from a group of grinning schoolboys. Henry helped her up, grimacing in embarrassment, while Alice played to the audience making a show of smoothing her dress.

Laughter and calls filled the air. Groups of people conversed together and smiled, drinking tea. The males discarded their jackets and loosened their ties in the warm air. The females, aunties and mothers, all in colourful summer dresses and broad-brimmed hats, talked and laughed. Alice made a further show of herself, putting on a La Di Da accent and laughing like a donkey. Henry kept his head down and smiled when necessary, looking as if he would rather be planting potatoes or weeding the scallions.

Alice and Henry were full of pride and satisfaction. Their three big boys had come up trumps. They were no doubt particularly satisfied that their offspring had done so well amongst the children of the well-off parents from the private school, who were a variety of doctors, solicitors, and government officials. Henry, in his quiet way, looked very smart in his worn brown suit and shiny shoes.

He was very proud of his brown leather shoes. My! Oh! My! Did he polish them! His handsome features, build, and height stood him out from the crowd, when really he would have rather melted into the background.

"Yes! Your boys have done very well, Mrs. Harris," congratulated Johnnie Blazer, the Assistant Head Master—the leader of men, the god on his pedestal, superman. Alice had rounded the three boys together and cornered him before he disappeared behind the pavilion. *Surely he isn't going for a pee?* Brendan wondered, there being no toilets on the ground.

He was looking very hot and flustered in his heavy tweed jacket and worsted tie. He had no doubt intended to look sporty, but looked more like a frustrated brown bear.

"Yes! They have done extraordinary well." Smiling at the three boys, he stepped closer to Alice, who had caught his arm.

"They are also doing so well in their lessons, aren't they?" she stated, while giving one of her devastating smiles.

"Yes! Yes! Of course they are, Mrs. Harris." Johnnie Blazer no doubt had never seen Billy before. Brendan was one of the many, and Jono did his best to keep up in the class. This seemed to satisfy Alice who, turning quickly to the three boys, unfortunately pulled Johnnie around whereupon he lost balance and, to steady himself, put his hand on Brendan's shoulder.

His face appeared in front of Brendan's, and his breath filled the air as he gasped. Brendan recoiled from the smell of bad breath. Reputations and respect can be lost in an instant. He was mortal; he was only human.

The senior 4 by 400-yard relay race finished the day's sporting activities and all parents gathered around the pavilion. Eddie Byrne, the Head, made a small speech about the future and how sporting activities were the background of a healthy nation, and a healthy nation was a wise nation and the future was secure due to the outstanding performances today.

To a resounding cheer and a hearty "Hear! Hear!" he passed the responsibility of announcing the prize winners to Johnnie. Still sweating in his heavy suit, Johnnie read out the names. His assistant, the severe Mrs. Jackson, dressed as if for a funeral in dusty black, passed the prizes from the creaking trestle table. The Harris name became quite noticeable after the fifth call. Brendan got a great cheer when he collected the cup for the 440 yards. He felt very nervous and shaky walking out in front of the audience, but did feel very good otherwise.

After the prize giving, congratulations were offered all round and various school friends came over to shake hands. Jono was a bit sad, as this was his last sports day; he was leaving school to start work.

Gathering all the many prizes—books, vouchers, fountain pens, and silver cups—the family piled into the large Ford Consul, the Wolseley had given up the ghost the year before, and made their way home, all feeling very pleased with their day.

14

Latin Class

One of Brendan's pet hates at school was Latin. Now fourteen years old and just starting in the senior school, he was managing to cope with the plethora of subjects deemed necessary to prepare him for the rest of his life.

However, when he moved into the fourth form, Latin was a new subject to manage. Was Latin a language? Nobody in the whole world spoke it. Was Latin just books of complicated verbs created to confuse an immature teenager? Was Caesar's Gallic Wars deliberately written in Latin to make life difficult?

The Latin teacher, Mr. Kenny, was a formidable, balding, middle-aged, short-tempered man. Possibly a happy family man loved and ad-mired in life outside the schoolroom, but to Brendan and many others in the class he personified the Latin language. Something to avoid, some-thing to fear, keep your head down; don't raise your head above the para-pet or Kenny might pick you out to ridicule.

Indeed, Brendan did not like Latin, but every Wednesday afternoon at two o'clock, the class would await the entrance of Caesar.

The classroom door opened with a flourish. Caesar would stride in, wearing a master's black gown with a mortarboard balanced on his bald head. He would give a slight smile—no greeting, no recognition of the twenty teenagers, most wishing they were elsewhere.

Walking with precise steps he'd move to the rear of the classroom and turn with his back to the window. From this vantage point he could survey the whole class without them seeing him. Unless, of course, they turned their heads. If anyone were so bold as to do so, there would be the barked command of "Look forward!"

"The verb 'amare' to love," is how the lesson would begin, without any introduction, in his droning inflexible monotone. Twenty minutes of parsing the verb "amare" and others, in the infinitive, the present active, the perfect active, perhaps looking at the indicative mood, amo, I do love, I am loving. The thought of Mr. Kenny loving anybody brought a surprised burst of incredulous laughter from some in the class.

"If there are any further outbursts, I will have the culprit reported," would be the stern warning. By the time he had come to the pluperfect passive subjunctive, amatus essem (I might have been loved, I would have been loved), the class would all be dreaming and considering the different possibilities of being loved or would have loved—if only!

The droning voice would continue, with the odd surprise question to the unsuspecting pupil, who would flounder at the answer.

The sound of a distressed bluebottle zooming its erratic path across the classroom would catch the attention. Where is it? Has it been loved or might it have been loved? Perhaps it would have been loved if it wasn't a bluebottle. Such thoughts would cross the mind of tomorrow's leader of industry or politics. Oh, the sheer stultifying boredom of the subject and its presentation! Would it ever end?

"O'Shaughnessy! O'Shaughnessy! Are you paying attention?" The sudden higher tone, the voice raised in exasperation. "O'Shaughnessy! Answer me, boy."

Everyone's head rose in interest. What was "Oh So" up to? "Oh So," easier to say than O'Shaughnessy, was older than most in the class; he had been held back at the year end as he was somewhat slow and prone to making comments out of context. His head was resting on his Longman's Latin Verbs textbook. Surely he wasn't asleep? Yes! He was! Oh, the poor guy. He was in for it.

"Yes, sir," came the sleepy reply. Raising his head, the poor confused lamb to slaughter looked at the blackboard. Where had the voice come from? There was no teacher. Looking frantically around, his bleary eyes must have caught sight of the black shape outlined against the large window.

"Jesus, it's the devil!" The class collapsed into nervous laugher, relieved for the break in the boredom, but fearful as to what was to follow. The indignant Mr. Kenny, reddened in face, strode across the room and, catching poor "Oh So" by the tail of his jacket, dragged him into the front of the class and remonstrated him with pointed finger for sleeping when he should be listening.

"Outside the door, boy. I'll give you devils." Opening the door of the classroom, he bundled the poor, weeping, terribly confused, and frightened "Oh So" into the corridor.

There was a gasp from the audience. Poor "Oh So." Mr. Kenny strode back to his haloed pedestal and instructed the class to continue parsing the verb amo.

And so Brendan's schooling continued along its undetermined path. He drifted along with his French lessons, stumbled through mathematics and accepted algebra as of possible importance. English history was a list of facts to be remembered whilst Irish history was just folklore. Geography had potential, English poetry was confusing, and essay writing was interesting. English grammar was a chore. French language had a chance in Brendan's estimation, however, as there were some people on the continent who spoke it. Irish language was a waste of time as there were apparently only a half dozen or so souls, in the barren west of Ireland, who spoke Irish as a natural language, so why waste time on it?

The Irish Government, in their misguided wish to keep alive the mystic folklore days, made the Irish language a compulsory examination subject. Everyone had to learn it. A backward move, in Brendan's estimation—perhaps if the Irish teacher had made the subject interesting, he would not have consigned it to the waste bin along with Latin.

Brendan wandered his way along the education trail, picking up bits of knowledge here and there, hoarding the sweet nuts and discarding the unpleasant weeds. At fourteen he was finding his way around life. He knew that his parents were poor, or professed they were, so how could they afford his school fees? The cottage roof was leaking badly. He was aware that the clothes he wore were scruffy in comparison to his peers at school. He was good at sports, such as hockey and would have liked to play cricket, but did not have the uniform required. The whites, the flannels, and the special cricket boots all cost money.

Whilst he found it difficult to become accepted amongst his wealthier classmates, Brendan retained his optimism and his ambitions and entered into activities where finance allowed. He scraped by with a second-hand hockey shirt, his ever-trusty runners as footwear rather than boots. He played left wing in the junior hockey team, becoming a dab hand with the reverse stick, and did a lot of running up and down the side of the field awaiting the magic pass. Sometimes it came.

He made some friends. Billy Boland, for example, the son of a travelling salesman who never seemed to stop travelling, and whose mother was never seen. Billy always smelled of urine and always had money for sweets. Billy gave Brendan half a crown to be his friend. Half a crown—a small fortune. Brendan took it, but never told his parents.

15

A Day's F---in' Fishin'

With the summer holidays stretching out ahead of him, Brendan put his problems behind him and considered the next few months. Perhaps he could do a bit of fishing in the harbour, go sailing, cycle over to Killiney Bay, or drop down to the Dunlaoghaire Baths for some swimming. Yes! The holiday months stretched ahead. After the success at the recent sports day, his confidence had returned and, though he did now and then feel very tired and lethargic, he thought no more of it.

On the first day of the holidays, with the sun shining, Brendan and Billy decided to do a bit of fishing in the harbour. They had seen some guys catch a few mackerel from the harbour wall and, after quizzing them on the necessary tackle, had been down to Perry's yachting outfitters and bought two lengths of twine, each about thirty feet long, and some fishing gut. The general store near the harbour sold small packets of fishing hooks. Tying a six-foot length of gut nylon to the end of the line, and attaching three hooks to this with a lead weight attached to the added gut nylon, they were ready to clear Dunlaoghaire harbour of mackerel.

Arriving at the harbour wall just down from the yachting basin, after propping their bikes against some bollards, they walked over to the edge of the wall to find three tough-looking lads sitting with their legs dangling above the water, the surface of which was some twelve feet below them. Each had a fishing line stretched out into the water.

The biggest of the three called Brendan over.

"Saw ye the other day, sonny. Did ye get yer tackle?"

"Shure I did," replied Brendan, emptying the tackle out onto the wall beside the big guy.

"Wait a minute. Jesus, I've got one. F---in' hell!" Leaping to his feet, the big fella holding the taut line started to pull it in overhand. "God, I think there must be a half a f---in' dozen of the buggers on it."

Just then, one of the other lads struggled to his feet.

"Hey! Gar, I've got a f---in' dozen on mine." Not to be outdone, the third fisherman started heaving in his line.

"Christ Almighty! I've got a f---in' hundred on mine."

Between the three of them, amongst great laughter and leg pulling, they pulled in five shiny mackerel between them. They had hit a shoal.

"Quick! Let's get our lines in the water, Billy," encouraged Brendan.

"No hurry, lads," advised Gar. "They go around in shoals. We might not get another for an hour or so. The tide's cumin' in, shud be a lot around den. Here, let me sort out your lines for you."

Before looking at their tackle, he re-baited the four hooks on his fishing line and, lifting the end with the weight, started to whirl it around in a circle. With a mighty heave, he sent the weight with the line attached miles out into the harbour. Tying the shore end to a stick jammed between the flags, he looked at their tackle.

Paddy, fishing next to Gar, came over and between them made the boys' lines fish-worthy, even providing some spare line as their cords were not long enough.

"Good, you've got some f---in' herrin'. Sorry—nice herrin'," exclaimed Gar, grinning at the two boys in mock apology. Taking a knife from his pocket and, after gutting the fish, cut the silver body into strips and attached a single strip to each hook.

"Now you're ready, me boyos. Throw it in and let 'em f---in' come."

Looking at each other, Brendan and Billy raised their eyes at the language. Not used to the "F" word being used in everyday conversation, it was a bit of a shock. Gar seemed to realise it must have sounded a bit offensive to the two youngsters and tried to moderate his language.

Billy, always attempting to be the first and the best at anything, hurriedly started to swing the line over his head. Brendan and Gar had to crouch over as the baited hooks whistled over their heads and watched the thrown line sail straight up in the air and land on the jetty in a tangled heap.

"Now youngster, let me do it for ye. You'll be okay, big fella," he confirmed to Brendan, who had started to put some momentum into the swing of the lead weight on the end of his line.

"Don't stand so near the water. I can't swim," shouted Gar, as Brendan lost his balance and stumbled closer to the harbour edge. Trying again, Brendan got a lot of line out and settled down on the edge of the harbour with his legs swinging over the water. He glanced at Billy and they grinned at each other and thanked Gar for the help.

Sitting on the wall in the warmth of the sun, his feet swinging over the seawater below, with tendrils of seaweed swinging in the rise of the water and the tide coming in, Brendan felt very relaxed. This is the life. Come on fishes!

The day was getting warmer with a light breeze ruffling the water. There were a few yachts lazily tacking their way to the harbour mouth. The mailboat was approaching the harbour entrance on its way to Holyhead, its decks lined with passengers waving to the small figures grouped at the tip of the East Pier. Howth Head, on the northern end of the bay outside the harbour, was shrouded in a diminishing light mist. The seagulls were swooping and calling over the fish trawlers recently returned from their nighttime fishing.

A tug on the line. "Oh, Golly! Have I caught one?"

"No! Nothing more. Settle down, Brendan boy, settle down."

"I've got one!" exclaimed Billy, who started to pull in the line as quickly as he could. "No, it's gone. Oh! Bugger!"

"Must be a shoal passing," called Gar. "Yep! I've got a whale."

Pulling his line in, he landed another wriggling, shiny mackerel. Paddy followed with another two and they all settled down to await the next shoal.

"Pull in your lines, you two," suggested Gar. "They may need some herrin'."

"Yes! Of course," exclaimed Brendan excitedly, pulling in the line and attaching herring strips to the bare hooks. Billy did the same and, after a couple of attempts, they got the lines out into the water and settled down awaiting the next shoal.

Activity in the harbour increased. Small motorboats, taking owners to yachts, left a surge of water at the feet of the fishermen as they swept by on their important errands. A large cabin cruiser sauntered in and, with a deal of sudden activity, tied up to the quay further down from the fishermen.

"Dey must be from England," stated Paddy. "Look at that bugger. God! Look at the f---er." Roaring with laughter, the fishermen's eyes were attracted by the sight of a large man making his cautious way down the gangplank from the cruiser. Wearing sparkling white shorts that would have made enough sail for a large yacht, a huge red shirt and topped by a florid red face with sunglasses and a wide-brimmed Stetson cowboy hat, the Englishman—for he could only be English, as nobody in Ireland could afford to fill a body that size—stepped off the gangplank, allowing the cruiser to settle back with a sigh of relief onto an even keel.

"Are you there, Elizabeth?" the body called back to the cruiser as a tall, shapely female in white slacks and a sun hat appeared at the top of the gangplank.

"Yes! Coming, Hector," the vision replied. "Wait a mo'."

The three fishermen, enthralled by the sight of this affluence, rose to their feet and, in mock English accents, called out in unison.

"Yes! Coming, Hector. Wait a mo'."

Grinning, the three of them settled back to the important job of fishing, laughing amongst themselves.

By now the tide was at full and the water had reached within four feet of the boys' bare toes—they had decided to take off their sandals in case they fell off into the water. As Gar and the others had shed their shirts in the warm sun, both Brendan and Billy did the same. Their thin white bodies were in sharp contrast to the sun-tanned, muscular bodies of their three friends.

As there had been no action on the fishing front for some time, Brendan pulled in his line to discover that a couple of the herring strips had fallen off. Replacing them, he made his best cast of the day and, sitting down on the warm water's edge, he looked over at Billy.

"Bet you I get one now."

With that, Billy's line tautened and, in great excitement, he pulled in a leaping mackerel. Getting it onto the wall, he tried to catch it as it leaped about on the end of line. Gar, with his big hands, caught the fish and, dislodging the hook from its mouth, placed his first two fingers in the fish's mouth; with his thumb on the back of the head he pressed down, breaking the mackerel's neck.

"There ye are boys. Dat's how you do it. Well done, young fella."

Patting a smiling Billy on the head, he went back to his line.

"Show the young f---ers how to do it," he commented to his two associates.

Time began to pass slowly. The day was getting warmer and the water began to recede. Gar said the fishing would be poor and he and his brothers were now going to have a jar. Wishing the two boys happy fishing, the three of them swaggered off with their haul of mackerel.

After half an hour with no further action, the two boys decided to cycle home, having learnt a great deal about f---ing fishin'.

16

Reading the Lesson

Churchgoing was an expected practice in the early fifties. Brendan Harris went to church on a Sunday morning more to support his parents than as a christian duty. Alice Harris, ever the person to make an appearance, liked to show off her charming husband and three tall sons to the Protestant community. So the four males would follow mother to church and comply with the ritual. Henry, when approached by Brendan, who wished to know the reason why churchgoing was so important, tried to explain.

"Son, it's easier to agree than to disagree. I go to church as your mother wishes it. It's up to you, son, to make up your own mind."

With the piece of sound advice that "mother knows best," Brendan saw no problem in complying with mother's wishes. However, due to her close connection with the church, the following transpired one Saturday morning.

"Brendan, will you come here a moment, please."

Hearing his mother's voice from the sitting room, the voice she always put on when the Vicar was around, Brendan made his way up the hallway wondering what she wished. Mr. Draper or, to give him his correct title, the Right Reverend Kilkenny Douglas Barnabas Draper of the Parish Church, had just called. Draper was a frequent caller on church business, as Alice was now "Chief Mother" of the Mothers Union and Henry was Chief Warden in the Church.

Draper gave the appearance of being a very lonely man. Living by himself in the large rectory up the road from the cottage, he always appeared embarrassed and confused when spoken to. He bumbled, stuttered, and reddened in the face when approached for an opinion.

A large, well-fed man, big in girth rather than height with a well-rounded figure, he was quite bald, had a rather large nose, and always wore a light grey, very long raincoat, buttoned up to the neck. The coat was badly stretched, with the odd tear and some subtle gravy or soup stains. When invited to take his coat off, he would always refuse. No, Mr. Draper was not the ideal figure to complement the prominent middle-class members of his flock.

Brendan, as with most fourteen-year-old boys, was very critical of those who did not conform to his expectations. Mr. Draper certainly did not have the expected aura of a spiritual leader of men.

"Yes Ma! Comin'."

Leaving his attempt at painting a country scene with poster paints, Brendan made his way up the hallway, wondering if Draper wanted him to read the Sunday Lesson. After last Sunday's church service, Brendan had voiced some criticism of the lesson reader, as he couldn't understand a word old Murphy said. He was surprised to hear a voice that seemed similar to his own saying he could do better if old Draper would like him to give it a go.

Entering the sitting room, he saw Draper sitting in the armchair with his back to the window, the sunlight accentuating the loose grey hairs on his pate. Wearing the usual raincoat, now with a further stain on the sleeve, he got to his stockinged feet—he always took his shoes off before coming into the room.

"Hello! Hello!" Stutter, splutter. With his large soft hand outstretched, he stumbled against the small coffee table. "Brendan, how are you?"

Brendan caught the hand and returned it quickly.

"Hello, Mr. Draper."

Returning to his seat, Draper stumbled backwards, catching his feet at the base of the armchair, and collapsing in a jumble of raincoat with a relieved smile.

Brendan leaned forward and, with a sidelong grin to his mother, re-plied to the question of his health in the affirmative.

"Mr. Draper, I think you are sitting on your hat," he continued.

"Oh! Goodness me! Am I? It must have—where is it?" Like a whale coming up for air, the raincoat rose from the chair, turned to look back at the seat, discovered the crumpled head cover, recovered it, placed it on his head and, in one smooth movement, swung around and collapsed into the creaking armchair. His stockinged feet rose off the floor like the last surge of a whale's tail before disappearing under water.

"So sorry. Thank you. So sorry."

Trying not to laugh, Brendan sat in the chair opposite the visitor and looked quizzically at his ma.

"Brendan, Mr. Draper has something he wishes to ask you."

"Oh! Yes! Oh! Yes! Yes!" came the stuttered acknowledgement from Draper, as his large hand rose from the raincoat to remove the hat perched askew on his head.

"Don't need that, do I? Ha! Ha!" he spluttered. "Not leaving yet, am I? Ha! Ha!"

Placing the crumpled hat on his knees, the uncomfortable figure started to explain his reason for calling. Amongst the stuttering and spluttering, Brendan discovered that Mr. Murphy had died suddenly and that Draper needed a replacement to read the church lesson in the morning.

"Would you, Brendan, be so kind, as I know you young men are so, so busy these days."

The reverend glanced towards Alice, who smiled in affirmation. He looked at Brendan with great anticipation.

Well, Brendan thought. *If old Murphy could do it, then so can I.*

"Yes, Mr. Draper, I'll have a go. What are the lessons and what do I do?"

"I have a piece of paper here somewhere, somewhere."

Fumbling in his coat pocket, he brought out some crumpled pieces of paper and started to smooth them out, one at a time, on the small table.

"Yes! Yes! Here we are. Oh! No! Ha! Ha! That's not it. Where is it?"

The confused figure disappeared into his own world whilst he deciphered the numerous notes written in a very neat, copperplate hand.

"Always be prepared." Raising his head, he smiled in embarrassment. "Be prepared. I was a boy scout. Ha! Ha!"

Sitting to attention, the sorry figure brought his right hand, closed in a fist with the first two fingers making a "V" sign, to the side of his forehead.

"I dib, dib, dib."

Brendan, being in the wolf cubs at school, knew Draper had made the wolf cub sign instead of the scout sign but, rather than extend the embarrassing, if humorous, moment, did not correct Draper.

In his attempt at humour, the ungainly figure had scattered his notes. Brendan, with the resigned air of the young, collected the papers from the floor whilst Draper apologised again.

"Here we are. Is this it, Mr. Draper?" asked Brendan, showing Draper a paper with the words "Isaiah 6:1–11 and Rev 4:1–9" written on it.

Offering his profuse thanks again to Brendan for finding the piece of paper, he confirmed the readings and promised he would have markers put in the Bible for the next day, Sunday. He then subsided with relief into the armchair, crossing his feet to hide the hole in his left sock.

"Would you like a cup of tea, Mr. Draper?" Alice enquired in a voice that hoped for a refusal.

"Oh! Yes! Yes! How kind of you, Mrs. Harris! Alice! How kind of you. Thank you, Mrs. Harris. Thank you."

Frantically fumbling under his unopened raincoat, he produced a large silver watch on a gold chain. Opening the sprung cover with surprising dexterity he announced in an apologetic voice,

"Sorry, so sorry Mrs. Alice, I have an appointment. I must go. Thank you, thank you. Thank you, Brendan. Good boy! Good boy!"

Rising to his feet with a great effort and recovering his hat from the floor, Draper placed it on his head, apologised for dropping it and stated he intended to buy a new one. He walked backwards toward the closed exit door still apologising, bumped into it and, turning around with a further apology, opened the door, closing it with a bang behind him. By then Brendan and Alice were doubled up in laughter, gasping for breath. The door opened again. Draper, raising his hat again to them both, excused himself.

"My shoes, my shoes. Riding a bicycle is difficult without." Pushing his feet into the awaiting well-polished pair of leather shoes, he folded the oil-stained trouser legs into his socks. Excusing himself again, he backed out in confused embarrassment and hastened down the garden, pushing his large sturdy cycle before him.

Brendan, not being very well acquainted with the Bible, found the verses in Isaiah were full of creatures called seraphims flying around with some poor souls having red-hot coals put in their mouths. Revelations was all about a guy called John and his seven churches and that Jesus Christ was the first begotten of the dead. How did one pronounce the word "Uzziah"? Not understanding the messages in the lessons, he made sure he could pronounce any difficult words.

The following morning, after a full breakfast with the rest of the family, all dressed in their Sunday best, he walked down to the church. Alice, with her arm in Henry's, proudly led her three tall sons past Mahony's newsagents with its high window and dark interior, nodded to the smithy shoeing a horse in the forge—unusual to find him working on a Sunday—and wished a good morning to some of the neighbours returning from Mass.

Walking past the rectory on Glebe Road where Draper lived his spartan life, they met up with Mrs. Todder and her large daughter. The Todders were poor Protestants, and quite unpleasant people—all fat and smelly. Henry, in his affable manner, was very pleasant with them. However, Alice gave them the cold shoulder. The rumour that Mrs. Todder had expressed visions of her daughter marrying a Harris son had not been too well received by Alice. Brendan and Jono were not too enamoured by the thought, either, and quickened their pace after wishing the family a good morning.

"Wonder where Mr. Todder is?" grinned Brendan in an aside to Jono.

"Poor man, probably back in the house making the dinner."

Moving quickly, the Harris family rounded the long corner after the Rectory and walked alongside a large field of swaying wheat and joined the Butlers, who were distant cousins, as they came out from their farm-house on their way to the church.

"Donggggg! Donggggg!" went the church bell calling the devout, all dressed in their best clothes. Large cars dropped their passengers off at the church gates. Alice waved to the many smiling mothers. Henry nodded his head to other husbands, whilst Jono and Brendan looked at the girls. Billy, being the youngest son at nine years old, was more interested in getting away from all the unnecessary fuss.

Feeling quite nervous due to his impending trial, but feeling quite proud of himself, Brendan took his usual place in the family pew at the rear of the church. Kneeling down on the worn hassock, he viewed the activity through open fingers as he made the pretence of praying for the poor people in Africa. There was Mary Yardley, a tall pretty girl. Did she look over his way?

"You're supposed to be praying," said Billy, nudging him. Both Alice and Henry were hustling around on church business.

Yes! There's the lectern on the right of the church. I'll have to walk down the aisle, past Mary Yardley, turn right and then step up to the lectern. Hope Draper has prepared the Bible, thought Brendan. *Should I go up and check?*

Draper was shaking hands with everybody and smiling at everything. Coming down the aisle he noticed Brendan and lifted his arms in recognition. He leaned into the pew and, in a loud hushed voice, confirmed he had prepared the Bible for the lesson.

"Good. Good boy, Brendan. Good, good. Tut, tut."

Wringing his hands, he backed away to interfere with somebody else. With the church bell ringing its message to the community, Brendan sat back in the hard pew and looked around as the church began to fill up.

There was old Traynor on his way up to the front pews. The Anderson family were sidling into their pew—grandfather first, followed by grandchildren and parents. Mrs. Anderson is a looker, nice pair of legs. Who's that? A striking-looking teenager with long blond hair and pretty face came into view, looking around anxiously.

"Who's she?" asked Brendan.

"She's Tommy Traynor's cousin from England," whispered Billy.

At eleven o'clock exactly, the church bell stopped ringing. The wave of talking ceased and, in the hush, the vestry door opened. A transformed Draper appeared. Gone was the washed-out raincoat and the dishevelled appearance. Here was a different man. Dressed in a white surplice with black cassock, he strode purposefully to the front of the church and commenced the church service.

Brendan was becoming more nervous as time passed. *What if I make a fool of myself?* he thought, beginning to wish he hadn't volunteered to do the lesson.

With the psalm finished off with "Glory be to the Father, the Son, and the Holy Spirit," Brendan took a deep breath and stepped out onto the carpeted aisle.

With a set smile on his face, the brave soldier made his way to the front through the trenches of smiling faces, believing he was the centre of their attention. Arriving at the front of the church, he stepped up onto the marble base. With the impressive lectern in front of him, a marble post surmounted with a polished golden eagle, its wings spread holding the substantial leather-covered King James Bible, he placed a nervous hand on the brass support of the lectern and looked up. The congregation all sat and waited for him to start.

I have the power! he thought to himself. *If I do nothing they get nothing. I could start singing Mollie Malone. I could tell them a joke. No! I had better read the lesson.* He smiled to himself. There was the odd suppressed cough amongst the faces looking expectantly towards him.

Looking down at the large parchment page of the old Bible, he moved the embroidered cloth marker to the side of the page and, in a nervous voice, started.

"Here beginneth the sixth chapter of the book of Isaiah, verses one to eleven," Looking up again at his audience, the young Laurence Olivier waited whilst the dedicated churchgoers found the relevant chapter in their bibles. When silence again reigned, Brendan started to read. "In the year that king Uzziah died I saw also the Lord sitting upon a throne—" Gaining confidence, Brendan continued reading, raising his voice and lowering it where he thought would be suitable. He read the lesson as if he knew what it was all about, putting great emphasis on the line, "Then said I, Woe is me! For I am undone: because I am a man of unclean lips and I dwell in the midst of a people of *unclean lips . . .* " He raised his head and paused slightly. *How many of you lot have unclean lips? Whatever that means,* he wondered to himself.

With added confidence, he continued reading for some minutes until the final verse, raising his voice on the words "and the houses without man, and the land be utterly desolate." Raising his head and looking at the many faces before him, Brendan finished.

"Here endeth the first lesson."

He stepped down and sat in the front pew with his back to the congregation. Sweating heavily, his nerves jangling and feeling very lightheaded, he stood with the rest of the congregation to mutter the words of the Te Deum Ladamus.

"O Lord, in thee have I trusted," he whispered, and stepped up to the lectern again. "The second lesson will be verses one to nine from chapter four of Revelations."

After the shuffling of feet and turning of bible pages among the congregation, he started reading again in a now very confident manner, putting emphasis on the "beholds," "cometh," and "haths." He began to enjoy himself and, by the time he came to the final words, was rather loath to stop.

Reaching the final verse he raised his head, looked again at his audience and ended his reading in a firm voice. "Here endeth the second lesson." He then started to close the heavy Bible. As the lectern began to sway a bit due to the movement of the very heavy Bible, he left well alone and started his triumphant return to his pew.

Stepping down from the lectern in the silence, whilst Draper prepared himself for the church announcements, he strode down the aisle looking straight ahead, ignoring the hopefully admiring glances from Mary Yardley and the congregation. With a big grin, still feeling a bit light-headed, he sat down in the family pew and acknowledged the smiles of congratulations and pride from his parents.

Very relieved that it was all over, Brendan, still shaking a bit and feeling very hot, sat on the hard seat wishing he could go out into the fresh air. As Draper began to announce the next meeting of the women's guild and the visit of the mission to Africa, his voice became distorted and Brendan began to feel his body sinking into the seat. He glanced towards Alice and called out to her.

"Ma! I feel awful. I'm going . . ."

Falling forward in a faint, Brendan crumpled like a ragged doll and fell into the narrow space of the pew.

Weighing some eleven stones, Brendan was not easy to lift in such a restricted space, but they stretched him out as best they could and rested his head on a dusty hassock. Fortunately, within a minute he recovered his senses and, helped by his father and a very anxious mother, was able to slump on the seat of the pew. With people all asking how he was, Alice and Henry decided to walk Brendan to the back of the church. Feeling quite weak, he walked with the aid of his parents out to the sunlight and sat in the churchyard on a chair placed by Billy. One member of the congregation, observing Brendan's plight, offered to drive him home.

Feeling much better and wondering what all the fuss was about, Brendan joined Alice and Billy in the car and returned to the cottage. Henry had to stay on due to his responsibilities as Church Warden, and Jono had to walk, as there was no room in the small car. That evening it was decided a visit to the doctor would be the best thing to do.

17

Heart Problem: Friends in the Woods

"I want to make an appointment for my son to see Dr. Folly, please! No! It's quite urgent. All right, next Thursday will be fine, at ten in the mornin'. Mrs. Alice Harris. Yes, that's right. Good-bye."

"There you are, Brendan, next Thursday. We'll see about your dizzy spells and get it sorted out."

On the chosen day, Alice dressed in her finest and Brendan with his new suit, feeling a bit of an imposter as he felt quite well, took the bus to Dunlaoghaire to see the doctor.

"Now, Brendan, you're to be on your best behaviour when we see the doctor. He will have the answer to why you fainted in the church. Now straighten your tie and don't make any funnies when we see him."

Arriving at the address, they climbed a half dozen or more granite steps to a very large, heavy front door. Looking at rows of names listing doctors and solicitors, Alice picked out the name of Dr. Folly and pushed the bell button. After what seemed like hours, the heavy door slowly opened and a prim, skinny woman stepped back to allow them to enter.

The hallway was tall and wide, large enough to garage a row of double-decker buses. They were shown into a plush waiting room with a high ceiling and heavy curtains. There was a muffled silence, with a large ornate clock in the corner slowly ticking the time away. Tick, tock, tick, tock.

Alice picked up a yellow *National Geographic* magazine and pretended to read it. Brendan wandered around, looking in cupboards and examined the ornaments on a small table beside the large impressive fireplace.

"Wonder if they roasted an ox in there," said Brendan pointing to the large grate.

"Sit down, Brendan, and don't break anything," cautioned Alice.

Tick, tock, tick, tock.

"Ma! The clock says a quarter past ten. When will he see us?"

"Doctors are busy people and we have to wait for them. But I am getting a bit fed up anyway," retorted Alice. "We'll give him another ten minutes."

Tick, tock, tick, tock.

Brendan opened the door and looked out into the hall. The only movement in the large hallway was the dust shimmering in the sun's rays.

"Shut the door, Brendan, and sit down."

"Wait. There's a door opening down the hall, Ma. There's someone comin' out. It's an old lady."

An elderly well-dressed lady, escorted by the prim woman, stuttered past on shuffling feet. Opening the heavy door to the swish of expensive carpet, Miss Prim called good-bye, in a posh voice, to Mrs. Lovegrove and wished her a good day. Then with another swish of expensive carpet the door closed and the carpet settled down.

Miss Prim gave Brendan a disdainful glance as she passed, tall and erect.

"The doctor will see you shortly, young man," she admonished as she entered the rays of dusty sunlight and disappeared back behind the door.

Tick, tock, tick, tock.

"Ma, I wanna go to the lav."

"Can't you wait, Brendan? It won't be long now."

"No, Ma! I really need to go."

"All right then, but be quick."

Tick, tock, tick, tock.

A door banged shut. Voices were heard down the hall, then silence.

Tick, tock, tick—dong! Half past ten.

Brendan returned and sat down in the waiting room.

"Ma, you should see the lav. It's got pictures on the bowl and real fancy paper—nutin' to read, no newspaper. Go on, have a look," suggested Brendan, grinning at his mother.

"I'm goin' to find out what's goin' on. It's gone half ten," stated Alice in exasperation, rising to her feet. But before she got to the door it swung open and Miss Prim walked in.

"The doctor will see you now," she announced.

"About time, too," muttered Alice, pushing Brendan ahead of her.

Following their leader, they were escorted down the soundproof hallway and along a short dark corridor to be halted by a raised hand.

"Please wait here, madam and sir," came the instruction from Miss Prim, whilst she tapped on a large door and then ushered them into the room.

"Hello, Mrs. Harris, so sorry for keeping you waiting. And you also, young sir," came the affable welcome and instruction from behind a large desk.

"Do sit down."

Alice, in her dignified pose, quite ready to complain about the wait but taken aback by the friendly greeting, acknowledged it. She and Brendan sat down in the oversize armchairs in front of the large desk.

After Alice had described the problem, the overweight and bespectacled expert on medical matters came waddling out from behind his fortress and, waving his stethoscope like a magic wand, had Brendan take his shirt off and began to examine him. With a number of "tut-tuts" and "humphs" he returned to his seat behind the desk, folding his tool of office into a black bag, and cleared his throat.

"Mrs. Harris," he announced, "your son has a slight heart murmur. Nothing too serious, but it is advisable he rest and reduce his activity level. After some time he should get better. Now, young man, you have to do what your mother says and remain in your bed for the next month. After that you are not to run or exert yourself. Come back and see me in six months."

Returning home after the devastating news, Brendan's parents, never thinking to question the doctor's decision, bundled a fit young man to bed for a month. By the end of the first day, Brendan had read all the books he possessed and was nearly screaming with the boredom. After the second day it was decided that if he walked slowly and didn't exert himself in any way he could get up and sit in the front room.

The front room became the front garden. The walk to the toilet became a walk around the house and by the end of the first week, he was getting up in the middle of the morning and trying his hand at watercolour painting, walking to the shop, and feeding the chickens.

"You are not to run, Brendan, not even walk fast. It would be folly to do so," advised Alice, smiling at her use of the word. By the end of the second week Brendan was doing a bit of slow gardening and taking the odd slow bus ride to the library in Dunlaoghaire.

During one of his slow walks up to Moran's pub to catch the bus, he and Alice were approaching the stop when the bus rounded the corner and, instead of them both running, which would only have been natural, Alice raced the fifty yards, waving frantically to the conductor to wait for her little sick boy. Little? Sick? Nearly six feet tall, weighing eleven stone and looking very healthy, Brendan felt like a fraud as he walked the fifty yards from Moran's to the bus stop.

Quite embarrassed, Brendan stepped onto the platform to be welcomed by the long-nosed conductor.

"Well, if it isn't the big grammar school boy. Your Ma says you're not well, laddie. Now come and sit downstairs."

This was all said and done in a friendly manner with no apparent malice, as the smiling official showed Brendan to a seat downstairs.

To fill in the long summer days, Brendan went for walks down to the fields; whether this was wise or not due to his supposed condition, nobody told him. As it was summertime he wore a short-sleeved white shirt and khaki-coloured shorts with a pair of scruffy white runners. One favourite walk was into the woods to the fountain with the angels.

As he walked along a narrow path through the bushes one day, three youngsters jumped out and startled him. Each one had a homemade bow with arrows made from thin branches; they had chicken feathers in their hair and all tried to look fearsome.

"Halt! Who goes there? Hans up," was the command from the oldest, who looked about ten. As with the other younger children his skin was an attractive light brown and his voice had a foreign twang to it. All wore scruffy short trousers and runners without socks.

Brendan, putting his hands up, getting over the initial scare, answered in a deep voice, "The Lone Ranger. Who are you?"

"Let's kill him. He's a Golem," suggested the smallest assailant, aiming his armed bow in Brendan's direction.

"We own this land. You shuddent be here," advised the eldest.

"I was here years before you ever came," stated Brendan, annoyed that somebody else was claiming his secret place.

"We live in the house," announced the third member of the gang, "So you're trepassin."

With that, the three of them started to dance around Brendan making yodelling noises, leaping up and down and shouting, "Kill! Kill! Kill the Golem."

Brendan, beginning to enjoy himself, lowered his arms. "Bet you can't catch me," he called out and turned and ran down the grassy path.

Rounding a clump of bushes, he leaped behind a large rhododendron bush. The three Red Indians came racing after him and past his hiding place. Brendan, who had practised the ability to make a particular shrill and loud whistle with two of his fingers, stopped the three killers in their stride. They looked around confused, trying to place the noise.

"Put your hands up. I've got you covered," ordered Brendan as he stepped out from behind the large flowering bush, pointing a branch he had broken off in their direction. "This is a six shooter and I'm Billy the Kid."

The eldest of the three, playing the game, threw down his bow and put his hands in the air.

"You've got us there, Billy. We surrender."

"No, I don't, Johnnie," shouted the smallest, trying to fire an arrow at Brendan. Pulling the string back on his bow and letting it go, the arrow, a thin angular piece of branch, fell in front of Geronimo, the middle-sized child.

"Bang! Gotcha, you're dead," shouted Brendan, taking the advantage.

"You missed," shouted the smallest one, starting to load another arrow. Brendan, firing another shot and shouting "Bang!" started to run again. Enjoying the exhilaration, he ran down the grassy path, leaping over bushes into a small field, back into the jungle, to hell with his murmur. Run, run.

Suddenly arriving at the clearing with the fountain, panting with the exertion, he stopped and leaned on the wall around the water.

Janey Mac, he thought to himself. *I shouldn't be runnin'.* Taking deep breaths, he did not notice the three Indians creeping up behind him.

"Han's up, Golem. We have got you now."

Brendan turned around with his hands in the air to see the three Indians with their bows loaded with various shaped arrows pointing at him. Dropping his "revolver" and still recovering from his run, he sat down on the grass and invited the three to have a pow wow.

Johnnie, Solomon, and Levi Speilman were all from England and were now living in the Gate Cottage of the estate.

"My Dad is a famous man," said Johnnie. "He helped win the war."

"My Dad runs the Dublin Gas Company."

"Golly, he must be important," exclaimed Johnnie. "Where do you live?"

"Down the road in the cottage, an' my name's Brendan."

After a few more questions and answers the four of them rose as Johnnie, with the agreement of his two brothers, decided to show Brendan their camp.

"You're not to tell nobody, cross your heart and hope to die," instructed Johnnie. Brendan crossed his heart and said he would keep their camp secret for the rest of his life.

Crouched over, they tiptoed in single file, with Brendan at the rear, away from the fountain towards the big house. Looking over his shoulder to check all were following him, Johnnie instructed his two small brothers to climb the lower branches of a nearby tree to keep a look out. Motioning Brendan to follow him, he pushed through the bushes at the side of the path. Crawling on hands and knees in the thick carpet of old leaves and pushing aside obstructing small branches, Johnnie suddenly stopped.

"Wait here, Brendan," he said. Lifting some broken branches to the side, he disappeared behind the trunk of a large tree.

"All clear now. Come on, Brendan," came the instruction from Johnnie. Brendan obeyed the request and rounded the tree trunk. About four feet tall by six feet wide, the "camp" was made of leafy branches balanced on a couple of planks of wood nailed to the tree trunk. There was a scruffy cream blanket spread on the ground.

"What do you think?" asked Johnnie, with pride in his voice, as he picked a snail off the blanket.

"Janey Mac, it's smashin!" replied Brendan. "Did your Dad help?"

"No, we did it on our own."

"What's that, Johnnie?" interrupted Brendan. "Did I hear sometin'?" Listening intently, they heard Levi call out.

"White man comin'."

"Yes! Brendan, it must be the enemy. Come on."

The two boys crawled out of the entrance. Johnnie replaced the covering branches and they scurried off on hands and knees through the undergrowth. When far enough away from the hide, they started walking nonchalantly along the path toward the fountain. The two others joined them as they saw a woman walking into the opening.

"There you are," the woman said. "It's your tea time. Who's that you've got with you?"

"It's our new friend, Mammy. 'The Golem.' We found him in the woods. Isn't he big? Can he come to tea?"

The woman looked across at Brendan initially with suspicion, then smiled a greeting. Her thin dark-skinned face lighting up, her long brown hair framing her face, and the slim body dressed in a red working skirt and white blouse made a very attractive picture. Brendan found himself blushing as she came towards him.

"Yes! Do please. That would be nice. What's your name? Mine is Annette Speilman. Hello!"

"Brendan, Mrs. Speilman," answered Brendan, blushing more than ever and taking her thin hand as it was held out to him. "How do you do? What's a Golem?"

"The Golem's blushing, look at him!" laughed Solomon. "It's only my Mammy."

"I'll have to go home and tell my mother, Mrs. Speilman."

"All right, Brendan, see you shortly. By the way a Golem is a friendly clay giant who helped to watch over the Jews in the city of Prague three hundred years ago."

Brendan, turning on his heel, raced back to the haycock field, forgetting he should not be running and thinking of how nice the three boys and their mother were. He ran back to the cottage and told his mother who insisted he have a wash and tidy himself up.

"And by the way, Brendan, have you been running?"

"Just a little bit, Ma. I forgot."

"Remember what the doctor said. Now, away with you and have a nice tea."

He made his way back to the gate lodge, where Mrs. Speilman had laid out a table with mugs of orange juice and a large wooden board in the centre covered in a mound of jam sandwiches.

The lodge was sparsely furnished and looked very temporary. There was a wedding photograph of Mrs. Speilman with her husband—a tall, severe-looking man wearing a uniform and a large peaked cap. Quite entranced by this gentle, slim woman, Brendan would make many visits to the woods, always hoping to meet her.

Later in the year, on his return from a holiday in Wicklow, upon calling at the lodge he found the door locked and the windows boarded up. Asking around, nobody knew where the family had gone.

"Anyway, the father was a load of trouble. The police were after him," was the decided opinion of the locals.

Brendan's health had improved greatly over the months and, when Alice rang in the September to make an appointment with Dr. Folly, she was told he had retired. As there had been no further faints or problems, they decided to save the money and not bother any further.

18

The Tinkers

In the nineteen fifties, the politicians in Dublin had a surge of conscience and decided they should help the poor tinkers. Some people called them gypsies, others tinkers, but whatever they were called, these people lived outside the norm expected. They didn't live in houses, they didn't have regular work; instead, they wandered around the country earning a bit here, a bit there, helping themselves to the odd loose object. Really, what the politicians wished was to tidy up the countryside. Were the tinkers asked if they wished to be housed? Did they want help? Brendan very aware of those less fortunate than himself, found himself questioning his own and his mother's social conscience.

"Would you look after the O'Toole family den for us, Mrs. Harris? They're down in a house in Mountain View," pleaded Michael Flynn. Michael worked for the Dunlaoghaire Council; he was a youngster of twenty, related to the Flynns from the cottages and a bit out of his depth.

"Shure Michael, I'm only too happy to help out," Alice replied. "How's your mother keeping? She's expecting another soon, isn't she? A lovely job you've got here. Did your big brother become the priest, then?"

Michael, very conscious of his new job and new suit provided by the council, smiled at the barrage of questions and didn't hear any of them.

"Ye know, Mrs. Harris, there's twelve of dem and dey have vans an' a horse an' cart an' dey don know how to live like us,"

"Don't worry Michael, I know what to do. We can't have them living as they do. It's no good for them. I'll go down to the house right away. Which one is it?"

"I'll take ye down there now, missus," said a relieved Michael.

"Hav' ye got a bike?"

"Of course I've gotta bicycle, young man. Brendan," she called out, "are you there? Good—I'm goin' with Michael here to the tinkers in Mountain View."

A small hamlet called Mountain View, a short mile down the road from the cottage, five charming cottages, with a view of the distant Dublin Hills, had been determined uninhabitable. The grudging occupants had been moved into some newly built council houses and now the cottages were being used to house the "homeless."

"Okay, Ma! I'll come with you," answered Brendan coming up the hallway to see whom Alice had been talking with.

"Well! If it isn't the bold Michael Flynn. God! You look smart, Mick. Got a job with the council then, have you?" Brendan exclaimed, standing back in mock admiration of the embarrassed Michael in his new suit and tie.

"How's Marcella? I hear she's a nun now. Is Patrick a priest yet?"

"Yeh! Brendan, you're right der. Patrick is down the country training to be a priest. Charlie's workin' on the bins an' Jean is married now with two childer'. De other three are still goin' to school. Marcella changed her mind an' 'gon' to Lundun."

"How's your Ma and Da?" Brendan asked, remembering the many times he had seen Ma and Pa Flynn staggering home after an evening in Moran's pub.

"They're fine, Brendan. Oh! There ye are den, Mrs. Harris."

Wheeling their bikes onto the road, Brendan and his mother followed the council official as he led them on his new blue council bike, proudly acknowledging the looks of admiration from the passing villagers.

"There's young Flynn. He works for the council. Hasn't he done well?"

The three of them cycled down to Mountain View, Alice on her upright lady's bike with the wicker shopping basket attached to the handlebars, and Brendan on his prized possession, a Hercules bike with three speed gears and straight handlebars past the "dump." The dump was a large convenient depression in the land, open to the road, with mounds of steaming household waste and discarded rubbish hidden by the wheeling white clouds of screaming gulls and black crows.

Twitching their noses at the unwholesome smell, the three cyclists continued their journey along the narrow road. Rounding a corner shrouded by a hedge, the impressive Our Lady of Lourdes Hospital for the Incurables dominated the skyline to the left. Run by the religious orders and staffed by hundreds of black-garbed nuns, the whole edifice exuded the atmosphere of finality and death, somewhat akin to the final resting place of the community's rubbish.

The secluded cottages of Mountain View appeared to the right. The once neat and tidy hedges and gardens were now overgrown and hidden by a mixture of old cars and carts with horses tethered to the front gates.

Dismounting, the three cyclists wheeled their bicycles past the horse tethered at the gate of number three and went into the garden. Michael produced a long chain with a small padlock.

"A great idea, Mick," Brendan exclaimed. "I wondered how we were goin' to stop them from being stolen. We could lock them to that old bedstead in the roses there. What do you think?"

"There ye are den, Mr. O'Toole," stuttered Michael as he nodded to Brendan, locked the three cycles together and lifted a hand in greeting to a small stocky man who had appeared at the doorway. Wearing torn brown corduroy trousers held up with baling string, with brawny arms folded across his chest in a defiant pose, Mr. O'Toole did not appear to be very welcoming to this visit by officialdom.

"Remember me, Mr. O'Toole? Said I would call back with de lady. Can we come in?" pleaded Michael, embarrassed at being caught locking the bikes. Mr. O'Toole, with a withering look at Michael, turned without a word, and pushed his way back into the cottage past the gawping children and scruffy dogs now gathered around his legs.

Entering the low-roofed cottage, Brendan, having to stoop due to his height, was taken aback at the sight of the rubbish-strewn floors and the dreadful smell.

"Are ye all right den, Mr. O'Toole? Is Mrs. O'Toole in the back den?" enquired Michael, trying to speak without breathing through his nose.

"Mary, cum here woman," ordered O'Toole brusquely. "I to'd ye to clean up before the council came. There's a crowd of dem here now."

A worried-looking, attractive-featured woman in her late thirties came submissively into the room, wiping her hands on a torn cloth apron that covered a light cotton dress. With her head down, she stood in the corner.

"Are ye al right den, Mr. O'Toole?" repeated the council official, pushing the dirty grasping hands of the three grinning youngsters away from his new suit.

"Wha' do ye wanna know, mister?" grunted O'Toole in reply.

"Mrs. Harris is here to help ye," replied Michael, trying not to show his difficulty in breathing and waving his arm in Alice's direction, whilst backing toward the door to reach the fresh air.

"What's that awful smell, Mr. O'Toole? It smells like dog dirt, Mr. O'Toole," asked Brendan, looking toward a dark corner of the room.

"I don' smell nutin'," muttered O'Toole in reply. "I don' smell nuttin'. Will ye be after leavin' us alone. We don' need the bother. Will ye all go th' hell."

And so the interview continued. Alice, with her handkerchief to her nose and Brendan taking gasps of air in unison with Michael, discovered the family had been sleeping in the vans and using the cottage as a lavatory.

It was obvious the O'Tooles considered there was nothing amiss in the way they lived and what business was it of anybody else?

Michael and Alice pleaded with O'Toole to try and adapt to this new way of life, for the sake of the children at least. With the youngsters pulling at Alice's clothes and touching Michael's new suit, begging for money, and the greyhounds cocking their rear legs in the corner of the room, Brendan caught Alice's arm and pleaded with her to leave.

"We're wastin' our time, Ma. Come on, before we catch something," pleaded Brendan.

"But look at the children, they haven't had a meal in days," retorted Alice, pointing to a particularly scrawny girl with wispy, dirty, long blond hair, showing a mouth of broken teeth and gobs of snot dripping from her nose.

Noticing Alice looking at her, the child pinched her nose with two fingers and deposited the white mucus on her torn dress and, in a whimpering voice, pleaded for a "bit of bread," rubbing her stomach with the free hand.

In unison, the other equally scrawny children called for "a bit of bread missus, we're starving," while rubbing their small, swollen bellies.

"I've had enough," finalised Brendan. "Come on, Ma. Let's get out of here. You're wasting your time," he called out, backing toward the cottage door. Alice reluctantly followed Brendan and glanced toward Michael, who hastily followed her.

"Bloody hell, Ma! Look, they're trying to pinch our bikes," shouted Brendan as he exited the cottage door.

A couple of youngsters were pulling at the chained bicycles and trying to break the locked chain with a crowbar. The youngsters, hearing Brendan's shout, jumped up and ran away, laughing and shouting obscenities at officialdom.

Recovering their bikes, the three failed welfare workers made their way back to Laurel Cottage, and Michael returned to work on his report for his boss. Brendan was glad to see the back of the problem, while Alice began to wonder what further she could do to feed the "starvin childer."

Some weeks later, returning from a days fishing, Brendan recognised a couple of dilapidated vans parked outside the cottage. He pushed open the front door and called out, "Ma! I'm home. Are you there? Ma! Those tinkers' vans are parked down on the lane and a horse and cart loaded with old bedsteads. Ma! Are you there?"

"Yes, Brendan. Down here in the kitchen."

I can hear voices. Wonder what she's up to, thought Brendan. *They're tinkers' vans on the road. God! Surely she hasn't?*

There was Alice, his mother, the wife of the church warden, an associated member of the British Legion, the chair of the women's church committee, dressed as if she were on her way to church, serving plates of boiled new potatoes and fried mince to a table full of ill-dressed adults and children, all happily spooning the food into their greedy faces.

"Brendan, would you fill the kettle? Our guests would like a cup of tea."

The guests, a full dozen of them, sitting around the long table in the kitchen, three adults and nine children, with two greyhounds, all looked up anxiously at Brendan as he entered the kitchen.

Mr. O'Toole, in need of a shave and wearing an old pullover of Brendan's, stood up, placing his spoon on the now empty plate.

"Will ye be quiet now, the lot of ye. The master of the house is here," he admonished the table as all heads turned.

"Thank ye kindly, surr, fer inviting us to dis meal and the missus. 'Tis not often we are invited. God bless ye, surr."

"Thank ye, surr," was the chorus from the rest of the table, as empty plates were held out to their hot and now quite dishevelled benefactor.

The two gas stoves were working at full capacity, with pots of potatoes simmering under clouds of steam and a couple of frying pans with delicious-smelling fried mince. Brendan looked over at his mother who raised her head in defeat, imploring him to help her out.

"Ma! What are you up to?" Brendan asked out of the side of his mouth as he took the large kettle to fill it at the sink.

"Are they all here? There's none of them loose in the house, I hope,"

"Mr. O'Toole, all your family are here, aren't they?" Alice asked.

"No! Mam, not all of dem me brudder is in Dublin an we had to leave the young 'un in the hospital. Other dan dat Missus dere all here. Dey are Mary? Aren't dey, now?" O'Toole replied, glancing over at the woman beside him.

"Yeh! Sean. All here now," answered Mary, pretending to count the heads with her spoon. "They're all here, Missus, an' why shuddent dey be?"

"No reason, Mary everything's all right," replied Alice looking at Brendan. Before Brendan could retort there was a sudden shout from Mr. O'Toole.

"*Albert!* What are ye doin' in the corner there? Yer not havin' a piss, are ye? Jea-sus Christ child, don' be stinkin' out the luvley woman's house. Go out in the yard. Sorry, Missus, can't have it—an' all yer doin fer us."

"Oh! That's all right, Mr. O'Toole, he wasn't to know."

"Ma, what are ye doin?" implored Brendan.

"Oh! I see ye've got some mackerel, Brendan. We can have them for tea tonight."

"No! No! Ma, don't change the subject. I'm shure there's more of them."

"They're nearly finished now," Alice interrupted. "Look, the little girls are putting the dishes away, isn't that good of dem?"

"Ma, the dishes are still dirty."

"Oh, they're not to know," replied Alice, leaning against the kitchen door, exhausted.

"Right, Mr. O'Toole. Get yerself an' the family out of here, pronto," ordered Brendan, realising his mother had had enough.

"Come on. No, leave the dishes, young 'un. Where are ye going, young fella?" he asked, stopping young Albert from going up the hallway and in exasperation, bundled the wiry body out the back door.

"Don ye touch me childer, mister, or I'll be havin' the council guards on ye," remonstrated Mr. O'Toole. "Cum on, all of ye. I know when we're not wanted. Cum on Mary, Patrick. Cum on now."

Standing back, counting the heads as they exited the cottage, Brendan realised two of the party were missing.

"Ma! There's a couple of them in the house."

Running up the hall, he heard one of the youngsters calling out. "Matt, dat bastard is comin'. Run fer it." He arrived in time to see two scrawny figures disappearing out the front door. As they joined the departing family, who had come from the back of the cottage, the two turned and laughed, making the fingers sign to Brendan.

Mr. O'Toole stopped at the gate, turned, pointed his finger and, in a loud voice, threatened Brendan an' his missus "Dat he would be tellin' the council." He then turned, slamming the green door behind him, and the air was soon filled with the roar of engine noise and laughter.

"Come on, Ma. Come on, let's get tidied up before Pop comes home," exclaimed Brendan, as he now realised his mother was not the infallible person he had always considered her to be.

19

Back to School—Intro to the Doc

Brendan was enjoying himself in the latter months of 1954. At the advanced age of fourteen and a half, his health had improved after the heart scare. However, the important years for his education were not being used properly. He was conscious of this and spent a lot of time in the public library reading and at least trying to improve his word power. One of the books that caught his attention was the *Kon Tiki* expedition by the Norwegian explorer and writer Thor Heyerdahl.

Brendan's imagination was also captured by the book by Captain Joshua Slocum on his famous circumnavigation in 1895, in his sloop, the thirty-seven-foot Spray. It took Slocum over three years to circumnavigate the world. For a fourteen-year-old in the 1950s, whose world consisted of home, school and parents who spent their days searching to find the monies to live on, he wondered how a man could spend three years sailing around the world doing nothing. Sailing wasn't work. Where did he get the money from to live on?

"The boy looks very well now, doesn't he, Henry? Let's send him back to school and see what happens. Old Folly has retired, silly ould fool. Who did he think he was to do so without tellin' us? Never liked him anyway."

So Brendan returned to school, after four months of idleness, wondering what the future held for him. Could he go sailing around the world? What a thought! See the world, call into those exotic-sounding islands in the Pacific Ocean, or visit some famous cities in Europe. What about America, or Scandinavia? Was his destiny to get married, have children and spend the rest of his life scraping around for enough money to live on as his father was doing?

Dreams were only what they were—dreams. No around the world adventures for him. It was back to school and into a new classroom with its rows of desks, new teachers, and the same old difficulties of trying to adjust to the unequal lifestyle of his peers. The list of new textbooks was quite daunting.

"There you are, Brendan, five shillings. That's all we can afford for books."

So it was a long bus ride into Dublin to visit the many bookshops, especially Fred Hannas, the second-hand specialist. What books were more important? What subjects? Maths—maybe get one with the answers. French, English literature and geography. Forget about Irish; maybe get the one on Latin. Need the one on Euclid. Do I need the one on poetry? Oh yes! History, both Irish and English. Jono has a few I need.

On his return from Dublin, pleased with most of the books he had bought, especially the maths book with the answers, Brendan hoped his parents could get him a school blazer, as all the other boys were bound to have one. Long grey trousers were also needed and a new shirt and new shoes would be wonderful.

Some dental work was needed. "Take them out," advised the dentist. "Once out, they can't bother you again." As Alice and Henry were forever complaining about their false teeth, Brendan suggested he would rather have the teeth repaired. Agreeing with his wishes, they had the dentist fill those he could and remove the ones gone beyond redemption. Luckily, those that needed taking out were all back teeth.

A new blazer was not forthcoming, due to price, so he had to do with Jono's old sports jacket and one of Henry's old shirts. New long trousers were bought and, fortunately, the large turn-ups helped to hide the white runners he had tried to blacken. Brendan was not looking forward to returning to school.

As salaries in the 1950s were not geared to the luxury of school fees Alice started to take in holidaymakers and once again began to advertise her cream teas.

Holidaymakers, particularly from Scotland, arrived over the summer months, with Alice spending her time making beds and cooking. They made some new friends, but not very much money. The "Teas Inside" effort brought a few inquisitive walkers in for a cup of tea and a scone, but Alice soon gave it up, as it was not worth the effort. No American customers came, like last time. Every week the crossword competition results were examined with great anticipation. As the months went by without any success, the anticipation lessened.

Life continued with Henry going into work early and coming home late and tired. Alice did her best to earn a few pennies and eke out the small salary brought home by Henry. Realising they could not pay the fees required for the two remaining boys to continue in the school, they met Mr. Blazer, the deputy head, and pleaded that the two boys should be able to continue. Alice was at her sparkling best and they returned home with an agreement to pay what they could and that the debt would roll over, whatever that meant.

Jono had left school and was bringing home a few shillings. He had started in an accountancy firm under the guise of trainee accountant, but more the tea boy and messenger.

Brendan found school quite difficult. Girls were a mystery, as they were to most young men of Brendan's age. His body was sending confusing signals. He wondered if there was something wrong with him, due to his body's reaction to the sight of a bare female leg or when a girl would speak with him directly. He knew it had something to do with reproduction, but it was quite uncomfortable.

Also, what career should he follow? Banking, law, accountancy—it all seemed so boring and beyond his abilities. Most of the class appeared to have their futures all decided, for example going on to Trinity College to get a degree or going to work in their father's firm. Brendan knew he couldn't afford to go to Trinity College, and working in the gas company as a collector was not an attractive proposition.

What Brendan needed at this time was someone to give him a fresh look at life, someone to show him what the world had to offer a young man in his teens. His parents, with their very restricted knowledge of the world and opportunities available, did their best. Would good fortune provide this mentor?

At a morning assembly in early November, it was announced that a new teacher, a doctor of philosophy no less, would be teaching history and geography. Mr. Forsyth had to leave suddenly, "due to unexpected family problems" as explained by the headmaster. Everyone, of course, knew he had been sacked.

The following Monday morning, sheets of cold rain lashed against the classroom windows. The sky was a dismal grey. Brendan had been caught in some heavy showers cycling to school and his trouser legs were very wet, the front mudguard of his bicycle being not too effective. The last boring hour had been spent conjugating Latin verbs with the dour Mr. Kenny. The smell of drying clothes and smelly bodies was quite stifling. Brendan, sitting at the back of the classroom in a two-seater desk, had Hans Sheckter beside him.

Whilst Brendan himself did not wash too often, Sheckter's body probably had not touched water for a year or two. His breath smelled pretty foul as well. Brendan was also in a little discomfort as the shirt collar he had on was too tight and the couple of pimples on his face and back were very painful. New shoes, to replace the scruffy runners, were blistering his heels and he hadn't been sleeping too well. Life was at a low ebb.

The class was quite subdued. O'Shaughnessy and Sutton were starting to quarrel, their voices beginning to rise. The ever-sensible girls, most of whom sat in the front row of the class with the brainy boys, Williams, Kershaw, and the superior Porteous, interrupted their chattering to turn around and attempted to shush the quarrelling boys.

The next class was to be history, Irish History, shades of Forsyth. Of course! He had left! Maybe it would be the doctor of philosophy.

It had gone eleven. Better get the textbook out. Interesting how much thicker the book is now that half the pages have been underlined. Some of the pages were cut through from the use of a sharp pencil. With constant use, the book was beginning to fall apart. *Must read it sometime,* thought Brendan, attracted by the sight of Prue Smith's pleated dress caught up under her bum. She was in the desk in front of him, and he could see a tantalising glimpse of pink. Nudging Sheckter, he indicated the attraction and the two of them leaned on their cupped hands and fantasised. Prue Smith, sensing she was under scrutiny, turned in her desk to see the two immature faces staring intently at her rear.

"What are you looking at?" she called out indignantly. Both boys dropped their eyes and pretended to examine their textbooks. Looking down, she noticed she was showing some leg and knicker.

"Oh! You dirty minded boys. Oh! I thought better of you, Brendan Harris. Oh!"

She turned her back in disgust, straightening her skirt and covering her embarrassment with indignation.

Roll along twelve thirty, thought Brendan. *I can escape for an hour. What's this? It's the General and he's got someone with him.*

The "General" was the reverend, the small friendly man with a dog collar and puckered eye, headmaster of the school.

"Attention, everybody. I wish to introduce you to your new teacher, Dr. James Courcy. Dr. Courcy will be taking you for Irish History and Geography. Thank you!" Nodding to Dr. Courcy, he turned and exited the room, closing the door behind him.

Dr. Courcy looked very interesting, wearing the customary black gown thrown carelessly over a green tweed jacket that partially hid an off-white shirt with crumpled collar and green tie. His brown corduroy trousers were loosely wrapped around his thin frame and a pair of black dusty brogues peered out from the corduroy folds.

This untidy man had an interesting face, a mobile face, thin with a prominent beaked nose and badly shaven. His thinning hair showed a large forehead, with blue eyes that shone and told everybody they were interested in them. Eyes that searched out everybody, eyes that made the weary pupils sit up and take notice.

"Good morning, you dreadful people," were his first words in a soft Irish voice, a voice which carried around the room. A voice loaded with interesting tones offering further novel sentences.

Stepping out from behind the large desk with his hands behind his back under the black gown, he commenced to enthral the twenty pupils with a potted history of his recent past and his view of Irish history and how interesting it could be. He asked the class what they thought of the subject. He instinctively picked out the class leaders to hear their views on the subject. Asking Harold West, the brain, who always sat in the front row of desks, for a comment, he produced the usual careful, well-enunciated reply.

However, West always blushed furiously when approached. Whilst Brendan suffered from the same ailment, his efforts were nothing compared to the striking red sunset glow that emanated from Harold. By the end of the lesson, which passed in a flash, every pupil wanted to speak with the doc, wanted to be noticed by him. When he thanked everybody on his way to his next class, he left a room of rejuvenated youngsters talking amongst themselves, not realising they had been in the presence of one of the most gifted and intelligent men that Ireland had produced in its troubled history.

Dr. Courcy or the "doc" as he was affectionately known, was to have a positive effect on the lives of many of the pupils in that class, and particularly that of Brendan Harris.

20

The Parochial Hall Dance

In his early to mid-teens, Brendan was a tall, thin young man, weighing in at a lean and bony eleven stone. When wearing swimming shorts he believed he resembled the pimply scrawny youth in the "before" pictures in the Charles Atlas adverts. Looking for possible quick success in body-building, Brendan borrowed Jono's discarded Charles Atlas chest expanders. Upon gripping the large metal handgrips that were divided by three solid unforgiving springs, he took a deep breath and attempted to expand his chest. Wow! He struggled and heaved but could not pull the grips apart more than an inch. Even by attaching one grip to a hook on the wall and putting his whole weight behind it, he only doubled the result to two inches. At the age where instant success was required, he gave that up.

He was very conscious of his appearance. Whilst both his brothers had been endowed with attractive black curly locks, Brendan had been supplied with a head of unattractive hair, mousey in colour and straight as a ruler. In the 1950s, for those with straight hair a quiff was all the rage for a young man. To form a quiff one allowed the front hair on one's head to grow to six or seven inches. The resulting length of hair was then combed back in a sweeping wave over the top of the head. Some of Brendan's school friends had the most wonderful and enviable quiffs, but his attempts always ended in failure. He could never get his hair to bend as required.

If having the customary pimples, lack of muscle, and straight hair of the 1950s teenager was not enough, Brendan had another negative to conquer—his proclivity to blush. Not a faint reddening of the face, but the full grandeur of the midday sun or the redness of an electric fire on full output, the pulsating glory of a rosy red apple, the throbbing intensity of a furnace.

Clothes were difficult to find. Rather tall for his age, he found off-the-peg sports jackets always had arms that were too short. There was never a pair of trousers long enough, which always meant there was a crease in the cloth where the turn-up on the end of the trouser had been dropped.

However, life went on. Dab some camouflage cream on the pimples, force the recalcitrant hair into some shape, put the shoulders back, don't let the imagination go into overdrive when talking to a girl, try to ignore the blushing, wear the trousers with the twenty-two inch bottoms, and remember what your mother said: "You're taller, more intelligent, and better looking than all of them."

The church, the youth guilds, amateur dramatics, the boy scouts and girl guides, the boys' brigade, and the weekly dances in the church hall mainly offered social activities at the time.

Brendan thought about joining the Boys Brigade to see if he could play the trumpet. Turning up at the Masonic Hall in Dunlaoghaire on the Tuesday evening when the brigade met, Brendan introduced himself to the leader, who was very keen that he join. Trumpets were in short supply, however. With the thought of having to wear the tight uniform, especially the pillbox hat, and with the absence of girls (it being a boys-only brigade), he declined the offer.

At the age of fifteen, like all young males of this age range, Brendan and a school pal named Jim, always on the lookout for talent, had decided the best way to meet girls was to go to the weekly dance at the Church Hall. Jim was a year older than Brendan and had a glorious quiff, was pimple free and his main activity was the pursuit of the opposite sex. He was not as tall or broad as Brendan but gave the appearance of being a man of the world.

Brendan, ever the man to be prepared, some weeks prior to the dance borrowed a book, from the Carnegie Library in Dunlaoghaire, entitled Modern Ballroom Dancing by Victor Sylvester. He invested in a seventy-eight-rpm record by the Joe Loss Band and, with the help of Alice and after a lot of laughter and stumbling about, got some idea on how to present himself on the dance floor. After a few practice rounds, Brendan considered he was ready to put his dancing to the test, so he and Jim decided to go to the summer dance in the Church Hall the next Saturday night.

Dressed in his finest, wearing his suitably altered sports jacket, Ra-el-Brook white shirt with tie, slacks and highly polished leather shoes, Brendan reckoned he looked the part. With five shillings in his pocket, his pimples blessedly subdued, and with a fair pretence of a quiff, Brendan was feeling very pleased with himself and looking forward to the evening. Jim was, as ever, the dapper, smooth-complexioned, well-dressed man about town.

Arriving at the hall about half past eight in the evening, the pair sauntered into the dance hall having paid their two bob at the door. They stood just inside the entrance amongst the many other dashing Lotharios, casting their eyes around the groups of chattering talent, seeking their victims.

The local band, with Fred "Liquorice" Glansworthy on the clarinet and sax, Len "Fats Domino" Murphy on the piano, and Pat "Krupa" Kennedy on the drums, was on the stage tuning up. Fred was a tall, angular young man with black hair heavily Brylcreemed and sprinkled with dandruff. "Fats," as his nickname implied, was fat, but he could play a good piano, and Pat was a striking-looking youngster with his hair in a DA (a hairstyle so named when the hair at the back of the head is brought to a point shaped somewhat like a duck's bottom).

All three were very conscious of their audience, giving short tuneless bursts of music on their instruments and talking to each other. The girls, in their varied dress styles with their enamelled hair and pouting lips, were all sitting around the room eyeing up the bold lads gathering inside the entrance door. Those who were already couples from earlier times were drinking tea in the adjoining tearoom, waiting for the dance to start.

With a roll on the drums from Pat Kennedy, everyone's attention was drawn to the stage. Fred stepped forward with the clarinet cradled nonchalantly over his left arm and cleared his throat; he was a heavy smoker, and tipped fags were only for sissies. This was noticeable in his heavy, wet, glottal voice.

"Evenin', ladies and gentlemen. Let's start with a Paul Jones. Everyone on the floor, please. Ladies on the inside gentlemen on the outside."

With a short cough, he stepped back from the microphone, nodded to the rest of the band and awaited the girls to form a circle, facing outwards and holding hands, whilst the boys formed a circle around the girls facing inwards. When Fred was satisfied, he nodded again and the band launched into a lively semblance of "A Life on The Ocean Wave."

The boys began to circle counter-clockwise, whilst the girls moved in the opposite direction. Brendan had his eye on a particular smart, attractive girl wearing a short dress flounced out by petticoats. Her blond hair was lacquered up in a tall beehive. With a lively, smiling face and a pair of silver high heels, she looked like fun.

Moving in the circle to the tune, Brendan's target, the girl in the silver heels, was way on the other side of the circle. *What's this? Jim is holding me back,* thought Brendan. *What's he up to?* With a nod of his head, Jim pointed out a shapely-looking blonde goddess parading rather stiffly toward him. With that, Jim started to move clockwise to keep in front of her, when fortunately for him, the music stopped and he took the goddess off in a stumbling quickstep.

Oh God! thought Brendan as he faced his expected partner—the doughty Monica. Monica was five foot ten. She must have weighed twenty stone and had rolls of flesh under her loose blouse. She was in the same class in school as Brendan.

"Hello, Brendan. Done your homework?" enquired Monica, trying to keep up with Brendan's complicated quickstep. Brendan had not yet mastered the second step forward in a dance. Not being very confident that the partner would move her left foot back, he would swing his right foot over his left and move his dancing partner to his right, ending up dancing in a constant turn to his left. Brendan, concentrating on the dance and trying to check where silver high heels had gone, realised how rude he was and replied, not hearing her question.

"Very well, Monica. How are you?"

Before Monica had time to answer, the band went into the Ocean Wave again and all partners split up to form a circle and heave each other around to either plant themselves in front of chosen partners or to try and avoid certain bodies. Trying to time the stop-off point in the gyrating circle, Brendan saw silver shoes and pushed into the rapidly moving circle with beautiful timing to find she was standing in front of him when the music stopped.

With sparkling eyes and outstretched arms, she stepped closer to Brendan and they waltzed around the floor, circling like mad. Leaning back, she looked up at Brendan with her large blue eyes and asked in a husky voice, "Do you come here often?"

Brendan, lost in the smell of her perfume, the feel of her slender body moving under his right hand, the reactions of his own body, and trying to avoid the silver shoes with his size elevens, wanted to reply with some witty and grown-up reply but found himself apologising for stepping on her toe.

The Ocean Wave returned and they parted to join the circling throng. After a few more revolutions and hurried dances, he met up again with Jim.

"Her name is Sonja. Did you see her? Isn't she beautiful? I'm in love," extolled Jim as he stood up as high as he could to find his goddess.

"Have you found anything yet?"

"Don't worry Jim, I've got my eye on something," Brendan replied in his grown-up voice.

"Look, she's coming this way." The slim figure, with golden hair and silver shoes, accompanied by a dumpy female partner, passed by deep in conversation. Looking up, she happened to catch Brendan's eye and floored him with her smile.

"You're away there, me lad," said an envious Jim, as Fred announced the next dance. Rather than trust his luck too far with silver shoes, Brendan asked a surprised girl onto the floor and danced the foxtrot; it was the same step as the quickstep, only slower.

Gathering his nerve when the next dance, a waltz, was announced, Brendan made a self-conscious stride across the dance floor to silver shoes. *Will she say yes? I will feel a fool if she says no,* he thought Fortunately, she rose to her feet like a ballerina, excused herself to dumpy, and floated into Brendan's arms.

The evening continued with the hall getting hotter with all the gyrating bodies and the atmosphere getting denser from cork-tipped Gold Flake and Craven A cigarette smoke. The brave lads started coming in from the local pub at about ten o'clock, adding to the noise. Fred and the boys seemed to swirl in the smoke, all members of the band puffing away. Fred always had a fag balanced on the edge of a chair beside him, taking puffs in between runs on the clarinet.

Brendan had grabbed the opportunity to dance again with silver shoes and had discovered that her name was Polly and that she would like a cup of tea. Jim joined them with the goddess on his arm; she appeared to be taller than he, but maybe it was the height of the hair.

The four of them went into the adjoining tearoom. Jim, ever the man of the world, stood them all a cup of tea and a Marietta biscuit. He could not take his eyes off Sonja, the goddess. She was a large girl with striking Germanic features and all the hints of a voluptuous Roman Goddess body and spoke in a sexy, broken European accent. Poor Jim was gasping and could not stop nudging Brendan to congratulate him on his conquest. Sonja, who apparently was on holiday, happened to bring into the conversation her passion for sailing.

"I am passion for the sailing of leetle boats. Oh! Zee freedom of zee sees. I like zee man who sails zee leetle boat."

Knowing Jim's Dad had a yacht moored in Dunlaoghaire, Brendan thought to himself, *here's your chance, Jim boy, but don't forget your friends.*

"Sonjaaaa," croaked Jim, holding her hand as if to propose marriage.

"Sonjaa, I have zee—a boat in the harbour, we could go for a sail tomorrow."

"Oh! Jimlee," replied Sonja. They were both now wallowing in their respective names. Polly gave Brendan a nudge in the ribs and started to giggle.

"Oh! Jimlee. You have zee boat? Oh! Goodee, goodee. How big is zit?"

Leaning over, she brought her hands together, with Jim's face between them and planted a big Germanic kiss on his now reddening face.

"Oh! I am so happee we all go tomorrow, Jimlee. You say okay! What?"

Having had a confirmatory nudge in the ribs from Polly, Brendan, with a big grin on his face, leaned over towards Jim.

"What a great idea. We would love to come, Jimlee. What time? Is the whaler still at the yacht club?"

Jim, by now reconciling himself to the fact that he was going to have to share his day of anticipated passion with Sonja, agreed that they should all meet at the jetty in the morning at ten o'clock and to bring some wet weather clothes to be on the safe side.

Tingling with anticipation, Brendan led Polly onto the dance floor.

"You really want to come on Jimlee's boat tomorrow, Polly?" he asked in delight. When Polly nodded her head in agreement and squeezed his hand he could not help grinning. He could hardly credit his luck that this marvellous, smart, good-looking girl was keen to go out with him.

Holding her tighter, he tried to follow the rhythm of the music now being played. Fred's girlfriend, Mary Turbitt, a large smiling woman in her early twenties, had begun singing to the band's attempt at the Rosemary Clooney classic "Can't Tell a Waltz from a Tango." Brendan, turning to the left in Brendan style, was having difficulty with the rhythm: he certainly couldn't tell his waltz from his tango and neither could Polly, so they got closer to each other and shuffled around the floor, enjoying the feel of each other's bodies.

The evening went by in a romantic daze—holding hands, looking into each other's eyes, touching, talking nonsense until the final dance. Fred, with a flourish on the saxophone, instructed them all to stand for the National Anthem.

After a few compulsory bars of the "Soldier's Song," Fred and the band wished everyone goodnight. Polly said good-bye to her dumpy friend, who had joined in with a group of chattering sparrows, and they made their way out into the warm summer evening.

"Let's go for a stroll along the seafront," suggested Brendan. "It's still early."

"Yes, let's," replied Polly, catching his hand and starting to run along the pavement down to the sea front.

"Race you to that lifebuoy." Letting Brendan's arm go, silver shoes, with her bouncing petticoats and arms pumping, started to race ahead. Brendan let out a whoop of delight and raced after her.

Reaching the buoy at the side of the water, they caught each other's hands and ran down to the water's edge. With the wind blowing in their hair, the salt spray in their faces, the smell of the drying seaweed on the rocks, they took off their shoes and splashed in the water.

Racing along the water's edge, Polly stumbled in the soft sand and was caught by Brendan before she fell in the water. As he held her in his arms, they kissed without any shyness, tasting the salt on their lips, the feel of their bodies touching. Holding each other tightly, they stood with the waves swirling around their feet. After what seemed like an eternity, Brendan realised he had been holding his breath and let out a gasp, drawing a long intake of air.

Stepping back out of the water Polly, still holding Brendan's hand, but averting her eyes, suggested they get their shoes on. Running back in the sand, hand in hand, Brendan wondered if he had done something wrong. Should he have kissed her? His body was at a height of expectancy. Had she felt it, and maybe was offended?

"Take me home, please, Brendan," said Polly.

"It's getting late."

Finding their shoes in the dark, they walked back to the beach wall and sat apart whilst they dried their feet. Polly put her stockings in her large handbag and slipped on a pair of walking shoes, whilst Brendan struggled with his woollen socks that were soaked in seawater. Giving up the task, he put the leather shoes on his damp bare feet and slid off the low wall, wondering if their lovely evening was over and this was good-bye.

He turned to find Polly's face was on the same level as his and, catching her eye, he saw the mischievous smile reappearing on her face. Instinctively they kissed again and hugged each other in delight; they both knew something special had happened.

Helping Polly to her feet, Brendan caught her hand and they walked slowly back to the bike shed at the back of the dance hall, contented in each other's presence and anticipating the delights to come.

21

The Yacht Trip

After walking Polly home, Brendan had cycled back to the cottage in a very happy frame of mind. Life was good. He was feeling very well within himself; the bad heart scare, when he was thirteen, had resolved itself. He was now approaching sixteen years of age with his life ahead of him. He had met a smashin' girl, he had some good friends, school was finished and his exam results were due in September. He thought he had done reasonably well and was now trying to forget everything for the next few weeks and enjoy himself.

The evening itself seemed to agree with his feeling of well-being as he cycled back home, a cloudless black sky with a multitude of sparkling stars and a friendly moon lighting the path before him.

With the exhilaration of the wind in his hair, he pedalled hard until the bike reached speed. Lifting his feet, he would freewheel down the hills, swoop around corners, letting out the odd whoop of sheer enjoyment of life.

Approaching the cottage, he stopped alongside his parents returning home from an evening at Moran's pub, with their arms around each other and weaving a bit unsteadily.

"Brendan, boyo," called out Henry. "Will you put on the kettle and a bit of toast when you get in"

"Shure, Pop!" answered Brendan with a grin. "You both seem to have had a good night."

"Now be getting' on with yerself and get the kettle on, I'm parched," ordered Alice with a laugh.

"I'm parched, too," advised Henry. "So be getting on with it."

They waved Brendan on. Smiling at each other, they continued their carefree, if unsteady, walk towards their home, their arms around each other. A unit of contentment, any problems they had were forgotten for this moment.

Cycling up the avenue alongside the cottage, Brendan left his bike under the trees and again marvelled at the wonderful night, the smell of the pine trees, the height of the star-speckled sky, the silence of the night, the shadows thrown by the moon.

He opened the back door that led directly into the kitchen—it was rarely locked—and stepped into the warm homely smells of living. By instinct he avoided the broken floor tiles as he made his way, in the darkness, to the light switch. In the dimly lit interior, lit by one sixty-watt bulb in the centre of the dusty ceiling, he filled the large kettle from the water tap over the stone sink. Humming the tune, "Hey there, you with the stars in your eyes," he heard the front door being unlocked and the sound of his parents making their way down the long dark hallway.

In great humour, the three of them sat around the kitchen table, drinking the strong tea from large mugs and enjoying the rounds of thick bread cut off the large fresh pan of bread and toasted on the gas stove.

Brendan, full of his exploits of the evening, told them all about Polly and what a smashin' girl she was.

"She seems quite a girl, Brendan. Will you be bringing her home, then? We've got to see her."

As was the custom whenever either Jono or Brendan met a new girl, Alice always voiced the wish to "have a look." No harm in it, of course, as both boys liked to show off their conquests. There had been a few of Jono's victories displayed before the critical eye. Alice would ask her usual question: Was she a Protestant or a Catholic?

"So you met her at the church dance. She'll be a Protestant, den?"

"Yes! Ma! She probably is. I never asked her," answered Brendan.

"Will you be going to church in the morning?"

"No, I won't, Ma," answered Brendan.

Rather than get into any discussion about church going, as discussions with his mother when she had had a few jars invariably turned into arguments, arguments into rows and rows into upset relations and unpleasantness, Brendan continued.

"I'm away to bed now, see you in the morning," and before Alice could retort with one of her cutting asides, Brendan smiled to them both and turned away, giving Henry a slight wink.

The following morning, with a hundred or so birds singing their merry heads off in the orchard and the smell of frying bacon coming from the kitchen, Brendan awoke.

"Wonder what time it is? Wish I had a watch. I'd better get up. What a great life. What a night!"

Untangling himself from the loose sheets, Brendan rolled out of bed with a big grin on his face and made his way into the adjoining bathroom, singing the well-known song from the musical *Oklahoma*, "Oh! What a Beautiful Morning."

After a quick wash and the honorary morning ritual of a shave, he scraped a razor over the light fuzz on his face and thought of the day ahead.

"Brendan, are you up? I'm frying some rashers. Do you want an egg?" was the call from the kitchen.

"Coming! I'm a coming, Pop. I'll have all you've got."

Following the delicious smell of frying food, Brendan trotted through the next room, giving Billy a shake. "Up you get, you lazy sod."

"There you are then, Brendan, me lad. Get that into you," smiled Henry placing a breakfast of hot fried bacon, crispy fried bread, and a fried egg done the way he liked on the table.

"There's plenty of tea in the pot."

He waited until Brendan had sat down at the table before continuing. "Brendan, your Ma was a bit disappointed you're not going to church this morning," he said, as he and flipped the hot delicious-smelling fat over the large egg in the frying pan.

"I know, Pop," Brendan smiled resignedly.

"It's not my faith she's bothered about. She just wants to show off the family. Anyway, Billy will go, won't he? Do you think I should go in an' say good mornin'?"

"No," cautioned Pop, "don't do that. She has one of her headaches."

Relieved, Brendan started into his breakfast. *Must ease up on the fried stuff,* he thought to himself. *No good for the pimples.*

Eager to get going, but to mollify his conscience, he offered to wash the dishes when he came home that evening, bade his father good-bye, wheeled his Hercules bicycle out from under the pine trees, and started the mile and a half run to Dunlaoghaire. He had arranged to meet Polly at the Roman Catholic Chapel at the top of Marine Road in the town. Luckily it was all downhill from Killoughlin, as the three speeds on the bike had somehow stuck on high, the cruising speed.

Racing down Patrick's Street, he arrived outside the large Catholic Chapel with a squeal of brakes and came to a shuddering halt alongside Polly. As the bike only had a front brake, the sudden stop nearly threw him over the handlebars. Falling back on the narrow saddle with a painful jolt, he bid the startled Polly a good morning.

Dressed for seagoing, he wore the off-white roll-necked sweater knitted by Alice, with a large pair of grey slacks used for gardening and a well-used pair of white runners. The right one had always been a bit tight and was beginning to wear badly over the toes. He had his raincoat and sou'wester hat clipped on the carrier over the back wheel. Ready for all weathers.

Greeting Polly, he apologised for being late. As this was the first time they had seen each other in the daylight, they were both a bit wary as the circumstances were now so very different from the music-filled evening.

However, with the initial nervousness being broken by Brendan's abrupt arrival, Polly burst out laughing and asked if what she was wearing was all right as she hadn't been on a boat before.

Brendan couldn't take his eyes from her. The cream roll-neck sweater accentuated her attractive shape. *Gosh, what a pair of diddies,* were his fleeting thoughts recalling when he and Jono had danced around the fountain in the woods pointing at the bare breasted nymphs. Wearing a pair of loose trousers belted at her narrow waist, her small feet in a pair of white runners, her dark blue eyes, clear complexion, laughing lips and long blond hair tied back in a pony tail, she was all he desired.

"Polly, you look smashing," were Brendan's admiring words as he swung his leg over the Hercules, while Polly mounted a rather old and rusty ladies' bicycle. This had high handlebars, a chain guard and a wicker basket attached to the front containing her raincoat.

"Before we go, Polly," cautioned Brendan, "I must tell you we're meeting Jim and Sonja at the Royal St. George Yacht Club. Jim's Pop is a member. I've never been in there. Have you?"

"Good God! No! I've never even bin in a boat before. Wait until I tell my Ma."

"Let's go then," decided Brendan.

Freewheeling down Marine Road with its large Victorian houses on each side and the imposing Royal Marine Hotel on the right, the impressive harbour appeared in front of them. With Brendan's right arm signaling to the sparse traffic, they swept down in front of the Royal St George Yacht Club, coming to a brake-squealing stop alongside the impressive cars in the car park.

They locked their bikes together to the railings and collected their raincoats. Brendan, saying he must attempt to look the part, put his off-colour black sou'wester over his head. Laughing together, they took each other's hands and made their way to the imposing entrance doors.

"Hey! Brendan, over here," was the shout from the far side of the park.

It was Jim and Sonja getting out of his old MG sports car parked behind an immense Daimler Saloon.

"God! Would you look at the pair of them, Polly," exclaimed Brendan in mock astonishment. "Is it Errol Flynn and Rita Heyworth we're goin' with?"

Jim dressed in a cream-coloured blazer with white shirt and blue cravat, white slacks and, of all things, a yachting cap at a jaunty angle, came striding across the park. The Viking maiden, Sonja, followed him. Dressed in designer slacks and shapely jersey emphasising her wonderfully formed chest and wearing a peaked blue cap, she looked like a model from a Yachting magazine.

"Blimey, Brendan," stuttered Polly. "Don' they look a right pair? I want to go home," she exclaimed jokingly, looking down at her slacks and worn runners, "and take that stupid hat off," she ordered under her breath to Brendan as the beautiful pair approached them.

Jim, with his charming smile, went straight up to Polly, catching her hands and telling her how lovely she looked. He looked in dismay at Brendan's appearance, muttering as they entered the imposing entrance. "I'll have to pretend you're my assistant or something. You scruffy sod."

"We're going for a sail Jim, not a mannequin parade," retorted Brendan, giving Jim a playful punch.

"I do like your partner, though. She's something, isn't she?"

"It's the charm, Brendan, me boy. Something you country boys would know nothing about," replied Jim, returning the punch and following up with news that was to have a great effect on Brendan's future.

"I've got some great news, Brendan. Blue Funnel has accepted my application for a midshipman's post. I go to sea in the next six months. You know Brian Neeson has joined Eagle Star Tanker Co. as an Officer Apprentice? You should be thinking of it for yourself. Not that you are real officer material. Just look at you—my God!"

Laughing together, they passed through the main doors and, after Jim had signed them in with a flourish, telling the desk clerk how lovely she looked, they made their way down a short corridor to a large door, which brought them out onto the yachting slip. The slip, a concrete base sloping down to the water, was crowded with a multitude of every size yacht under the sun.

Jim acknowledged a few greetings, introducing Brendan to captain somebody or other and to his good friend Mal.

"Remember Mal? He was in the Fastnet last year."

"Where is ze yacht, Jimsee?" called Sonja, looking up at all the imposing hulls of large sailing yachts and cabin cruisers.

"In the harbour, my lovely. Follow me, you lucky people," he instructed as they all made their way to steps leading down to the water.

"Okay there, Paddy?" called Jim to a young boy who was sitting in a small dinghy awaiting his passengers.

"Right yur are now, Mr. Jim," replied the young boatman, as he helped Sonja into the bows of the small craft.

"We'll go first," advised Jim. "Paddy will come back for the pair of you."

With that, the youngster pushed off and, leaning into the oars, took his passengers out to a large, white robust-looking yacht, very different to the many sleek eighteen-foot Nationals, Fireflies and other small racing dinghies tied to buoys. The sunlit air was full of small clinking noises resulting from the rigging hitting the swaying masts.

Jim's news had started Brendan thinking. Could he go to sea as a midshipman? He thought they were Royal Navy. Or as an officer apprentice like Brian Neeson? Brian was a year older and he and Brendan had lost touch. Maybe Doc Courcy could help.

"Sorry, Pol, I was daydreaming," apologised Brendan as he turned to Polly. Taking a deep breath of the salt-laden air, he resolved on his return home to start making enquiries about a sea career.

"Are ye alright there, surr?"

"Sorry, Paddy, Pol." Brendan again apologised as he stepped into the wobbling dinghy and held out his hand to assist Polly onto the boat.

With his body pressed against Polly's in the stern of the small dinghy, they looked at each other and smiled in anticipation of the day ahead. With his free hand, Brendan pushed the dinghy from the steps.

"This is exciting," exclaimed Polly as they moved out into the harbour, with Paddy skilfully avoiding the moored yachts. Ahead they could see Jim and his long-legged, Nordic goddess attaching the canvas sails to their respective masts. She appeared pretty skilful, hoisting the mizzen sail, and appeared to be directing Jim as to what to do next.

The yacht was more like a large rowing boat; in fact, it was a robust working sailing boat known as a whaler. Broad of beam and about eighteen feet long, it had two masts, one in the centre to take the mainsail and a smaller one in front of the tiller to take the mizzen sail. The hull was made of slats of white wood, each piece overlapping another. "Clinker built" was the technical name.

Paddy commented to Jim as he pulled the dinghy alongside the whaler.

"Yu don' see many of these beauties around dese days, surr."

Jim, nodding to Paddy, took Polly's hand to help her on board whilst Brendan nodded his thanks to Paddy.

"I wouldn't be goin' too far out in the bay, surrs, as the wind is expected to get harder later in the day."

"Thanks for that, Paddy," replied Jim as he helped Brendan scramble on board the whaler. While helping Polly step onto the larger boat, he had been left straddling both boats and needed help to recover his balance due to the rapidly widening gap between the two.

Expecting Jim to take control, especially as he was nearly a sailor and his Dad owned the boat, Brendan was surprised to hear Sonja call to Jim to let go of zee moorings go as she took the tiller. The mizzen sail took the wind, which was strengthening, and they started to pull out between the moored yachts.

"Polly, vill yu sit here beside me? Vee get ze men to do ze vork," suggested Sonja to Polly, patting the thwart beside her. Brendan looked at Jim as he fumbled with the jib. He gave a dismissive shrug of his shoulders as if to say, "She seems to know what she's doing."

"Jimsee, loose zee Jib now please," was the order from the stern. With a crack of wind-induced sound, the sail opened and took the wind, with the water beginning to chuckle alongside.

"Now Brendie, please be you to lift ze what you say, the beeg sail please? Tank you."

They had miraculously passed through all the moored boats. The whaler was beginning to move quite swiftly, lifting up and down to the increased wave action. They passed quite close to the one third of the Irish Navy, a Second World War corvette painted in camouflage grey, at anchor in the harbour, getting a cheerful wave from a member of the crew.

Hoisting the mainsail increased the speed dramatically. With the boat heeling to starboard, Brendan and Jim propped themselves on the raised port side, leaning back over the water to balance the boat as it sailed with increasing speed between the two arms of the harbour mouth.

The heavy boat was now beginning to move faster and rather than ride the increasing waves as a lighter boat would have done, was buffeting through the water and throwing spray back over the boat. Brendan, hanging onto the main sheet, was leaning dramatically over the side of the boat and getting very wet, but was exhilarated with the movement. He caught Polly's eye and they smiled to each other. However, her smile turned to one of shock as a larger than expected wave hit the side and threw cold stinging water over her.

Jim's smart clothes were beginning to look somewhat creased and damp. Undismayed, holding on with one hand to the sail sheets while the other was raised in triumph, he and Brendan rode the waves as the boat sped through the water at some speed.

The two girls sat at the stern with the strong wind blowing their hair and their faces reddening in the water-filled wind. Sonja's designer slacks were getting quite wet, as was the rest of her, but she and Polly were shouting out loud in exhilaration.

Swinging to starboard, Sonja shouted to the lads to tighten the sails as they were getting closer to the wind, and they buffeted their way along with the coast to their right. They spent the next ten exhilarating, if exhausting, minutes literally flying across the waves, the wind having increased considerably.

Sonja, who the boys later found out had sailed boats all her young life, realising the return passage to the harbour would take some effort as they were sailing into the wind, signalled to the boys she was going to "go about." By now everyone was soaking wet, the wind was beginning to chill their skin and the initial euphoria was beginning to diminish.

Jim, to regain some authority, quite needlessly shouted back to Sonja,

"Tighten the sheets and come around to starboard. We will then come into the wind."

"Okay!" Sonja, signalling her agreement, pushed the tiller to port. The boat turned to face into the wind and, with a rattle of blocks and tackle, a crack of the sails and with the sheets pulled tight, the boat started to speed back the way they had come.

With the wind increasing and the waves beginning to steepen, the motion of the boat began to become somewhat unpleasant. Both Jim and Brendan huddled down to protect themselves from the biting wind as they tacked out to sea, realising that Captain Sonja really knew what she was doing. Polly was soaking wet and looking quite miserable.

"About we go!" was the shouted order from Sonja as the boat swung to port and Jim and Brendan had to hang on grimly to the sheets to keep the sails tight into the wind. It took a further hour of exhausting sailing before they re-entered the calm of the harbour, all relieved to return safely.

With rapid orders, the mainsail was lowered and Captain Sonja skilfully approached the mooring buoy. Instructing Jimlee to attach it to the boat, she brought the whaler to a stop by turning into the wind.

There was a splatter of applause from the few boats in the vicinity, which Jim acknowledged by bowing and pointing with a hand to Sonja, implying that it was really nothing to do with him.

Tingling with the exertion, faces glowing after the water-sodden wind, they recovered rapidly and were full of praise for Sonja.

Paddy rowed them back to the shore and, as they staggered slightly on reaching firm ground, Jim suggested they might all like a cup of coffee in the clubhouse.

Brendan hastily took Jim aside as the two girls walked ahead.

"Jim, love to have a coffee, but I've no money on me. I'm broke."

"Don't worry, Bren boyo. I'll put it on Da's account. Now tidy yourself a bit, you scruffy bastard. Come on."

22

Farm Work and Drive to Limerick

The year 1956 was quite a year for Brendan. Still suffering from the scourge of pimples and the lack of a decent hairstyle, Brendan, now sixteen was very tall for his age, a bit underweight and very conscious of his appearance. He was concerned about his future as so much depended on his final exam results. He had always been led to the assumption that, upon leaving school, a young man would map out a career until retirement. It was, therefore, very important to start in the correct career. His peers were considering starting in accountancy or the law, or perhaps studying to be a doctor, all very boring and unadventurous.

There was also, however, the lack of ready cash so it looked like he would need a job, for the summer at least, and then see what would happen. He was still dating Polly, taking her to weekend dances and the pictures—or, rather, she was taking him as she paid more often than not. A temporary job, then, looked like the only option. There was always plenty of work around, especially at the local farms, if a person was ready to work and get his hands dirty.

Brendan presented himself to Jerry Duffy, the Farm Manager who used to chase him when he was a youngster. The local Reformatory School owned the farm Duffy managed. This school was filled to the rafters with young men who had either got on the wrong side of the law, were from broken homes, or were orphans. These young men were kept under close surveillance. Even with this bountiful supply of labour, Duffy was more than pleased to hire Brendan and had him initially picking potatoes for twelve hours a day, rain or shine, for a shilling an hour.

After a few days of backbreaking labour, a weary Brendan put it to Duffy that unless he was allowed to work at something else in the farm he would leave. Duffy, a most abrupt and difficult man who always had a frown on his face, suggested that the big fairy Brendan could go and milk the cows and feed and clean out the pigs.

Brendan tried his hand at milking and settled into the morning milk with a group of boys from the school who looked at him with suspicion as an outsider. However, with his easy manner he got on well with most and joined in the morning race to draw the fastest bucket.

Most cows were cooperative and were given names by the milkers. There were the usual difficult and sly ladies, but especially one who was aptly named the Kicker. With a friendly smile, she would stroll into her stall and, when the milker had sat on his three-legged stool, with his head resting on her flank and his fingers gripping her teats would suddenly start mooing and kicking. Buckets and stool would go flying.

There was great glee amongst the boys on the first day when Brendan was presented with the Kicker, especially when he ended up on his backside in the drains. Prepared for the worst, Brendan had another try and was cheered when the first satisfying sounds of a strong stream of steaming milk swished against the side of the galvanised bucket.

Brendan always had to keep one step ahead of the boys from the school, as some were very disturbed and constant mischief-makers. Not knowing very much about pigs, Brendan had been ordered by Duffy to speak with the charge hand and do what he instructed. The charge hand, a lad not much older than Brendan, looked at Brendan with a sneer on his sly face and made a motion of slitting his throat with an imaginary knife. In a thick country accent he warned Brendan that, unless he obeyed instruction, the knife would be used. Brendan found out later that Aloysius O'Hara was in the Reformatory School because he had attacked his father with a knife and put him in hospital, and his mother died in suspicious circumstances.

"Will ye be after getting' dat barrer there and fill it with cooked spuds te feed the pigs," instructed Aloysius, pointing to a large and heavy wooden wheelbarrow, with high sides encrusted with dirt, and nodding toward a brick building.

Brendan, disturbed by the threat from Aloysius, wheeled the unsteady barrow toward the open door of the brick building and noticed a small furtive-looking boy followed him.

"Don' be worried by dat big shit Aloysius, surr. He's just full of wind and piss. Here, let me help ye get de spuds."

With his new friend, Brendan dipped a large galvanised bucket into the steaming vat of lovely-smelling new potatoes and half filled the barrow.

"De pigs are over there, sur. Now, I'd better be goin' or Duffy will lash de back off me."

Left on his own and nodding his thanks to the little fella, Brendan made his way through the cobbled yard, pushing the heavy barrow through the slimy water and dirty straw to arrive at the low-walled pig sties. The smell from the sties was quite overpowering in the still air and the sight of the big pink snorting bodies, as they snuffled their way through the dirt, was most unappealing.

"Brendan, me boy, would you be after givin' that one der, on the left der, the spuds yuv' got?"

The charge hand, materialising behind the straining Brendan, pointed to a small walled sty apart from the others. The designated sty had a solitary large pig looking through the bars of the gate, his piggy eyes staring at the steaming wheelbarrow. There was green goo oozing out under the gate and a strong smell of rotting food, wet straw and pig droppings.

"Giv' him half the barra' load, Brendan, me boyo," came the order from behind.

Brendan, now a bit wary, pushed the gate open with the barrow between himself and the immense grunting malevolent pork chop. He was standing in the pig muck in his runners with the goo up to his ankles, ready to tip the barrow forward to serve the pig his dinner, when the pork chop began to get excited. He had got the smell of the new boiled potatoes and started to push against the barrow.

Brendan pushed harder; the pig squealed and seemed to lose its temper, getting its nose under the front of the barrow and turning it on its side. Most of the spuds fell out into the mud and Brendan, trying to right the barrow and avoid the squealing mass of flesh, fell forward on his knees and toppled sideways into the heaped muck against the wall. Nearly crying in frustration and horror, Brendan pulled himself up by the small wall and looked up to see a row of grinning faces enjoying his discomfort.

"What are you useless nose pickin' shits doin? Get back to yer work or I'll beat the livin' daylights from ye," roared Duffy from the far side of the yard as the he came storming through the muck, brandishing a hayfork. By the time he reached the sty where his new employee was struggling to his feet, the onlookers had raced away to their respective duties.

"God! An' what are ye doin' down there, ye eejit? Does yer mudder not feed ye?" Leaning on the hayfork he stood by as Brendan rose to his feet, his runners full of smelly water, his trousers soaking with rotting straw stuck to them, his hands filthy and the back of his shirt as wet as his trousers.

"There's a tap down the yard. Get yerself washed off and get back to work, young fella."

"No thank you, Mr. Duffy," retorted the sodden Brendan in a resigned voice. "I've had enough of this bloody business. I'll come for my money at the end of the week."

So ended Brendan's first attempt at working on the land. At one shilling an hour, he felt it was not worth it.

Where next? What about driving? If he had a driving licence, that would open some doors. Brendan had had a try at driving the car left by his Uncle Cecil, a little Ford Prefect Saloon built in 1942, ten-horse power, pretty rusty with soft tires. Uncle Cecil, Alice's brother, had disappeared to England, leaving the car parked under the pine trees at the back of the cottage. With some help from a lad who worked in the local garage, and permission from his father, Brendan got the engine turning over and, after a few runs up and down Red Clay Lane to charge the battery and to get some practice, he started his journey into Dublin to buy a driving licence.

With the ten shillings he had earned at the farm and a loan of a pound from his mother, he put a gallon of petrol in the car and drove into Dublin. After standing in a queue for the best part of the day he bought a driving licence for a pound. Now he was a licensed driver he could drive anything on four wheels.

Later in the same week Brendan was taking a rewarding pint in Moran's pub, after helping the publican take delivery of his weekly supply of Guinness, when a local trader, Sean Devlin, approached him. It was well known that Sean had recently started a painting and decorating business, on a very threadbare shoestring, and was always on the scrounge.

After the customary verbal sparring of "How are ye's and how's your mother?" "Is your father working yet?" and "Isn't the weather fierce?" Sean bought Brendan a pint of Guinness. He nodded him over to sit on the side seat near the roaring fire and away from the sound of Radio Luxembourg.

"Brendan! Ye know I've started dis painting and decorating business?" stated Sean.

Brendan nodded his affirmation, wondering what he wanted.

"Well, I've got dis big job down in Limerick. It's with Our Ladies Convent. God Bless them, don't they do a fine job, the nuns. Well, you know that miserable sod Patrick? He's gone and let me down. Now, I hear you're at a loose end and I'm sure you could do with a few bob? I hear you've now got a drivin' licence. Is dat right?"

On Brendan's nod of agreement, Sean detailed his problem. He was desperate for someone to take the wages and a few pots of paint down to the site in Limerick. As Patrick had let him down and he, Sean, was going to Belfast in the morning, could Brendan do it for him?

Well, thought Brendan. *I'm doing nothing tomorrow so I might as well have a go.* After negotiating a fee of £5 for the trip, it was arranged that Brendan would cycle over to Sean's house in the morning, collect the van and wages and drive to Limerick.

The following morning Brendan cycled over to Sean's house, a three-mile journey, and found the house in a narrow unkempt street near the main road to Dublin. Part of the street was still cobbled, with two-storey terraced brick buildings lining each side, all looking very weary. Number eleven was on the corner alongside some waste ground. There was a scruffy 1950 dark blue Ford Van amongst the flourishing weeds, leaning dejectedly against the wall with a sodden blanket covering the bonnet.

Ringing the doorbell without response, Brendan hammered on the heavy timbered door. Some minutes later, after the sound of bolts sliding and keys jangling, the door opened a few inches and a boy in his teens, dressed in scruffy pyjamas, acknowledged Brendan's presence. This was Sean's son, Mick, who led him into a rusty kitchen and commenced to fill a battered kettle from a noisy backfiring tap.

"It's okay, Mick, I won't bother with a cup," said Brendan.

"Jus' give me the wage packets and some directions and I'll get away."

"Okay den," grunted Mick, "wasn't going to make ye a cup anyway. Dad's lef' a note on the table in the front room with a list of paints. The ladders are in the shed at the back. The pay slips are all made out. The keys for the van are with the list and you can collect the money from the Hibernian Bank just down de road. Now, I'm goin' back to bed."

With that, Mick took his steaming mug of milky tea and disappeared upstairs. Wondering what he had let himself in for, Brendan pushed open the front room door. The room had style—a lovely ornate ceiling and a carved wooden fireplace peering out from behind columns of various sized paint pots. Yes, there was the note, under one of the pots, listing the paints to take and ladders to load.

Brendan prised open the back door of the van after untying the heavy string holding the doors shut and started piling the various sized cans of yellow, blue, and white emulsion and enamel paint with a thousand paint brushes, small step ladders and scrapers, into the battered interior. Job done, he shut and tied the door handles together with the string supplied.

Manhandling the large multi-extension ladders from the back of the house, having pulled Mick out of his bed to aid him, he lashed them onto the roof rack. This rack stretched from the back doors of the van to the front of the bonnet, encasing the van in a steel frame. The longest ladder section extended some four feet in front of the bonnet and stretched the same distance behind, making a full length of some sixteen feet from front to back, giving the appearance of large, upside down toboggan.

Rather than dare drive the van to the bank—that experience could wait—he got Mick to run down and get the money from the bank and on his return, started to fill the pay packets.

That task finished, Brendan climbed into the overloaded van, settled into the worn leather seat, and ran his hands over the large shiny steering wheel. Feeling somewhat apprehensive with so little driving experience, he found the ignition on the side of the steering wheel and checked the foot pedals. All there. He wobbled the long brake lever and looked around the interior. The ashtray under the dashboard was overflowing with ash and cigarette butts and there was a roll of greasy newspaper pages that smelt of vinegar on the passenger seat.

A hand-drawn map supplied by Devlin rested on the side seat. Now, if you look at a map of Ireland you will find Dublin to the East and Limerick to the West, some 120 miles nearer America. Whilst some fifty years later with motorways, 120 miles could be done before breakfast, 120 miles across Ireland in the 1950s was like a journey into an undiscovered country. A map of Ireland, torn out of an atlas, had an arrow pointing to Limerick, the address of the convent with a few town names, and a statement that the foreman of the site, Paddy, would be expecting him in the afternoon.

Great, thought Brendan. *Now, which way is west?*

Reaching to the long gear lever with the shiny, well-worn knob, he forced this into neutral. He pulled out the choke and, after a half dozen turns, the engine gave a half-hearted attempt to fire. The windscreen wiper, all the while, was attempting to scrape the glass off the windscreen. After a couple more turns the engine spluttered into life and with a few little prods on the accelerator, settled into a loud steady sound.

Into first gear, clutch out, no movement; the engine was beginning to roar madly.

"Maybe it's the choke better push it back."

The engine started to splutter. He pulled the choke out again. The engine regained life and roared its delight. With the engine nearly screaming, the ladders rattling and the paint pots beginning to jump and a cloud of steam or smoke enveloping the van, Brendan desperately got the gear lever into second.

He let out the clutch and the overloaded workhorse lurched forward, breaking its hold in the muddy earth, and fell out onto the road. Brendan's foot hit the accelerator with too much pressure; the van leaped forward, there were sounds of falling paint cans, but they were moving. Looking through the small gap in the dirty windscreen, Brendan gave a cheer and started his journey west, or east, or wherever. He was moving.

Joining the light traffic on the main road, Brendan got the van into top gear and, after a few miles, noticed the petrol gauge was registering zero. Fortunately he had borrowed a pound note from his father to pay for something to eat. He had forgotten about petrol, and so had Devlin. If he put ten shillings' worth in maybe it would get him to Limerick. The foreman at the convent could, hopefully, give him enough to get back with.

Fortune favours the foolhardy, as the petrol station for the area appeared like magic and Brendan pulled alongside the petrol pump. The attendant came out of his steamed-up office.

"Put in ten bobs' worth, please. By the way, am I pointing right for Limerick?"

"Shure you are!" replied the attendant. "Head into the city and take the Naas Road South. Ye'll be there by tomorrow. By the way, there's some lovely yella paint dripping out of your van."

"Oh, God," exclaimed Brendan. He then remembered there was a loud noise in the back when he started. Something must have fallen over.

Leaping out and around the grinning attendant, he saw a steady drip of yellow and white paint seeping out under the back doors. He untied the string, the door sprang open, and an avalanche of paint pots fell out onto the concrete. Fortunately, only two of the tins had opened, but the others were quite dented.

Repacking the van and getting paint on his hands and clothes, Brendan paid for the petrol, apologised for leaving a pool of paint for the now scowling attendant to clean up, and climbed back into the van. Leaving a trail of white and yellow footprints, he recommenced his journey.

As the rush hour had died off he made good time following the road signs towards Dublin. The road to the southwest of Ireland would take him to his destination so, with added confidence, he turned left at the next sign pointing toward the west and followed directions along the Grand Canal to the Naas Road. He was getting somewhere.

Beginning to enjoy himself, and with the road pretty clear ahead, Brendan decided to increase speed. Thirty-five miles an hour, forty, forty-five. The wind began to hum through the ladders on the rack. The rattles in the back ceased. He was flying. Up to fifty miles an hour—what's this? The steering wheel started shaking violently and the body of the van shuddered as though in great pain. Everything started rattling. *Better slow down*, thought Brendan. *Is the darn thing going to fall apart?* Easing down to forty, the vibration ceased.

"Must be the way I loaded the ladders. It must have unbalanced the van," Brendan said to himself as he continued the journey.

Through townships and past fields, over rivers and forward into the rain-laden sky, Brendan flew across Ireland at a steady forty miles an hour. *I'll be there by three*, he thought.

Coming towards Portlaoise, about midway on his journey and thinking of a cup of tea, he joined a line of traffic crawling along behind an overloaded tractor. For the next ten minutes, Ireland slowed down to cow speed.

No time for the tea, better keep goin', Brendan thought.

Into Portlaoise, free of the town, speed at forty. With fields on either side separated from the road by drainage ditches, the road stretched ahead clear of traffic, with a right hand bend in the distance. *Let's try to go a bit faster*, thought Brendan. Up to forty-five and the shuddering started again. *Let's do fifty. Yep, that's better.* The shuddering had eased.

Oh! The corner, it's tighter than I thought. Slow down, going too fast, brake, road muddy, shuddering starting again, going into a slide, good-bye road, hello, ditch . . . SPLASH!!!

Ditches in Ireland in the fifties were of varying depths. They were all over the country—deep ones, shallow ones, ones filled with water, some even with resident ducks. Fortunately for Brendan, he had landed in a shallow one. It was still a good two feet deep, however, and the van was resting with two wheels on the edge and lying at an angle of forty-five degrees.

Brendan, after the initial shock of finding the road had disappeared, took a deep breath, switched the engine off and started to open the van door. He thought he had better try and get some help. The van gave a sudden lurch to the left. Brendan froze. There was a scraping noise on the roof and a few ladders fell off the rack. The van settled back with some dull falling sounds from the back.

Oh God, the paint! Not again, he thought.

As he sat in the driving seat wondering what to do, he heard the roar of a tractor pulling up alongside and a loud voice calling out in a west of Ireland country voice.

"What do ye tink yer doin' down there, ye silly eejit?"

Brendan, with great relief, clambered out of the cab and helped the scowling farmer attach a towrope to the front of the ill-begotten van. After a few attempts, they had it back on the road, with ladders hanging from the rack and the ominous sight of a multicolour stream of emulsion running from under the back door.

"Are you all right den now?" enquired the farmer. "I won't be chargin' ye fer the tow. Gud luck te ye now." Without waiting for a reply, he clambered back onto his snorting tractor and disappeared in the approaching rain.

Brendan, by now resigned to whatever fate had in store for him, untied the doors in the back of the van, stood the fallen pots back on their base, sealed the opened lids and, regardless of the emulsion on the floor, climbed in to secure the pots against the side of the van.

Tying the door securely, he pushed the now twisted ladders back on the roof rack, tying them up as best he could. In great relief he found the engine still made comforting motor sounds and the wheels still pointed forward.

Back in the van he started on the last lap to Limerick. All seemed well; there was only light traffic ahead. Speeding along at forty-five miles per hour, the van started to shudder again. He slowed down to thirty before the vibration eased. Through small villages he swept along at a stately thirty miles an hour.

"Pray nothing else happens," said Brendan to himself, "I should be at the convent by five o'clock."

The note from Devlin advised that the convent would be found on the right, just before entering Limerick. He should be there now. Was that it? A large building with a big lit cross attached to the wall appeared out of the rainy gloom. *This will be it,* thought Brendan with relief and swung into the entrance, narrowly avoiding a group of men advancing towards the van. He switched off the engine and, with a large sigh, both driver and van relaxed; they had arrived.

The group of men came toward the van and Paddy, the foreman, in an accusatory tone demanded to know why he was so late. Brendan started to explain, but realised nobody would believe him.

"Take de van over there to the right and we'll start to unload," instructed Paddy. Brendan started the engine again. The van gave a leap forward, scattering the workmen. A weary Brendan pulled up alongside a large door to the side of the chapel.

"Dat won't have done any good to the paint in the back," he said to himself and started to clamber out to make his way to the back of the van.

"God! You're in a mess," exclaimed the foreman as he looked at Brendan, whose trousers were liberally covered in white and yellow emulsion, as were his hands and face.

"Look at this, Paddy," exclaimed one of the men. "The ladders are all twisted." Another voiced in concern. "I hope he's remembered our bloody money!"

By now the back doors had been opened and the jumble of paint and brushes were on view.

"Me boy," asked Paddy in astonishment, "what in the name of Jasus have ye bin doin'? What a mess. Okay, lads, let's get the lot into the shed and sort it out tomorrow. You, young fella! Give me the wages and then go and ask for Sister Theresa—she'll give ye a cup of tea or sumptin'."

Brendan passed the wages parcel to Paddy and wearily stumbled in the direction he pointed towards.

Entering the convent building he found Sister Theresa who, after the initial shock of his appearance, found some newspapers to put on a chair and fussed over him with a cup of tea and some toast, tut-tutting over the mess. These Dubliners were odd creatures, weren't they?

Some twenty minutes later Paddy came in, leaned over Brendan and told him the van was now empty, that he would have a word with Devlin when he got home and that he could now make his way back to Dublin.

Getting a loan of ten shillings for some petrol, Brendan resignedly pulled himself back into the weary van and started the engine, which reluctantly coughed into life. He put it into second gear—first wasn't working, remember—let out the clutch, and pressed the accelerator. The van lurched six inches forward and the engine stalled. He went through the process again but this time the van would not move at all. Giving plenty of acceleration, the van simply held its ground and the engine stalled again. In exasperation, Brendan climbed out, thinking there must be something in the way. He walked to the front of the van. What's this? The front offside wheel is pointing to the right. Gosh! The nearside is pointing to the left. What if that had happened when the van was doing fifty miles an hour. The van would have probably somersaulted off the road and I would be a dead man.

A somewhat relieved Brendan patted the despondent van on the bonnet in thanks and went back into the convent to ask Sister Theresa for another cup of tea.

23

The Drunken Woman

As the prosperity of Ireland improved, the land in Killoughlin began to be bought by developers to build houses for the "nouveau riche"—accountants, solicitors, and businessmen. By this time most of the old two-room cottages built to house the workers at the now closed pottery works had been declared uninhabitable and the occupants offered homes on a newly built local council estate.

There was one surprise for Alice. She had always considered her family the envy of Killoughlin, as they owned land and were Protestants, and that the local poor thought her the lady of the manor. When all the council houses had been allocated and the local "poor" in great glee were moving their furniture in wheelbarrows, prams and go-carts, a few of the mothers and wives commiserated with Alice for not getting a new council house and hoped that she may be lucky next time.

Alice thanked them very kindly for their commiserations, but pointed out she was buying her own house and was quite happy where she was.

The Vee Cottage, the house at the fork of the road leading to Laurel Cottage, retained its old world frontage, but the interior was converted into a workshop for a new car garage and petrol station, all built on the green by the owner of the grocery close to the cottage. Red Clay Lane began to get very busy, with large lorries passing up and down with building materials for building developments down where the tinkers had been re-housed.

Laurel Cottage retained its own old world charm, hidden behind the high wall and laurel hedge. Alice and Henry were approached many times by developers wishing to buy, but Alice, who scorned the get-rich attitude, repulsed the buyers.

The cottage, however, was falling into decline and needed a lot of money spent on it, but Alice still believed she was a cut above the rest and that everyone envied her the home. A number of the rooms had been closed and let to mildew, but outwardly everything looked prosperous and comfortable.

A large field down the lane from the cottage had been sold by a local farmer, and within the year a row of large detached houses were erected. The houses rapidly filled up with businessmen and their young families and Alice, now in her forties, made a point of calling on each one to welcome them to the area and suggested they might wish to call to the cottage to view its old charm and to meet her and Henry.

One such couple were Tony and Jean McNulty, with their only child Robin. Tony ran his own small business manufacturing important parts for important pieces of machinery and spent most of his time touring the country. Robin went to a nearby grammar school and Jean was really at a loss what to do with her days.

One early evening as the daylight was going, there was a ring on the porch doorbell. Brendan in the hallway called out to his mother who was in the kitchen.

"I'll get it, Ma."

Approaching the porch door, he could see a figure through the frosted glass. Pulling the door open with some difficulty—it always scraped over the tiled floor in the porch—he saw a tall, attractive, slim woman standing in the darkening light wearing a short dress with a tight sweater and high heel shoes. She looked to be in her early thirties.

Wow! Was Brendan's initial response. What's this?

Brendan, now in his mid-teens was very conscious of the opposite sex. Or, at least his body told him to be. He had searched for something to explain his needs, but there was absolutely nothing. His parents avoided the subject. There were no books or magazines due to the severe censorship in the country and so, for a tall, well built, fairly good-looking young man, the female of the species was an item of constant curiosity. Women's magazines with pictures of corset-clad ladies with steel brassieres were the nearest he got to the hidden female form.

"Hello, lovely boyo," spoke the attractive shape, in an educated, husky, if slightly slurred, female voice. "Why now, you must be Brendan. Is your Mammy in? I'm Jean McNulty. I'm yur new neighbour."

"Oh! Mrs. McNulty, do come in," invited Brendan, stepping back to let this interesting woman into the porch.

"Ma! You've got a visitor," called Brendan, as the very attractive shape stepped into the porch and swayed against him.

"So sorry, big boyo," she apologised, supporting herself with her right hand on Brendan's shoulder whilst holding tightly to an open bottle of whiskey with her left hand. What with the sharp smell of the whiskey and the smell of perfume from her lacquered hair, together with the feel of her body against him, Brendan's imagination went into overdrive. Daring to put his right arm around her shoulders to support her, Brendan walked the soft yielding body into the sitting room and, with reluctance, placed it in an armchair.

"Tanks, Bren," came Alice's voice from the door. "Hello Jean. Come in, come in. I see you've met Brendan."

"Yes! Isn't he gorgeous? Hello! Alice, you did say to call in any time. I brought a bottle of light refreshment."

Jean held up the bottle of whiskey like a trophy.

"Now, what on earth would you want to do that for?" Alice replied in her put-on voice. "Shure, we have plenty of our own." Walking over to the small table beside the fireplace, she produced a couple of whiskey glasses from behind her wedding picture.

Brendan thought this was the time to retreat and backed out through the sitting room door as the two ladies settled down. Tingling a bit from the touch and smell of the female body, he gave up on his studies and decided to go out in the back yard to chop up a few logs in readiness for the winter. His mind was occupied by confusing thoughts. If only she weren't so old. If only she wasn't Ma's friend. If only . . .

"Ah! Well, such is life," he said to himself, smashing the axe down on the innocent piece of wood.

Later that evening while in the kitchen making some tea and toast with Henry, Brendan commented on the giggling and laughter coming from the front room.

"They're both getting a bit sozzled," Henry suggested with a rueful grin. "Ah well! Ma is enjoying herself and that Jean seems to be all right. I don't know about her husband Tony. He's away so much. He's down in Limerick at the moment. . . ."

"Oh, is he?" interrupted Brendan. "Where's the young fella staying, Pop?"

". . . leaving a woman like that on her own. The young fella? Oh, I heard Jean say he's staying at his grannies," Henry answered, rubbing a drop of hot butter off his trouser leg. "A nice bit of toast this, but the butter's a bit runny."

Hearing the sitting room door opening, they looked at each other as Alice's slurred voice called down the hallway.

"Are yu der, Brendan? Wil ye cum up here for a mo"

Grinning, Brendan rose from his chair whilst Henry shook his head ruefully.

"Dangerous ground there, Brendan. I'm staying out of it."

"Chicken!" retorted Brendan as he manfully squared his shoulders and strode out into the hallway. Alice was halfway down the hall, a bit unsteady on her feet. With her forefinger up to her mouth, she shushed while pointing with her free hand into the sitting room.

"Bren, me darlin', will—It's all right Jean, it's only Brendan," she answered the call. "Brendan, will you do me a favour. Oh, I've had too much whiskey!"

With a loud whiskey-laden burp she grinned at Brendan. "Jean is not feeling very well."

With her finger to her mouth, making more shushing sounds, she nodded her head to the sitting room door. "Cud ye walk her home?" Burp. "I'd do it only I want to go to the lav. He's comin', Jean. Hod your hosses, de Lone Ranger is on his way."

Patting the grinning Brendan on the bottom, Alice ushered him toward the sitting room. Brendan was enjoying himself. He was sorry to see his Ma so squiffy, but was looking forward to his escorting duties. Whilst he had encountered the odd drunken woman at the many parties at the cottage, he had never felt as he did now.

"Okay, Ma! Hi Yo Silver, away the lads! You go ahead Ma, I'll look after the little lady."

"No, no, no, no, no, it's all right, Alice. Tanks, Brendan, boyo, I'll make me own way home," came the slurred voice from the sitting room as Jean came stumbling out into the hallway.

"No ye can't, Jean," Alice declared. "You're drunk. Shure, look at ye."

With that, Alice let out a loud fart and started giggling. "Yu look after her, Brendan, I've gotta go." Turning around she hastily staggered down the hallway to the toilet in the pantry.

"All ri' den, Bren. Walk me home, hic. Maybe I need some fresh air, with all this fartin' goin' on. Jesus! I feel a bit groggy. Here, giv's a hand, Bren."

Reaching out her hand in the general direction of Brendan, she stumbled towards the porch door. Brendan hastily stepped forward and grabbed the unsteady body by the waist and leaned over to open the porch door. As Jean's body was between him and the stubborn door, her body pushed up against Brendan's, he felt the desire to wrap his arms around her and do something.

Wow! thought Brendan. *I'd better back away a bit.* Holding the slim body in his left arm, he wrenched the door open and the knight in shining armour, with damsel in distress, stepped out into the cool night air. However, if truth be known, this was more the knight in distress rather than the damsel.

"Les go for a walk, Bren," came the slurred words full of innuendo, as Jean put her right arm around Brendan's waist, sliding her hand under his trouser belt.

God! Brendan thought as he began to panic. *What's she doing now?*

"Now look, Mrs. McNulty, I've got to take you home. You better take your hand away or we can't walk." Enjoying the feel of her cool hand on his backside, secretly hoping she wouldn't move it, he was by now coming to boiling point and needed to adjust his pants to make himself more comfortable.

With the swaying body held up by his left arm, her right arm caressing his backside, and her left hand trying to unbutton the front of his trousers, Brendan's mind was in turmoil.

What the hell do I do? he wondered. Pushing the demanding left hand away, he started up the dark road with the intention of getting what was now becoming a problem back to its house and perhaps see what would happen then.

Coming towards the next door grocery shop with its light stretching across the road, Brendan became aware that Paddy, the owner, was standing in the doorway looking with interest as two of his customers stumbled by.

"Hello der, Brendan. Out for a walk are you den?" he chuckled.

"Would that be Mrs. Mac you have in your arms den? Hello, Mrs. Mac! It's a lovely night for a walk, isn't it now?"

"I'm just taking Mrs. McNulty home, Mr. Heffernan. She's not too well," answered Brendan as Mrs. Mac suddenly started to walk briskly, taking her hand from his bottom.

"Dat's quite right, Mr. Heff-hic-nan," slurred Jean. "Walkin' his baby back home. Now you go a'd serve your customers and mind yur own bluddy business! That's tellin' him, isn't it, Bren' me darlin'?" Jean stated as they moved out of the arc of light into the darkness again and her right hand slid back onto his bottom.

"Cum on quick, Brendan me boyo, and let's get over to me house."

Releasing his rear and catching his left hand, she started to stumble forward in the darkness.

Brendan, relieved to have the decision made for him, started after the now fast-moving body.

However, finding he couldn't move too freely due to the restriction in his groin, he began to trot after her, wondering what the outcome would be.

Stopping suddenly, Jean put her face up to Brendan's.

"Bren, me darlin', dis is our little secret, isn't it?" she asked in a husky voice, as she moved Brendan's hand to her groin. "Isn't it? Do you really want to?"

"Yes! Oh God, yes, missus! I want to."

Not being exactly too sure what she wanted, he knew he wanted it, whatever it was. This was certainly new ground for a young man whose only knowledge of the sex act was that a man and a woman did things together that they apparently enjoyed.

They crossed the road towards Mrs. McNulty's house, where Brendan saw there was a light on in the front room.

"I leave the light on jus' in case of burglars," she explained. "Cum on, quick."

Moving quickly, though still a bit unsteady, Jean led Brendan, whose imagination and body were at the height of expectancy, down the garden path past the double garage and started to fumble in her handbag for the door key.

As she leant against the front door, concentrating on her task, the door suddenly burst open. Without the support, Brendan's dream of fulfillment, the answer to all his lusts and dreams, fell into the hallway at the feet of what must have been Mr. McNulty.

"Where have you been, you bitch? Out drinking again! Who's your fella this time? Now piss off child!" were the hissed words as McNulty slammed the door in Brendan's face.

Standing on the doorstep with an aching groin, dreadfully disappointed but faintly relieved, Brendan turned and slowly limped back to the cottage.

24

A Visit to the Local Pub

"Well, if it isn't young Brendan, comin' to let us have the pleasure of his company. An' what is it that ye will now be drinking, young fella?"

"I'll have a glass of mild then, Mr. Fagan. An' thanks very much."

"A glass of mild? Bloody hell, dat's a drink only for wee babbies and little girls. Here, Marcella, give the young fella a pint of stout, it'll put some hairs on his bloody chest."

Not wishing to offend his newfound, if slightly inebriated, friend, Patsy Fagan, Brendan nodded his agreement to Marcella. With a sideways look at him, Marcella, a small thin girl in her late teens and daughter of the landlord, admonished Patsy for his language and passed Brendan a glass the size of a bucket, a bucket full of swirling black porter with a head of froth forming on the top. "There ye are, Brendan, me boyo. Knock it back. There's plenty more of it," ordered Patsy Fagan.

"Thank you, Marcella," Brendan said to the smiling barmaid as she went to serve her next customer.

"Thank you, Mr. Fagan, and here's to yer good health," smiled Brendan as he raised the glass of thick black porter to Patsy and the other onlookers. *Will he take a good swig of the stuff or will he sip like the girls do?* he could almost hear them thinking.

Brendan, knowing he was on show put his head into the bucket, closed his eyes and swallowed two large mouthfuls. Raising his head in triumph from the swirling liquid, with froth adhering to his nose and cheeks, he placed the bucket down on the bar top, relieved to have got that over with.

"Ah! I needed that," he pretended with a loud and satisfying sounding burp.

This, as the reader may gather, was Brendan's first pint. In fact, at sixteen, he should not have been served beer at all but, as he looked older and everyone knew him, what of it?

"Knock it back then, boyo," was the relieved call from the audience and the various conversations continued.

It was seven-thirty on a Saturday evening and Brendan had agreed to meet a couple of his friends in Moran's Pub. Moran's Pub was at the corner where the bus came up from Lower Killoughlin on its way to Dunlaoghaire, a couple of hundred yards up the road from the cottage. They had arranged to meet there and then go on to a dance.

So, dressed in all his finery to dazzle the girls, and with two pound notes in his pocket, he was feeling well within himself. There would be enough for a few drinks, the entrance to the dance and loose change to fund any success that night. The bar was empty, it being so early in the evening, and the smell of stale cigarette smoke still filled the air.

"Are you away den, dancing tonight?" enquired an envious Marcella in her relaxed Dublin accent, as she wiped down the bar top. Her fingers touched his hand as she lifted the glass of porter, now half full, to wipe the counter.

"That I am, Marcella. Meeting the lads and we're off to the Laurel Park in Bray."

"Brendan," Marcella whispered as she leaned over the bar to get his attention. "Patsy's glass is empty."

"God! Yes! Thanks, Marcella. What's that you're drinkin' then, Mr. Fagan?"

"I'll be havin' a shot of Irish, lad, tanks very much den, young man."

Turning to the three others in his group, he announced, "De lad's buying, boys. Dat be alright with you, Brendan lad?"

"Shure, that's fine Mr. Fagan," agreed Brendan. *Three more whiskeys and I'm nearly done. There should be at least enough to get into the dance*, he thought to himself.

Relieved to hear orders for three pints, being cheaper than the whiskey, he smiled, helping Marcella pass the slopping glasses over to the four locals who were thinking they were onto a good one here.

Brendan looked at his new companions. Tom Doyle, a farm worker, was still in his working clothes with the smell of cow dung on his boots. Stormy Doyle, Tom's elder brother, was one of the town's characters who didn't have a job, but seemed always to have plenty of drink in him. Sean Thomas was the youngest of the group in his early forties, worked on the bin lorries.

And then, of course, there was Patsy Fagan. Patsy owned the forge along the road from the pub. The forge had a horseshoe-shaped stone entrance off the road, leading into a dark pit with a glowing fire. There was always the smell of hot metal, the acrid smell of burning hoofs and the clang, clang of a hammer beating the metal into shape. The large dark workplace was full of discarded horseshoes, and farm machinery waiting to be mended, and always a patient horse standing with its head down waiting to be shod.

"How's the forge goin' den, Mr. Fagan?" Brendan's voice was getting a little bit slurred as he had finished the bucket of porter and, whilst not really wishing to drink any more of the awful stuff, wasn't going to leave until he got some return for his outlay.

"Shure! Son, are you all right den? Give him another pint, Marcella. The forge is dyin'. There's no bloody horses left an I'm goin' to have to shut down soon, so I'll have to be diggin' deep fer me drink in future."

Marcella pushed another bucket of porter toward Brendan who, leaning over the bar, touched her fingers before she had released the glass, giving her a smile. He turned back around to address Fagan.

"Where's your custom come from, Mr. Fagan, den?" he asked, his voice beginning to slur a bit. "There's lots of farms around arrant there. The milk dray needs shoes. No! I mean—I mean the horse does. Ha! Ha!"

"Look, son, I kno' me business, It's no laughin' matter," replied Fagan in a dismissive tone.

"Now, what were yu saying, Stormy? When we were rudely interrupted??" he continued, turning his back on Brendan.

"He don' mean it, Brendan. De bank hav' closed him down," advised Tom, noticing Brendan's surprise at being rebuffed.

"Oh! I'm so sorry to hear it, Mr. Fagan, I didn't know."

"Dats bloody right, ye didn't know. In yer bloody big house."

Standing up with his pint in his left fist and a riding whip in his right, he whipped the table beside Brendan.

"Ye bloody toffs are the death of me. Holy Mother of God. Jesus Christ." Whipping the table again, he drained the glass, flung it with some force into the fireplace, and stormed out of the startled room.

"What's goin' on here?" came a surprised voice from the open doorway.

"I see Patsy Fagan must 'a got sometin' in his eye he don like. Ha! Ha!"

The newcomer was dressed in a long, green, woollen coat adorned with brass buttons, wearing odd-coloured shoes and a leather bag over his shoulder. When told what had happened, he held his hands up to the ceiling.

"Oh dear! Not the forge! Next, it'll be the pub. Ah crone, ah crone, the end of the world is nigh. Marcella, me darling bit of a girl, I need a pint with undue haste, or even due haste."

"Av'e ye got the money dis' time, Timothy?" asked Marcella with a resigned smile.

"Would I have the money? The wench asks, be the Jesus here am I, Timothy Spangles, the singing voice of the fifties. I'm rollin' in it. I've got a silver pocket, listen . . ."

Pointing to his shaking pocket, the sound of coins could be heard rattling in the folds.

"Now, could I be after havin' a glorious pint of your nectar please, young lady?" he asked in a surprisingly deep melodious voice for such a scrawny, emaciated-looking individual.

Shaking a bit from Patsy Fagan's noisy exit, Brendan balanced his long frame on a bar stool and sipped at the remains of his pint glass, smiling at the newcomer. Before he could stop him, Sean Thomas had placed another pint on the bar beside him.

Golly! Brendan thought to himself. *What am I goin' to do? Another gallon of the stuff. Better go have a wee to get rid of some of it.*

Thanking Sean and making his excuses, Brendan made his way I to the gents, only to be assailed by the stench of urine and the sight of stained decorative enamel. Hurriedly finishing his task, Brendan returned to the bar to see Timothy Spangles Esquire taking his melodeon out of the leather case to the accompanying cheer from the ever-increasing crowd in the bar.

"Marcella, me dear, ye don' mind if I entertain your customers with a song or two?" enquired the diminutive figure, pulling himself onto a table at the side of the now fairly crowded room and slipping the melodeon harness onto his shoulder.

Smiling her agreement, Marcella continued pulling the endless pints of porter for the men folk and pouring small glasses of port or sherry for the wives of the regulars.

Swirling into a medley of Irish songs, Timothy sang "The Mountains of Mourne," "Biddy Mulligan the Pride of the Coombe," and "Molly Malone," with the whole room singing away to the catchy rhythms in the swirling cigarette smoke.

Sean stood forward and gestured to Timothy.

"Gi' us the Moonshiner den, Timmy, me boyo."

Changing the rhythm to a waltz tempo, Sean, in a creditable tenor voice, started to sing.

"I've been a moonshiner for many a year. I spent all my money on whiskey and beer. I'll go to some hollow and set up my still. I'll make you a gallon for a two-dollar bill."

The room then in one voice continued the chorus:

"I'm a rambler, I'm a gambler, I'm a long way from home. If you don't like me, just leave me alone. I eat when I'm hungry; I drink when I'm dry. And if moonshine don't kill me, I'll live till I die."

With resounding cheers for Timothy and calls for more drinks, the hum of conversation increased. As Mr. Spangles put his cap on the bar beside him, he raised his voice as he called out.

"Yees, will all be thinkin' of me den as yer spendin' yer money. Won't ye all?"

"Wha' about de Mountain Dew, Timmy? Now, ders a lovely song?" came the call from the back of the smoke-filled room and, in his attractive melodious voice, Timothy Spangles, smiling his thanks as some coins were dropped into his cap, went straight into the catchy tune.

"Let grasses grow and waters flow in a free and easy way. But give me enough of the rare old stuff that's made near Galway Bay."

And so the evening progressed with Brendan finding himself singing away, while drinks were offered all around. Everybody was everybody else's friend. His two friends called to collect him for the dance, but Brendan, by now so immersed in the atmosphere and his two pounds having been reduced to five shillings, decided he couldn't afford the dance.

Also, Marcella had been relieved by her father and she had come out from behind the bar squeezing alongside him. He was now in his element with a pint in one hand and a girl in the other.

However, he was feeling rather lightheaded after all the unaccustomed alcohol. Putting his arm around the willing Marcella, something he would normally never have dared to do, Brendan decided to forget the beer and concentrate on staying on his feet. The cigarette smoke was also getting quite heavy. Somebody suggested they open the door to let some air in and, with a staggering gait, Tom wandered across the room with his arms outstretched in mock, if not real, drunkenness. As the door swung open to let in a shaft of cold air, there stood an abject Patsy Fagan.

"Cum in, Patsy, ye 'ould eejit, yare forgiven. Cum on in," was the spontaneous call from the room and the door was shut again before any smoke had escaped.

Due to the sudden rush of fresh air and the swirling smoke, the pints of unaccustomed porter inside Brendan began to heave.

"Excuse me Mar . . . ," he spluttered as he ran, as quickly as he could, to the outside door. When the cool air hit him, the torrent of foaming porter gushed out of his heaving innards spraying the heaped crates in the yard. Leaning over an old pram, Brendan heaved in spontaneous gusts. Coming up for air, clearing his nose of bits of undigested food and porter, he vowed to himself never again.

"God! I want to die," he muttered. "I can't go back in there again. My jacket is covered in the stuff. Is there any way out?"

With the yard in darkness, he stumbled his way over to a gate in the wall. It was locked.

"Can't go back in there. Look at the mess I'm in. I'll go over the wall."

There were some empty beer crates against the high wall and Brendan, after falling back on the damp ground a couple of times, finally climbed unsteadily to the top of the weed-strewn wall and peered over the top.

The ground looked miles away as he threw his right leg over the top of the wall. *Oh! Me suit will get all dirty!* With both legs now dangling in the darkness, trying to touch the bottom, he lowered himself gently to the ground. Sliding down further, his suit tore on the sharp bricks as he lost his grip on the wall and fell backward about five feet.

His fall was cushioned by a mound of soil, a mound unfortunately covered in stinging nettles. Getting to his feet, with his hands already beginning to heat up from the nettle stings, he heaved the remains of the porter into the nettles and staggered down the road to the cottage feeling very, very drunk and sorry for himself.

25

Decide on Career in Merchant Navy

"Pop and I will see you down in the Legion about half past seven. Now, you'll be sure you'll get something to eat, won't you?" Alice called out as Brendan, in his sports jacket and cavalry twill trousers, his suit now being cleaned after the episode in Moran's pub, freewheeled his bike down the avenue at the side of the cottage.

Sweeping out onto the road, Brendan stood up on the pedals of his bike to get more purchase. Speeding along past the now closed forge and past Moran's Pub, he turned right towards Dunlaoghaire and sped along on the well-oiled and shiny bicycle.

With thirty shillings in his pocket he was a millionaire; he had worked a few long days at the farm and this Saturday afternoon he was on his way down to Dunlaoghaire to meet Polly at her home and have tea with her mother. His parents were expecting them both at the legion for a drink or two around seven-thirty.

Wonder what Polly's ma is like? thought Brendan. He had learned that Polly's father had died in a work accident, and that she had two brothers and a sister, all older than herself. *Well! Hope she likes me.*

Down past the grammar school, he turned into Crosthwaite Park Avenue, a sheltered road of stately terraced houses with oak and chestnut trees in the park opposite. Dismounting behind a smart, low-slung Austin Riley parked at the pavement, he self-consciously carried his bike up the wide steps to the large impressive front door. He had noticed the curtain twitching in the window to the left of the door, so he knew he had been seen. Before he reached the door it swung open like the barricaded gate on a western fort and, feeling like a frontiersman leading his horse into the unknown, he entered the fort interior.

"Leave your bike there, Brendan," Polly advised, pointing to the hat stand at the side of the large hallway. Brendan, continuing his frontiersman fantasy, patted the bicycle on the saddle saying, "There's a good horse now."

"How de do, par'ner," he mimed in an American accent. "Had many Indians attacking lately?"

Taking her hand in his and wondering whether or not he should kiss her, he realised from Polly's puzzled look that she did not understand his nervous humour. Brendan let himself be led down the hallway and up a wide staircase towards a large closed door in what appeared to be a carpeted wall.

"Here we are, Mom, this is my new friend, Brendan."

Towering above the small woman in the large armchair, Brendan smiled, leaned over, and put his hand out.

"Hello, Mrs. Hughes. How are you?"

"My! Oh! My! You are a big boy for my little girl, aren't you? Pull up a chair near me and tell me all about yourself," were the quietly spoken words from the heavy-set, pleasant woman. Leaning forward, she placed the daily paper and her glasses on the table beside her before stretching out her plump hand to be grasped.

Brendan shook the limp offering a few times, carefully returning it to its owner before sitting down as instructed on the low, stiff-backed elaborate chair beside the smiling woman. With his knees now higher than his waist, and having hitched his cavalry twills up to protect the crease, he noticed he was showing a lot of white leg and his socks, whilst both brown in colour, had a subtle difference in their hue; one appeared well sun-tanned whilst the other had been washed to a light brown.

Stretching his legs out in front of him to ease the trousers and hide his legs and socks, his foot pushed the elaborate trolley with the large wheels and expensive ceramic teapot in its no doubt fur-lined caddy, and sent it rolling toward the huge carved fireplace. Leaping up, Brendan was just in time to stop the impending disaster and, by lifting the teapot in a smooth movement, offered his hostess a cup of tea. Laughing, both women congratulated him on his dexterity and signalled he sit in a more comfortable chair.

"Would you like a cup, Brendan? It has only just been brewed," Mrs. Hughes offered.

Mrs. Hughes, in the polished manner of the well-educated woman she was, soon put Brendan at his ease and after a few cups of tea and half a dozen fairy cakes, he was quite relaxed and enjoying himself. Polly had also relaxed, sitting on the arm of Brendan's chair holding his hand. During one of those moments of silence, there was a loud bang in the hall outside and the door opened to admit a smartly dressed man in his early thirties.

"Mom, I'm just . . . Why, hello! You must be the owner of the bike. Polly's new beau."

"Yes! Gordon, this is Brendan. Brendan, my elder brother, Gordon"

Brendan, leaping to his feet, wondered how recent the last beau had been. Shaking hands, Gordon explained he was on his way to band practice and hoped the Old Riley would keep going "Haw! Haw!"

Leaning over to give his mother a peck on the cheek, Gordon strode out of the room and could be heard revving up the "Old Riley."

"Mary has left me a few sandwiches for my tea, Polly. I'm sure your big lad here would like something a bit more substantial," Mrs. Hughes suggested to Polly with a wink.

"Come on, Brendan, I'll fry a few eggs and do a sausage or two for you."

Pleased to have the chance to be alone, the two of them made their way down to the kitchen in the basement of the house. It was spotlessly clean and filled with all modern kitchen appliances such as a gas cooker, built-in range, fridge, and a large clean sink, with not a cobweb to be seen. *Wow!* Brendan thought. *It's all so clean.* It was nothing like the cottage.

As they entered the kitchen, their bodies brushed against each other whilst passing through the door.

"Brendan, will you get a couple of aprons from the top of the cupboard for us, there?" Polly requested, pointing to a low cupboard against the wall. Thinking she was looking particularly pretty, Brendan donned one of the maid's aprons and put his arms around Polly to tie her apron string. With spontaneous accord, they both called out to one another.

"Oh Brendan! Oh Polly! Oh! Yes!" Enveloping Polly in his arms with hers around his neck, they kissed deeply. After some minutes of sighing and squirming and gasps and more hungry kisses, they parted, with Polly running towards the open door.

"What if somebody had seen? Gosh, what came over me?" she gasped, half laughing. "Let's get cookin'. Two eggs, three eggs, how many do you want?"

With his body and mind whirring around in delight and anticipation, eggs were irrelevant. Still feeling the wonderful sensation of the fresh smell of her clothes and touch of her lips, Brendan skipped towards a retreating Polly who sidestepped him and raced around the kitchen, shrieking in delight.

The next ten minutes were spent frying eggs and sausages, interrupted by tentative touching and sighs and searching glances and whispered intimate words. Sitting down at the spotless deal table, with their feet touching, they ate their meal and, after saying good-bye to Mother, they made their way to the Legion in the warm evening sunlight.

They walked hand in hand, skipping when the mood took them, or drifting along with their arms around each other in the dream world of perfection and completeness. Their eyes would meet and they would laugh at the sheer delight of the new understanding between them. Not wanting to break the spell, when they arrived at the Victorian doorway Brendan looked at Polly as they stood holding hands.

"Do we go in? Do we break this wonderful spell?"

Smiling at each other resignedly, they pressed the bell in the polished mounting and entered the hushed, heavily carpeted hallway with the muffled sound of conversation and odd bursts of laughter coming from the lounge bar.

The uniformed porter welcomed them and showed them to the lounge bar. Alice and Henry, who were with a small group of friends, signalled them over and with introductions made all round, space was made for them around the long low table.

"What'll you have to drink den, Polly?" asked Henry. "I'll get a whiskey with a drop of water for you, Bren. That okay?"

"A white wine would be lovely, Mr. Harris," agreed Polly as Brendan, smiling his thanks to his father, sat on the low couch between Polly and Mr. Elder. Mr. Elder was the father of one of the boys Brendan had been in school with.

"How are ye den, Brendan? Must be grand having finished school. Have you got a job lined up yet?" enquired Elder in a broad Lancashire accent.

"Not yet, Mr. Elder. I was thinking of accountancy, or maybe goin' to England. Has Brian decided anything yet?"

Elder, a small fussy man dressed in an expensive double-breasted suit, was the owner of Elder and Smith, reputed boilermakers, and a self-made man.

"Oh! Brian is startin' in the firm as under manager at the Roscommon Branch," replied Elder, proudly. "He's on holiday in France at the moment."

Oh! Lucky him, Brendan thought. *He's got it made.*

Having overheard Brendan, Alice leaned over. "I didn't know you were goin' to England, Brendan."

"Jus' thinking about it, Ma, jus' thinking about it," he replied, very embarrassed. He wished she wouldn't ask him any more questions, since he felt he was losing face here. Alice, however, worsened Brendan's position by following up with an attempt to rectify her social error.

"Of course! Yes, of course," she exclaimed, striking her forehead.

"Brendan, your Uncle Desmond in London is interested in discussing a manager's post with you. Yes, George," she continued, directing her voice towards Elder, "my brother runs a small exporting firm in London. He's married to one of the Royal family, ye know."

Uncle Desmond, in fact, ran a trader's stall in Smithfield market in London and was married to a girl who had once worked as a maid for a member of the Royal family.

"That's grand to hear," answered Elder with a superior smile. Brendan looked at his father who raised his eyes fractionally. "That's mother for you" was the message passed. The conversation drifted into a monologue about business prospects and how stupid the countries' politicians were.

Whilst trying to appear interested in Elder's discourse, Brendan glanced around the room at the other small groups and Ellen caught his eye. Ellen was the wealthy widow of a British businessman. On his earlier visits to the legion, Brendan had danced a few times with Ellen and she had taken quite a shine to him.

She was sitting at the other side of the lounge under the large framed print of Queen Elizabeth and Prince Philip that adorned the wall over the fireplace. A small, interesting-looking man with thinning hair and a well-weathered face who was talking animatedly accompanied Ellen. She was giving him her full attention with a happy smile on her face. Ellen, noticing Brendan, waved over and mouthed the words "come over" and, pointing to Polly, she mouthed "introduce me."

Polly, noticing the signal, smiled her agreement and after excusing themselves, they made their way over to the welcoming Ellen.

"Hello, Ellen," smiled Brendan as he bowed slightly to the seated Ellen. "May I introduce my very close friend, Polly? Polly, this is Ellen."

Ellen and Polly exchanged smiles and handshakes, one, a fresh-faced youngster and the other an ageing, grey-headed woman contented with her life.

"Brendan, I would like to introduce you to this great friend of mine," Ellen said, smiling at her companion.

"Knowing your interest in the sea I am sure you would like to meet Captain Michael Walsh. Michael," she continued, turning to her companion, "this is my friend, Brendan Harris. Remember I mentioned his interest in the sea?"

"Hello, young fella and young lady," was the greeting in a voice roughened by many cigarettes.

He rose to shake hands with the two youngsters. Dressed in a smart, double-breasted, dark blue blazer with grey slacks and white shirt, he exuded stories of the sea. Brendan was drawn to him instantly. Polly pressed his hand in agreement. Ellen, noticing their interest, went on to tell them that Michael was an old friend of her late husband.

"You went to sea in oil tankers didn't you, Michael?" Ellen questioned, looking at Walsh.

"Yes, for some twenty years with CP Tanker Company until I retired a few years ago," answered Walsh. "Ellen tells me you are interested in ships, Brendan. Is that right?"

"Well! Yes, Captain. Two of my friends from school have recently gone to sea as cadets. One of them has joined Eagle Oil and the other is with Blue Funnel."

"Eagle Oil, yes. The San boats, saw a few of them over my years. Remember the San Demetrio? Her crew reboarded her after being set on fire by the pocket battleship Admiral Scheer in 1940. Good luck to the lad. He should have a few adventures on the San boats."

With a smile, the captain continued. "The Blue Funnel boats, you find them everywhere. Wish the youngsters all the best. What do you intend doing yourself, Brendan? There's a great life to be had at sea. Recommend it to ye."

So the conversation continued. Brendan's interest in seagoing was increased by the tales from Captain Walsh—his time as an apprentice deck officer with the CP Tanker Company, his progression through the ranks to that of captain, and his overall aura of independence and well being.

Would I be able to go as a cadet? I must read up something about it, Brendan later thought to himself. He realised that the results from the school exams would be more important than ever. They were due out in September—just a month to go. *Maybe if I write to a few shipping companies telling them about myself,* he thought, *they could say whether they wanted cadets or not.*

Noticing his parents looking towards him, no doubt bored with the tales from Mr, Elder, Brendan and Polly excused themselves and returned to their table.

"Ma! Pop! I'm going to go to sea. The captain over there has helped me make my mind up. If Jim and Brian can do it, so can I."

Relieved to have at last made a decision on his future career, Brendan finished his whiskey like it was orange juice. Alice was quite pleased he had at last decided what to do, but was apprehensive about losing her favourite boy. Henry was overjoyed and ordered drinks for the table, inviting Ellen and the captain over to join them.

Brendan, having downed a few well-watered whiskeys and Polly two or three glasses of wine, were both enjoying themselves. Brendan, remembering his recent evening in Moran's Pub, thought of the difference between the two ways of relaxing and enjoying oneself. Here everything was very ordered, everybody was refined and well spoken—there was no swearing, just the murmur of voices with muffled laughter. Of course, it was still early in the evening. No Timothy Spangles to liven the evening with his melodeon, or Patsy Fagan throwing his glass into the fireplace. Most of all, there was no singing. *God!* he thought. *Say I was to start singing "The Wild Colonial Boy" or some rebel song. I'd be taken out at dawn and shot.*

Later that evening, Jono arrived with his latest girlfriend, Eileen. At five-foot-ten, she was an interesting looking woman. She had already been introduced to the family and Alice thought she was smashin', as did Henry.

"If Jono's going to marry, let it be this one," Alice had proclaimed to the family. Jono, at eighteen, was now in the British Army and strode around with military bearing. He was on leave for a few days. Billy was staying overnight with a school friend.

Jono was delighted to hear of Brendan's career decision. He congratulated him and offered him another drink.

"A whiskey and water would go down very well," said Brendan, not really enjoying the stuff. At least it didn't fill him up like the Guinness. In fact, he felt quite disappointed that he felt so sober. *This drinkin' is a weird business. It would be cheaper just to drink orange juice,* he thought to himself.

As the evening wore on, the talking got louder, the laughter more relaxed. Captain Michael was entertaining a small group with his seafaring exploits. Alice was flirting with Elder. Polly was talking confidently with Eileen, and Ellen had fallen asleep. Henry was talking to the barman about the price of potatoes, and Brendan was pretending to listen to Mrs. Elder talking about her back problems, when suddenly there was a commotion at one of the tables where a group of younger men had been downing the bottled Guinness.

"Bloody say dat again and I'll knock your bloody head off," proclaimed one fit-looking young man, dressed in slacks and a sports shirt, knocking his chair over as he rose from the table.

"Now, Colin, keep it quiet, don' make a fool of yerself," appealed one of the group to the swaying figure.

There was no need to quiet him. The Guinness decided to return, covering the poor peace monger with a liberal coating of vomit. The aggressor gently subsided to the floor in a crumpled heap. The rest of the group, looking very sheepish, pulled the offending body out to the toilets, apologising to the staring audience.

"If they can't keep it down, they shouldn't down it," proclaimed Henry in a pompous slurred voice, nodding his head wisely.

"That's right, Henry," agreed Elder, missing the side of the bar as he went to lean on it. Giggling, he recovered himself before continuing. "Henry, isn't your Alice a luvley woman? God, she's gorgeous. Must go fer a widdle, a twiddle, or even a piddle."

So, singing gently to himself, Elder wandered towards the lav, already starting to unbutton his fly.

Brigadier Darling, who had been sitting at the end of the bar all evening, snorted into his brandy. Sitting back, twirling the sodden ends of his moustache with nicotine-stained fingers, he proclaimed, "Damn youngsters today. If I had my way they would be out square-bashing and doing a decent day's work," Snort! Snort! Tsch! Tsch! "Here, fill this again, barman."

The separate groups all returned to their huddles. The hum of conversation began to get louder, the odd glass bounced off the carpet, and the cloud of smoke from the Senior Service untipped cigarettes, and the St. Bruno pipe tobacco swirled around the room. Brendan, beginning to feel he would rather be out in the fresh air, squeezed Polly's hand and glanced towards the door. She nodded her agreement.

"Ma, Pop, we're away now. I'm going to collect my bike. Got a lot to think about."

"Okay, Bren, shure enough," replied Alice. "We hav' a lot to talk about. See you at home shortly. Wha's the time?"

She pulled Jono's jacket sleeve back to look at his watch.

"It's 'leven o'clock. See you at home, den. Nice to see ye again, Polly. Henry!" she called out loudly. "Bren an' Pol' are' leavin'.'"

Waving a farewell to all, the two made their way out into the fresh air. Holding hands and breathing in the clean sea air, they both let out a whoop of delight. Very relaxed with each other, but with their hormones buzzing at a high pitch, they ran down the steep steps onto the road making their way back to collect Brendan's bike. They went the long way, stopping at frequent intervals to kiss and fondle each other. Reaching the house, they were loath to part, both eager to explore and discover each other's bodies.

Promising to meet again the next day, they kissed again and Brendan, very carefully, mounted his bike, waved good-bye to the figure at the top of the steps, and started to cycle home with his mind thinking about the future. *Hope I can get to sea!* he thought. *Hope the exam results are good enough.*

To hedge his bets in his job quest, Brendan had written to a few insurance and solicitor firms in Dublin in the hope they might consider him and was delighted, during the following few days, to receive a letter offering an appointment. Paddy Moran had also suggested that a Seamus Loughlin, the owner of the general store in Dublin, might be interested in speaking with him.

The following week, Brendan donned his slightly misshapen suit, hoping it would not be too noticeable that the sleeves were a bit short and that his trousers hung very badly (it was assumed, apparently by the manufacturers, that a man with a long leg also had a large belly). With his shoes polished to a brilliant shine and his hair forced into the semblance of a quiff, Brendan boarded the bus to Dublin. He went past the posh houses in Foxrock, fantasizing that one day he might be rich enough to own something like that.

Arriving in the city some time before his appointment with Shield and Munster Insurance, he decided to go for a stroll in Stephens Green, a park in the centre of Dublin. Entering through the large gates, he joined the many students either strolling past the manicured lawns or conversing in foreign languages. He noticed the dark-suited businessmen hurrying past with their bulging briefcases, and wondered to himself if he would be one of them one day.

With his eye being taken by one particular smart lassie walking briskly toward him, her long shapely legs and trim body in colourful short skirt and sweater demanding his attention, he unfortunately stepped into one of the many dog deposits on the pathway. Hopping over to a bench and sitting down alongside a badly dressed man dozing with a small suitcase tied to his wrist, he started to dislodge the smelly substance with a twig picked up from the path. With the twig breaking, he took off the shoe and cleaned most of it off by scraping it along the leg of the bench. He hopped over to the grass verge to remove most of the balance with a tuft of grass.

Asking a passing woman the time, he realised he had better get moving to his appointment in Dame Street. Donning his shoe, he walked briskly to the appointment with the accountants.

"Welcome, Mr. Harris. Do sit down. I am Mr. John Brown and this is Mr. Peter Smith. We are in charge of recruitment . . ."

As the voices droned on and Brendan stuttered his replies, he noticed both men were beginning to lose interest and giving the odd sniff. Brendan was himself beginning to get a strong odour of dog shit over the smell of furniture polish and realised he must have missed some of the dog dirt. Looking down at his trouser leg, he noticed there was a piece of caked dirt contained in the turn up and some he had missed on his shoe.

By now, Brendan knew he was in a losing battle and was somewhat relieved when the two interrogators looked at each other and nodded. John Brown stood up, thanked Brendan, and dismissed him with the statement, "We'll let you know, Mr. Harris."

Relieved to be free of the claustrophobic atmosphere, Brendan closed the heavy door behind him and used the frill cover on the armchair in the hallway to clean his shoe.

Next stop, Loughlin's stores.

"Jus call in the nex' time you're in Dublin. I'll giv' Seamus a ring to let him kno' yer comin'," had offered Paddy Heffernan, the owner of the shop next door to the cottage.

Brendan entered a large mixed goods shop with a long wooden counter on the left and clothes hanging from the wall on the right. A small notice pointed upstairs to the shoe department. Asking a young girl leaning on the counter for Mr. Loughlin, she put down her comic and yelled at the top of her voice,

"Seamus! There's a young fella here wantin' ye."

"Sen' him up, Mary, I'm in ladies' shoes," was the response from Seamus.

"Up the steps der, mister," pointed Mary to some bare wooden steps at the side of the counter, still looking at the pictures in her comic.

Mounting the wooden steps, a large hand-written sign directed the customer to the ladies' shoes on the right. Brendan made his way past shelves stacked with shoes of all sizes and colours and stepped down into the ladies' department. There was Seamus Loughlin, a bulky overweight man wearing a red striped t-shirt, canvas trousers and white runners.

"Yes, young fella," asked Loughlin in a bored voice. "Wha' de ye want?"

Brendan, already deciding career prospects here would be pretty miserable, opened the charade.

"My name's Harris, Mr. Loughlin. Mr. Heffernan suggested I give you a call to discuss a trainee manager's job."

"God! I remember. Paddy did ring. Never said ye'd be in a suit. Anyone workin' here hasn't got time to wear a suit. Trainee manager? I shure need someone at the moment, but not a bloody trainee manager. Hav' ye ever worked in a store?"

"No, Mr. Loughlin," answered Brendan.

"Now, look here young fella. I'll be straight with ye; there's no future here. I'm selling out and emigratin' to America. I've had enough of this God-fearin' country. If I were you, I'd get out as well."

Stepping out into the melee of Moor Street with all its stalls and shouting vendors, Brendan, very disappointed in his first endeavours to find a job, made his way back to the bus and started the long journey home. He was now determined, more than ever, that it was a career at sea that he wanted.

26

Work in Local Sawmill

"Right," Brendan said to himself after the disappointing job interviews "I've got two options—either go to sea, or find work here in Ireland."

He had earlier written to a couple of shipping companies, one of them the new Irish Shipping Company. Doc Courcy had given him a name to write to. A negative reply was received from them, but Calvex Petroleum had said they would consider him subject to his exam results. They required three "A" level passes in the English GCE exam, to include English Composition and Mathematics, before he would be considered for an apprenticeship. They didn't want to know anything about his religion, which made a change.

Being turned down for a job because of religion seemed a pretty stupid way to run a business, but Brendan accepted it as the way of the world.

However, in his heart and soul he did not really wish to enter a career in the legal profession or accountancy. He had his mind set on going to sea, so the results of the final exams taken at school would determine his future career.

At the end of the summer a small, indifferent-looking brown paper envelope with a local postmark arrived addressed to Brendan.

Are these the exam results? he thought to himself. *Does this scruffy envelope contain my future? Have I passed?* With an anxious hand, he opened the unsealed flap and found the envelope contained a postcard-sized piece of paper with his name typed on it.

"Well, this couldn't be the results. Surely not! Wait, there's writing on the other side. Janey Mac, it's from the school. It's the results. Oh God! What are they . . . *Failed.*"

He had *failed.* The word jumped out and hit him between the eyes. "*Failed* the examination, as a whole." As a whole! Yes! Irish, of course! The stupid government had made Irish language a compulsory subject and he had failed the examination—as a whole.

However, the English and mathematics results were honours standard, as were geography and history. He had failed Latin and passed in art and French. Rather annoyed at the pettiness of the examining authorities, but pleased with the other results, he considered his next step.

As the postcard itself didn't look too impressive, he thought he would get a reference from Mr. Blazer, the deputy head, confirming the results and maybe a statement that an honours result was equal to an English GCE "A" level. So, after telephoning the school and making an appointment to meet Mr. Blazer, Brendan donned the grey suit, which was now getting a bit short in the legs and tight across the shoulders, mounted his bike and cycled down to the old school.

Dismounting at the school gate, as pupils are requested not to cycle on the drive, he walked his bicycle down towards the school entrance remembering the time, some ten years previously, when he had started in the kindergarten class. Nothing had changed; the immaculate lawn and flower beds were still there, the Virginia creeper still climbed the walls in orderly fashion, and the gowned figure of Mr. Kenny was standing in his customary position at the classroom window, his back to the drive. Brendan thought of the wasted hours listening to the droning voice going on about Latin verbs and Caesar.

"Glad that's all over," he said to himself.

Leaving his bicycle at the entrance door in a certain defiance at the school rules—bicycles must not be left at the school door—he entered the vestibule.

With its familiar smell of chalk dust, ink, and wood polish, he walked self-consciously along the windowed corridor between the classes; being tall he was able to see into each classroom. There was "Granny" Smith wasting her pupils' time with her Irish lessons; there was Miss Read speaking in French to the few interested pupils. There was the headmaster, cane in hand, ordering the attentive faces to understand Euclid.

Close to Blazer's study, Brendan noticed the doc, the only teacher he admired, talking animatedly to his receptive audience. He stopped to savour the sight and recalled the interesting lessons he had learned. Noticing Brendan, the doc turned with a beaming smile on his thin face and strode over to the door.

"Well, hello, Harris. Mr. Blazer said you were coming in to see him," he said, shaking Brendan's hand vigorously. "I hear you might be going to sea?"

"Yes, sir!" replied Brendan delightedly. "I've applied to CP Tankers and I'm coming to ask for a reference from Mr. Blazer"

"Glad you're doing that, Harris. Do give a call to tell me all—I am most interested. Must get back to these dreadful children."

Shaking hands again, the doc returned to the class obviously referring to Brendan, as all heads turned and stared at this tall lucky senior who had finished school. Feeling very pleased with himself Brendan knocked at the study door and was welcomed by Blazer.

Shortly after this meeting with Blazer, Brendan was delighted to get a letter confirming the honours results he had gained in the exam equalled the British General Certificate of Education standard.

Now, he thought, after he posted the letter to CP. *I'd better hedge my bets. I may not get the apprenticeship with them and I need to earn some money quickly.*

There had been a dismissive note from the accountants. The dog dirt on his shoes couldn't have helped. The work on the farm was not worth the money—one shilling and thruppence an hour, plus all the potatoes one could eat. No future there.

He had received a reply letter from Chipperfield's Circus offering a job as a tent man, which sounded interesting.

Brendan mused to himself as he sat down to consider his future.

He was sixteen, going on seventeen, with reasonable exam results. Should he get a job like his father and work his socks off for very little and a poor pension? Should he start in a business and work up from the bottom? That fellow in the store in Dublin seemed to think that because he was a Protestant there wasn't much chance of work in Dublin.

He decided he would have another attempt, maybe try the large bookshops in Dublin, especially those where he had changed his school textbooks.

So the following day, wearing the ill-fitting suit, with his shoes polished, he once more made his way into the city by bus to put himself at the risk of being offered a job.

He reached Dawson Street where most of the large bookstores were located and entered the familiar entrance to the store where he had exchanged his used school textbooks. The door and woodwork had not been painted for many a year and the interiors of the two floors were full of dust, but were also full of the magic of books. There were a few customers browsing, and a bored and very young-looking assistant moving books around in an aimless fashion. When asked for the manager's name, Brendan was advised Mr. Flynn would not be in until lunchtime.

"What's it like working here?" Brendan asked.

"Borin'," replied the girl. "Borin'. I'm leavin' here the end of the week. If you're looking for a job, Flynn might be interested."

"Right, I'll be back," replied Brendan with interest. "What time would be best?"

"Come in at one. I'll be knockin' off for me dinner so he has to be here. If'n he isn't, I'll have his guts for garters. He told me," said the youngster, leaning behind the counter and producing a square of stiff cardboard, "to put this notice outside the door."

Brendan looked at the notice. "Assistant Required. No Protestants."

Somewhat taken aback and very disappointed, Brendan stared briefly at the youngster.

"Why no Protestants?" he asked.

"Oh! Flynn is from the north and his parents were killed by the Prods. So if'n you're a Prod yersef', I wouldn't be botherin' comin' back."

Rather deflated and disillusioned with the world of employment, Brendan went and sat for a while in Stephens Green, thinking Ireland didn't want him. So, it seemed as if everything depended upon CP employing him.

"Brendan, Dr. Courcy from the school wants you to ring him."

Returning from his abortive trip to Dublin, Brendan, rather tired and frustrated with life, perked up when Alice told him there was a call from the doc.

"Hello, Harris," answered the doc in his effusive style. "I could do with some help preparing the building for the maritime museum. If you have some spare time, could you come down this weekend?"

Feeling quite pleased that the doc had thought of him and wanted his help, Brendan agreed immediately. Yes! It would fill in the time and take his mind off job hunting.

So that weekend, Brendan met up with the doc and a number of others from the school and set to clearing out the rubbish accumulated over the years in the now empty building at the harbour front. The doc had always had a hankering to open a museum in Dunlaoghaire, to show the many visitors the maritime history of this famous harbour some ten miles south of the capital, Dublin.

Over the next weeks, after a lick of paint and a few repairs to the woodwork, the doc started to put the few pieces he had gathered over the years on display. These pieces, along with many other parts of Irish maritime history, helped to make an impressive show of Ireland's place, as with that of Dunlaoghaire, in the maritime world.

With the need for money uppermost in his mind, whilst he was in town early one morning, Brendan had called into a small sawmill to see if there was any work. The doc had suggested it, as he knew the owner.

Brendan remembered the sawmill built at the entrance to the western side of the breakwater, close to the beach at Seapoint. He had noticed it many times when going for a swim in the bay. Passing through the high rusty gates at the entrance to a yard full of waste machinery and the odd rusty, discarded saw, Brendan was not too enamoured. The sight of the brick-built warehouse with a stained corrugated roof and blank wooden doors muffling the loud screeching of a saw in action did not offer much encouragement.

He continued around to the back of the warehouse, passing the curtained windows of an added building. He thought this must be where the manager lived, and pushed open a small door in the main building. The door, with a rotting base and old white paint covered by greasy handprints, as with everything else, did not impress.

The sound of the rotating band saw welcomed Brendan as he entered the warehouse. He saw to his left a group of men in a cloud of dust balancing a large horizontal tree trunk with wooden props as it screeched its way through a tall frame holding a vibrating saw.

There were a few small tables around the grimy and littered floor with different shaped saws resting on their tops and wood of all ages and shapes lying on the floor and propped against the walls. The attractive smell of fresh wood, however, helped to dispel the grey scene.

He made his way over to an unpainted, stained door to the right and knocked self-consciously on the door. The door swung open quite easily to show a greasy wooden table and an assortment of chairs with three half-filled mugs on its surface. A row of dank coats, hanging from metal hooks, helped to complete the depressing scene. The naked light bulb hanging from the dusty ceiling suddenly swung in the draught caused by a further door, on the right, swinging open.

The sight of a short, skinny man dressed in a pair of ill-fitting pyjamas with a scowl on his unshaven face, standing aggressively in the doorway, took Brendan aback.

"Who the f---ing hell are you?" was the snarled enquiry from the pyjama-clad figure, as he brushed the strands of long matted hair back over the top of his bald head.

"Wha' ye want?"

"I hear you're looking for staff . . . Mr. Flynn?" Brendan asked politely. "You are Mr. Flynn?"

"No matter who I am, go see Jack Smith, he'll sort ye out. Now let me git bac' te me f---ing bed."

Turning on its heel, the apparition disappeared behind the closed door.

Gosh! Brendan thought. *What a miserable little man.*

Nothing daunted, Brendan made his way over to the group of men who were lowering a large, sharp-edged slab of sawn wood off the trolley.

"Mr. Smith?" enquired Brendan, in his grey suit and polished shoes. The three dishevelled, roughly dressed men looked up at this startling apparition.

"Yeh!" answered the older of the men, a tall wiry man with broad shoulders and muscular arms.

"Mr. Smith," said Brendan, "Mr. Flynn said to talk to you about a job."

"Right there lads, have a brew an' I'll look arter 'dis. Now, what do ye wan' young fella?"

After a short discussion, during which Jack Smith expressed surprise that a young man of Brendan's like wanted to work in the mill, eventually offered him £4 a week to come in daily to learn the job. He would be expected to work at cleaning and helping where necessary from eight in the morning to five in the evening, with a half day on Saturday. Brendan, willing to try his hand at anything reasonable that would realise some money, agreed to start the following morning at eight o'clock and cycled home wondering what he had let himself in for.

When he arrived at the cold and dark warehouse the next morning Smith and his two cohorts bade Brendan a curt welcome and directed him to the kitchen. There was no sight of Flynn. "There's the pot and kettle, young fella; take Mr. Flynn in a cup, no milk or sugar, an' make enough for us three, den come out an' I'll show ye what to do."

And so the day went by, making tea, sweeping sawdust and stacking wood. Attempts to make conversation, with any of the men, resulted in a shrug of the shoulders and an unintelligible grunt. Flynn came out at ten o'clock, had a few words with Smith, ignored Brendan and drove off in the old Ford Popular that was parked alongside the mill. Over the next few days Brendan's attempts to speak with Flynn were ignored; the gang of three had very little to say. Approaches to Smith resulted in a direction to speak with Flynn. Flynn would storm into the mill, issue orders, and disappear into his office demanding a cup of tea.

At the end of the first week, Brendan had decided to stay for a week or two to get some money in his pocket as there appeared to be no future prospects in such a place. When ready to leave for home on the Saturday, he was instructed by Smith to report for work at seven o'clock on the following Monday.

It was with some trepidation that Brendan arrived at the sawmill on a dark, cold, and wet Monday morning. He immediately put the kettle on to supply the ever demanded cups of tea and took a cup into Flynn's quarters, a sour-smelling, one-room apartment. He placed the cup on the floor beside the overflowing ash tray and gave the snoring body a tentative poke. Flynn grunted in his sleep and turned over, snorting and spluttering. Brendan's task completed, he left the unsavoury room thinking to himself he was worth more than this.

Shortly afterwards, Flynn came out of his den demanding another cup of tea and had a word with Jack Smith who was, as were his two buddies, dressed in heavy coats to ward off the cold. When approached by Brendan for his wages, Flynn turned on him asking him who the hell he thought he was. Couldn't he see it was only early in the morning and that he would get his wages when he was ready? Quite shaken, Brendan's spluttered retort was lost as Flynn stormed away.

After the morning cup of tea, Smith called out to his two shadows.

"Cum on men, de sooner we go the sooner we're back." Smith looked over at Brendan. "Yer comin wit us young fella, git yer coat."

Brendan grabbed his raincoat as the three men went out into the yard where a large, over-worked, dilapidated Ford lorry with cab and open back was parked.

"Right son, git up der on de back. Der won't be any room fer ye in the cab," was the instruction from Jack Smith as he and his two fellow workers climbed into the cab of the lorry. Brendan, when he asked where they were going, was ignored, and he clambered reluctantly onto the open back of the lorry.

Some twenty minutes later, the lorry stopped in front of a roadside café and the three buddies made their way over to the entrance. Brendan, now quite cold and very wet, jumped down from the trailer and stumbled after them. Ordering tea and toast for themselves, the three sat at a Formica-topped table amongst the other steaming mounds of damp clothes, eating their toast and balancing their woodbines on the overfull ash trays.

Luckily, Brendan had a sixpence and bought a slice of toast and mug of tea and sat at a table beside a hunched figure deeply immersed in the Sporting Herald.

After an interminable journey in sleeting rain and cold wind, the lorry turned off the main road into a large forest somewhere in County Wicklow and bumped and swayed over rough roads through the dark funnel formed by the high trees on either side.

God! Where am I going? What am I doing? There must be a better life than this, Brendan thought to himself, hanging onto the sides of the lorry to avoid being thrown out. Suddenly, they came to a rain-drenched opening and lurched to a stop. Tree trunks of every size lay scattered around, with lorries waiting in a small queue to take their turn in loading the freshly cut wood.

The dark, cloud-filled sky kept a steady drizzle of cold sleety rain sweeping down into the clearing. There was movement from the cab: the three made their way over to a small hut at the side of the clearing and disappeared inside.

Brendan, very cold and shivering quite violently, made his way over to the side of the clearing to relieve himself. With his hands so very cold, he wet his trouser leg to add to his misery. Walking to the small hut, he found it to be full of lorry drivers all dimly seen through swirling cigarette smoke. As the air was warmer he rid himself of his sodden raincoat and stamped his feet to get the circulation moving again.

Standing in his steaming clothes, Brendan waited until it was their turn to load their lorry. He followed Smith and his two buddies out into the clearing and, after a lot of heaving and swearing, the four of them manually lifted a number of the long, heavy, thick tree trunks onto the lorry and lashed them down. When they were ready to move, Brendan made to push his way into the cab, but was repulsed.

"No room, son. Use this to tie yersef' on wit," and was handed a short length of rope.

Nearly crying in his frustration and indignation, Brendan climbed onto the sodden logs and, looping the rope around a protruding branch stub, made a harness for himself and squeezed down between the rough wet bark. The jolting drive back to the road moved the tree trunks, which pinched his body and caused some bruising. However, this eased a bit when they reached the smoother road.

So, in the incessant rain, the miserable journey continued until they arrived back at the mill. In the dark and now freezing sleet, Brendan staggered over to his bike and made his way home to the cottage, exhausted.

The following morning, revitalised by a good night's sleep and fried breakfast, but coming down with a cold, Brendan cycled down to the mill, ready to give Flynn a piece of his mind, get his cash, and leave. The day had brightened up with a biting easterly wind blowing in from the sea. The lorry, with its cargo of tree trunks, stood forlornly at the entrance.

Brendan noticed the door to the tearoom was open when he entered the warehouse. The three stalwarts, in muted conversation, were huddled around a small glowing brazier.

Wondering if Flynn was in, Brendan entered the tearoom and poured himself a cup of tea from the heavily stained pot and was surprised to be greeted by Smith with a muttered, "Mornin'."

"I'd better take a cup into Mr. Flynn an' hope he's got some money for me," replied Brendan, getting a raised eyebrow from Smith.

"Right, let's get to work, lads," instructed Smith. Followed by the heavily dressed, shivering workforce, he opened the large double doors, letting in a blast of freezing air. The lorry engine, after many attempts, reluctantly fired with a roar and with full choke, was reversed into the warehouse. The workers were then delegated to roll the trunks off the lorry as quickly as possible in order to get the doors shut.

Brendan lent a hand, even if it was only to get some circulation in his body. With the lorry driven out, the sullen workforce settled down to finishing the work they had left before their run out the previous day.

With the doors shut, the windows covered in years of grime, and the light from two naked bulbs in the high ceiling dimmed by the sawdust, the mill interior was full of shadows. Smith called Brendan over to sweep the mounds of sawdust that had gathered on the floor under a very large tree trunk balanced on the saw trolley.

Brendan swept the floor under the trolley, whilst the three dark shadows prepared the large trunk before it started its journey through the bandsaw.

"Right, young fella," instructed Smith as he switched on the band saw. "Git back there now will ye', an start the trolley motor."

Brendan, startled by this sudden recognition of his presence, pointed to the button on the Bakelite box on the side of the trolley and, on Smith's nod of affirmation, pushed it. With a loud roar the engine fired and the trolley started moving the tree trunk through the fast revolving band saw.

In the gloomy light, with sawdust spraying in a fountain of dust, the saw screeched in torment as the slabs of wood sliced from the tree trunk got heavier. Halfway through the third cut, the sound from the tortured saw got deeper and the saw blade began to shudder.

"Stop the motor," screamed Smith to Brendan. Before Brendan could punch the button on the bakelite cover, the saw exploded into a twisting sword of steel; it had stuck in the heavy wood and snapped. Brendan was fortunate to be behind the small protection offered by the engine housing but one of the men closest to the moving trolley received the full force of the twisting sword and screamed as the moving blade severed his right leg and narrowly missed the rest of his body.

Brendan stopped the motors and stood in silent shock as the screaming continued. Everything was moving in slow motion for Brendan. Smith came leaping forward like Bambi in a Walt Disney cartoon. The dust-filled air lessened its frantic swirling. The only sound was the sobbing screams from the injured man as Smith tried to stop the bleeding with a wad of cotton waste.

The spell was suddenly broken by a shaft of sunlight from the entrance door as Flynn strode in. "Jay-sus Christ! What's happened? Where's the saw? Here, out of the way. God! Jack! What's gone on here?" he shouted in exasperation, noticing the huddled group and the sobbing man on the floor. "Go on, young fella, ring for an ambulance."

Brendan, still somewhat dazed, ran over to the office and dialled 999. After the ambulance had taken the injured man away, Flynn called Brendan into the tea room and gave him his money for the previous week and in his gruff, uncompromising manner instructed Brendan to return to his work. By now, Brendan had recovered some of his composure and in a somewhat quavering voice told Flynn what he could do with his job and made his way home.

27

Interview with Calvex Petroleum Tanker Company

Returning discontentedly from the sawmill and wondering why this business of finding a job was so difficult, Brendan called out as he entered the kitchen of the cottage, making his way to the pantry.

"I'm home. Anyone in?"

"Is that you, Brendan?" was the teasing call from his mother in the front room. "Brendan! Yoo hoo, Brendan. There's a letter for you! Yoo hoo! It's from the Cee Pee. I have it here in the front room. Do you want it?"

A letter from CP. Wow! He raced up the hallway into the front room to find Alice sitting beside the coal fire with one of the neighbours, having a cup of tea.

"Where is it, Ma? Where is it? Hello, Mrs. Traynor."

Brendan looked at the white envelope. *This has my future. What is it going to be? Gosh! What if I open it and it's a no?*

Tearing open the sealed envelope, he unfolded the heavy sheet of paper, feeling the embossed letter heading. His eyes fell on the words ". . . meet Spinney House Liverpool, 10th January 1957." The relief! The anticipation! The potential!

Looking up he said quietly, "I've got the interview. I've got the interview. Yippee! Goin' to Liverpool in January."

Hugging Alice, he then danced around the room. "I must tell Polly and the doc."

Meeting up with a delighted Polly, the family had a celebratory evening of fish and chips and a visit to Moran's pub.

During the following weeks, and over the Christmas period, Brendan got a part-time job serving in Moran's Pub and prepared himself for the interview. One of the presents he got at Christmas was a new, off-the-peg suit.

And so the big day arrived. Dressed in his new suit and overcoat with a small carry bag, he was driven into Dublin docks by his parents accompanied by Billy, and boarded the MV Munster, the B&I ferry boat to Liverpool, at eight o'clock that evening. Waving good-bye to his parents as the ship pulled away from the docks, Brendan drew a deep breath.

"This is it. It's up to me now. Gee, this is the first time I've ever left Ireland. I've got to pass this interview."

He stayed up on deck to see the lights of Dublin receding in the background with the dim glow of Dunlaoghaire to the left. Brendan leaned on the side rail of the deck and adjusted his balance to the increasing roll of the ship as it exited from Dublin Bay into the Irish Sea.

The wind began to pick up and, feeling cold, he stepped back into the never-ending corridors with their streams of constantly shuffling people, balancing themselves against the ship's movement. Most were smiling self-consciously as their frantic feet and hands tried to balance against the sudden roll of the deck. There were suitcases and paper parcels everywhere, with groups of roughly dressed men holding grimly onto their pints of stout, shuffling involuntarily with the movement of the ship. The smell of stout and beer was beginning to fill the air, mixing with the constant cloud of cigarette smoke. One corner of the lower deck had been taken over by a card school.

Another shipload of disaffected Irishmen on their way to bother the world, Brendan thought to himself.

Not having secured a cabin for the night due to the expense, Brendan tried to find somewhere to rest for the next eight to ten hours. He walked aimlessly up and down stairways, through a constant moving mass of people, stepping over recumbent bodies, through cafés, along corridors with seats, all occupied by noisy children and resigned parents.

He wrapped his overcoat around his body and settled into a corner at the end of a row of occupied seats. Taking out his copy of *Kon Tiki* by Thor Heyerdahl that he had borrowed from the library, he settled down for a good read. Feeling somewhat uncomfortable, he resigned himself to a long night.

He had managed to doze off for a while, when he was suddenly awoken by a loud bang and raised voices. He looked up to see three roughly dressed men, no doubt Irishmen, with large half-filled tumblers of black stout grasped in their hands, remonstrating with each other.

"Will ye now be after lisnin' to me, you f---."

"Who de ye tink ye are . . . ?"

Like three hissing geese, they circled each other until one flung his slopping tumbler onto the wooden deck and, with fierce determination, swung a loose fist at a swaying body. Missing his target, he fell on a sleeping form huddled against the wall. The huddled form, jumping to its feet in startled confusion, swinging its arms in self-defence, tripped over its attacker and fell against the two remaining geese. These two, who had become more like drunken ducks with their wings entangled around each other, started to hit back at their innocent assailant.

The sudden noise and the raised swearing voices had disturbed the sleeping groups, resulting in aggrieved female voices remonstrating.

"Will you hush the noise, you bloody eejits, and stop the bloody swearin'? There's children lisnin'."

By now, the three "fighters" had punched themselves into exhaustion and were now the greatest of friends, as apparently they all came from Mullingar, a small country town in the middle of Ireland.

With his solitude disturbed, Brendan noticed the clock on the wall showed one o'clock.

Oh God! Another five or six hours to go. Where can I get a cup of tea or something to drink? Staggering on the swaying floor, he shuffled to the café only to find it closed. "Maybe get a drink of water? In the toilet, of course!"

Stepping over the suitcases and boxes, and the odd twitching recumbent form on the floor, he made his way to the gents' and, twitching his nose to ward off the smell of vomit, drank some water from the tap over a large sink.

With the smell of beer, unwashed bodies, and cigarettes and the ever-moving walls and staircases, Brendan decided he would go for some fresh air. Staggering along the corridors and swaying staircases, he found an exit door and forced it open against the heavy spring. He stumbled out onto the wooden boat deck, and with a deep breath of the fresh air, he looked around.

In the starlight, everything was swaying to the right and, to the left the cloudless sky was covered in bright groups of swinging stars and a leaping moon. Taking deep breaths, Brendan felt quite exhilarated; the fresh air and the movement made him realise how big the world was. There was so much to look forward to.

Sitting down on a deck seat with his overcoat wrapped around him to protect his suit from the moist air as much as to warm himself, Brendan started to doze a bit. He was disturbed by a voice swearing about the conditions. Rousing himself, he became aware of a young man, not much older than himself, huddled on the seat beside him. Brendan, ever eager to talk and discover others, introduced himself and found out his new companion was returning to Birmingham, having been to see a relative in Dublin.

In his Birmingham accent, in great contrast to Brendan's soft Irish brogue, his new companion started to ridicule the Irish people, their lack of business expertise, their drunkenness and their fear of the church. Brendan, beginning to bristle a bit from the criticism of his home country and fellow countrymen, remonstrated as best he could.

Quite enjoying the banter, Brendan, trying to defend the lack of business acumen of his fellow countrymen, lost the argument. However, he got his new companion to agree that the Irishman could apparently drink an Englishman under the table. When it came to religion, whilst Brendan agreed the church was too strong in Ireland, he was amazed when the young man beside him proclaimed he was an atheist. That he didn't believe in any stupid Jesus and God.

He was astonished that somebody could be proud for not believing in a God. Didn't everybody believe in God? He asked the Englishman to explain why he was so pleased to be an atheist. After a brief lecture on reality and the facts of life from this independent and, in Brendan's mind, lost young man, Brendan put forward the final devastating question.

"You mean, you believe man is worth no more than a dog?"

There was silence for a long moment before the young man from Birmingham agreed with a shrug of his shoulders.

Somehow there was nothing more to say and the two youngsters, with their respective thoughts, staggered away in different directions.

Making his way inside the ship again, Brendan made himself as comfortable as possible and dozed until six in the morning, when the ferryboat eventually began to make its way through the lock gates to tie up close to the famous Liver Buildings.

He had arrived in Liverpool, the stepping-stone for the thousands of Irish on their way to America. There was the River Mersey, the docks, the Liver buildings, the smells of salt air and horse dung. Even at this early hour there were vast numbers of people, all hurrying to their destinations. Standing on the gangway leading down to the dock, at seven o'clock in the morning, hearing the chimes of the Liver clock, Brendan took a deep breath and, with great expectation, joined the moving mass of bodies.

There were ships berthed to his right, an engine and carriage passing by on the overhead railway to the left, and lots of family groups with their assorted parcels and grumbling children on their way into the city. Stepping aside as important workers pushed their loaded trolleys to their destination, he asked one of the workmen where he could get a cup of tea.

"Te de rih ye'll fine de lanny'. Gerra cuppa there," the man replied in a strange guttural voice. None the wiser, Brendan smiled at the now rapidly disappearing form and followed the flow of people.

Coming to the exit gates with the Liver Buildings ahead of him and a small church across the road to the left, he followed a stream of people moving to the right toward the river.

What's a "lanny"? Maybe he means the landing stage down there? Brendan thought to himself.

Surrounded by strange smells, strange sights, and even stranger voices, he joined a small queue for the café. Finishing an awful cup of tea and slab of toast, he wandered around for a bit, making his way into the city to look for Spinney House. His interview was at half past ten.

He asked a cloth-capped old man, surrounded by newspapers and shouting out an unintelligible message to the passing people, where Spinney House was. The reply was spoken so fast he could only catch the odd word: "neu billdin, chirch stree', oposit wollies." The language barrier wasn't helped either as, in between the strange words, he waved a newspaper followed by the shout "Daily pos'gerram 'ere."

Buying the Daily Post to read later, Brendan started exploring the neighbourhood, as he had plenty of time to fill in. Seeing Woolworth's store amongst all the vendors' stalls erected on the pavements, he decided he must be on "Chirch Stree" and, sure enough, opposite "Wollies" there was Spinney House.

With his destination resolved, he wandered around the city centre for a while, had a cup of tea in Lewis's store, a wash-up in their impressive toilets, and made his way, albeit reluctantly, towards the interview.

After he had climbed numerous flights of stairs and wandered down some ten miles of empty, distempered corridors, Brendan eventually found the door with the CP shield. After introducing himself to a pleasant young lady behind an imposing desk, he was offered a cup of tea and asked to wait. Quite nervous now, Brendan began to realise that this moment could be a turning point in his life. *This is it. If I don't get this interview where do I go? What do I do?*

His negative thoughts were soon interrupted by the appearance of a tall, impressive-looking, middle-aged man dressed in a uniform. The three roundels of gold braid on his jacket sleeves denoted his captain's rank.

"Mr. Harris," he smiled, standing back from the door with his gold-encrusted right hand awaiting a handshake.

"I'm Captain Ken Marsh. Did you have a good crossing?"

Brendan, returning the welcoming smile, unhinged his long frame from the low sofa and entered the interview room ahead of the captain. The room was vast, with the sun streaming through wide windows. The high-panelled walls were adorned with impressive paintings of CP tankers, while ships' flags hung from flag posts. Brendan, his pulses racing and feeling quite sick in apprehension, heard a friendly, deep male voice introducing himself.

"Good morning, Mr. Harris. I am Commodore Walsh."

Brendan, still smiling, bid a good morning to the other gold-braided uniform as it advanced from behind a ship-sized desk to shake hands and sat down in the tall chair, placed some six feet in front of the desk.

Commodore Walsh returned to his commanding position behind the desk and went into some detail about CP and its place in the world and how important its ships' officers were and how essential it was to realise the right calibre of apprentice deck officer.

Asked why he thought he was a suitable candidate, Brendan went into nervous overdrive saying how enthusiastic he was, how ambitious he was, how well he had done in school, and how he had been a cub leader and captain of the junior hockey team.

When he paused for breath, a smiling Captain Marsh started to ask some further questions. On the subject of examination results, Commodore Walsh referred to the failure in Irish language. Brendan, in a flash of inspiration, rather than saying that the Irish teacher "Granny" Smith was useless, said he had thought it wiser to spend the time on other subjects. Walsh, with a smile to Marsh, agreed that the need to be able to speak Irish when loading a cargo of oil in Mina-Al-Amadhi was pretty remote.

Noticing Brendan's quizzical look, the Commodore explained Mina was an oil port in Kuwait. *Where's Kuwait?* Brendan wondered.

The interview continued for some further thirty minutes, by which time Brendan had relaxed. With smiles all round, the two officers agreed that, if Brendan passed the customary medical and eye tests and references, they would accept his application for an apprenticeship with CP.

In somewhat of a daze, Brendan thanked the two sailors and after collecting a form to apply for his travel expenses, found himself outside on the pavement and feeling quite exhausted. Tired from lack of sleep and elated by the success of the interview, but again slightly apprehensive at the thought of undergoing a medical and remembering the supposed heart trouble diagnosed by Dr. Holly some three years earlier, all Brendan wanted to do now was get home.

The long, wet, and weary hours that Brendan had to endure until the ship set sail again that evening were spent walking around shops to keep out of the rain, or down to the docks when the rain abated. He did have a few hours respite in the Tatler Cinema watching, in between periods of sleep, Mickey Mouse and Tom and Jerry cavorting around the screen.

The journey home across the Irish Sea later that night was quite uneventful. He slept on the floor of the passenger lounge for most of the time and welcomed the sight of his parents waiting for him when the ship arrived in Dublin early the next morning.

"Three things I have to do, Ma," he said, when he finally arrived home.

"Have a medical, an eye sight test, and get good references. They give eight pounds a month for the first year, Ma, increasing to twenty pounds in the fourth, rent free. Isn't that great?"

Alice agreed, realising with sadness that another of her brood was on his way into the big wide world. Jono had joined the British Army and now her Brendan was on his way to joining the Merchant Navy.

Within the week a letter arrived instructing Brendan to make his way into Dublin for an eyesight test and a medical at posh doctors in Dublin. He also had to provide two character references, one from the professions, and one from his school.

"You can get a reference from the Reverend Folly, and what about the one you had from the deputy head, Mr. Blazer?" suggested Alice.

"Better to be on the safe side—I'll get another from the doc. Yeh! The doc! I'll give him a call. I'd like to talk with him anyway," answered Brendan.

"He should be home from the school now it's gone six."

The doc was delighted to hear the news about CP and agreed to write the reference. Brendan cycled down to Dalkey to collect it and have a talk with him. The doc wasn't like any other teacher Brendan knew. He dressed to suit himself, so nothing matched; a worn brown jacket with grey baggy trousers, scruffy shoes, unkempt grey streaks of hair on a mottled pate, a three-day-old unbuttoned shirt under a nondescript tie. All this faded into the background when the lively eyes, the smiling face and the keen brain addressed its audience, whether it be a multitude of hundreds or a sixteen-year-old youngster looking for attention and advice.

Welcomed into the doc's cottage in Dalkey, a small seaside village close to Dunlaoghaire, Brendan was introduced to Mary, his wife, a pleasant woman and led into the doc's study.

Listening to Brendan's request, the doc, whilst writing the required reference in longhand, regaled Brendan with his experiences in Irish Shipping and his association with the Dunlaoghaire Lifeboats, and expressed his admiration at Brendan's decision to go to sea. After an hour or so drinking rather strong tea, eating stale biscuits and discussing Irish and French politics, or rather listening intently, Brendan left with the Doc's best wishes and a great feeling of confidence in himself.

The request for a reference from the Reverend Folly was met by an effusive affirmative on the phone and a suggestion that Brendan call to the Rectory to collect it. A further short ride on his bicycle brought him to the impressive Victorian building hidden behind a number of untidy trees and wandering bushes.

A little old lady of at least fifty years of age, wearing an apron, answered his ring and led him into a stale-smelling, heavy curtained drawing room, with unwashed window panes and a thick carpet with a faded square mirroring the window. Whilst waiting, Brendan wrote with his finger in the dust on a large oval dining table and stood back to admire the words: Captain Brendan Harris.

Hearing the door reopen, he hurriedly wiped the words off with his sleeve and stepped forward to greet the blustering reverend who, apologising for the dust, shook hands with Brendan, mistakenly grasping his left hand and dropping it hurriedly to take his right hand, asking at the same time how Brendan's parents were.

Whilst tossing Brendan's hands around and asking questions, he produced a piece of paper from a small folder and presented it to Brendan.

"I-I-I-do-do hope this is what you require, Brendan. I-I don't ha-ha-ve a typewriter—complicated things. Ha! Ha!"

Amused by the exhausting figure, Brendan looked quickly at the written words, quite readable in a fine copperplate hand in dark ink. Thanking the reverend for the reference, Brendan brought him up to date on his application to CP and said the kind words would be a great help.

Shaking hands again, Brendan backed out through the doorway with the reverend nodding his head and wishing him every good fortune, saying he looked forward to seeing Brendan in church the next Sunday.

The next step was the medical. Slightly apprehensive due to the supposed heart problem diagnosed by Dr. Folly, Brendan climbed the wide stone steps to the impressive doorway in Fitzwilliam Square. In the Victorian grandeur of the large building he disrobed and subjected himself to a medical examination. When asked by the doctor if he had had any heart trouble, he thought it best to own up to the diagnosis. The doctor nodded his large head, made a few tut- tutting noises and, leaning against his stethoscope, requested Brendan to cough. After a few more tut-tuts he told Brendan to get dressed and that he could leave.

As the doctor did not volunteer any information as to success or failure of the medical, Brendan left the chilling atmosphere as quickly as possible. The eyesight test followed in the shipping offices in Burgh Quay alongside the River Liffey. This was passed without any trouble so, putting together the references and sight certificate, Brendan posted the envelope to CP to await the result.

28

Good-bye Ireland

"Well, Brendan, you're nearly there. What are you waiting for now?"

"The okay from CP and what I do next, Polly. The medical worries me, but if I get the all clear I'll have to get the uniforms and clothes and whatever else and then it's up to CP when I join my first ship."

"What about us, Brendan? Will you still want to know me after you've seen the world?"

"Oh, Polly! Let's not worry about that at the moment. Come on, let's go dancin' tonight and live it up a bit."

So very close now to his dream, Brendan did not want to know Polly's worries. He was only sixteen and the world awaited him.

That evening over the table at teatime in general conversation, Alice asked if anyone would be interested in taking part in some of the church activities. She was now quite involved with the church, as was Henry, who was Church warden.

"What's on offer, Ma?" enquired Brendan with a grin on his face.

"What do you suggest?"

"Well, there's the Bring and Buy sale this weekend in the hall," Ma replied in a hopeful voice. "The Rev is also looking for help to do the garden at the rectory. There's a play being considered for Easter to raise some funds to send a donation to the poor black people in Africa. They need . . ."

"Maybe the Bring and Buy, Ma. Billy and I could do a second-hand bookstall. What do you say, Billy? I don't fancy the gardenin'."

With Billy's nodded agreement it was decided he and Brendan would organise the bookstall.

"What about the play, Ma?" At the recent prize giving at the school, the doc had written a short satirical play about politicians in Roman times and Brendan had enjoyed his brief moment as a leading proconsul before he was beheaded for dissent.

"Any parts going for a budding actor?" he asked jokingly. It would be something to do until he knew the result of his medical and, anyway, if they did want him to start it surely would not be for at least a couple of months.

"Dunno. The brigadier asked me if I knew anybody who might be interested in taking part. I think he's a bit desperate as very few people are interested."

The brigadier was a retired Englishman living in a large house in the prosperous area of the parish. Of erect bearing, a loud commanding voice and a bristling moustache, he was quite unapproachable in Brendan's eye.

"No, Ma. As I said, I'll do the bookstall on Saturday and wait until I get the answer from CP. You never know, they might want me to start sooner than we think."

That weekend, Billy and Brendan spent the Saturday selling books at the Bring and Buy. Being a frosty day with a bit of snow, it being January after all, the customers were few, but it filled in time for Brendan whilst waiting for the news from CP.

A few days later, whilst he was out in the garden cutting up some logs, there was an anxious shout from the kitchen.

"It's CP, Brendan, its CP on the phone. Quick! Brendan, it's long distance . . ."

"Right Ma, I'm comin'. I'm comin'. Gosh, it's CP. Hope it's good news."

Running in from the garden, Brendan hastily took the phone from Alice.

"Yes! Brendan Harris here . . . Yes, May sixteenth, South Shields . . . a letter in the post . . . with forms and Indenture papers for signature. Thank you. Good-byeeeeee . . ."

"I've got it, Ma! I'm in. I'm to join a ship in South Shields, England— God knows where that is—I must have passed the medical. I'm in. Gosh!"

Punching the air, hugging his mother, running in and out of the room, and jumping up and down, Brendan celebrated the news.

"Must tell Polly! Tell the doc! Pop will be pleased! May the sixteenth! That's two and a half months away. The lady says the forms are in the post. Gosh! Lots to do."

Yes! There were lots to do. On receipt of the papers from CP, there were instructions to have Indenture papers signed and returned, personal details to complete and uniforms to buy. The ship he was to join, as a navigating deck apprentice, was the Calvex Renown, a 16,000-ton tanker just built and commissioned to CP.

The following Sunday, after another confusing sermon by the reverend, the congregation gathered outside the church in the sunshine, gossiping and saying their good-byes. Brendan and Alice had decided earlier to see if the brigadier would take them on as actors in the play he intended to produce. They approached him as he began to pronounce, to a group of listeners, on the inabilities of the British government to put the rascal Nasser in his place.

Noticing Alice, who was looking very attractive in her best dress and short coat with her ash blond hair reaching her shoulders, he stopped his lecture. With a smile on his large red face, he greeted Alice, taking her hand and bowing slightly. When asked about the play, he jumped at the opportunity to recruit Alice.

"You would be ideal, young lady. So glad you offered. Now, what about you, young man?" Standing some six inches taller than this condescending buffoon, Brendan noticed Alice's astonishment at being considered for a part.

"A comedy about the British Royal Air Force, *A Worm's Eye View* by Delderfield. Do come along, both of you, to a meeting in the hall tonight. I am sure there will be parts for you both."

Twirling his long moustache, the portly figure in his brown, well-tailored suit turned to his admiring audience and continued his lecture on the present disappointing results in Egypt.

That evening Brendan and Alice, both slightly apprehensive, arrived at the church hall as the Brigadier lifted himself onto the stage calling for quiet; he announced in a severe tone that, when he was speaking, he would rather nobody else spoke. Knowing heads nodded to each other. "Yes! The brigadier is on form tonight."

"The play I propose directing is the war time comedy, *Worm's Eye View*, and is a story about a group of billetees, cottagers, and airmen staying at the Bounty household. There's a cast of eleven—three females and eight males. Now, I have read the play and harrumph! Find it quite painful, Airmen you know. Tsch Tsch. Flying around looking down on the soldiers doing the fighting: harrumph! But needs must. Now for the cast. Alf, give everybody their copy of the script, advising which part I suggest they take."

Alf, the brigadier's sergeant, walked around the room handing out sheaves of papers to the aspiring actors. Looking at those passed to him, Brendan saw the part of Sydney Spooner. Before he had time to look at the script, the brigadier coughed for attention.

"Everyone got one? Good! Each of you has the part I intend you taking. We are short of actors for three parts: Bella, the squadron leader and the duke. Any questions? Harrumph! Ask me now."

"Or forever hold your peace," was the muttered comment from Alice.

Whilst the brigadier discussed who would be prompt, sceneshifters and other not so important parts, Brendan saw his ma was rather disappointed.

"What's wrong, Ma?"

"I'm Thelma, the maid. I wanted to be somebody important. What part has he given you, Brendan?"

"Sydney Spooner, Ma! Hope I can do it. There seems to be a lot to say."

"Right, all actors gather around me now. Alf, get some chairs in a circle. Is everyone happy with their part?"

Looking around with an expression that suggested no dissent, the brigadier noticed Alice's unhappy face. Smiling, he stated how pleased he was to be able to offer such an important part to her and, before she had time to comment, had turned to answer a question from one of the regulars.

Throughout the evening the brigadier discussed the layout of the stage. Alice, after having spoken with Alice Spencer who was taking the part of Mrs. Bounty, and who had pages and pages of lines, realised that perhaps the part of Thelma would be enough after all.

With weekly rehearsals arranged, Brendan and Alice walked home wondering what they had let themselves in for, but quite excited with the prospect of acting on stage.

The following morning, Brendan made his way into Dublin to the tailors, Murphy and Wilson, in Shaw Street to be measured for his officer's uniform—tropical whites, shorts, shirts, long socks, shoes. On reading the list of requirements supplied by CP, there was a suggestion that a tin trunk would be most suitable, particularly when the proposed traveller was expected to visit the tropics. Alice, wishing to ensure her son was equipped with everything required, had Henry buy a large "Treasure Island" trunk, with rounded top and reinforced with strips of wood banding the whole dreadful embarrassing monstrosity. As it had apparently taken some time and effort by them both to procure the trunk, Brendan did not have the heart to refuse.

The opening night for the play was planned for the second week in April, just before Easter, so the following months were quite busy. Rehearsals were a bit of a shambles to start with. The brigadier had roped in the remaining cast required and spent the early days shouting at everyone to "smarten up and learn their lines" as quickly as possible.

Brendan was beginning to enjoy his part as the distasteful son of the landlady, Mrs. Spoonert, while Alice, in the part of Thelma, found it a great opportunity to act the rather bawdy middle-aged maid.

The makeshift props and the overbearing attitude of the brigadier constantly complaining about attitude and commitment and the requirement to go over the top, lent the rehearsals an air of tenseness. There were some tears and some funny episodes during rehearsals.

During one rehearsal, where nerves were getting a bit frayed with the brigadier hitting the stage in irritation with his riding whip, Squadron

Leader Briarly, a kindly soul, had been called in to pacify an indignant Sydney. Sydney was incensed at the unwelcome approach, in Sydney's eyes, of one of the airmen to his young sister.

In the scene, Sydney enters from right, spluttering in indignation. From his height of six-foot-two, he was ready to put the squadron leader in his place. He makes his way to the settee, the back seat of an old ford car. Now, this old leather seat stood only some eight inches from the stage floor. It had been decided, due to the height differences of the two protagonists, the squadron leader being only five feet two inches, that they sit alongside each other. The kindly squadron leader settled himself onto the car seat, without any problem. Sydney, however, pointing his finger and admonishing the squadron leader in an irate manner, started to lower his long frame to the very low seat. With his free hand searching for the surface, which was only eight inches from the floor, he lost his balance and fell backwards onto the seat with his legs in the air.

The ridiculous pose started Sydney giggling nervously, and the squadron leader started to laugh. This started the rest of the cast snorting until there was uproar of nervous laughter and rehearsals had to be stopped for some time until everyone recovered. The brigadier was not too pleased.

And so the weeks passed. Brendan and Alice spent time learning their lines. Brendan had a fitting for his new and expensive Merchant Navy uniform.

Shortly after Easter, the rehearsals for the play ended and, proficient or not, the first of three performances was to be played in the Church Hall. The Reverend Folly announced the performance in church notices the Sunday prior to the first night of the play.

"The Dramatic Society will be holding their play, *The Bird's Eye View*, next Thursday," he beamed.

The brigadier, who always sat two pews from the front of the church with his large wife, corrected Folly in his booming voice:

"*A Worm's Eye View* for three nights, Mr. Folly. I repeat, *A Worm's Eye View* for three nights."

A flustered Folly dropped his notes on the floor while apologising to the congregation for his mistake. The congregation didn't know whether to laugh or cry when there was a loud tearing sound when the poor man, upon standing up after retrieving the fluttering notes, apparently had stood on the back of his long gown. The brigadier, sitting down, dismissed the whole episode with a further loud "*Harrumph!*"

Thursday night arrived, cold and damp. The hall was half full when the curtain opened and the play rambled along. The odd lines were missed. Alice, in stage fright, forgot her lines in hers and Brendan's scene.

However, with a bit of adlibbing the play continued. A real sofa had re-placed the car seat, so there was no repeat of the giggling episode.

By Saturday night, Brendan was glad to see the end of the play, having fluffed his lines a few times to a near empty hall. The Saturday night was played mainly to families of the actors, as they were the only persons who braved a heavy snowfall that had lasted most of the day.

The brigadier acknowledged the plaudits from the audience at the end of the play and, swishing his riding crop against his legs, thanked each of the cast. He made a special note of wishing Sydney Spooner every success in his career. Brendan, embarrassed, nodded his thanks from the stage and felt well pleased with himself as he and his family walked home later that evening in the deep snow.

Brendan spent the following weeks preparing for his career in the Merchant Navy. The uniform took some time from being measured to the complete package: a double-breasted jacket and trousers in heavy navy twill. He journeyed into Dublin to purchase shirts and shorts for the tropics and for formal wear and warm clothes for the colder temperatures.

The apprentice's indenture papers arrived on impressive heavy paper, outlining the terms that were, briefly, as follows:

"The said Brendan Harris hereby voluntarily binds himself unto the said company and their assigns for the term of four years. He will be taught the duties of a deck officer and receive the sum of £575 paid over the four years as outlined with twelve shillings yearly in lieu of washing. After four years of satisfactory service a further £30 will be paid. It is necessary to provide a fee of £20 to register this document at Maritime House."

The role of a navigating deck apprentice, from the booklet supplied, was to learn the workings of a ship, about cargoes, ship handling, navigating as expected and a million and more other things. There would be six-monthly examinations on all the subjects mentioned and, after four years, a major examination to become a deck officer.

When the signed and witnessed indentures, witnessed by none other than the brigadier, were posted to CP by return, Brendan was instructed to join the Calvex Renown at the port of South Shields in Northumberland on 16th May 1957 as a navigating apprentice.

Promising his parents he would help pay back the money they had spent, he agreed to send home £4 a month from his first year's earnings of £96. This wasn't going to leave very much for a young man to spend, but at least he wouldn't have to outlay any money for lodgings. His only regular expense would be the shilling a month for washing.

The final day of the fifteen of May 1957 arrived. Brendan waved to his anxious parents on the Dublin quayside as the British and Irish ferry pulled out into the River Liffey. He was on his way to a new life with his large leather suitcase, dreadful sea chest, and a head full of great expectations for the future.

Lightning Source UK Ltd.
Milton Keynes UK
UKOW041955081112

201916UK00002B/72/P